"Please make a point of meeting the Gillman family. Scott, the husband and father, is busy saving the world from the ravages of climate change by pedaling his recumbent bike around the United States on a summer-long tour. His wife, Ellie, and daughters Misha and Abbie, are busy saving everything else. Judith Arnold is such a terrific writer and such a gifted observer of American family life. She sees and illuminates the everyday drama of friendships, plugged toilets, weather-related mishaps, and workplace treacheries. As the titular "Girls Aloud" confront the rigors of getting by without the immediate presence of Scott, they come to the slow realization that they're neither powerless nor hobbled. Indeed, they have talents to assert, love to share, and a recasting of the order to impose. Arnold's fine prose—always on point, occasionally hilarious, never intrusive—carries the story along with a knowing and deft touch. This is a fine novel."
— Craig Lancaster, award-winning author of *Dreaming Northward* and *And It Will Be a Beautiful Life*

"Wise and funny and smart, *Girls Aloud* is a bright feminist tale of a woman coming into her own power to find her voice. Populated with lively, real-life characters and the daily problems of modern life, it's a book that's guaranteed to make you cheer."
— Barbara O'Neal, bestselling author of *This Place of Wonder*

"As always, Judith Arnold's prose is captivating. I stopped many times to enjoy a beautiful phrase or an apt metaphor. And throughout the book is Arnold's trademark humor. I smiled as I read this wonderful novel. Another winner here that makes the world a better place!"
— Kathryn Shay, *New York Times* bestselling author of the *Brothers of Fire* series

GIRLS ALOUD

Judith Arnold

THE
ST●RY
PLANT

The Story Plant
1270 Caroline Street
Suite D120-381
Atlanta, GA 30307

Copyright © 2023 by Barbara Keiler
The Library of Congress Cataloguing-in-Publication Data is available upon request.

Story Plant hardcover ISBN-13: 978-1-61188-375-6
Story Plant e-book ISBN-13: 978-1-61188-384-8

Visit our website at www.TheStoryPlant.com

First Story Plant Printing: February 2024

Printed in the United States of America
0 9 8 7 6 5 4 3 2 1

To my daughter-in-law, Katie Bach, who is brilliant, brave, and gloriously aloud.

.

DAY ONE

And we're off!

I crossed the New York State line, and I'm feeling great. No problems, no snafus, no aches or pains. I know I'll hit roadblocks — both figuratively and literally — along the way, but so far, so good. I found a clean, inexpensive motel just up the road from a McDonald's. Of course, "just up the road" could be a several-mile stretch, but this time it wasn't. I made it to the McDonald's and back on my own power, which is the whole point. Making it on our own power.

McDonald's is not the most carbon-neutral eatery. But what the hell. I was hungry, and there it was.

Time to call my wonderful girls, and then I'll shower and get some sleep. Back on the road tomorrow.

CHAPTER ONE

Ellie hadn't expected this.

She had assumed a handful of people might show up to wave Scott off. A few neighbors, maybe a couple of his students. Not what appeared to be at least half the student body of Shelton Middle School, some carrying a banner reading: "Mr. Gillman Is Our Hero!" and some, no doubt members of the school chorus, serenading Scott with a surprisingly sweet rendition of "What a Wonderful World." Also a dozen of his former students, high schoolers now, one armed with a trumpet on which he played the familiar military bugle fanfare that was usually followed by a commanding officer shouting, "Charge!" And a van from one of the local Boston TV stations, which disgorged a cameraman and a reporter who had makeup as thick as stucco slathered on her face and a hairdo so heavily lacquered that the steady breeze roiling the morning air couldn't budge it. And three pint-size Girl Scouts in uniforms who insisted on donating boxes of Thin Mints and Samoas for Scott to snack on along the way.

The atmosphere reminded Ellie of a carnival, minus the Ferris wheel and the corn dogs. However, a real dog was present: Lucy, who romped around the front yard, sniffing at people's ankles and toes in search of anything that smelled edible.

The reporter was babbling into a hand-held microphone, but Ellie couldn't hear her above the cacophony of cheering, singing, and trumpeting fans gathered in front of the house, eager to wave Scott off and wish him well.

"Daddy's going to be on TV." Misha, standing to Ellie's right on the front porch, looked awed. "That is *so cool.*" She punctuated her statement by clapping her hands and executing a little kick-step.

Abbie stood to Ellie's left, not clapping or kicking. At fifteen, she was five years older than her sister and much too blasé to be easily impressed by transient television fame. "I hope she doesn't interview us," she said, glaring in the direction of the reporter. "I'm not wearing any mascara."

"Which is very fortunate," Ellie said, "because if you were, I'd make you wipe it off."

Abbie sighed dramatically. Life was tragic when you were nearly sixteen and your mother didn't let you smear cosmetics all over your face as if you were, for example, a TV reporter.

Across the front yard, in the street, Scott basked in all the attention. Attention was what he wanted, why he was pursuing his mission. Bicycling around the country to raise awareness of climate change was important. It was noble. It was also arguably insane. But the whole point was to gain attention, and he was succeeding.

Thanks to the money he had raised on a GoFundMe page, he had bought himself an elaborate recumbent bike for the journey, along with a trailer to carry his gear. "It's called a 'Beast of Burden,'" he'd informed Ellie and the girls as he hooked the trailer to the bike and then attached a bright orange flag to the trailer's bumper to make him more visible on the back roads and byways where he would be riding. Misha had helped him to adorn the Beast of Burden with signs. One side held a silkscreened cloth reading "Save The Planet," the other a graphic rebus of sorts, with the letter "I," a picture of a red valentine, and a blue circle with latitude and longitude lines superimposed on it, along with silhouettes of the western hemisphere's continents. On the back, below the orange flag, another silkscreen: bright red letters on yellow fabric read "RE:CYCLE!"

"Get it?" Scott had beamed a bright grin, obviously proud of his pun. "*Regarding the cycle* and *recycle*! I've ordered some T-shirts that read 'RE:CYCLE' too."

The shirts had arrived a couple of days ago, sunshine yellow with blood-red lettering, like the sign on the Beast of Burden. Scott was wearing one of the RE:CYCLE T-shirts now, layered over a long-sleeved Henley shirt because the late-May morning held an unexpected chill. He had stashed half a dozen other RE:CYCLE shirts in his duffel so he could rotate through them while he rode.

This bicycle trip was his crazy, glorious idea. He had planned and prepped for more than a year. He'd studied maps, coordinated routes, contacted supporters in towns across the continent. He'd trained for it. As a science teacher, he understood the threat of climate change to the earth's future on a deeper, more technical level than most people, and he felt compelled to do something about it, something beyond eating vegetarian twice a week, watering the yard less often, and making sure all recyclables were disposed of in the green trash bin with the big black triangle on it.

Ellie was proud of him. She felt deeply threatened by climate change, too. She hearted the Earth. A part of her wondered whether biking across the country would change anything, but the fact that he was trying, exerting himself, attracting the attention of so many people... Well, that was why she loved him. He did things like this.

Scott was certain his trip would make a difference in Mother Nature's grand scheme. "I'll stop at schools and town centers along the way. I'll talk to people. More than five hundred people sent money to my GoFundMe page. This is going to be big, Ellie. Writing letters to the editor and calling our representative's office — that's too localized. We need to make our case to the nation. I'll prove that we can travel without polluting the atmosphere. If I can bike from New England to the West Coast without spewing greenhouse gases, it will open people's eyes. People will see me or hear about me, and they'll think about using their own muscles to make trips," he predicted. "Every able-bodied adult should have a bike or a three-wheeler with a trailer. They could pedal to the supermarket and back. Think of the exhaust fumes all those cars in the Whole Foods parking lot pour into the atmosphere. If those shoppers biked instead, our air would be a hell of a lot cleaner."

Ellie wished Scott's enthusiasm was contagious. Sometimes she allowed herself to be caught up in it. Other times, apprehension overtook her. What if he got hurt? What if he skidded off the road and fell into a ditch and lay there, undiscovered, for days? What if an eighteen-wheeler smashed into him? What if his GPS developed a glitch and sent him in the wrong direction, and he passed no eateries for days, and he perished from starvation? So many things could go wrong.

He assured her nothing bad would happen. "It's all going to be great," he'd insisted. "I'll be heard. I'll raise the nation's conscious-ness. I'll meet new people and open their eyes. I'll be fine, I prom-ise." As if he could promise that no eighteen-wheeler would flatten him beneath the deep treads of its oversized tires.

He was so passionate about this trip, so confident, so fervent. His passion, confidence, and fervor were a large part of why she'd fallen in love with him so many years ago, why she still loved him today. He had a vision, and he was committed to it. He was taking action. Biking across the country to alert people to the threat of climate change was his dream, and he was making his dream come true.

Between her job and her daughters, Ellie wasn't even sure what her dream was. Some days, her dream was only to make it through the day without needing a nap. Sometimes she felt envy when she thought of Scott and his coming-true dream. Sometimes she simply felt awe.

The reporter made her way up the front walk to the porch steps, the cameraman traipsing along after her, his camera perched on his beefy shoulder and his eyes shielded by sunglasses with mirror lenses. From the bottom of the porch steps, the reporter called up to Ellie: "You're Mr. Gillman's wife, correct?"

Ellie smiled and nodded, and wondered whether she should have put on some mascara. Abbie might have spoken the truth about the importance of appearing well groomed on TV.

"May I come up on the porch and ask you a couple of ques-tions?" the reporter inquired.

"Say yes," Abbie murmured. "You don't want her aiming the camera up at you from the bottom of the steps. It'll make your nos-trils look gross."

Ellie hesitated. Inviting the reporter onto her porch was nearly the same as inviting her into the house. Too intrusive. Too intimate.

But she didn't want her nostrils to look gross on the local news, either.

She descended the three steps to the front walk. The reporter's smile widened. Ellie wondered whether the woman gargled regularly with bleach; her teeth were blindingly white. Abbie remained on the porch, out of camera range, but Misha followed Ellie down the stairs, her steps bouncy and her cheeks dimpled from her grin.

"Your name is Ellie, correct? That's what your husband told me."

"Eleanor," Ellie said. People she invited onto her porch or into her house could call her Ellie, but this reporter, with her pasty cosmetics and her rigid hair and that phallic-looking microphone clutched in her manicured hand, did not fall within the category of personal guests.

The reporter's smile remained rigidly in place as she rotated to face the camera. "Scott Gillman's wife, Eleanor, is here to wave Scott off on his cross-country bike trip. Eleanor?" She thrust the microphone at Ellie's chin. "How do you feel about what he's attempting?"

"There's nothing more important right now than reversing climate change," Ellie said. The words sounded rehearsed to her, and perhaps they were. She had certainly heard Scott speak them often enough. "It's Scott's dream to do something big, to make people sit up and take notice of the peril our planet is in. If we can't save the Earth from the devastating effects of climate change, nothing else matters. To Scott, this isn't just an adventure. It's a crusade."

"And he gets to go biking every day, and meet people all over the country," Misha said, unable to contain her excitement.

"Do you like to bike?" the reporter asked, lowering the microphone to Misha's chin.

"Of course," Misha said, her tone implying that she thought the question was inane, which it was. "My daddy's a hero. See the sign?" She gestured toward the banner the students in the street were holding up. "Oh, look, Mom — Luke is here." With that, Misha bolted across the lawn, Lucy racing after her as she vanished into the crowd of school children. Luke Bartelli had been Misha's best friend since they'd wound up on the same peewee soccer team when they were in kindergarten. This year, as they'd graduated to playing on the larger soccer fields, they'd joined a league that offered only single-sex teams, all-girl or all-boy. It was the first time since they'd both fallen in love with soccer that they were not on the same team. But they were still best friends.

Misha wasn't really a tomboy. She loved sports, especially soccer, but she had also enjoyed ballet the three years she'd studied it. She had especially loved the tutus and the sparkly tiaras she and the other dancers got to wear during their recitals. And she had eagerly adopted the nickname her teacher had given her. "My name is Michelle," she'd told Madame Coursey.

"I shall call you Misha," Madame Coursey had declared, "after the greatest ballet dancer of all time."

Only later did Misha learn that the Misha Madame Coursey had referred to was actually a man — Mikhail Baryshnikov. But he was a revered ballet dancer, and Misha had insisted that the nickname sounded more like a girl's name than a boy's name. When she was in third grade, her ballet lessons conflicted with soccer practice, and Ellie told her she would have to choose one activity or the other. Mikhail Baryshnikov notwithstanding, she'd chosen soccer. Fortunately, she didn't ask people to start calling her Pelé. She remained Misha, and she carried her ballet skills onto the soccer field, her posture ruler-straight as she ran, her fingers arched elegantly, her toes pointed as she kicked the ball.

Ellie spotted Misha amid the teeming mob of middle school students clogging the road. This coming fall, she would start middle school herself, and she seemed to fit right in with the older students. Ellie experienced a pang at the realization that her baby was growing up, that soon Misha would be an official teenager, demanding to wear mascara.

She glanced behind her at the porch, where Abbie remained, her hands on her hips and her lush brown hair fluttering in the breeze. Abbie's gaze was locked on her father, who chatted with the Girl Scouts. He was probably explaining the ozone layer to them, or the perils of fossil fuels. They were a cute trio in their matching khaki vests, and they peered up at him with intense, slightly giddy expressions, as if he were the lead singer in their favorite boy band.

Soon they would be teenagers, too, happy to dismiss anything adults told them.

"Are you worried about your husband's safety on the road?" the reporter asked, dragging Ellie's attention back to her.

Ellie tried not to wince. Scott's safety was her biggest fear. But the viewers of this reporter's news story didn't have to know that. "He's very careful," she said, "and he's got that bright orange flag. I'm sure he'll be all right."

"I bet you'll miss him, though."

"I'll miss him very much," Ellie agreed. Those words didn't convey just how much she would miss him. He would be gone for three long months. His hope was to be back home in time to resume teaching in the fall term, although the Shelton Middle School principal had lined up a substitute teacher in case Scott's return was delayed for any reason. "What you're doing is educational, too," Scott's boss had assured him. "And you'll be sending regular tweets for the children to follow, doing those remote zooms and whatever. But I'll need a warm body at the front of your classroom if you don't get back to Shelton in time for the fall semester."

Unfortunately, the school district would not be paying Scott's salary if he was somewhere in Utah or Alabama next September, zooming and sending tweets back to the middle school. Thank heavens for the GoFundMe page and Ellie's salary. Unlike him, she would be working at her job all summer, taking care of the girls, maintaining the home front. Making sure the lawn got mowed. Making sure the bills got paid. Making sure Lucy's poop got scooped up and thrown away.

Observing Scott's bright yellow shirt and his brighter smile as he explained the recumbent bike to a cluster of teenage boys, she acknowledged that she would miss him for a whole lot more than the fact that until he came home, she would be in charge of everything that went into keeping the Gillman household functioning. No fellow adult to lean on, to turn to, to make sure the girls disposed of Lucy's poop. No man in her bed at night. No silly puns. No one to back her up if she had a conflict with her daughters. No one to rant about fossil fuel companies over dinner. No one to wrap his arms around her every morning, kiss her cheek, and say, "Love you, sweetheart. Thanks for breakfast. Have a great day."

Abbie and Misha never thanked her for breakfast or told her to have a great day. She tried to remember the last time either of them had said they loved her, and came up empty.

The reporter remained on the lawn, yammering about what a brave journey Scott was undertaking. Ellie shifted her gaze from the reporter to Scott, who had plucked Misha from the swarm of children and led her up the front walk to where Ellie was standing. He held Misha's hand and Misha peered worshipfully up at him. As he neared Ellie, he beckoned to Abbie to come down from the porch and join them. She made a face but complied.

"I've got to leave," Scott said, once their little nuclear family was gathered on the front walk. The reporter was only a few feet away, and Ellie wanted to order her back to the street, but she couldn't do anything that might wind up making her look grouchy on the evening news, so she did her best to ignore the woman.

Scott wrapped one arm around each of his daughters. Lucy scampered over, apparently sensing that this was a family conference and staking her claim as part of the family. The dog head-bumped Ellie's shin, then sniffed Misha's canvas sneakers and Abbie's san-daled feet, her toenails polished a bright purple. Eventually, Lucy discovered Scott's streamlined bike shoes and rested her head on his insteps.

"I was thinking, maybe the girls could grab their bikes from the garage and accompany me as far as the town line."

"Yes!" The idea pleased Misha so much, she gave a little jump.

Scott pivoted to Abbie, who nodded.

"Go get your bikes and your helmets," Scott said, nudging the girls in the direction of the garage. When they were gone, he turned back to Ellie. "You're going to be okay?"

"We'll be fine," she assured him, swallowing the catch in her throat. Sure, she and the girls would be fine. But she would miss him so much. Her hero, her environmental warrior, her partner — he would be gone all summer, dodging malevolent eighteen-wheelers and pedaling through rain and sleet and snow and hail — or at the very least, occasional rain. His absence would leave a vacuum which would fill up with worry about everything bad that could happen to him on his journey. Nature abhorred a vacuum, after all.

He eyed the reporter, then shrugged and gathered Ellie into a tight hug. "I'll phone every day."

"You don't have to," she said. "Seriously. If you're tired, or you're doing an interview or whatever . . . We can follow you on that biking website."

"I'll phone." He touched his lips to the tip of her nose. "Thank you for letting me do this."

"Someone's got to save the planet. It might as well be you," she said.

He shot the reporter another quick look. She was watching them intently, as if she expected them to do something newsworthy, like exchange body fluids in a steamy farewell. He sighed and gave Ellie another light, chaste kiss, this time on her mouth. "Too many people around," he murmured. Evidently, exchanging body fluids would have suited him if they'd had a bit of privacy.

It would have suited her, too. But not on the front lawn, in view of a television camera and all those cheering children. She and Scott had indulged in their passionate farewell last night, after Abbie and Misha had gone to bed and Scott had reviewed the contents of his bags one last time. Ellie had tried not to cling to him afterward, not wanting to burden him with concern about how much she would miss him, how much she would miss their lovemaking, how big and empty and lonely the bed would feel for the next several months while he was away. But they'd cuddled together, his breath whispering over her hair as he'd drifted off to sleep. She hadn't slept much at all. She'd wanted to remember every minute of that night, every ounce of warm weight as his arm looped around her rib cage, as his chest pressed into her back.

She could either smile or weep at the memory of their final night together. She smiled. "Go. And be careful. There are a lot of crazy drivers on the roads."

"Come on, Daddy!" Misha hollered from the driveway.

Ellie looked past the reporter to the driveway and saw both her daughters straddling their bikes, wearing their helmets. Abbie's helmet was royal blue, slashed with jagged stripes of silver light-ning; Misha's was plastered with so many decals, it was impossible to determine what the helmet's actual color was.

Scott gave Ellie a final brisk kiss, then waved the girls down to the street as he jogged across the lawn to his bike. The crowd parted for him, the trumpeter played another fanfare, and the children holding the banner began undulating it as if it were a dragon at a Chinese New Year parade. Shouts of "Good luck!" and "Go, Mr. Gillman!" rose from the throng like bubbles from a street-wide vat of seltzer.

Ellie remained by the porch steps, watching as Scott mounted his bike. Flanked by Abbie and Misha, he started slowly down the street, his Beast of Burden trailing behind him, its orange flag flut-tering cheerfully. They reached the end of the street, turned the corner, and disappeared from view.

A wave of pride washed over Ellie, followed by a wave of . . . not quite grief, not quite despair, but soul-deep anxiety.

He was a hero, but he was also *her* hero. He wanted to save the world, but he was also *her* world, hers and Abbie's and Misha's. He could pursue his dream if he had to, but right now, her only dream was that he return in one piece, soon.

CHAPTER TWO

After Abbie and Misha rode off with Scott, the crowd dispersed, the singers and the trumpet player and the news reporter decamping as soon as the savior of the planet had pedaled out of sight. Ellie was amazed by how swiftly the street outside her house emptied.

She was equally amazed by the detritus left behind. With Lucy trailing behind her, she strode across the lawn to gather the candy bar wrapper crumpled against the curb, the popped balloon lying limp on the asphalt, a shred of silver foil, and several scraps of orange paper with indecipherable ink marks on it.

So much for saving the planet, she thought. If you want to save the planet, the least you could do is not litter.

She returned to the house with Lucy, tossed her collected debris into the trash can, and scrubbed her hands at the sink. Lucy wandered over to her water dish for a drink, then stared plaintively out the screen door to the back porch, as if expecting Scott to materialize on the patio, next to the barbecue grill.

The house was too quiet. Too empty. Ellie was tempted to join Lucy at the screen door, but she knew that doing so would not make Scott miraculously reappear.

Rarely did she have the entire house to herself. Most mornings, she departed for work right behind Scott and the girls, and they were usually home by the time she pulled into the driveway at five thirty. Even if one of the girls had an after-school activity, the other would be around. And Scott rarely stayed at the middle school past four o'clock.

Every now and then, Ellie wished for just this — an empty house, the peace, the freedom of knowing every room, every wall, every cubic inch of air belonged only to her. Well, to Lucy, too, but she was a generally calm, easy-going mutt who demanded little beyond an occasional belly scratch and an open door to the yard when she had to pee. Ellie wished her daughters were as mellow as their dog.

These days, it seemed, Abbie lurched from crisis to crisis, her crises usually on the order of a broken fingernail, a rumor that someone in school had said something to someone about someone else, or a homework assignment that, according to Abbie, was stupid and an utter waste of time. Abbie could fight like Rambo in a Southeast Asian jungle over such life-or-death issues as her desperate need of a certain kind of mechanical pencil and Ellie's failure to drop whatever she was doing and drive Abbie directly to the store to buy that pencil. Or her parents' unforgivable stinginess in refusing to subscribe to every single one of the streaming services available on TV. Or the outrageous injustice of Ellie's denying her the right to plaster her face with makeup.

Misha was easier, but only because her hormones hadn't fully kicked in yet. She was in the early throes of preadolescence. She had sprouted little bumps on her chest and spent an inordinate amount of time studying her reflection in the full-length mirror in the upstairs hallway, demanding to know when, if ever, she would have cleavage — and whether having cleavage would interfere with her ability to play soccer. She had discussed shaving her legs and tweezing her eyebrows with Ellie, even though she didn't need to do either yet. She wanted to know if the fact that Luke Bartelli was her best friend meant she and Luke were gay. She wanted to know if she was smart enough to get into the honors math class once she started middle school.

Ellie assured her she was smart enough. And if she really wished, she could start shaving her legs in sixth grade, although her eyebrows seemed nicely shaped without any tweezing. A stretch bra might be appropriate, but Misha said she didn't want to wear one yet. And whether or not she or Luke were gay had nothing to do with the fact that they were buddies.

Ellie and Misha didn't have to argue about any of this. Misha was usually upbeat and enthusiastic, even about trivial matters like accessorizing her sneakers with rainbow-hued shoe laces or spotting a chipmunk scampering across the back yard, or taking second place in a classroom spelling bee. So many things seemed to energize her; so few intensified into a crisis.

And then there was Scott. He was a loyal husband, a devoted father — and far from upbeat when it came to the state of the universe, about which he could fume fiercely and endlessly, even when Ellie was trying to cook dinner or solve the crossword puzzle in the newspaper. "Our atmosphere's average temperature has risen nearly two degrees Fahrenheit in the past five years," he would rant. "We can switch over to electric cars, but then we have to mine lithium for the cars' batteries. Do you have any idea how dirty lithium mines are?"

Scott, Abbie, and Misha were all gone right now, and Ellie ought to savor the silence of her house on this sunny Sunday morning. She ought to welcome it. But it made her edgy.

She picked up her phone and tapped Connie's number. "Hey," Connie said. "Is the man of the hour gone?"

"The man of the hour is going to be on the news tonight," Ellie told her. "Are you free? I'm making a fresh pot of coffee, and I think I've got some blueberry scones in the fridge, if Scott and the girls didn't eat them all."

"I'm on my way," Connie said.

Ellie disconnected the call and prepared the coffee. Belatedly, she checked the refrigerator's contents. The box containing the scones was still on the bottom shelf, with two scones inside. She had bought a half dozen yesterday, detouring to Trumbull's Bakery after she'd finished her weekly supermarket run. Scott had muttered about the scones' lack of nutritional value, but she had argued that the family ought to eat something special for his farewell breakfast before he headed off on his cross-country bicycle trip, and besides, blueberries were nutritious. She herself had been too nervous about his impending departure to eat anything when they'd all arisen that morning, but Scott had wound up eating two scones, and Abbie and Misha had each eaten one. That left two in the box for Ellie and Connie.

The coffee maker beeped to announce that the cycle was complete just as Ellie heard the sound of a car idling and then shutting off in her driveway. Connie knew to walk around to the back yard and use the kitchen door. "Hello!" she called through the screen before opening it.

Lucy backed away from the door and let out a happy bark as Connie entered. After sniffing Connie's espadrilles, the dog trotted over to her water dish, the exertion of greeting Connie apparently having dehydrated her.

Connie was dressed more formally than Ellie had expected — tailored slacks and a smooth knit shell with lacy trim along the neckline. Before Ellie could comment, Connie said, "I'm hosting an open house from one to three." She had taken courses, passed the licensing exam, and become a real estate agent five years ago. Ellie was impressed that in her forties, Connie had tackled a new career and was flourishing in it. When they'd met, Connie had been working part-time in a gift shop in town, the sort of job you got when you married straight out of college after graduating with a degree in anthropology and harboring no interest in traveling to a remote island nation to study its native inhabitants.

Abbie and Connie's daughter Merritt had been classmates at the Koala Cub Club, a preschool just a few blocks from the Shelton Town Hall, where Ellie worked then — and still worked now. Once Ellie and Connie had bonded as fellow mothers of koala cubs, they'd arranged countless play dates for Abbie and Merritt, but the girls didn't like each other. Now in high school, Abbie complained that Merritt was much too goth, dressing in funereal outfits, dying her hair black, and moping around the school as if a storm cloud constantly hovered above her head. Connie told Ellie that Merritt was suffering from depression and seeing a therapist. Ellie had no idea if Merritt had serious psychological issues or was merely pretending. But Ellie was relieved that Abbie had grown in a different direction, playing junior varsity volleyball, studying the clarinet, and leaving her chestnut-brown hair undyed.

Fortunately, their daughters' failure to click had no bearing on Ellie's and Connie's friendship. The moms no longer had to arrange play dates for their children in order to see each other.

Connie made herself comfortable at the kitchen table while Ellie poured two cups of coffee and carried them, two plates, and the bakery box to the table. "Ooh, these look delicious," Connie said as she lifted the lid. "Trumbull's? Their stuff is so good."

Ellie settled into the chair across the table from Connie and helped herself to a scone. Connie took the other one and broke it carefully in half, catching the drizzle of crumbs on her plate. "So tell me about Scott's send-off. He's really going to be on TV?"

"I may wind up on TV, too," Ellie said. "A reporter from Channel 7 interviewed me and Scott, and Misha added her two cents. You know they run that hour-long news broadcast every night. They obviously need filler."

"Nonsense," Connie argued. "It's not just filler. What he's doing is newsworthy."

"Maybe, but it's also crazy, don't you think?"

Connie tasted her scone and smiled. "Delicious," she said around a mouthful of pastry. She chewed, swallowed, and reverted to the topic of Scott. "You must be so proud of him, Ellie. Not just because he'll be on TV, but honestly, he's like a warrior, marching into battle. Or pedaling into battle, I guess. Doesn't that turn you on?"

Ellie laughed. "When he first told me he wanted to do this, yeah, it turned me on. How can you not love someone who wants to save the world? But now that he's actually doing it . . ." Her smile faded. "I'm worried. I already miss him, and I keep wondering why he had to do this. He could get hit by a car. He could . . ." She drifted off, once again imagining all the catastrophes that could befall him. "Does he really think he can change the world by riding his bike to California?"

"He's got vision," Connie said, then took another delicate bite of her scone. She was a petite woman, her face angular, almost pinched. Ellie was pleased to see her devouring the treat. She was always on a diet, even though she didn't need to lose any weight. According to her, her husband thought she was pudgy.

Then again, her husband was an asshole. Ellie often shared her opinion of him with Connie, and Connie invariably agreed with her.

"Scott thinks beyond himself," Connie said. "The only time Richard ever thinks beyond himself is when the Patriots are playing. Then he thinks about the Patriots."

"It isn't football season now. Richard could think about other things."

"The Red Sox," Connie said, then sighed. She lowered her scone, took a sip of coffee, and leaned across the table. "I opened my own bank account," she whispered.

Why was she whispering? The only person in the kitchen who could hear her confession was Ellie. Lucy wasn't a person, so she didn't count. "Richard doesn't know?"

Connie shook her head. "I'm going to put a portion of my earnings in it with each house I sell. He won't even notice."

He probably wouldn't. Richard Vernon earned oceans of money as a fund manager. According to Connie, he regarded her real estate commissions as pocket change, pin money, nothing more than an added hassle when his accountant prepared their tax returns.

"And if he does notice," Connie continued, her voice fractionally louder, "I'll tell him I donated that money to charity. It's not exactly a lie. I'll be donating to the Connie charity."

"Are you going to leave him?" Ellie asked. Connie often moaned about how difficult Richard was, how selfish, how domineering. She'd been contemplating divorce for some time. Once, a few years ago, she had even talked to an attorney, but she'd decided the time wasn't right.

Evidently, it still wasn't right. "I can't afford to yet. And anyway, Merritt's so fragile. I want to wait until she leaves for college. By then, I should have a decent nest egg in my secret bank account."

"You don't have to wait until you can afford it," Ellie told her. "You could make him support you if you got a divorce. He could pay alimony."

"Right. Like he's going to pay me alimony if *I* leave *him*. He'd fight me tooth and nail, and then he'd demand full custody of

Merritt, even though he doesn't spend any time with her. He'd do it just to spite me." She popped the last bit of scone into her mouth, swallowed, and smiled. Merely thinking about leaving her husband seemed to cheer her. "You're so lucky, Ellie. Scott is a saint."

"No, he's not." Ellie dismissed Connie's comment with a laugh. "He can be self-righteous, and sanctimonious — "

"Isn't that what being a saint is all about? Sanctimony and self-righteousness?"

"He's trying to save the world. You need a pretty big ego to believe you can do that."

"So he's got a healthy ego." Connie shrugged. "Trust me, Ellie. He's a saint. You don't know how lucky you are."

Ellie opened her mouth to dispute Connie's statement, then closed it without saying a word. She did know how lucky she was. Scott was a terrific guy, even if he wasn't a saint. Who would want to be married to a saint, anyway?

Of course Ellie supported him in his mission. How could she not? The planet he was trying to save was her planet as much as his. He wasn't abdicating responsibility; he was making an enormous sacrifice, spending so much time away from his family.

And yet.

He was going to be gone for the whole summer. He was going to abandon his family for three months, maybe longer. He was going to leave Ellie alone, without another adult under her roof to back her up, to pick up the slack. To pick it up before it became slack.

When Abbie and Misha bickered, Scott was the one who got them to stop. They didn't listen to Ellie the way they listened to him. When one of the warning lights on the dashboard of Ellie's car flashed on, Scott was the one who added the fluid or checked the air pressure in the tires. When some telemarketer phoned during dinner, Scott always gleefully took the phone and had fun with the caller. "You want me to buy hearing aids? Huh? Could you speak up? I can't hear you!"

This wasn't the first time he'd left her and the girls alone. He attended his high school and college reunions without her, and he'd stayed a week at his mother's house after his father died. Ellie could handle a few days here, a week there. She was competent. She was sensible. She kept the refrigerator full, made sure the bills were paid, oversaw the girls' schedules, the parent-teacher conferences, the permission slips, the laundry. All those Mommy things.

But she'd never had to be a solo parent for months on end — and she'd never had to do it while wondering if that little orange flag on the back of Scott's bike trailer would keep him from getting run over by a car on some back road in Indiana or Arkansas.

"I am lucky," she admitted, taking a sip of her coffee. Everything would be fine. Despite being a cranky, moody teenager, Abbie was mature and well-behaved. Despite being a little hyper at times, so was Misha. They would manage without their father for a few months. Before she'd married Scott, Ellie had taken care of her own car, a much older, more decrepit car than the hybrid she was currently driving. She could take care of her car now.

He would be gone, but he would come home. His little orange flag would protect him, and he would save the world and then come home.

CHAPTER THREE

"He ate at McDonald's, and we have to eat tofu stir-fry," Misha complained.

They had just ended their phone call with Scott, which had interrupted their dinner but was nonetheless welcomed. He had reported that, indeed, he'd eaten two hamburgers and a wilted salad from McDonald's. He'd told them his first day had gone smoothly. He'd spotted more squirrels than he could count along the side of the road, and a few bunnies, and lots of cars, but not too many trucks because trucks mostly stuck to the Interstate, where cyclists weren't permitted to ride. "I had to breathe in some auto exhaust fumes, but no truck fumes," he'd told them. "That's a plus."

"I like tofu stir-fry," Abbie said as she delicately poked the tines of her fork into the last button mushroom remaining on her plate. "I thought it tasted good." She punctuated this critique by popping the mushroom into her mouth.

Ellie smiled, wondering what privilege Abbie was going to request. She rarely wasted her breath complimenting a meal Ellie served. Her praise for that evening's dinner undoubtedly meant she wanted something from her mother. Permission to wear mascara, probably.

"It tasted okay," Misha allowed. "But Daddy ate at McDonald's. We never eat there. When was the last time we ate at McDonald's?"

"You should feel sorry for your father," Ellie pointed out. "He had to eat a greasy, flavorless hamburger."

"*Two* hamburgers," Misha corrected her. "He ate two."

"I tell you what." Ellie knew the girls were restless. She'd been as aware as they were of Scott's vacant chair at the kitchen table, the empty placemat, the absence of his deep male voice harmonizing with their high-pitched female voices, the lack of his lame jokes and indignant proclamations and interrogations about the homework they would be turning in to their teachers on Monday. All three Gillman women needed something to distract them from the fact that Scott was gone. Something to cheer them up. "How about if I make some popcorn and we watch a movie this evening? You both finished your homework, right?"

"*Field of Dreams!*" Misha shouted. It was Scott's favorite movie.

Ellie glanced at Abbie, who nodded. "Yeah, we should watch *Field of Dreams* in Dad's honor, since he's not here."

"Fine." Not the funniest movie, and by the end they would all be sobbing, but they would be sobbing happy tears. Ellie stood, gathered the empty plates and silverware, and carried them to the sink. "Go set up the DVD player and I'll make the popcorn."

The girls scampered into the den, Abbie ahead of Misha because she was bigger and older. Ellie grinned as she rinsed the plates and stacked them in the dishwasher. Abbie might be a teenager, might believe she was quite sophisticated, might insist that she should be allowed to wear as much makeup as she wanted, wherever and whenever she wished. But the thought of a family movie accompanied by a big bowl of popcorn still excited her. She was not as nonchalant as she might believe.

Once the dishes were done, the table wiped down, and the popcorn popped, Ellie joined the girls on the sofa in the den. It had once been a vivid brown, but now it was faded to a vague grayish-taupe, the fabric shiny in spots, the cushions permanently depressed in the shapes of variously sized butts. Ellie would love to buy a new couch. For that matter, she would love to buy new living room furniture, a new runner rug for the hallway, a new armoire for the master bedroom — on the old one, one of the doors never closed properly — and a new kitchen table with a heavily lacquered surface, impervious to spills and stains. But while solidly middle class, the Gillmans weren't rich. They deposited a significant chunk of Ellie's monthly paycheck into a college fund for the girls and did their best to cover their day-to-day expenses using only Scott's schoolteacher income.

Ellie was acutely aware that while Scott's school agreed to pay his salary through the end of the current term, he would not be earning any money teaching summer school this year, and if his save-the-planet bike tour caused him to miss the beginning of the fall term, he would not be granted a paid sabbatical. Scott had set up his GoFundMe page to finance his trip, but that money was dedicated solely to the trip. He could pay for dinner at McDonald's using those funds, and his motel room, and whatever other expenses he incurred as he saved the planet, but Ellie could not use a penny of his GoFundMe money to splurge on scones for breakfast, let alone a sofa, a rug, and all the rest. Tomorrow, the girls would be back to breakfasts of cereal and milk, although lately Abbie had taken to augmenting her morning meal with a half cup of black coffee, which she choked down while insisting it tasted delicious. She stubbornly refused to make the coffee more palatable by adding sugar and cream. "The whole idea is it's got no calories," she explained to Ellie as she sipped the bitter black brew in her mug and grimaced. "What would be the point of drinking it if it made me fat?"

As soon as Ellie settled onto the sofa, Misha pressed the "play" button on the remote control and the movie began.

Ellie had arrived in the den armed with distractions along with the popcorn: the magazine from the Sunday *Boston Globe*, a pencil, and her phone. She checked her phone first. Scott had told her he would be contributing regularly to a website called Wheeling and Dealing, which allowed long-distance bicycle riders to post photos and updates about their trips. "It's a good way to stay in touch with all those generous people who donated on the GoFundMe page," he'd explained. A good way to stay in touch with his fans, too, Ellie thought. A good way to remain in the spotlight, however dim that spotlight might be.

She was able to access his Wheeling and Dealing page on her phone. He had posted pretty much exactly what he'd told Ellie and the girls during their phone conversation: he had crossed into New York State, he'd found a cheap motel for the night, he'd bought supper at a McDonald's down the road from the motel. He didn't mention the squirrels and rabbits in his post, but Ellie supposed that in time, he would write longer entries and offer more detail. It would be pretty boring for him to post *I biked 150 miles and ate at McDonald's* every day. Then again, squirrels and rabbits could be kind of boring, too.

She glanced up at the television in time to watch the Boston-set scene from the movie, during which Kevin Costner would track down James Earl Jones and they would attend a baseball game at Fenway Park. Ellie always felt a surge of hometown pride during the movie's Boston section, even though the Gillmans lived twenty miles from the city. She and Scott had met in Boston as college students. They'd dated there. They'd fallen in love there. They had even ridden their bicycles through the city, although Ellie had always felt nervous when they did, given Boston's twisting streets and maniacal drivers. Scott was undoubtedly much safer biking across the continent than he'd been biking from Back Bay to the North End.

Abbie was already sniffling a bit, even though the movie hadn't gotten sad yet. Its overriding tone was wistful, and the soundtrack music was poignant. Misha would undoubtedly need to wipe her eyes and blow her nose soon, as well, but right now, she was too busy stuffing popcorn into her mouth. She was as thin as a blade of grass, even as she consumed vast quantities of food. That she could cram fistfuls of popcorn into her mouth after polishing off a heaping plate of stir-fry — she'd devoured a gluttonous portion despite her disappointment that it wasn't hamburgers — made Ellie wonder whether she was undergoing a growth spurt.

What if she grew two inches while Scott was away? Would he still recognize her when he got home?

Ellie reached across Misha's lap to scoop a few popcorn puffs from the bowl, then opened the magazine to the puzzle page. The actors' voices drifted through her brain, along with the sounds of traffic and the wind and whatever else was going on in the movie. Ellie had viewed it enough times — Scott liked to watch it at least once a year — that she didn't need to watch it now. She was content just listening to it with her daughters seated next to her, her dog under the coffee table gnawing on a plastic chew-toy shaped like a T-bone steak, and the salty fragrance of popcorn in the air.

By the end of the movie, as Ellie had predicted, Abbie and Misha were both sniffling, but smiling despite their moist eyes. "It's like Daddy," Misha said. "The hero has this dream, and he makes it come true, and it changes everything."

"Daddy's dream is a little more significant than building a baseball field in a cornfield," Ellie pointed out.

"He's not just building the ball field," Abbie reminded Ellie, gesturing toward the TV. "He's also reconciling with his father."

Ellie suppressed a smile at Abbie's word choice. She was already studying vocabulary lists in preparation for the standardized college tests she expected to start taking next year. *Reconciling* wasn't a word she used on a regular basis.

"You're right," Ellie said. "Fortunately, your dad doesn't have to reconcile with his children. It's a school night, so time for bed, Misha."

"No! I have to stay up to watch the news. Daddy's going to be on it. And we are, too."

True enough. The news would start at ten p.m., and the story of Scott's bike ride wasn't major enough to appear in the first half hour. But Ellie couldn't *not* let Misha watch it, even if she would have to stay awake past ten thirty to do so. "Go get washed up, get into your PJ's, organize your backpack, and then you can stay up — just until the report about Dad is on. I don't want you falling asleep in class tomorrow."

"If Ms. Gorshin talks about the thousand paper cranes again, I'll fall asleep in class even if I go to bed right now," Misha predicted. "I mean, it's a good story, but she talked about it all last week. We all know how it ends. The girl dies."

"Go wash up anyway," Ellie ordered, softening the command by kissing the crown of Misha's head.

Both girls rose from the couch, Abbie carrying the empty popcorn bowl, and vanished into the kitchen. Ellie heard the spray of the water in the sink as they cleaned the bowl, and then their footsteps as they climbed the stairs. After completing the crossword puzzle, she tapped her phone awake, clicked to the Wheeling and Dealing website, and read Scott's entry once more. He would probably be deeply asleep in his motel room by now. All that biking — he'd be exhausted from today, and in need of a good night's rest for tomorrow.

She, on the other hand, couldn't imagine falling asleep. She was tired. It had been a hectic day after a restless night. But how could she sleep when worry niggled at her? It was a faint white noise inside her skull, reminding her of everything that could go wrong on Scott's trip, how far away he would be, how unreachable. Sticking to the back roads, he could have an accident and discover that he had no cell phone signal. Or the accident might break his phone altogether. He would surely encounter precipitation — he'd packed waterproof outerwear with that expectation — and the wet roads would be slick. Even worse, in those vast Midwestern states he might encounter tornadoes. She had watched *The Wizard of Oz* almost as many times as *Field of Dreams*, and the image of Mrs. Gulch pedaling her bicycle through a twister, while Dorothy's house spun through the air before landing in Oz, had always made Ellie laugh. Not anymore.

She shook herself free of negative thoughts once the girls returned to the den. Abbie was still dressed, but Misha wore her jammies, the cotton worn nearly to transparency and the flowers in the pattern faded beyond recognition. The bottoms fell barely past midshin on Misha's legs. She was definitely growing.

Ellie heaved herself off the couch and carried her magazine to the kitchen, where she added it to the recycle pile. Then she let Lucy out into the backyard for her final pee of the day. If Scott were home, he might have poured himself and Ellie a glass of port, a treat they often enjoyed at the end of a long week. But she wouldn't drink port without him, especially not with the girls around. Most Sundays at this hour, Misha was asleep and Abbie was shut up inside her bedroom, texting with her friends.

Ellie had guessed correctly; the report about Scott's bike trip didn't appear until after the weather forecast at ten thirty, although the newscast showed several teasers about it, the anchorwoman gushing, "And coming up soon — this Shelton man is using his bicycle to spread the word about global warming!"

"Climate change!" both Abbie and Misha shouted at the television each time the anchorwoman said "global warming." Scott had explained to them that not all climate change was about the planet's growing warmer, although the rise in atmospheric temperature was the underlying cause of many weather disturbances. "When you say 'global warming,' someone always says, 'If the planet is so warm, how come we got two feet of snow yesterday?' or 'Bring on the warming! I'm tired of these subzero temperatures!' The problem is that weather extremes used to be aberrant, and they're not anymore. Do you know what *aberrant* means?"

Scott had defined the word for them enough times that they knew it now. If it appeared in the vocabulary portion of Abbie's SAT test next year, she would be prepared.

Finally, after the meteorologist described the upcoming weather for the week — no tornadoes forecast for the Midwest, thank God — Scott's story came on. There was their house, their street, the children with the banner, the school choir, the trumpeter, the Girl Scouts with the cookies. There was Scott, looking remarkably sexy in his bright yellow RE:CYCLE shirt and snug biking shorts. He had been in excellent shape even before he'd started his training regimen for this trip. Now, his calves were even more contoured with muscle, his thighs taut beneath the shorts, his arms lean and sinewy; they were hidden by the long sleeves of his Henley shirt, but last night those strong, naked arms had held Ellie close. His hair danced gently in the breeze, mostly a dark blond with a few strands of silver woven through the waves. He squinted slightly in the bright sunlight, and his smile folded his lean cheeks into dimples.

"He looks good!" Abbie said. It was unlike her to be so enthusiastic about anything, let alone her parents. But she'd only spoken the truth. He did look good.

More than good, he looked amazingly confident. He looked like someone who intended to save the planet and believed he was capable of it. In the news feature, with the reporter babbling about his trip in a gee-whiz singsong voice and the school children cheering for him as if he were a pop music idol, he was getting a great deal of attention — which was what he'd wanted this trip to be about. At least on his first day, things were going precisely as he'd hoped they would.

"There we are!" Misha bounced on the couch, not the least bit sleepy despite the late hour. "Look, Mom!"

Indeed, there Ellie and Misha were. Misha looked as eager as her father did, but less squinty-eyed in the sun's glare. In the background, on the front porch, Abbie was a faint silhouette, but she still cringed and covered her face with her hands as the camera panned the length of the porch. "Ugh," she groaned. "I look awful."

"You look beautiful," Ellie argued, not adding that Abbie's eyes were lovely without any makeup on them.

She remembered the pat phrases she'd said in answer to the reporter's questions. Listening to herself speak in the broadcast, she decided she sounded articulate and knowledgeable, and while not as pretty as either of her daughters, she appeared reasonably presentable in her slim jeans and cotton sweater. But she wasn't looking straight at the reporter, or at the cameraman directly behind. Her gaze angled a bit past the camera, settling on Scott. And her eyes appeared worried, her lips tense, her hands curled into fists. Loose fists, but fists just the same.

What had she been thinking when she'd talked to the reporter? That her husband would be riding off toward the horizon on a skimpy bike with little protection other than his helmet and that orange flag? That he would be gone for months?

Or that when he came home, he would be different? Not dirty, although she was sure he would be scruffy. No matter how many showers he took and how many loads of laundry he ran, road dirt would cling to him. He might decide, after a while, to forgo shaving. His hair would be even longer.

But those differences were cosmetic. What if he changed inside? What if he truly did believe himself worthy of all the attention he was receiving? What if he honestly was convinced that he had saved the planet?

What if he came home a saint? How would she be able to live with someone like that?

DAY FIVE

All went well at Millardville today. I arrived at the primary school later than expected (road construction, a detour, and hills, hills, hills!), but thank heavens for cell phones. I contacted the school, and they were able to push my presentation back to two o'clock.

The kids loved my presentation! They watched my PowerPoint slides and listened to my talk. They asked good questions. (Well, some of those good questions were asked by teachers, not students.) They were very curious about the bike itself. Most of them had never seen a recumbent bike before. And the Beast of Burden was a novelty to them. A couple of them mentioned those screened, zippered child carriers adults sometimes attach to their bicycles, but not a trailer for carrying gear, which is a necessity if you're using your bike in place of a car. Bikes don't have trunks, right? You need that Beast of Burden to carry your groceries home from the supermarket — or your clothing, snack supply, and laptop across the country.

Anyway, the kids were a terrific audience. They wanted to pose for pictures with the bike, and with me. The third-grade teacher (Millardville is small enough that they have only one class per grade) used her phone to take a group shot of me surrounded by her students. As soon as the fourth graders saw that, they asked their teacher to take a picture of me with them. And then the second graders wanted their turn, and the kindergarteners, and all the other students.

I felt like a movie star, posing for photo after photo. Some of the photos were posted to the school district's website: www.millardvillepublicschools.edu. *As you can see, I look a lot more like a long-distance cyclist than a movie star. But my RE:CYCLE shirt photographs really well, doesn't it?*

More later.

CHAPTER FOUR

"**Y**our husband is famous!" Wayne boomed as Ellie entered the office suite she shared with him in the town hall. Wayne McNulty was officially the town manager and Ellie was his assistant, but in truth, she performed most of the work his job entailed. Wayne owed his position to the Shelton Select Board, which had hired him. He specialized in shaking hands, slapping backs, and making sure the members of the select board thought he'd hung the moon. He had sculpted hair as thick as a mink's fur, the neon smile of a game show host, and the robust personality of a politician, even though, unlike the select board members, his wasn't an elected position. He answered to the board, and they in turn answered to the town's residents who had voted for them.

With his glossy appearance and glib manner, Wayne was skilled at addressing town meetings, delivering the explanations and mission statements that Ellie prepared for him, and taking credit whenever anything went right.

As his assistant, Ellie made sure most things went right.

While she found Wayne overweening, and she sometimes — often — resented having to take orders from someone five years younger than she was and nowhere near as competent, she loved her job. She had majored in urban planning in college, and while Shelton was more suburban than urban, she knew how to do whatever needed to be done to keep the town functioning smoothly. She had worked in several of the town's departments en route to her current job as the assistant town manager, and her resume and experience far outshone Wayne's. But she lacked his talent for backslapping and handshaking, and her hair fell in a drab, brown, shoulder-length pageboy. Clearly, the select board placed a great deal of value on backslapping, handshaking, and impressive hair. They adored Wayne McNulty.

Ellie had spent most of the afternoon at the public safety complex down the road from the town hall, explaining to the fire chief that he could not get a new state-of-the-art fire truck every year. The fire engine he craved carried a sticker price in the mid six figures, and the town simply couldn't budget that much so Chief Mulroney could have all spanking-new engines. "Every three years, minimum," she'd informed him after sharing her budget projections with him. There was a limit to how high property taxes could go. There was a limit to how much blood she and Miriam Horowitz, the town controller, could squeeze from a stone. "The older trucks still work. They might not have all the bells and whistles, but they've got excellent sirens."

Chief Mulroney had smiled weakly at her joke. She knew he was disappointed. She knew that every department in town — Police, Public Works, Public Health, Education — wanted the latest, the newest, the best. They wanted fancy buildings and fancy vehicles and tractors that could simultaneously clear snow from the sidewalks and sprinkle chemicals that would melt the ice. As someone who walked on those sidewalks, she would love to provide the public works department with such tractors. But . . . Property taxes. Blood from a stone.

Of course, Wayne didn't want to be the one who said no to the town's various department heads. He wanted to be popular, to be loved. So he had Ellie handle that unpleasant chore. It made sense that she should be the one to tell the department heads their wishes would not be fulfilled, since she also prepared the budgets and worked with Miriam to monitor revenues. She knew better than Wayne did what the town could and could not afford.

Sometimes she wondered whether she ought to be the town manager, rather than the assistant town manager. She wondered whether she ought to get the title, the glory, the bigger office, the bigger salary. She would definitely appreciate the bigger salary, but the rest of it? If the job meant kissing up to elected officials all the time, she wasn't sure she'd want that. She wasn't sure she'd be terribly good at it, either.

"So," Wayne said, "Joe Schumacher told me your husband was on the Channel 7 news the other night. We found a video online, so I was able to see for myself. You were in the video, too."

Although it was nearly four o'clock in the afternoon, this was the first time she'd talked to Wayne since she had arrived at work that morning. He hadn't found his way to the town hall until she had already left for her meeting with Chief Mulroney. Evidently, he'd spent part of that morning with Joe Schumacher, who was the town counsel, another glad-handing political hack. Given that it was a lovely spring day, they had probably conducted their business on the golf course at the ritzy country club where Wayne was a member. At some point — perhaps while indulging in an expense-account lunch in the clubhouse after the eighteenth hole — they'd plugged in a laptop or done a search on their phones and found the news report of Scott's festive departure.

"So your husband's famous," Wayne said now.

"He's trying to raise awareness about climate change," Ellie said. "Any news coverage is welcome."

"Good luck to him. I wouldn't want to ride across the country on a bicycle myself. For one thing, I think my ass would get pretty sore, all that time on a bike seat. For another, what does he do if it rains?"

"He has a rain slicker and waterproof pants," Ellie said.

Wayne shrugged. "I'm a suit-and-tie guy myself," he said, although at the moment he was wearing a dark gray sport coat, khaki slacks, and a polo shirt. No tie. "Gotta hand it to the guy, though. He's making quite a splash."

He'd make a bigger splash if it was raining, but Ellie didn't mention that.

"So, how'd it go with Dan?" Wayne asked. Of course he was on a first-name basis with the fire chief. During her session with him that afternoon, Ellie had called him Chief Mulroney, as she always did. He had never invited her to call him anything else. But then, since she was nearly always the one delivering unwelcome news, he probably didn't consider her a friend.

She filled Wayne in on her meeting with Chief Mulroney, conveyed his disappointment, and explained the numbers she and Miriam had come up with to justify their denial of the fire chief's coveted new fire engine. Wayne listened with a vague expression, as if he were already thinking about what wine to drink with his dinner that evening.

"Chief Mulroney told me you'd promised him a new fire engine this year, Wayne," she said, allowing a little steel into her tone. "You knew the budget couldn't accommodate that. Why on earth did you promise him?"

"I didn't exactly *promise* him," Wayne defended himself. "I told him we'd do our best to get him one. I'm sure you did your best."

"He seemed to think it was more of a commitment than 'doing our best.' You've got to check with me before you make promises like that, okay? I'm looking at our property tax revenue for the next few quarters, and the money just isn't there."

"Okay, okay." Wayne sounded like a petulant teenager who'd come home an hour past curfew, smelling of beer. "I didn't *promise* Dan anything. He must have misinterpreted what I told him."

"Don't tell him anything," Ellie warned, "unless you check with me first."

Wayne nodded, properly chastened. At the threshold between her office and his, he hesitated and turned to face her. "Almost forgot — your daughter called while you were out."

"My daughter?" Ellie cautioned herself not to panic.

Today, Abbie had orchestra practice after school, but Misha could handle being on her own in the house for a couple of hours. She wouldn't have had to be alone if Scott hadn't bicycled off to save the world, but she had assured Ellie she could manage until either Ellie or Abbie got home. "I'll have a snack and do my homework," she'd told Ellie. "I'll let Lucy out in the backyard in case she has to pee. I'm almost old enough to babysit. I think I can take care of myself. And

I can always call Mrs. Kupferman if I need help." Nancy Kupferman was their next-door neighbor. In her late sixties, her children grown and scattered around the country, she moaned about not getting to see her grandchildren often. She clearly didn't view Abbie and Misha as surrogate grandchildren, since most of her interaction with them involved her telling them to make Lucy stop barking at the squirrels who scampered through their adjacent yards. But she'd assured Ellie that the girls could always phone her in an emergency.

Misha hadn't called Mrs. Kupferman, which meant she probably wasn't dealing with an emergency. But she'd called her mother's office, and Ellie couldn't help but worry. "When did she phone? Did she sound all right?"

"Oh, she was fine," Wayne said with a dismissive wave of his hand. "What an imagination. She told me she was named after Michelle Obama."

"She *was* named after Michelle Obama," Ellie said.

Wayne's eyebrows arched in surprise. His forehead was surprisingly smooth for a forty-year-old. But then, he never seemed to worry about anything. Why would he have frown lines or stress wrinkles? "You named her after Michelle Obama? Are you friendly with the Obamas?"

"No," Ellie said, racing through her explanation so she could end this discussion and return Misha's phone call. "My parents always told everyone I was named after Eleanor Roosevelt. When my daughters were born, I decided to continue the tradition by naming our daughters after First Ladies. Abbie was named after Abigail Adams, and Misha after Michelle Obama. And the dog was named after Lucy Hayes."

"Lucy who? We had a president named Hayes?"

"Rutherford B. Hayes," Ellie answered, stifling the urge to tell Wayne he was an idiot. Seriously — the town manager, the person charged with making sure the town of Shelton functioned successfully — didn't even know the names of the presidents? "I really need to call my daughter back."

Wayne seemed mystified, although why he would think it was perfectly sensible to name his boys after two beloved Boston Bruins hockey players — he'd told Ellie his sons Cameron and Philip were named after Cam Neely and Phil Esposito — but odd that Ellie and Scott had named their daughters after First Ladies, Ellie couldn't say. She watched him step into his office and shut the door, then dropped onto the swivel chair behind her desk, pulled her cell phone from her purse, and called home.

Misha answered after two rings. "Misha, is everything all right?"

"I guess," Misha said, although she didn't sound all right.

"What happened?"

"I hate Luke Bartelli. He's so mean!"

Luke? Her best friend? "What did he do?"

"He started this club, in honor of Daddy. They're going to follow Daddy's bike trip on a map, and do little bike rides around town to tell people about what Daddy's doing."

"That sounds wonderful," Ellie said.

"Yeah, but he wouldn't let me join. He wrote me this note that said, 'No Girls Allowed.' Only he didn't spell it right. He wrote a-l-o-u-d. 'No Girls Aloud,' like we're supposed to be silent or something."

Ellie relaxed in her chair. She didn't want to minimize Misha's indignation. Of course Misha was hurt. Of course discriminating against girls was bad. Of course misspelling the word "allowed" was stupid. But at least the house wasn't on fire. At least Misha wasn't lying on the kitchen floor, gushing blood.

"Honey, you should have called me on my cell phone. I was out of the office, but you could have reached me."

"I didn't want to bother you. I figured if you were out of the office, you were probably doing something important."

"I do important things *in* the office, too," Ellie said. "But with Dad gone when you get home from school, and you're all alone in the house, I want you to be able to reach me, no matter where I am." Ellie would also prefer that Misha not engage in meandering conversations with Wayne, who apparently had nothing better to do than answer Ellie's office phone when she wasn't able to answer it herself. "I think Luke is being very small-minded, and I don't blame you for being mad."

"I hate him," Misha said, her voice wavering.

"Right now, you do. Maybe he'll come to his senses and realize what an idiotic thing he's doing by banning girls from his club."

"Especially 'cause it's *my* father. I bet Daddy would be really pissed if he knew Luke had made this club in his honor and then told me I couldn't be in it."

"I'm sure he would be," Ellie said. "Don't use words like 'pissed.' They're crude."

"I don't care. I'm so mad." Misha's voice wavered even more. She sounded on the verge of tears.

"I'll be home as soon as I can," Ellie told her. "I've got some documents to file, and I have to make sure Mr. McNulty isn't making any promises he can't keep. And then I'll come home. Will you be all right until then?"

"I guess so." Misha sighed damply. "I might have to eat some cookies."

"Don't spoil your appetite," Ellie warned before telling Misha she loved her and ending the call. And realizing that, given how thin she was, Misha could probably eat an entire package of cookies and still have room for dinner.

Ellie pulled into the driveway just minutes before Abbie arrived home. "Torie Shinako's mom drove me home," Abbie reported as she swept into the house, her backpack dangling from one shoulder and her clarinet case in her other hand. "So I didn't have to take the late bus." She uttered the words *late bus* with a grimace and a shudder, as if the route the late bus took passed through several circles of hell before delivering the students to their stops.

"I'll have to give Torie's mother a call to thank her," Ellie said, dropping the leather tote that served double duty as her purse and her briefcase on the kitchen counter and bracing herself for Lucy's enthusiastic greeting. Fortunately, Lucy was not much bigger than a loaf of rye bread, so she didn't knock Ellie over with her joyful headbutt. She might have tripped Ellie, though, especially since Ellie was searching the room for her other daughter. "Misha?" she shouted toward the ceiling, figuring Misha was upstairs in her bedroom. "We're home!"

"Don't call Ms. Shinako," Abbie said, as if to do so would be a grotesque faux pas. "I'll die if you call her."

"Why will you die?"

"Because. It's embarrassing." She dropped her backpack onto one of the chairs by the kitchen table. "I thanked her. What's for dinner?"

Ellie hadn't given dinner much thought. She'd been distracted by worry about Misha, and now she was additionally distracted by the understanding that she owed Meg Shinako a favor. Would she be able to leave work early to pick up Abbie and Torie at the high school the next time they had a late orchestra rehearsal?

Before she could sort out the asset-debit ratio on her mental balance sheet of mommy-favors, Misha clomped down the stairs, her feet thudding ominously on each step. For a skinny ten-year-old, she could make a lot of noise on the stairway.

She stormed into the kitchen, her expression glowering, a bag of chocolate chip cookies clutched in one hand. She hadn't polished off the entire package, Ellie noted with some relief, and she wasn't crying, Ellie noted with even greater relief.

"Wow," Abbie said, assessing her sister with an intense stare as she unzipped her hoodie. "You look like you want to bite someone's head off."

"Luke Bartelli's head," Misha said, setting the cookies on the counter. "He'd probably taste gross, though. Like raw tadpoles or something."

On that appetizing note, Ellie swung open the door of the refrigerator to see if it contained anything that might be easy to cook. Vegetables for a salad, but she wasn't going to feed the girls beans or cheese for their protein. She would have to defrost something. She was reasonably certain the freezer didn't contain raw tadpoles.

"I have the information for the end-of-the-year concert," Abbie told Ellie, unclipping the strap on her backpack and folding back the lid. "The times and everything. I can't believe Dad's going to miss it. He never misses my concerts." She sounded more sorrowful than annoyed about this. Her next comment was directed at her sister. "What did Luke do?"

"He started a club all about Daddy's bike trip, and he said I couldn't join because I was a girl."

"You're kidding! What a douche!"

"What's a douche?" Misha asked.

Abbie shot her mother a pleading look. Ellie shrugged. If Abbie was going to use that word, she could damned well define it for her sister. "It's, like, he's disgusting," Abbie told Misha.

"And you know what he did?" Misha continued, her tone bristling with righteous anger. "He said, 'No girls allowed,' only he misspelled 'allowed.' He spelled it a-l-o-u-d." Evidently, Misha considered this spelling error at least as offensive as his banning her from his club. She had raged about it to Ellie on the phone, and now she was raging about it to Abbie.

"Well, that just proves he's a —" Abbie caught herself before calling him a douche again. "A total moron." Swinging toward the cabinet where the pots were stacked, she yanked open the door and pulled out a skillet and a lid. "Here," she said, banging the two together as if they were cymbals. "Let's be *aloud*!"

The clamor nearly made Ellie drop the frozen salmon fillets she'd pulled out of the freezer. Misha let out a shriek and raced across the kitchen to grab her own instrument — in her case, the pot Ellie had used to make oatmeal in that morning, and a spatula from the utensil holder beside the stove. She banged the spatula against the pot as if it was a tom-tom, and howled like a banshee.

Abbie joined the chorus of howling. The two of them stormed around the kitchen, screeching and bashing their improvised instruments. Had they ever made this much noise before? Maybe when they were infants, wailing with hunger at two a.m.

Ellie tossed the salmon onto the counter and turned from the freezer, prepared to demand that they quiet down — but they looked so fierce, so fervent, so... free. That Abbie would be supportive of her pesky kid sister touched Ellie deeply. Abbie caught Ellie's eye on one circuit around the kitchen, and the grin she gave Ellie was more exuberant, more ecstatic than Ellie had seen since adolescence had swamped Abbie with hormones and pseudo-sophisticated apathy.

How could Ellie possibly tell them to stop?

"We're loud!" Abbie bellowed.

"We're *a*-loud!" Misha chorused.

"We're the *Aloud Girls!*" Abbie roared.

"*Girls Aloud! Girls Aloud!*" Misha shrieked.

They were so *aloud*, Ellie almost didn't hear the phone ring. She grabbed the cordless handset, hurried into the living room where the noise was half a decibel lower, and answered. "Hello?"

"Hey," Scott said, then paused. "What the hell is going on?"

"They're girls aloud," Ellie said, then laughed. "Girls may not be aloud everywhere, but they're aloud here. This is the 'Girls Aloud' house." She shouted toward the kitchen doorway, "Girls? Dad's on the phone."

A swell of giggles, a few more clanks and clunks on the pots, and then the noise died down. One room away, she could hear them panting, struggling to catch their breaths. More giggles.

"What the hell was that all about?" Scott asked again.

Ellie could hear him much better now that her daughters had subsided. She considered her answer. Did Scott really need to know? Did she have to explain? He wasn't a girl.

"You wouldn't understand," she said, realizing that her answer was a bit smug. But he was off biking — somewhere in Pennsylvania, if she wasn't mistaken — and he had a troop of boys, one of whom used to be Misha's best friend, celebrating his heroics.

He was a guy. He was *allowed*.

He wouldn't understand.

CHAPTER FIVE

"**H**ey!" Connie swept into Ellie's office, dressed in an outfit that all but screamed that she was a real estate agent: a blazer and tailored trousers, an eggshell-white blouse, modest heels, and a colorful silk scarf knotted loosely around her throat. "I just escaped from a brokers' open house down the block," she told Ellie, flopping onto one of the visitors' chairs, her posture the exact opposite of her crisp, polished apparel. She looked weary and bleary. "The house was hideous, not that the selling agent knocked herself out to stage it. Ratty old furniture, faded drapes, stained wall-to-wall carpeting, and an atmosphere of *eau-de-kitty-litter*. And garbage in the driveway. Sheesh. You'd think the selling broker would have tidied up the area around the trash cans." She wrinkled her nose, then grinned. "Of course, if I can find a buyer for it, I'll happily pocket my commission. But..." Another wrinkle-nosed grimace. "Given the price point, it's not going to do much for my personal checking account."

Ellie grinned. She was delighted that Connie had opened her secret personal bank account. Ellie couldn't imagine doing that herself — she and Scott had joint accounts; what was hers was his and what was his was hers — but then, if she were married to someone like Richard Vernon, she would want her own private cash stash.

The door to her office, which was essentially a large anteroom leading to Wayne's office, was always open. People came and went. Sometimes her visitors were town residents eager to lodge a complaint about the duration of the red light by the Whole Foods or a neighbor who was still displaying those dancing laser Christmas lights four months after the holiday, when the snow was long gone and daffodils were in full bloom. Sometimes her visitors were people who worked in the town hall, collecting signatures on a fellow employee's birthday card or searching for a stapler that didn't jam. And sometimes they were friends like Connie, who just happened to be in the neighborhood.

"I was wondering if you were free this evening," Connie continued. "Richard has a working dinner tonight. At least that's what he said. I figure if he's enjoying a three-martini dinner somewhere, I should be enjoying one, too."

Ellie would love a girls' night out with Connie, but she couldn't say yes. While Merritt and Abbie might be mature enough to be left alone at home for a few hours at night, Misha was still not quite ready for that much responsibility. Besides, Ellie couldn't abandon her girls when they were missing their father so much. His empty chair at the kitchen table at dinnertime every evening created a small but real pain, like a pebble in one's shoe. Ellie couldn't force her daughters to endure not one but two empty chairs. Two pebbles in one's shoe could be crippling.

"Why don't you and Merritt come over for dinner, instead?" she suggested. More full chairs would be far better than more empty chairs. "I can't promise martinis, but I can open a bottle of wine."

"Sounds great. I'll bring dessert."

"By the way, that's a beautiful scarf, but you don't need it."

"What do you mean, I don't need it?" Connie fingered the scarf. "I know it isn't cold out, but this is lightweight."

"Women wear scarves like that to conceal their wrinkly necks. Your neck is beautiful."

"Oh, it is not." Connie shook her head and waved Ellie's compliment away. "Richard says it looks like a lizard's skin."

"Richard is an asshole," Ellie reminded her.

"True." Connie sighed, then grinned and pushed herself to her feet. "I'll see you this evening. Merritt's gone vegan, by the way, but cook whatever you want. Just don't be insulted if she doesn't eat much."

"I'll make something vegetarian," Ellie promised.

"Good enough. She probably won't notice if you put milk in it. What time should we come?"

"Six o'clock," Ellie said. "And really, your neck is very nice."

Connie laughed and shook her head as she strode out of the office.

Ellie noticed a faint perfume lingering in the air, something soft and flowery. She wondered whether Connie wore perfume because Richard wanted her to — maybe he'd accused her of smelling like a lizard — or because it put her clients in the mood to buy expensive houses. Scott never wanted Ellie to wear perfume. He claimed that adding artificial fragrances into the air was a kind of pollution.

At least Connie didn't smell of kitty litter.

And anyway, who cared if Scott would approve of Ellie splashing some fragrance on herself? He wasn't around. Not that she owned any perfume, but if she did, she'd dab a little on, just because.

He had been gone eight days. Ellie tried to recall the last time she'd been apart for him that long. She was growing used to his absence, sort of. The empty chair at the kitchen table didn't bother her as much as it had the first few days he was gone, although it was still there, a presence announcing his absence, like a scar.

The nights were not getting any easier. She and Scott weren't acrobatic youngsters anymore, but they still enjoyed lovemaking. She slept much better after sex. She had gone this long without sex before — certainly in the first weeks after each of her daughters was born, when her body was recovering and she could have fallen asleep standing up if her howling babies would have allowed her to. And that week when Scott had been helping his mother cope after his father's death — no sex then, either. But she missed more than sex. She missed cuddling with him. She missed his tenderness, his kisses, his surprisingly gentle touch. She missed falling asleep with his arms around her.

Last night, she'd hardly slept at all. She had lain in bed, loyally remaining on her side of the mattress even though she didn't have to leave space for him, and thought about the celebration of noise Abbie and Misha had indulged in earlier that evening. Why hadn't Ellie described the girls' eruption to Scott when he'd phoned?

She'd felt he didn't have the right to know. He wasn't around. It wasn't his business. There had been something special about that racket, something magical. It had been so spontaneous, so rambunctious. So celebratory. And it had been initiated by Abbie, who had wanted to make her kid sister feel better. For those few noisy minutes, Abbie hadn't been a cool teenager, blasé and jaded. She'd been Misha's champion.

Scott hadn't been around to see it. He would have loved it — but he was hundreds of miles away. His choice. If you pedal off on a bicycle to save the world, you might just miss something precious back at home.

When Misha had taken her turn on the phone with Scott, she'd tried to describe what she and Abbie had done, but her anger at Luke Bartelli had been dissipated by the raucous outburst, and she'd dissolved in giggles. "We took spatulas" — *giggle, giggle* — "and oh, my god" — *giggle, giggle.* "I can't explain it, Daddy," she'd concluded, then giggled some more.

By the time Abbie had claimed possession of the phone, she had reverted to her standard adolescent personality, supercilious and uncommunicative. "I have no idea what Misha's talking about," she'd said to Scott, her voice lofty, her expression passive until her gaze collided with Ellie's. Then her mouth spread in a wicked smile and she turned away and started telling Scott about the school orchestra's June concert.

Scott would miss that, too. He wasn't around. He was off saving the world.

Damn, but Ellie loved her daughters. She had lain in bed last night, restless and pensive, and thought about how spirited and exuberant and utterly magnificent they were.

Then she'd thought about Scott. And about his side of the bed, as empty as his kitchen chair. And about her body, which did not have his arm draped protectively over it. And about the fact that she was horny.

Should she buy a vibrator?

Should she even think about such a thing while she was at work, with Wayne in the inner office, separated from her only by a thin wall, and the rest of the town hall humming with activity just beyond her door? The very idea of obtaining a vibrator made her cheeks flame with heat. She stared at the spreadsheet filling her computer monitor. Supplied by Miriam in the treasurer's office upstairs, it offered projections of tax revenue three years into the future. If the projections held up, the school system wouldn't be underfunded this year, but the primary schools wouldn't be able to hire the second reading specialist they'd been agitating for. They had one reading specialist whose time was divided among the three schools, and she seemed able to tutor all the students recommended for remedial support. A second reading specialist might ease her student load. But it was more likely that doubling the reading-specialist staff would prompt teachers to double the number of students they recommended for supplemental reading assistance. Did all those students *really* need extra help with their reading skills? Weren't their classroom teachers supposed to teach them how to read?

How much did vibrators cost? Where did you buy them? Surely Ellie couldn't waltz into the local Target to shop for one. She might run into someone she knew. And what if they were really expensive? She had to maintain a household budget as disciplined as the town's budget. Scott wouldn't be earning any summer-school money this year.

Forget vibrators, she ordered herself. *Focus on the budget projections.* No second reading specialist, but the class sizes wouldn't have to be increased next year, and every eligible child could attend full-day pre-K without property taxes being raised above the no-vote limit allowed by the state. The school superintendent would have nothing to complain about.

Public works, though…Ellie would get an earful about the need for those sidewalk plows that sprinkled salt. She would get the earful, because Wayne would assign her to talk to the head of the public works department. Wayne only delivered good news. Telling public works they weren't going to get fancy sidewalk plows was not good news.

Did vibrators come in different sizes? Should she get one that came close to mirroring Scott's size? Or should she experiment, buying one thicker than he was, or longer, or stubbier, and pretend she was having an affair with a stranger?

A laugh escaped her. Maybe she ought to skip the vibrator and march around the kitchen, banging pots and pans instead.

"Oh, yuck — she's bringing Merritt?" Abbie moaned as Ellie unpacked the grocery items she'd picked up on her way home. "Merritt's so weird."

"Why did you buy whole wheat pasta?" Misha asked. "It doesn't taste like pasta."

"It tastes like whole wheat pasta," Ellie told her.

"You didn't buy meatballs."

"I'm making pasta primavera. That doesn't have meatballs."

"Yuck," Misha said. Then she turned to Abbie. "Let's be loud."

They gathered a few pots and utensils and paraded into the living room, staying out of Ellie's way while she chopped vegetables and simmered them in olive oil and minced garlic. Perhaps if she were in the living room, the din would be deafening. But while she was in the kitchen, busy with her cooking, it was simply background music, the girls' clattering and rattling accompanied by Lucy's enthusiastic barking.

Once Abbie and Misha returned to the kitchen and stashed their noisemakers back in the appropriate cabinets and drawers, they were measurably more cheerful. Clearly there was a therapeutic benefit to being aloud.

"What if Daddy calls while they're here?" Misha asked, lifting the package of whole wheat penne, scrutinizing stiff brown tubes of pasta visible through the cellophane, and wrinkling her nose.

"We won't spend as long on the phone with him as we usually do," Ellie said. "We'll tell him we've got company."

"He keeps writing about what he's doing on that web site," Misha said. "Luke's stupid club reads the website. That's how they know what he's doing."

"He *wants* people to know what he's doing," Abbie said in her I'm-lecturing-a-fool voice. "That's the whole point."

"Okay, girls — please set the table. We'll eat in the dining room tonight."

"The dining room table has stuff all over it," Misha reminded Ellie.

True enough. They rarely used the dining room table for dining, so it had become a convenient surface to accumulate newspapers, advertising fliers, hair scrunchies, grass-stained soccer shin guards, school notices, school art projects, school research reports, and catalogs that had arrived in the mail the previous December but Ellie hadn't yet gotten around to perusing.

"Clear it off. Throw away anything that can be thrown away, and leave the rest on Daddy's kitchen chair for now."

"We have to recycle the paper stuff," Misha said. Clearly, the mere mention of her father — or at least his chair — was enough to remind her of her obligations to the environment.

"Of course. The newspapers and catalogs go in the recycle bin."

"You don't want to buy anything from those catalogs?" Abbie asked, sounding as if she herself might want to browse through them and make a few purchases.

"They're from Christmas. None of those prices are relevant anymore. Besides, who wants to buy an ugly sweater in May?"

"Who wants to buy an ugly sweater *ever?*" Abbie retorted as she wandered into the dining room, presumably to clear the stuff off the table.

Ellie continued with the food preparations, tearing romaine lettuce into a salad bowl, filling a large pot with salted water, pulling two wine glasses down from an upper shelf. No martinis, but she had a bottle of Chianti. That would have to suffice.

Connie and Merritt arrived punctually at six, just as Ellie was draining the pasta. As was Connie's habit, they strolled around the house to the back porch and tapped on the kitchen door, which launched Lucy into a flurry of operatic barking. Abbie and Misha had done a creditable job of clearing off the dining room table and setting it with placemats and cloth napkins — Scott had banned paper napkins from the house a couple of years ago — but wherever Ellie's daughters had vanished to, they were not available to answer the back door. Ellie left her colander of pasta dripping in the sink and let Connie and Merritt in.

Connie had changed from the real-estate-agent outfit she'd been wearing that morning. She looked comfortable in stylish jeans, a fitted blouse, and canvas slip-on shoes. No scarf; her exposed neck looked graceful and distinctly unreptilian. Merritt resembled a street urchin — an anemic one at that. Her hair was blacker than Ellie had remembered, her skin paler. Her eyes were circled in kohl to make them look hollow and even darker than they already were, and what Ellie initially mistook as a zit on the edge of her nostril was, in fact, a small silver stud. She wore a baggy, black T-shirt, a black skirt that drooped below her knees, and clunky black ankle boots. She carried a box; it was white cardboard with "Trumbull's" written across it in stylized black script.

"Hello, hello!" Connie chirped, evidently not sharing her daughter's glum mood. "Hey, there, Lucy!" She gave Ellie a quick hug, then hunkered down to scratch Lucy behind her floppy ears. Ellie, Scott, and the girls had adopted Lucy from a rescue shelter, where she'd lived for a few months after having been found scrounging around a dumpster behind El Pepe's Mexican Cantina on Boston Boulevard, a few blocks from the town hall. The shelter could only guess at her lineage — a beagle's black and brown splotches of color, a terrier's snubby face, and floppy ears like a spaniel's. Those ears loved to be scratched. Right now, Connie was Lucy's favorite person on Earth because she was scratching Lucy's spaniel ears.

"These are for you," Merritt mumbled, handing the box to Ellie.

"They're for all of us," Ellie corrected her, lifting the lid and grinning at the assortment of cupcakes. The white-and-black box might have matched the color scheme of Merritt's outfit, but its contents, the pastries festively crowned in pink, blue, and yellow frosting and freckled with multicolored sprinkles, did not. "Thank you. They look delicious. Girls?" she shouted into the atmosphere. "Connie and Merritt are here."

Abbie and Misha clomped down the stairs and entered the kitchen. Abbie greeted Merritt with a sullen nod, which Merritt returned. Misha seemed much happier about the presence of company for dinner, even if, as she loudly announced, the pasta would not be accompanied by meatballs. "Just vegetables," Misha said. "I guess it's supposed to be healthy. What's in the box?"

"Something not healthy," Connie told her, carrying it to the counter. "Thank you," she added in a whisper to Ellie. "Merritt might actually eat some dinner."

They were taking their seats around the dining room table, the salad tossed, wine poured for the adults and ice water for the girls, when the phone rang. "It's Daddy!" Misha shrieked, leaping out of her chair and racing back to the kitchen to answer.

"Tell him we'll call him back later," Ellie shouted after Misha.

Misha ignored her, remaining in the kitchen to chat with Scott for five minutes while everyone else sat at the dining room, doing their best not to eavesdrop as Misha babbled about the watercolor painting she was making in art class, her upcoming soccer game against a formidable team from Quincy, how her entire class — including Luke, who was a turd — was following his online blog, and what was Ohio like?

"We've been following Scott's blog, too," Connie told Ellie and Abbie. Abbie kept stirring her pasta and adding salt. Ellie suspected she wanted to sprinkle some cheese on top, but out of respect for Merritt's veganism, Ellie had left the jar of grated parmesan in the refrigerator. Merritt hunched over her plate, stabbing each tube of penne and each chunk of vegetable with vicious intensity, her eyes darting from Abbie to Misha's empty chair and back again. She said nothing.

"So he's in Ohio," Connie went on. "I saw today that he's going to be on a podcast tomorrow. That's exciting."

"Really?" Ellie hadn't read Scott's latest entry yet. "Well, he's trying to get publicity for his cause."

"He's a star," Connie said, her smile tinged with awe. "You must be so proud of him."

Misha returned to the dining room. "I told him you'd call him later," she informed Ellie. "He said don't call too late because he's tired and he wants to go to bed early."

"Of course he's tired. All that biking," Connie said. "How many miles does he go each day?"

"It varies," Ellie said. Her mind had snagged on Connie's earlier comment, about being proud of him. Ellie *was* proud of him, but…It wasn't as if he were Misha, scoring a goal in soccer, or Abbie playing the clarinet solo in the school orchestra performance of *Peter and the Wolf*. Or either girl bringing home an A on an exam.

He was a grown-up. He didn't need a mommy's pride.

There was still half a bottle of wine left when everyone was done eating. Abbie and Misha had each devoured a cupcake, and Connie had reluctantly split a cupcake with Ellie after bemoaning her nonexistent pudginess. Merritt refused to eat a cupcake because, she was convinced, it was infused with animal products. "Butter in the frosting. Eggs in the cake. I can't eat that."

"Can I have yours?" Misha asked Merritt, but Ellie intervened and told Misha that one cupcake was plenty.

Abbie and Misha cleared the table without being asked, and Connie suggested, rather firmly, that Merritt help them deal with the dishes. That left Ellie and Connie alone in the dining room. Ellie topped off their glasses and smiled at the peace that settled over the room like a cozy blanket once the girls were gone. No muttering from Merritt. No pompous pronouncements from Abbie. No surly glances exchanged between the two. No effusive babbling about art projects and Ohio from Misha. Just two women, enjoying their version of a three-martini dinner. Ellie believed Chianti tasted much better than martinis.

"This is nice," Connie said, leaning back in her chair, which squeaked slightly. The dining room set was old — Ellie had inherited it from her parents when they'd sold their house and moved to their condo in Boca Raton. Scott had said he would tighten the joints that held the arching backs to the seats and legs to eliminate the squeaking, but he'd never gotten around to it. So they continued to squeak.

"I'm just glad we were able to do this," Ellie said. "Any time Richard has a business dinner, let me know."

"Even if he doesn't have a business dinner." Connie grinned like a naughty child who had gotten away with something. "This is so much more pleasant than eating dinner with him. And Merritt ate a decent portion. She never eats my cooking at home."

"Why not? I'm sure you're a good cook."

"Yes, but I use butter and eggs." Connie shrugged and sipped her wine. "She usually just grabs a bag of roasted garbanzo beans and disappears into her bedroom."

"She's hanging out with Abbie now," Ellie said. Just a guess — it sounded as if the girls had finished with the dishes and vanished somewhere else in the house. Lucy wandered into the dining room and flopped down under the table, which Ellie took to mean there was no more interesting activity in the kitchen. "Hope springs eternal."

"Abbie is such a nice girl," Connie said wistfully. "I wish she and Merritt were friends."

Abbie could be a bitch, but Ellie didn't say that. "We can't live their lives for them," she said instead. "Hopefully, someday, they'll get past their affectations" — by which she meant Merritt's affectations — "and rediscover each other."

"What I really wish is that Merritt could visit you sometimes when Scott is around. She needs to see what a good man is like. Someone who's smart and interested in kids, and who cares about the environment. And who's physically fit enough to bike across the country."

"You idealize Scott too much," Ellie said. "He's got feet of clay, just like the rest of us."

"It must be hard to pedal a bike with feet of clay," Connie joked. "I'm sure he belches and leaves his dirty socks on the floor and screams at the TV if the umpire makes a bad call during a Red Sox game. But compared to Richard...well, that's not fair. Compare *anyone* to Richard, and that person is going to seem fabulous. Today was a good day because it didn't start with him snarling at me about how his coffee got cold — which is always his own fault, not mine — or complaining about how I didn't fold his handkerchiefs the way he likes them folded, or telling me my butt looked fat. He just left for work. He didn't carry his breakfast dishes to the sink. He left them on the table. But at least he didn't comment on the size of my butt."

"He's crazy," Ellie said. "Your butt is fine."

By the time the wine bottle was empty, Ellie looked at her watch and saw it was a quarter to nine. "It's a school night," Connie said with a sigh. "I should get Merritt home. It takes her half an hour just to scrub that eyeliner crap off."

"Tell her she can't wear it," Ellie suggested. "That's what I do. Abbie's on my case all the time, wanting to wear eye makeup. I tell her no."

"Abbie is a well-adjusted girl," Connie countered. "If I told Merritt she couldn't wear makeup, she'd probably do something awful, like swallow a bottle of Tylenol."

Connie shouted for Merritt, who descended the stairs with Misha. Abbie remained upstairs, out of sight, which was kind of rude, but Ellie let it pass. She thanked Merritt for coming, and Merritt grunted something that might have been thanks for the invitation. Lucy barked a couple of times, and Ellie and Misha escorted Connie and Merritt to the back door and waved them off.

Through the screen door, Ellie heard the engine of Connie's slick little Mercedes rev to life and then fade as Connie backed down the driveway and drove away. Connie had demanded the car after one particularly brutal argument with Richard, when he'd thrown a dinner plate at her. He'd insisted he was not aiming at her, claiming that if he had been, he would have hit her with it. As it was, the plate had shattered against a wall several feet from Connie's head. But Connie had threatened to report him to the police, and he'd suffered a moment's contrition and bought her the Mercedes. Connie loved it, clearly much more than she loved him.

"Can I have another cupcake?" Misha asked as Ellie closed the inner door. "There are extras."

"They'll keep until tomorrow," Ellie said. "They were humongous. Did you finish your homework?"

Misha's disgruntled expression gave Ellie her answer.

"Upstairs. Get it done. It's late."

Misha's gaze lingered for a long, yearning moment on the bakery box.

Ellie tucked in the lid and slid it onto a shelf in the refrigerator. "Homework," she said.

"Merritt is a weird name," Misha said.

"It's Connie's maiden name. I think Merritt's real first name is Elizabeth. But she likes to be called Merritt."

"She's cool," Misha said. "Did you see that stud in her nose? It looked cool."

"I thought it looked like a pimple," Ellie said.

Misha giggled. "Don't forget to call Daddy," she reminded Ellie as she clambered out of the kitchen and up the stairs.

Ellie lifted her phone and tapped Scott's number. The phone rang twice, and then he answered, sounding as if his mouth was stuffed with cotton balls. "Hullo?"

"Did I wake you up?"

"No." He cleared his throat. "Well, yeah. But that's okay. I'm glad you called."

If Ellie hadn't drunk that last glass of wine, she might have felt guilty about having disturbed his sleep. But it was only a little past nine, and she had been hosting a dinner party, and the wine pleasantly blunted the edges of her emotions. And he was glad she'd called.

"Connie and Merritt came over for dinner," she told him.

"With Connie's ghastly husband? What's his name again?"

"Richard, and no, he didn't come. We had a good time." Lots of wine, she almost added. "So, you're in Ohio?"

"Yeah. It's pretty flat where I am, thank God. My legs — I'm feeling muscles I didn't know existed."

"I hear you're doing a podcast tomorrow."

"Yeah." He sounded more awake, energized by this news. "It's called *Keep It Clean*, all about cleaning up the environment. The host, Mike Rostoff, wanted to interview me while I was actually riding, but I wasn't sure that would be safe. I've got the Bluetooth, I could talk to him and hear him while I was biking, assuming there was good cell phone reception, but I wouldn't want to be distracted. While I'm riding, I've got to watch out for the traffic. So we're going to record the podcast in the morning, and then I'll take off. I've got an interview lined up with a weekly published in a suburb of Cleveland, so I've got to bike there as soon as we're done doing the podcast. Then I have to head down to Akron. I think it's hillier there."

"You've got muscles," Ellie reminded him. "You'll be fine."

He laughed. "Easy for you to say."

"Mom!" Abbie shouted from upstairs. "Mom! We have an emergency!"

"I've got to go," Ellie told Scott. "We'll talk tomorrow."

"Love you, babe," Scott said, already sounding drowsy. He disconnected the call. She imagined him rolling over and instantly falling back to sleep. That was one of his talents: the ability to fall asleep less than a minute after he closed his eyes.

Ellie couldn't do that in the best of times. She certainly couldn't do it when Abbie was screaming about an emergency. She tossed the phone aside and raced up the stairs, her heart thudding against her ribs.

Reaching the second-floor hall, she spotted Abbie and Misha hovering in the bathroom doorway, gazing in. Misha was bouncing on her toes, her hands pressed to her mouth. Abbie shook her head and turned to Ellie. "The toilet's flooding," she announced. "Misha broke it."

"It's not my fault!" Misha's voice trembled around a shrill sob.

"She flushed a tampon down the toilet."

"A tampon?" Ellie jerked to a halt and gaped at Misha. "What are you doing with a tampon? Did you get your period?"

"Not yet. But three girls in my class already got theirs. Nikki Fluris, Joanna Benchuk, and Amy Flannigan. And Merritt said I should prepare myself, because I'm going to get it soon. She said I should practice so I can use tampons."

"She used *my* tampons," Abbie said, as indignant as if Misha had used her favorite blouse as a dust rag.

"They're not *your* tampons," Misha argued. "Mommy buys them."

"They're mine because I use them. And you're not supposed to flush them down the toilet."

"It said on the box you could flush them."

"This toilet is fifty years old," Ellie reminded them. Older houses might have their charms, but efficient plumbing wasn't among them. You had to run the kitchen sink for a solid five minutes before the water got hot. You couldn't run the dishwasher and the clothes washer at the same time. You couldn't flush the toilet if someone was showering. And you couldn't flush a tampon down the toilet.

She nudged the girls aside so she could peer into the bathroom and assess the damage. The toilet was filled to the brim — with clear water, thank God — and an inch-deep layer of water was spreading across the tile floor.

She would categorize this emergency as minor — except that she wasn't sure how to fix it. She was reasonably handy. She could shovel snow off the driveway. She could adjust the shelves in the refrigerator. She was a whiz at removing stains from clothing and splinters from her daughter's feet, and she could figure out most computer glitches. She had mastered the technique of smacking the thermostat with just the right amount of force when it got stuck.

But she had never dealt with an overflowing toilet. For some reason, plumbing issues had always been Scott's domain, not hers.

Scott was in Ohio, undoubtedly fast asleep by now, his muscles recuperating from the past week's exertion. As of this minute, plumbing issues were Ellie's domain.

"Don't go in there," she ordered the girls. "I have to do some research." She jogged down the hall to the master bedroom, where her tablet was lying on her night table, recharging so she could read in bed. She tapped it awake and Googled "clogged toilet."

A plunger. That was what she needed. She was sure she had one somewhere, in one of the bathrooms, maybe, or in the basement.

"I can do this," she said out loud, reading the instructions on how to plunge a clogged toilet. She searched the cabinet under the sink in the master bathroom. No plunger there.

Removing her shoes and socks, she returned to the girls' bathroom and splashed through the water to the vanity under the sink. No plunger there, either.

"Okay," she addressed Abbie and Misha, who remained hovering in the hallway near the site of the disaster. "Where do we have a plunger?"

"I think it's in my bedroom," Misha said, spinning on her heel and racing down the hall.

Why would Misha have a plunger in her bedroom? Ellie would have to question her about that. But first she had to unclog the toilet.

Misha returned, carrying a plunger with her. It was the old-fashioned kind, with a hemispherical rubber cup at the end. The online instructions she'd read had recommended a more modern design, but she wasn't about to drive to the hardware store at nine thirty at night to shop for a new plunger. She took the tool from Misha, waded back into the bathroom, and called over her shoulder, "Get the mop and pail from the broom closet in the kitchen. Once I fix the toilet, we'll have to mop the floor." Her confident phrasing — she *would* fix the toilet — gave her courage.

While the girls were downstairs retrieving the mop, she fitted the plunger over the hole in the toilet and pumped it up and down. She wondered if this was what women in ancient times felt like when they churned butter. The water in the toilet bowl sloshed and gurgled. She pumped some more. Louder sloshing and gurgling, and she noticed the water level slowly, gradually sinking.

"I can do this," she said again, this time not to bolster herself but to congratulate herself. More loud gurgling, and the water level dropped a little quicker.

The girls reappeared in the doorway, Misha holding the mop and Abbie a bright yellow bucket. Ellie's shoulders sore from all that plunging, she straightened and, sending a silent prayer heavenward, pressed the flusher.

The toilet flushed.

"Yay!" Misha jumped up and down again, this time in celebration rather than anxiety.

"Good work, Mom," Abbie praised her.

Ellie felt absurdly competent. Unclogging a toilet, she acknowledged, was not that hard. Preparing pasta primavera was harder, although it didn't cause her back to ache.

"Okay," she said, trying not to swagger. "You girls know how to use the mop. The water's clean, so you can empty it into the tub. And the plunger is going to stay here" — she wedged it into the vanity beneath the sink, shifting a four-roll pack of toilet paper, a half-dozen bottles of assorted hair products, and the box of tampons that had misinformed Misha about their flushability to clear a space for it — "and not in anyone's bedroom. Why was it in your bedroom, Misha?"

"I thought it looked funny," Misha said, as if that explained everything.

It didn't.

It didn't have to.

Scott wasn't around, and Ellie had fixed the toilet all by herself.

DAY NINE

I had a great chat with Mike Rostoff on his podcast, Keep It Clean, *this morning. Mike really knows his stuff when it comes to particulate matter. We discussed carbon footprints and smog. He suggested that if I'm riding in traffic, I should wear a face mask to protect my lungs from whatever the gas-fueled cars and trucks are spewing into the air. Good advice, except that I can get pretty sweaty on these warm afternoons, and a face mask would be uncomfortable. On rainy days, trying to breathe through a wet mask might be akin to waterboarding.*

But I liked what Mike had to say, and I guess he liked what I had to say, too. Keep It Clean *has an audience of over four hundred thousand listeners! That boggles my mind. Even more mind-boggling is the understanding that I'm reaching all those listeners, helping to raise their awareness of climate change to an even higher level. The link to the podcast appears in the comments below. Please give it a listen, and feel free to post your thoughts.*

Now on to Columbus, where I've got an interview lined up with a reporter for a local weekly. She said she'll want some photos of me and especially my recumbent bike and the Beast of Burden. I may not have time to shave and shower before she starts snapping photos, but then, what can people expect after I've biked 140 miles? At least it's not raining today. The cloudburst that nailed me two days ago . . . well, I posted the selfie. I won't look quite that bad today.

I'm going to spend the night in the Columbus area. My quads are really feeling it. But a good night's sleep and a hearty breakfast should fix that. I polished off the Thin Mints, but I've still got a box of Samoas. Thank you, Girl Scouts!

CHAPTER SIX

"The interview was phenomenal," Scott told Ellie that evening on the phone. "Both interviews, really. The podcast — man, that was fantastic! So many listeners! That I could sit in my motel room and talk to hundreds of thousands of people...I mean, wow!"

Wow, Ellie thought, silently chiding herself for not feeling more excitement. Of course reaching all those people was thrilling. Of course it was a wonderful opportunity for Scott — and for the planet, too, she supposed. But she'd had a rough day, and she was too tired to send up a cheer.

Her schedule had already been packed when Wayne informed her he needed her to meet with the town engineer and the developer who wanted to build a new fifty-five-plus condo development on the old Mumson Farm property on Route 29. "There are water and sewage issues," Wayne informed Ellie. "But I think you can work around them. If anyone can work with Carl Corrigan — that's the developer — you can. This looks like a winner, Ellie. The town needs this development, so work with Carl to make it happen. I emailed you and Nick the specs. I'm sorry I can't do this meeting myself, but I've got a lunch scheduled with the new health inspector. I know you and Nick can handle it."

"Nick" was Nakul Pawar, the town engineer. For some reason, Wayne believed that Americanizing Nakul's name was a sign of respect and camaraderie. It was not. Nakul had told Wayne on several occasions, with Ellie as his witness, that he did not like being called Nick. But Wayne persevered in using the nickname, usually with a big smile and a slap on Nakul's back.

Ellie had had to set aside her other work to review the condo development specs before her meeting with Nakul and Carl Corrigan. That meeting had taken up the entire afternoon. They'd debated the number of units, the fifty-five-plus age requirement, the contours of the acreage and the water table underneath it, the landscaping, the price range of the units, the possibility of adding solar roof panels to make the development more energy efficient, the parking accommodations, and on and on. Ellie hadn't had time for lunch, but she'd downed three cups of coffee during the meeting, and her stomach was now churning with caffeine and acid.

Dinner — a defrosting bag of frozen scallops, a box of rice, and a crown of broccoli — sat on the kitchen counter, awaiting her attention. She'd asked the girls to get the rice started while she changed from her work apparel into a pair of jeans and a soft, faded T-shirt, but Abbie had vanished into her bedroom with her clarinet and Misha had taken Lucy out for a walk, shouting over her shoulder that she would be meeting with her friend Hayley a couple of blocks over. If the Gillman family was going to eat dinner tonight, it was up to Ellie to prepare it.

Ellie wasn't even sure she was hungry anymore. She would have liked a glass of wine, but Scott had phoned before she could open a bottle. Probably just as well. She and Connie had indulged in all that Chianti last night. She didn't want to turn into an abandoned housewife, drowning her loneliness in booze.

Not that Scott had abandoned her. He'd just ridden off to save the world.

"So I wound up having enough time to shower and change my clothes before I did the newspaper interview," he continued. "You would have been proud of me, honey. I looked almost-sort-of well groomed. The journalist wasn't the brightest bulb in the chandelier, but my answers were much better than her questions. I also hyped the podcast a lot during her interview. I'd love to get invited back to *Keep It Clean*. Mike Rostoff is definitely the brightest bulb. At least 150 watts — LED, of course. When I think of all the people we can reach... Even if we change the habits of only ten percent of them, that would have an enormous impact."

Ellie sat up straighter on her chair at the kitchen table. She had been slouching from fatigue, and the ache in the small of her back reminded her that posture was important. The pile of junk mail and catalogs the girls had transferred from the dining room table still occupied Scott's kitchen chair. She needed to deal with that.

"After the interview," he went on, dragging her attention from the clutter on his chair back to their conversation, "I returned to my motel room and checked my phone, and there was a text waiting for me from someone at University of Illinois. They want me to do a presentation there. I started out with an elementary school, and now I'll be talking to university students. They've got an organization called Act Green, or Think Green — something like that. I'm biking down into Kentucky first, then across southern Indiana, so that's a few days off. I'll need a little time to prepare something more sophisticated than what I presented to the kids in Millardville. God, upstate New York. It seems like a lifetime ago."

Ellie nodded, then realized he couldn't see her nodding, so she said, "Yes, it does."

"And I've got to run a load of laundry tonight. There's a laundromat up the street, but I think they may have a couple of machines right here at the motel, which would be great. Thanks for making sure I packed that detergent. Do you know how much they charge for detergent in the laundromat? They don't always sell low-phosphate detergent, either. Just some cheap powdered stuff — which isn't cheap at all."

"I know." *Wine*, Ellie thought. She would much rather contemplate wine than the polluting qualities of overpriced laundry detergent.

"So, neither of the girls is around to say 'hello' to their old man?"

"Not right now." Even in her bedroom with the door closed, Abbie must have heard the phone ring, and Ellie had shouted up the stairs that the call was from her dad. She hadn't emerged and asked to talk to him, however. "Misha is walking Lucy," Ellie told him, "and Abbie's practicing her clarinet."

"That's okay. I'll talk to them tomorrow." Scott sighed audibly, a hiss of breath through the phone and into Ellie's ear. "God, I'm beat. What a day. A great day! But after a while, all those miles, and the weather... I'm not as young as I used to be."

"None of us are," Ellie said, wondering if she sounded supportive or resigned.

"I'll recover. A good night's sleep and I'll be fine." A silence stretched between them, and then he asked, "So, what's going on with you?"

"Not much. Work." Ellie glanced toward the refrigerator, wishing she could open it telepathically and, using mind control, get a bottle of wine to fly across the kitchen to the table where she was seated. "I unclogged the toilet last night."

"No kidding? Good for you!"

Don't patronize me, she almost snapped. But she stifled the urge. She couldn't blame Scott for her exhausting day, made doubly exhausting because she'd been stuck attending a meeting Wayne should have attended. Of course he couldn't attend; he'd had to eat his fancy lunch with the new town health inspector. He had his priorities. And now that she'd attended the preliminary meeting with Corrigan and Nakul, the project would be her responsibility. There would be more meetings, spreadsheets, slides, charts, topographical maps, sessions with the zoning board, sessions with the select board, sessions with Nakul, who was a sweetheart, and with Carl Corrigan, who was brash and mercenary and much too full of himself, and whose comb-over didn't really work. Meetings like that were supposed to be Wayne's job, not hers.

Scott's voice pierced the fog of resentment clouding her mind. "How did the toilet get clogged? Or shouldn't I ask?"

"You shouldn't ask." She wasn't about to discuss with him that Misha was already preparing mentally for the onset of her period. If she brought up the subject of menstruation, he would lecture her about those underpants women were supposed to wear and wash out every day because they were more ecologically sound than pads and tampons. It figured that women would be stuck performing this added chore on the planet's behalf, just as they were being pressured into reverting to cloth diapers so they wouldn't clog landfills with disposable diapers.

All well and good, Ellie acknowledged. No one wanted clogged landfills. But it did seem as if women were being asked to shoulder the burden of unclogging the landfills by scrubbing soiled diapers and absorbent undies, while men got to clean the environment by going on bike trips.

"I really should go," Scott said. "Gotta get my beauty rest. Love you, babe. Give the girls a hug for me." With that, he ended the call.

Ellie pressed the disconnect button and realized she was slouching again. Pushing herself out of her chair, she trudged across the room to where the bag of scallops sat on the counter and cautioned herself not to search for a bottle of wine, which would make her feel desperate. She didn't want to cook, but she needed to eat. Misha would be home soon, no doubt starving — she was always starving. Abbie would deign to descend from her room once all the labor of preparing dinner was done.

Ellie measured some rice and water into a pot, set it on the stove, and then pulled her tablet from her tote bag, which she'd tossed onto the kitchen table when she'd arrived home from work. She did a quick internet search for *Keep It Clean*, clicked on the link, then set her tablet on the counter, where she would be able to listen to the podcast while she cooked.

Scott's new best friend, Mike Whatever, greeted his listeners and introduced his guest. "If you haven't heard of Scott Gillman before, you've heard of him now," Mike Whatever said. "He's biking across America, stopping in all forty-eight contiguous states — guess you can't ride a bike to Hawaii, huh, Scott? — to spread the word about global warming, climate change, and the ways we can design our lives to have less of an impact on our environment. Welcome, Scott!"

Then Scott came on, his voice as clear and crisp as he'd sounded on the telephone just minutes ago when he'd praised Ellie for repairing the toilet as if she were a kindergartner who had just printed her name on a piece of paper with a crayon. "Well, we can't *not* have an impact on the environment, Mike. We're part of the environment. The key is to have a *positive* impact, not a negative one."

And they were off, discussing Scott's recumbent bike, ana-lyzing the calorie expenditure of biking everywhere instead of driving, chuckling about the particular challenges of riding in bad weather. They got along famously. They bonded over their shared contempt for single-use water bottles and fossil fuels. It was quite a lovefest. If Ellie were less insecure, she might wonder why Scott didn't heap praise on Mike Whatever for having mastered a simple toilet repair.

Yet that repair hadn't been simple. Maybe Ellie hadn't saved the planet last night, but she'd saved the toilet, something she had never done before. She deserved more than a "good for you!" from Scott.

She laughed at herself. He *was* saving the planet, or at least trying to. All she'd done was pump a plunger up and down in the toilet bowl. If she hadn't had to do Wayne's job along with her own today, she wouldn't feel so emotionally bruised now.

Misha bounded through the back door into the kitchen, Lucy scampering alongside her, announcing their arrival with a spirited bark. "Guess what, Mom?" Misha said as she unclipped Lucy's leash. "I'm going to start my own club. Hayley said she'd join. It's only for girls. And we can be as loud as we want."

"Sounds great," Ellie said. "Just don't be too loud inside the house. A little loud is okay, but not a lot of loud."

"But we're girls!" Misha declared, her voice booming. "We're *a*-loud!"

Her bellow must have alerted Abbie, who thumped down the stairs and swept into the kitchen. "What's for dinner?" she asked. "Scallops? Eew."

"You like scallops," Ellie said, arranging the contents of the bag in a cast-iron skillet, dropping several dabs of butter in, and sprin-kling the small white discs of seafood with seasonings. She turned to look at Abbie and frowned. Abbie's eyelashes looked darker than usual, and a little longer.

She was wearing mascara.

Ellie turned back to the stove, watched the butter melt and sizzle and bubble, and decided she just wasn't going to deal with

Abbie's eye makeup tonight. She didn't have the energy. Besides, if the planet was in such dire shape, needing Scott and Mike Whatever to rescue it from destruction, did whether or not Abbie wore mascara really matter?

DAY FoURTEEN

Okay, I'll admit it: biking in a downpour sucks big-time. A little rain isn't so bad, but a cloudburst that floods the roadways is really unpleasant. Even though I wore my rain gear, lubed the bike, added mud fenders, had all the stuff in the Beast of Burden protected underneath a waterproof cover, and rode eighty miles without a flat tire, which is a miracle in itself... Not fun.

My jacket is breathable (or so the manufacturer claims), but my waterproof booties had my feet sweating as if I'd run a marathon. Which is worse, being soaked with rain or being soaked with sweat?

I stayed on back roads because I wanted to minimize my encounters with cars. I couldn't avoid them completely, though. And you know what happens when a car drives through a puddle when it passes you, right? The tires launch mini-tsunamis at you. So yeah, I was wet from sweat, wet from rain, and wet from road puddles. After a ride like that, happiness is a dry towel.

My conclusion: you can still rely on a bike as your main mode of transportation, even in rainy weather. (Snow and ice are another matter.) Is biking in bad weather unpleasant? Sure. But you know what's really unpleasant? Rising sea levels, melting polar caps, droughts, out-of-control wildfires, stage-five hurricanes, and the disappearance of bees and polar bears from the face of the earth. I think we could all put up with a little splashing rainwater if it would prevent the extinction of life on our planet.

.

CHAPTER SEVEN

"**W**ayne's a schmuck," Nakul said.

Hearing him say the word *schmuck* was weird. The son of immigrants from Pune, India, Nakul had been born in New Jersey, but he spoke with a precision and formality that generally didn't allow for blatant insults, especially Yiddish ones. Nakul was polite and reticent, but, when necessary, he spoke his mind. As the Shelton town engineer, speaking his mind was often necessary.

He was the town officer who told the select board when the bridge over Hobson's Brook needed to be shut down for repairs, who demanded the installation of a traffic-control button for pedestrians in front of the high school, who brokered a deal with the Unitarian church to install a cell tower inside its spire so the tower wouldn't be an eyesore looming above the town green. He oversaw inspections, evaluated proposals, and reviewed all construction projects in town, invariably finding things wrong with them and irritating people with his criticisms.

Before taking the job as Shelton's town engineer, he had worked for a construction company, writing specs for public buildings that were generally deceptive. "We would offer a low-ball bid on a project and win the commission," he'd once explained to Ellie. "Then, after we had the contract, we'd say, 'Oh, wait, you wanted triple-paned thermal windows? Our bid was based on double paned.' Or, 'Oh, you wanted *this* thickness of rebar in the columns? We wrote our spec based on *that* thickness.' Or, 'You didn't specify brick walkways. We priced this out for concrete.' If you ever wonder why major construction projects always come in over budget, this is why. Construction firms underprice everything in their bids and then, once they have the contract, they charge for all the upgrades the client thought were included in their bid." It was a sleazy business, according to Nakul. He'd taken a cut in income to work for the town of Shelton, but, as he told Ellie, with this job, he could look himself in the mirror at the end of the day and not cringe.

Now they were seated across a small table in the corner of the local Starbucks, a few short blocks from the town hall, and Ellie could look at him without cringing. He was a few years younger than she was and a few inches taller, his physique long and lean, his skin tawny and his dark hair rising in messy spikes from the crown of his head. Ellie wasn't sure if this was a deliberate styling choice, or if he had madly raked his fingers through his hair while contemplating Wayne's schmuckhood. More likely the latter.

He had buzzed Ellie fifteen minutes ago and suggested that they head down the street to Starbucks. There was a staff lounge in the town hall building, with a functioning coffee maker and a minifridge filled with containers of skim milk and half-and-half, but the staff lounge was Gossip Central. Some secretary or select board member or clerk or minion was always seated at one of the Formica-topped tables, munching on a piece of fruit or an energy bar and mentally recording every word spoken by anyone else in the vicinity. It was not a room where a town employee could safely say, "Wayne's a schmuck." It probably wouldn't be safe even to *think* such a sentiment in the staff lounge. Some of those clerks and minions seemed able to read minds.

So when Nakul suggested Ellie join him for a coffee break at Starbucks, she knew he wanted to discuss something he didn't want overheard. Criticizing the town manager certainly fell into that category.

She didn't really have time to abandon her office; budgets, requests, and diagrams of the Mumson Farm property on Route 29 formed a neat, nagging stack on her desk. But she liked Nakul. If he needed to unload, she would listen. Especially if he was unloading about Wayne.

Nakul stirred a surprising amount of sugar into his venti dark roast. "I don't know what he promised Carl Corrigan, but that condo development has to be seriously downsized."

"And we're the ones who are going to have to break the news to Corrigan," Ellie said, sighing as she lifted her latte for a sip.

"I don't know why Wayne put you in charge of this project," Nakul said, studying his coffee and deciding he needed to empty yet another packet of sugar into it. "I called him this morning, and he told me to work with you on it. Not that I mind working with you," he added with a fleeting smile, "but it's *his* job. Not yours."

"Wayne thinks his job is glad-handing people and making everyone happy. Heavy lifting is not a part of his job description."

"You should tell him no," Nakul said, at last tasting his coffee and smiling, apparently pleased with the level of sweetness. "You should say, 'Wayne, it's your job. You have to deliver the bad news to Corrigan.'"

"First of all," Ellie said, "It's not going to be all bad news. The town wants this complex. Corrigan can build it. We just have to trim it back a bit and make sure he's doing all the green stuff we're demanding — the solar panels, the insulation levels, the sustainable landscaping. He might not make as big a profit as he'd like, but he'll get his complex."

"Not making as big a profit as he'd like will qualify as bad news," Nakul pointed out. "What's second of all?"

"Second of all, I can't risk my job by saying no to Wayne. We're a one-income family at the moment."

"Ah." Nakul nodded. "How is your husband doing? Still on his bicycle?"

"He's going to be on his bicycle all summer," Ellie told him. "Instead of earning money teaching summer school. I can't throw a hissy fit with Wayne. He'd fire me."

"He can't afford to fire you," Nakul argued. "If he fired you, he'd have to deal with Carl Corrigan himself."

Ellie shook her head and grinned. "He'd just hire another gofer to do his bidding for him."

"Too bad Wayne didn't ride away on a bicycle. Our lives would be easier if he did."

"We'd still be stuck dealing with Corrigan," Ellie said.

"Yes, but we wouldn't be simmering with resentment. At least, I wouldn't."

Ellie grinned again. Nakul's resentment was on her behalf more than his own. She appreciated that.

"So, I may as well tell you — since we're on company time here — there are some serious drainage issues with the Mumson Farm property," Nakul said. "Corrigan's going to have to work on that. He can probably create proper dry-bed channels, construct ducts, that sort of thing. But when you're building a condominium community, you have to worry about the owners suing one another if one unit's rainwater floods another unit's yard. Or worse yet, their basements."

"Should we schedule another meeting with him?" She drained her cup. "I can't explain dry-bed channels, but I can set up a meeting."

"Wayne should set up the meeting," Nakul muttered, then exhaled. "You had better set up a meeting. Wayne won't do it."

"Mom? Lucy threw up."

Ellie groaned. A day that had started so well — escaping with Nakul for some delicious coffee and even more delicious venting — was ending less auspiciously. As Nakul had suggested, she'd set up another meeting with Carl Corrigan, informed Wayne of it and said she really thought he should sit in on it, nodded skeptically when Wayne said he would try — which meant he wouldn't try — and was working her way through the pile of non-Corrigan-related paperwork on her desk when Abbie phoned Ellie's cell with this news about the dog.

"Was she in the garbage?" Ellie asked. "Did she eat anything she shouldn't have? Chocolate, maybe?"

"I don't know," Abbie said. "I just got home from school. Misha's at soccer practice."

Right. Soccer practice. Ellie had spent nearly an hour on the phone last night, making arrangements for one of the other team mothers to drive Misha home afterward. Usually, team parents were accommodating, helping one another when schedules got snarled, but today's practice seemed to be unusually problematic for much of the team. Marnie's mother had to drive Marnie directly from the field to her orthodontist to have her palate expander checked. Louisa's father was in a loaner car — his SUV was undergoing a brake job — and he had to get the loaner back to the rental place across from the repair shop before five p.m. or he would be charged an extra day for it. Hayley's mother had a root canal scheduled for that afternoon and was herself looking for someone to drive Hayley home from practice. Finally, Nina's mother agreed to drive both Misha and Hayley home. Which meant Ellie was now indebted to Nina's mother as well as Torie Shinako's mother.

"How does Lucy look?" she asked Abbie.

"Okay, I guess. I mean, how is she *supposed* to look?"

"Well, does she look sick?"

"I don't know. What does a sick dog look like?"

Whoever thought teenagers had a monopoly on eye-rolling had never been the mother of a teenager. Ellie's eyes were rolling like steel marbles in a pinball machine. "Is she droopy? Is she whimpering?"

"She's really quiet. She's lying on the floor and making little moaning sounds," Abbie said.

"Probably because her tummy hurts."

"And the garbage can in the kitchen was knocked over."

Shit. What had Ellie and the girls thrown away in there? They'd eaten chicken last night. There had been bones. "She's probably all right," Ellie said, hoping to reassure herself as much as Abbie. "Where did she vomit?"

"On the living room rug."

Shit. "Try to clean it up. I'll get home as soon as I can."

"Mom. It's *vomit*!"

Ellie considered reminding Abbie of all the times *she* had vomited as a child — from stomach bugs, from ear infections, from strep throat, from the Tylenol-with-codeine a doctor had prescribed for pain relief when she'd had surgery to repair the ankle ligaments she'd torn on a misbegotten ski trip a couple of years ago. Ellie had cleaned up Abbie's vomit every time, without complaint. It was what moms did.

But then, Abbie wasn't a mom. And Lucy wasn't her daughter.

"Get a towel from the rag bag in the laundry room," Ellie instructed Abbie. "Wet it and do your best to clean up the rug. And keep Lucy confined to the kitchen." The kitchen didn't have any rugs covering its tile floor. If Lucy threw up again, a mop would clean the mess. "Make sure the lid is tight on the garbage pail. I'll be home as soon as I can."

"Mom. It's gross."

"I know it's gross. Just do it. Love you, sweetie," she added, gentling her tone in the hope that Abbie wouldn't file papers requesting that a court declare her an emancipated minor before Ellie got home.

She disconnected the call and crossed to the door connecting her office with Wayne's. Miraculously, he was in his office, not at a golf course or in a restaurant. "I have to leave," she told him. "Family emergency."

He peered up from whatever he was reading. It looked like a magazine: glossy paper, glossy pictures. "Did you finish reviewing the public works budget requests?" he asked.

"I'll finish tomorrow. I have to get home to deal with this emergency. I'm a single parent these days, you know."

"This is why people should remain married," he muttered.

She refrained from reminding him that she and Scott were married. "Did you mark the meeting with Carl Corrigan on your calendar?" she asked him.

"Email me a reminder."

She rolled her eyes again, deciding that Wayne was significantly more of a pain in the ass than her adolescent daughter. Not trusting herself to say anything civil to him, she spun away from the door, typed a quick reminder email to Wayne on her computer, clicked "send," grabbed her bag, and jogged out of the office.

Driving home, she tried not to worry about Lucy, about whether she'd have to take the dog to the vet, about what the vet would charge for the visit. Because she'd left the town hall early, no rush hour traffic clogged the roads, and she arrived home in ten minutes. Entering the kitchen, she immediately spotted Lucy lolling under the table, alongside another puddle of vomit. The dog lifted her head and whimpered then lowered her head to her paws again.

Ellie strode to the foot of the stairs and hollered, "Abbie?"

"I'm doing my homework," Abbie hollered back.

Perhaps she was doing her homework. Perhaps she was simply claiming she was doing homework so Ellie would think she was engaged in something more important than cleaning up Lucy's vomit. Ellie dropped her tote on the table and hunkered down. "Hey, Lucy," she sing-songed. "Hey, honey. How are you?"

Lucy gave her a doleful look.

Ellie straightened up and headed down the hall to the living room. A white towel lay on the rug near the coffee table. Ellie tip-toed in and lifted a corner of the towel, which was wet. The towel hid a stain — part water, part vomit — on the rug. Abbie hadn't done a particularly effective job of cleaning up Lucy's mess, but at least she'd made an attempt.

Ellie made the rest of the attempt, scrubbing the towel vigorously over the rug's nap until she could see only water darkening the pattern. She carried the towel into the laundry room and tossed it into the washer, grabbed a second towel from the rag pile, and washed away the mess on the kitchen floor. Then she scrubbed her hands. Lucy still lurked under the table, disturbingly listless.

Sighing, Ellie phoned the Shelton Veterinary Hospital. Dr. Zhou had taken care of Lucy ever since the Gillmans had adopted her six years ago. Dr. Zhou had also taken care of the stray cat Misha had brought home after a play date with Luke Bartelli when they'd both been in first grade. Luke's parents had wisely vetoed the cat, which was missing a couple of inches of tail and a corner of an ear, and less than a year after Ellie and Scott had paid an exorbitant sum of money to Dr. Zhou to restore the bedraggled cat to health, it had run away. Misha had been inconsolable for a week, even though Ellie and Scott had assured her the cat had likely gone home to its true owner. But then spring soccer season had begun, as well as preparations for a dance recital in which Misha would be performing as a butterfly, complete with gossamer wings attached to her leotard, and she had forgotten about the cat.

A receptionist answered Ellie's call. Ellie described Lucy's condition and admitted she had no idea what, if anything, the dog might have consumed while no one had been home. "Our kitchen trash can fell over," Ellie told the receptionist. "Maybe she ate something from the garbage."

"You say she threw up twice?" the receptionist said.

"That I know of."

"You'd better bring her in," the receptionist advised. "More than once, we like to see the patient."

Ellie visualized another exorbitant sum of money flying out of her bank account and into the animal hospital's coffers. Sighing, she raced up the stairs to change into a pair of old jeans and a shirt she didn't care about — in case Lucy decided to upchuck en route to the hospital — and then tapped on Abbie's closed bedroom door. "Yeah?" Abbie called out.

Ellie took that as an invitation to open the door. She found Abbie seated cross-legged on her bed, her laptop open in front of her and a spiral-bound book — Ellie recognized it as Abbie's math textbook — resting on one knee. "I'm taking Lucy to the vet's," Ellie told her. "Misha should be home from soccer around five. If I'm not home by then, you and she could get dinner started. There are some defrosted cod fillets in the refrigerator."

Abbie lifted her gaze. She looked profoundly annoyed. "What am I supposed to do with them?" she asked.

"Season them and arrange them in the oblong Pyrex dish. Stick them in the oven if I'm not home by six."

"The dish is rectangular," Abbie said. "Not oblong."

Ellie was pretty sure a rectangular baking dish could be considered oblong, but she wasn't going to argue with Abbie about it.

"I'll phone from the vet's office once I know what's going on," she said, then remembered to add, "Thank you for cleaning up the vomit," even though Abbie hadn't done a particularly thorough job of that.

Abbie nodded, gave Ellie a long-suffering look, and turned back to her math homework.

Fifteen minutes later, Ellie and Lucy entered the waiting room at the veterinary hospital. Fortunately, Lucy hadn't puked on the drive over, although she seemed weary. Usually, a trip in the car thrilled her. She liked to perch her front paws on the door's armrest and poke her head through the open window, her tongue hanging out of her mouth and her ears flapping in the wind. Given Lucy's upset stomach, Ellie opened the car window today, hoping that fresh air would suppress any residual nausea. But Lucy didn't even nudge the open window with her snout.

Usually, when Lucy had to see Dr. Zhou, Scott brought her. He could get home from work a couple of hours before Ellie, leaving school as soon as he finished teaching his last class of the day. But since Scott wasn't around, Ellie was the one to leave work early today, so she would arrive at the animal hospital before it switched to emergency hours and charged twice what a regular visit would cost.

The place was busy. She had to share the waiting area with an elderly woman who held a fat gray cat on her lap, a mother and her young daughter flanking a small crate with a guinea pig inside it, and a lanky, bearded man with a poodle bedecked with a postsurgical cone that resembled a satellite dish, as if the dog might pick up signals from outer space. After checking in with the receptionist, Ellie took her seat near the cat woman and kept a loose grip on Lucy's leash. Lucy gazed sympathetically at the other dog, no doubt relieved she wasn't wearing a cone.

Three other patients, Ellie noted. She and Lucy would have a long wait.

A young woman carrying a bottle of pills and leading a bulldog by the leash emerged from the examining room. The receptionist told the cat lady to go in. Ellie wondered whether Dr. Zhou would recommend that the cat undergo gastric bypass surgery. It really was obese.

Her cell phone rang. She looked at the screen. Abbie. At least she knew Abbie wasn't phoning her this time to tell her Lucy had thrown up on the living room rug. "Hello?" she answered in a muted tone. The bearded poodle owner glowered at her.

"Misha's home," Abbie reported. "She said practice ended early because one of her teammates had a dentist appointment or something. We think you should bring take-out Chinese home for dinner tonight."

"Okay," Ellie said, partly because she didn't want to engage in a protracted conversation with Abbie while seated in the animal hospital's waiting area, and partly because, if she was going to get hit with an astronomical bill for this visit, what difference would spending a few extra dollars on take-out Chinese make?

"Get the lo mein."

"Fine."

"I want to talk to Mom!" Misha's voice reached through the phone to Ellie.

"Misha wants to talk to you," Abbie said.

Ellie heard a scuffling sound, the phone changing hands. "Mom? We figured out my club."

"Your soccer team?"

"My Girls Aloud club. There's five of us — Hayley, Eliza, Nina, Viveca, and me. Maybe we'll invite more girls. We haven't decided yet. But it's kind of a secret. And the way it works is, whenever something happens that can only happen to a girl, like getting your period or getting a soprano solo in glee club, or getting a bra, or you shave your legs, we all have to scream. We have to make a lot of noise."

"That sounds . . . noisy," Ellie said. The poodle owner's eyebrows flickered upward, although he pretended to be staring at the door to the examining room. The girl with the guinea pig leaned across the carrying case to whisper something to her mother.

"We won't do it in class," Misha said. "Like, at recess or something, when we're outside. We all get together and scream, or clap our hands, or bang on something. We're *aloud*!"

Ellie heard Abbie in the background, saying, "Some boys shave their legs."

"No they don't," Misha argued.

"Some of the boys on the high school swim team do. They think it makes them swim faster."

"That's stupid," Misha declared, her voice clearer as she addressed Ellie once more. "No boys are allowed in our club, no matter how you spell 'allowed.' Are you going to get Chinese take-out for dinner?"

"If that's what you girls want."

"Can you get chicken with cashews?"

"Okay."

"And lo mein," Abbie shouted.

"I know," Ellie said. "Lo mein and chicken with cashews."

"And extra fortune cookies," Misha said. "Is Lucy okay?"

"I don't know. We haven't seen Dr. Zhou yet. I might be here a while." The poodle owner snorted. Ellie wondered how long he'd been waiting to see the vet. And his poor dog — how long had it been forced to wear the postsurgical cone? "I've got to go," Ellie said.

"Tell Lucy I love her," Misha said. "Tell her I hope she feels better."

"Tell her not to barf on the rug," Abbie muttered, just loud enough for Ellie to hear.

"I'll tell her. Be good. Do your homework. I hope I can get home soon." She disconnected the call.

Lucy sighed loudly and sprawled out on top of Ellie's feet. For a small dog, she could make herself ridiculously heavy. Ellie wondered if the bones shaping her insteps would crack under Lucy's warm weight.

The cat woman emerged from the examining room. The guinea pig family was summoned. The poodle owner busied himself thumb-scrolling his phone. Ellie glanced at the magazines arrayed on a table near her chair. *Modern Dog. Catster. For Pet's Sake.* She'd rather stare at the wall than read any of them.

She should have brought her folder of notes on the Route 29 condo project. She and Nakul were going to have to notify the zoning board to see if Carl Corrigan could include a drainage easement in his design. That was something Wayne ought to be taking care of. It was his freaking job, not hers.

Her cell phone rang again. This time the screen indicated the call was from Scott. "Hey," he said when she answered. "I called home and the girls told me Lucy was sick. What's going on?"

"I'm at the vet with her," Ellie told him, twisting in her chair so she wouldn't have to look at the poodle owner, who was clearly annoyed by her phone chatter. Lucy growled in protest as Ellie shifted her feet, then resumed her sprawl across Ellie's insteps. "I don't know if she's sick or she just had an incident. The garbage pail in the kitchen was knocked over. She might have eaten something she shouldn't have."

"I hope it's nothing serious," Scott said. "Poor pooch. Give her a hug for me."

"I will."

"Did you read my post from last night?" he asked.

"I didn't have a chance," Ellie said. "Work was crazy, and then I had to leave early to take Lucy to the vet."

"Then let me tell you about the rain storm I biked through," Scott said, and he proceeded to do just that. He was still describing the depth of the puddles on a stretch of road in southern Indiana when the guinea pig family emerged, the little girl looking much more cheerful than before. The poodle owner was summoned, and Ellie relaxed in her chair. She was the only person in the waiting area, other than the receptionist. Her phone conversation couldn't disturb anyone now.

It wasn't much of a conversation, and it probably wouldn't have disturbed anyone because she said so little. Scott did most of the talking. He told her about his waterproof booties. He told her about the motel where he would be spending the night. He told her about the feedback he was getting from the *Keep It Clean* podcast. His buddy Mike Rostoff, the podcast host, wanted to record another podcast with him. They'd done such a solid job with the first podcast, and the comments from listeners were uniformly positive. Also, the University of Illinois would be moving Scott's presentation to a larger auditorium due to increased interest on campus. "The campus has its own cable TV station," Scott said. "They're going to broadcast my talk."

Ellie might have pointed out that cable TV — especially a campus station — wasn't the same thing as broadcast TV. But then, the University of Illinois was a huge school. Even if only a fraction of the students and faculty watched Scott's speech, he would still have a pretty impressive audience.

"That's wonderful," she said.

"I wish you were here," Scott said. "I could use your wisdom about my wardrobe. I never know what to wear to these things."

"Wear one of your RE:CYCLE shirts."

"I guess I'll have to." He laughed. "It's pretty much all I've got." He paused. "I can't believe how big this thing is getting, Ellie. Maybe I'm actually making a difference."

"You've already been on TV," she reminded him. "Your grand departure, remember?"

"Yeah, but that was just a local Boston-area station, and I'm a local Boston-area guy. Now... I'm going national."

"You're a star," she told him, feeling just a bit peeved. Yes, he was a star. Yes, he was going national. But *she* was taking care of the dog and a thirty-acre parcel on Route 29. Scott wasn't the only one whose actions might impact animal safety and land use.

Her irritation was petty. He was doing something spectacular, and doing it in bad weather as well as good, in his waterproof booties as well as his biking shoes. He was making a difference. People were listening. Maybe they were thinking more about the fate of the planet, and what they could do to make a difference.

Surely she could take care of Lucy, and the girls, and Carl Corrigan, and the future residents in those condos, even if the spotlight passed her by, even if there was no glory in such pursuits. They still mattered, she told herself. What she was doing mattered.

CHAPTER EIGHT

An hour and twenty minutes later, Ellie arrived home, carrying a bag containing lo mein, chicken with cashews, brown rice, and fortune cookies. Dr. Zhou had said Lucy wasn't presenting the expected symptoms of having eaten a chicken bone, but her abdomen was distended and she was listless and feverish. "She could have a bacterial infection, or she could have eaten something toxic. We should probably keep her here for the night and monitor her."

So Lucy was being monitored, and Ellie was visualizing the bill she would receive when she picked Lucy up — tomorrow, she hoped. She wondered if a vet bill might count as one of Scott's expenses, so it could be paid for out of his GoFundMe money. He would say no, of course. He was too ethical to spend on Lucy money his supporters had donated to finance his bike trip.

The cost of Lucy's overnight stay at the animal hospital worried Ellie. The trash she'd seen lying on the ground in the parking lot of the Chinese restaurant infuriated her. Several crumpled napkins, two empty packets of low-sodium soy sauce, and a cigarette butt littered the pavement near where she'd parked. Who even smoked cigarettes anymore? And why did one of the few lingering smokers think it was acceptable to snub out a butt and leave it lying on the asphalt? And who was the pig who'd dropped napkins and soy sauce packets onto the ground rather than carrying the trash back into the restaurant and discarding it properly?

Ellie didn't have time to clean up the litter, but she couldn't leave it lying on the sidewalk. Unlocking her car, she set the bag of food on the passenger seat, then gathered up the trash, which she carried into the restaurant. A quick dash to the restroom enabled her to wash her hands; touching a cigarette butt which had undoubtedly spent time in someone's mouth grossed her out. Fortunately, she rarely used her car's air conditioning, and the food remained warm during her ten-minute drive home.

Abbie and Misha greeted her effusively once she entered the house. She wasn't sure if their warm greeting was prompted by happiness that she was home or by the aromatic bag of Chinese food in her hands, but their enthusiasm cheered her up. "How is Lucy?" Misha asked.

"I don't know. She might have an infection. She had a fever, and she was dehydrated. Hopefully, she'll be able to come home tomorrow."

Both Abbie and Misha had the good taste to look concerned. They perked up a bit over dinner, though, wolfing down the take-out food with gusto. Misha talked a little about her soccer practice and her noisy new club. Abbie rubbed one of her eyes repeatedly and said it was bothering her. Ellie suggested that she wear less mascara. Abbie glared at her.

"I'm so sad about Lucy," Misha said once they were done eating, the dishes were taken care of, and the bag lining the trash can was tied up and carried out to the garage for disposal. "Can we watch a movie? I finished my homework."

"I finished mine, too," Abbie said quickly.

"*Field of Dreams*," Misha said. "Because Daddy isn't here and Lucy isn't here. We need to cheer up."

"We do," Abbie agreed.

"Go ahead," Ellie said. "But no popcorn. You two pigged out on the fortune cookies." Each girl had eaten three, and strips of paper bearing their fortunes littered the kitchen table. According to the cookies, it was better to light a candle than curse the darkness, a penny saved was a penny earned, living long was good but living well was better, and it was important to follow one's dreams. Had Ben Franklin risen from the dead to work at a fortune cookie factory?

Ellie threw away the fortunes, wiped down the table, and then pulled her notes about Corrigan's condo development from her tote and joined the girls in the den, where they had already started the movie. The wistful music began, the scenes of the Iowa farm, the scenes in Boston. Ellie occasionally glanced at the screen, but mostly she focused on her notes, wondering what would happen if she told the select board to veto the project. They were firmly in favor of it; not only did fifty-five-and-older developments bring tax money into the town, but the late-middle-age residents didn't add students to the school system, which consumed the largest portion of the town's budget. Any project that increased the town's revenues without increasing the school population was a win. The select board would never block the development.

But the drainage problem was an issue. And she and Nakul hadn't yet evaluated the prospective increase in traffic on Route 29. Would the town need to install a traffic light? How many residents in the complex would be retired, and how many would still be commuting to work?

Stifling a groan, she set aside the folder and lifted her gaze to the screen. There was Kevin Costner's wife, fretting over the farm's finances while Kevin cruised around the country, searching for an author and a doctor, and searching as well for the meaning of his dream about building a baseball diamond in the middle of his corn field. And his wife... his wife was worrying that the farm would be foreclosed on.

But her fear, her struggle to keep the farm from failing — he ignored that. His dream was too important.

Next to her, Abbie and Misha sniffled. A fortune cookie crumb was caught in Misha's hair, and Ellie gently eased it free of the strands. Misha glanced at her, and Ellie showed her the crumb cupped in her palm. Misha grinned, then steered her damp gaze back toward the screen.

Children were supposed to have dreams. Dreams were wonderful. They provided motivation. They awakened the imagination. They allowed people to think about things they might otherwise never consider.

But grown-ups had to deal with sick dogs and job demands and making sure those dreamy children were well fed. And sometimes they had to deal with keeping the farm from going under. Sometimes, the only dream they had was to get through the day without going insane.

Sometimes, it seemed, their dreams — whatever they might be — evaporated in the heat and light of everyone else's dreams.

CHAPTER NINE

"Five hundred dollars for an upset stomach," Ellie groaned. She and Nakul sat in the conference room down the hall from her office on the first floor of the town hall. Nakul's office was on the second floor. Evidently, the town realized that residents were far less likely to visit the town engineer than they were to visit the town manager, so Nakul, like Miriam Horowitz in the treasurer's office, wound up with second-floor offices, which were quieter, roomier, and sunnier, at least on days when the sun was shining. The Shelton Town Hall was an odd building perched on one end of the town green. It comprised a pillared main section constructed around the end of the Civil War and a sleek but bland addition that had been tacked on forty years ago. The building looked like the love child of an ancient Greek temple and a suburban dentist's office. Ellie's and Wayne's offices were located in what was still called the new wing, which compensated for its lack of charm with air conditioning.

Scott hated the fact that the building's new wing had central air. He hated air conditioning on principle, and he insisted that the thermostats in their house be set to seventy-eight degrees in the summer. Ellie never admitted to him that she relished being able to escape from the house on scorching August days and flee to her office to cool off.

It was the first of June, not a scorching August day, but the air outdoors was unpleasantly muggy. If he were here, Scott would point this out as proof of climate change. But he wasn't here. He was on a university campus in central Illinois, addressing a bunch of eco-warrior students while someone broadcast his appearance on the campus television station. Ellie would bet good money the auditorium where he was appearing was air-conditioned.

"The vet said she thought it could have been pancreatitis," she told Nakul. "She wanted to observe Lucy and rehydrate her. Turned out it was just a stomach bug, like what we humans get."

"Only we don't have to pay five hundred dollars and spend a night in a cage when we get stomach bugs," Nakul said sympathetically.

"Right. We just eat some chicken soup and go to bed."

Carl Corrigan chose that moment to enter the conference room. His face was slightly shiny, and sweat pasted the sparse strands of his hair across the bald dome of his skull. He wore a collared shirt and khaki slacks, the waistband of which underlined a budding paunch. "It's hot out there," he announced his arrival. "Thank God for air-conditioning, am I right?"

Ellie already knew Carl Corrigan, a developer pushing for approval of an oversized condo development on acreage compromised by the water table underneath it, was the anti-Scott. Of course he would love the air-conditioning.

He settled at the table, across from Ellie and Nakul, as if to emphasize that he was not on their team. He pulled a folder from his old-fashioned attaché case, opened it, and unfolded a blue-and-white plat of his proposed complex. "All right," he began. "We've redesigned the layout. By putting building H *here*," he indicated an elongated rectangle on the plat, "instead of the original location, we can extend the entry drive a bit and put in an extra drain for runoff. But I've gotta tell you, reducing the number of units is a nonstarter. We're entitled to make a profit on this, am I right? I've got investors I have to satisfy. Complying with all the MEPA regulations cuts into our margins, and then you're talking about solar panels. And let's face it, density housing is one of the best things we can do for the environment. Reducing the number of units reduces the density of the development, am I right?"

Ellie recalled a drinking game she and her friends used to play in college. When they watched an awards show on TV — the Oscars, the Emmys, the People's Choice — they had to take a drink of beer every time a winner thanked God in his or her acceptance speech. By the end of some awards shows, Ellie and her friends would be plastered. Right now, she was thinking she would like to drink something alcoholic every time Carl Corrigan said "Am I right?" Wine rather than beer; her tastes had matured.

MEPA regulations were the environmental rules the state imposed on all new construction. Corrigan shouldn't be complaining to her and Nakul about them. The town of Shelton didn't create those rules.

Then again, MEPA regulations were enacted because of people like Scott. They were fair and sensible. The planet needed to be protected — and condo developments needed to respect the ground on which they stood.

"I don't understand why Wayne isn't here," Carl griped. "When he and I discussed this project last year, he was all gung ho, am I right? He didn't mention all this stuff about the solar panels. He said the select board would give it a green light, easy-breezy. And now, all of a sudden, you're digging your heels in."

"We aren't digging our heels in, and it's not all of a sudden," Ellie said calmly, hoping her smile removed the sting from her words. "MEPA regulations have been around for years. You know all about them, Carl."

"And the engineering department has to provide its honest report to the select board before they approve or veto any development," Nakul added. "I'm sure Wayne reminded you of that."

"He didn't," Carl said. His smile looked as phony as Ellie's felt. "He said this was a no-brainer."

Ellie refrained from agreeing that *no-brainer* was the correct label for a project that needed a bit more thought put into it.

"I don't understand why he isn't here now." Carl pouted. "Nothing personal, but when push comes to shove, the top dog should be dealing with it, am I right?"

"We aren't vetoing this project," she reminded him. "We don't have that power. The select board will decide its ultimate fate. We're suggesting alterations that will make the board's approval much more likely. We want this project to be approved as much as you do." She was pretty sure that last statement was true.

True or not, it mollified Carl a bit. "I still don't know why Wayne couldn't be here. He and I understand each other."

Two buffoons. Of course they understood each other. And of course Wayne couldn't be here, because it was always Ellie's job to tell people things they didn't want to hear. Like, for instance, that they should reduce the size of the complex and include solar panels.

"There are things you could do to improve drainage," Nakul said, then launched into a technical dissertation on landfill and gravel and conduits. Ellie's education was in urban planning, not engineering; as far as she was concerned, Nakul might as well be speaking gibberish.

But she was happy to have him take over. She didn't mind telling Carl things he didn't want to hear, but she *did* mind doing Wayne's job for him. She didn't even know where he was this afternoon. Some vitally important meeting on a golf course or at a restaurant, no doubt.

By the time she got home from work, she felt like a damp rag, wrung out and clammy. She would have liked nothing better than to settle her butt into the contoured cushions of the old couch in the den, kick her feet up on the coffee table, and perform meditation breathing for an hour or so. She would have liked Scott and the girls to fix their own dinner, and clean up any messes Lucy might have made as she recuperated from her stomach bug, and then all go off on a long bike ride, leaving Ellie alone in peace.

That wasn't going to happen, though — not only because Scott wasn't around but because in about two hours, Abbie would be performing in the high school's end-of-the-year concert. Ellie had to fix a quick dinner, feed the girls and herself, deal with an inevitable apparel crisis — was the white blouse Abbie was supposed to wear with her black trousers clean? Had it been ironed? Why couldn't she wear sandals? Where was her belt?

There would also likely be a subsidiary clothing crisis with Misha, who would want to wear shorts and a T-shirt to the concert. Ellie would explain that a music concert was a formal event, even if it was at the high school and the performers were all students, and Misha had to show respect by not wearing the shirt from her soccer uniform but, at the very least, jeans and a top with nothing written on it — not her name, not her number, not the Shelton Youth Soccer Association logo.

The house was warm. Ellie adjusted the thermostat to seventy-four degrees and sighed — not quite a meditative exhalation, but a happy one — when she heard the air conditioning click on. All right, so she was destroying the environment. Scott wasn't here. He wouldn't have to know.

She broiled some chicken and threw together a salad for dinner. The girls seemed happy enough with that menu. Abbie confirmed that yes, her white concert blouse was clean, and no, it didn't have to be ironed; no one would notice if it was a little wrinkled. "I wish Dad was here," she said pensively. "This is the first time he's ever missed one of my concerts."

"You should do something *aloud*," Misha suggested. "Play your clarinet extra loud."

"Yeah, right." Abbie snorted. "I'd get kicked out of the orchestra."

Abbie had to be at the high school an hour before the concert began — that seemed a bit excessive, but the instruments did have to tune, and the conductor did have to run through a list of reminders and a last-minute bit of rehearsing. Ellie and Misha drove Abbie to the school and then returned home so Misha could change into respectable attire. "Daddy always brings Abbie flowers at the concerts," Misha reminded Ellie before she raced up the stairs to her bedroom to put on an outfit that met with Ellie's approval.

Ellie nodded. "You're right. Let's pick up a bouquet on the way back to the school." She recalled that Scott had also given Misha flowers after her ballet recitals. Misha had been so young then, five and six and seven, and she'd felt so utterly elegant in her little spangled leotard, her butterfly wings and tiara, carrying a bouquet of daisies wrapped in recycled tissue paper. Scott gave her no flowers after her soccer games, but she would have been embarrassed if he had. Until this year, she'd been on coed teams. Boys didn't get flowers after a soccer game. Therefore, she wouldn't want to get flowers, either.

But Abbie would want them tonight. She was missing Scott.

Scott was missing this concert.

Ellie felt a wave of pure exhaustion wash over her. Why did she have to do Scott's job as well as her own? Of course she knew one answer: her daughter deserved flowers after playing in the annual June concert, and Ellie wouldn't have her miss out on a bouquet just because Scott was absent. But really, was it fair? Was it fair that Ellie had to do Wayne's job during the day and Scott's job during the evening? If one aspect of saving the planet entailed preserving energy, why didn't Ellie get to preserve *her* energy? What would happen to the planet if her supply of energy was depleted?

Not much. The Earth would survive. But the Gillman household might not.

Ellie did not wish to expend any of her dwindling energy supply arguing with Misha over her attire. Misha clomped down the stairs dressed in her nicest blue jeans and a bright yellow RE:CYCLE T-shirt. Scott had ordered a few extras and given one to each of the girls. Abbie had yet to wear hers; she said it made her shoulders look too big. Misha had worn hers often enough for it to have gone through the washing machine twice. Because the weather was mild, Ellie had refrained from using the drier, honoring Scott's wishes and hanging the damp clothing on a clothes line outdoors. Without him around, tossing his sweaty bike clothes into the hamper on a regular basis, she was able to run smaller loads and get them hung and dried on the clothes line without too much extra effort. Abbie complained that clothing off the line felt like cardboard. It did, but running the drier was not the best way to save the planet.

She had discussed with Misha the importance of wearing apparel with no writing on it for certain occasions, but she knew that if she told Misha to change into a slogan-free shirt, they'd wind up arguing. Misha would insist that her father's slogan was a message the entire world, or at least the people attending the Shelton

High School Spring Concert, needed to see, and Ellie would wind up pissed off at Scott, and she was already pissed off at him because he wasn't around to buy flowers for Abbie. And because Ellie had to buy flowers for Abbie, she and Misha really had no time to argue, anyway. They raced outside to the car, made a quick detour to Whole Foods to purchase a bouquet — were the flowers organic? Was there such a thing as organic flowers? — and then cruised to the high school.

The parking lot was already crowded. Ellie hoped she and Misha would find decent seats in the auditorium. Misha raced ahead of Ellie to the school's main entrance. Ellie trotted along behind her, cradling the bouquet in her arms.

They were in luck; as soon as they entered the auditorium, Ellie spotted Connie standing beside a seat in the fifth row, surveying the crowd. When she spotted Ellie, she waved flamboyantly. "I think Connie may have saved some seats for us," Ellie murmured, clamping her free hand over Misha's shoulder and steering her down the aisle toward the fifth row.

Connie's husband Richard stood when Ellie and Misha sidled down the row to the seats Connie had saved for them. Good-looking in a bland, polished way, Richard wore a monogrammed shirt and crisp twill slacks, and he held a bouquet twice the size of the one Ellie gripped. Whether this was because he was twice as proud of Merritt's participation in the school chorus as Ellie was of Abbie's participation in the orchestra, or because he wanted to show off how much money he spent on flowers for his daughter, Ellie couldn't say. For that matter, she couldn't tell if the flowers he'd bought for Merritt were organic. The roses, lilies, and violets in the arrangement he held looked lusher and more colorful than the carnations and baby's breath in Ellie's bouquet, but who knew if they'd been nurtured with chemical fertilizers rather than cow manure, or whatever organic flowers might be grown in?

"Thanks for saving the seats," Ellie said to Connie as Misha pulled down the hinged base of her seat, kneeled on it, and searched the crowd for anyone she might recognize. "Nice to see you, Richard."

"Connie insists that if we don't drag ourselves to these school functions, Merritt will throw herself off a bridge or something," he said. "I think she's made of sterner stuff than that. So how are you doing? Enjoying the single life while hubby is off riding around the country on his two-wheeler?"

Not particularly, Ellie thought, but she would never utter a negative thought in Richard's presence. He was the kind of guy who would remember it and use it against her sometime in the future. "We miss Scott," she said, "but of course we support what he's doing."

"Scott's a saint," Connie said, her usual refrain.

"Still, a woman all alone?" Richard winked at Ellie. "Now's your chance to have some fun."

She smiled, even though she wasn't sure he was joking. Instead, she settled onto her seat and chased away a stray thought about vibrators.

The lights in the auditorium dimmed, and the chatter of parents and grandparents died down. The school principal, a stout, silver-haired woman named Dr. Lee, strolled to a microphone on the stage, welcomed everyone, gushed about how proud she was of the school's musicians, and reminded audience members to turn off their phones. The auditorium filled with rustles and clicks. Ellie dug her phone out of her purse and shut it off.

The first half of the concert belonged to the glee club. The students marched in, arranging themselves on risers. Connie nudged Ellie and pointed to the back row. Merritt was actually pretty easy to find. She had the chalkiest skin of any of the singers. She was wearing a requisite white shirt along with her dreary black skirt. Seeing her in a garment that wasn't entirely black was refreshing.

The glee club sang their songs competently. Ellie recognized a few of Abbie's friends among the singers. They seemed to be enjoying themselves, unlike Merritt, who hid behind the black binder holding her sheet music. Could she even see the conductor? Did she truly deserve that hundred-dollar bouquet her father had brought for her? Did Richard think the flowers would serve as evidence of his devoted parenting if he and Connie found themselves in a custody battle in the foreseeable future?

To Ellie's right, Misha shifted and fidgeted. She was clearly bored. Ellie let her squirm. At least she wasn't making any noise.

After the glee club finished their performance, a select a cappella group gathered at the center of the stage and performed a few numbers, managing the complex harmonies reasonably well. The singers assigned to make percussion noises were apparently having quite a fine time, while those carrying the melodies and harmonies seemed solemn, even a little grim.

Misha seemed a little grim, too. She yawned audibly.

During a brief intermission, the risers were removed from the stage and chairs were set up for the orchestra. "Finally," Misha muttered, dragging out each syllable.

The orchestra members emerged from the wings, carrying their instruments and folders of music. Ellie spotted Abbie entering, talking quietly with a girl carrying a flute. She took her seat, licked her reed, and set her music on the stand in front of her chair. Even before a note was played, Ellie felt her cheeks rise, pulling her lips into a smile. How many school concerts had she attended over the years? How many, starting when Abbie was in primary school and the young musicians could barely tune their instruments, let alone perform without errors? No matter; every concert had thrilled Ellie, just as Misha's ballet recitals and soccer games thrilled her. These were her girls. Her pride. Her greatest accomplishment.

The orchestra plowed through an early Beethoven symphony without any major clinkers. Then the conductor, a wiry young man with red hair that bubbled around his face like tiny springs, announced that the ensemble would be playing a medley of Gershwin songs. Misha stopped squirming enough to whisper, "Who's Gershwin?"

"He wrote *Porgy and Bess*," Ellie whispered back. "You know the song, 'Summertime'?"

Misha nodded.

Gershwin had also written "I've Got Rhythm," which was the first song in the medley. To Ellie's delighted surprise, Abbie played a solo in it. Connie dug her elbow into Ellie's ribs and Misha bounced in her seat. Bouncing was her default response whenever she got excited.

The rest of the medley went smoothly. The students seemed to enjoy playing Gershwin more than Beethoven. A violinist played a solo in "Summertime" and a boy Ellie didn't recognize played a trumpet solo on "Strike Up the Band." They ended with a cheerful, up-tempo rendition of "You Can't Take That Away From Me."

The audience clearly enjoyed Gershwin more than Beethoven, too. Exuberant applause greeted the final chord, and as the conductor gestured for his soloists to take a bow, Misha jumped to her feet and shouted, "That's my sister!"

Fortunately, Abbie didn't appear to have heard Misha over the clapping. Ellie patted Misha's shoulder, attempting to ease her back into her seat, but she refused. She bounced as much standing as she had sitting, clapping her hands above her head and hooting. Only when the applause waned and the orchestra members folded their music and meandered off the stage did Misha calm down. "It was a perfect *aloud* thing," she justified her behavior. "If Abbie plays a solo, girls should be *aloud*."

Ellie couldn't argue with that.

"I guess we should bring our virtuosos their flowers," Richard said, giving the bouquet in Ellie's hand a patronizing look. If she'd known Abbie was going to play a solo, she might have purchased a bigger bouquet for her. But then, probably not. Unlike Richard, Ellie wasn't a fund manager earning exorbitant sums. To be sure, if she earned even a third of what he did, he would probably be among the Shelton residents storming the town hall to demand that she be paid less, simply because civil servants weren't supposed to earn that much.

She and Misha struggled against the current of audience members streaming up the aisles toward the lobby. They made their way to the corridor adjacent to the stage door, where the musicians in their white shirts and black skirts and slacks milled around, flirting, yammering, and bumping fists. Ellie glimpsed Abbie surrounded by a group of her fellow orchestra members, all of them holding their instruments as they gravitated slowly toward the practice room where their music cases were stashed.

It took a while, and the push and pull of the crowd managed to tear a few petals from one of the carnations, but eventually Ellie and Misha caught up to Abbie just inside the practice room doorway. "You were fabulous," Ellie gushed, handing Abbie the flowers. "Why didn't you tell us you had a solo?"

"It was a surprise." Abbie smiled, her cheeks flushed, her eyelashes a bit darker and thicker than nature had intended. "Did you like it?"

"I screamed," Misha reported matter-of-factly. "I made a lot of noise, because, you know. *Aloud.*"

Abbie grinned. Clutching her flowers in one hand and her clarinet in the other, she navigated through the crowd to her instrument locker, where her clarinet case was stored. As she disassembled the instrument and inserted the pieces in their felt-lined slots, the orchestra teacher approached, his springy hair trembling and his dress shirt wilted from the heat.

"Ms. Gillman!" he greeted Ellie. "I'm Henry Streiberg."

"Yes, of course," Ellie said, shaking his hand. She was glad he'd introduced himself. Abbie and her friends referred to him as "Mr. Cyborg," and that was the name that had popped into her head when she saw him. She wouldn't have wanted to call him that to his face. "I'm so proud of Abbie. Her solo was such a surprise."

"I wanted to talk to you about that," Henry Streiberg said, and Ellie experienced a momentary pang of worry. Had Abbie done something wrong? Avoiding her teacher's gaze, she focused on wiping down the segments of her clarinet and arranging them in the case.

"I'm not sure how committed she is to her instrument," Henry Streiberg said. Ellie's worry spiked, until he continued. "But I think she needs more than my instruction once a week. She's enormously talented. If she's willing to make the commitment, she ought to be studying with someone at a higher level. Maybe she could study with one of the faculty members of the New England Conservatory. They have a summer program she might be interested in. And there are members of the Boston Symphony Orchestra who work with private students, as well. I think this is something Abbie ought to consider. *If* she's willing to make the commitment," he repeated, beaming a smile at Abbie, whose cheeks flushed even darker as she stared at the scuffed linoleum floor.

The New England Conservatory? The BSO? Was he kidding?

"She's my sister!" Misha bellowed. The noise level in the room was high enough that her shriek didn't seem terribly out of place. "Maybe she'll be famous. Our dad is famous. He's been on TV. So have I, for like a half a minute."

"I know about Mr. Gillman's cross-country ride," Henry Streiberg said. "And yes, maybe someday Abbie will be famous, too. The next Benny Goodman."

Abbie rolled her eyes.

"Well." Ellie collected herself. "It's certainly something we'll have to talk about."

"I hope you do," Henry Streiberg said. "I can continue to teach her in the meantime, but I think this would be a worthwhile investment for Abbie. *If* she's willing to make the commitment."

A big if, Ellie thought. Given the way Henry Streiberg kept repeating that, he clearly wondered whether she was willing.

"I'm very proud of Abbie," he said. "I'm sure you are, too." With that, he moved on to a cluster of violinists and their parents.

"Well, we know there'll be at least one A on your report card," Ellie teased Abbie as, a few minutes later, they left the school building and headed across the parking lot. The asphalt felt slightly spongy beneath Ellie's shoes, still soft from the day's heat, although now that the sun had set, the air had cooled down a bit.

"I'm getting an A in English, too," Abbie said. "And probably math."

Misha spotted the car and bolted ahead, burning off some of her energy. Ellie hoped she wouldn't bounce all the way home in the car. Even wearing a seatbelt, Misha could bounce.

Ellie remained silent as she inched the car through the bottleneck of traffic that formed at the parking lot's exit. Once they were on the road and cruising toward home, she glanced at her older daughter, who sat quietly beside her in the front seat, her clarinet case and her flowers balanced in her lap. "What do you think about what Mr. Streiberg said?" she asked Abbie. "I mean, besides the likelihood that you'll get an A in music this term."

Abbie aimed her big, dark eyes at Ellie. "I want to take lessons with someone from the New England Conservatory."

"We'd have to find out who might be taking private students, and how much it costs. And if they're located in Boston, we'd have to drive into the city, unless they give classes remotely..." Ellie's brain bubbled like a kettle of boiling water. "Money is a little tight with Dad not teaching summer school this year."

"I have a summer job," Abbie reminded Ellie. "I could pay a little."

Her summer job was as a mother's helper for five-year-old twins, three days a week, from nine thirty until two. The twins' mother wanted some free mornings, and their father was willing to pay Abbie ten dollars an hour to keep his wife happy. Entertaining two five-year-olds for four and a half hours was going to be a challenge, possibly more of a challenge than Abbie realized right now. But she was thrilled to be earning all that money.

"We've discussed your summer earnings," Ellie reminded Abbie. "You have to save at least half for college."

"But there's the other half."

"Which you're going to want to spend on mascara." Ellie smiled to let Abbie know she was teasing. "The real issue is commitment," she went on. "Mr. Streiberg said that word several times. If you wanted to lift your playing up a level, you can't just practice for twenty minutes a few times a week. You'd have to practice an hour a day, at least."

"I know," Abbie said, sounding slightly less enthusiastic.

"Why can't I get a job?" Misha called from the back seat.

"You're too young," Abbie shouted back.

"I signed you up for the town day camp again," Ellie reminded her. "You loved it last summer." And town employees got a discount on the fees, thank goodness. "Sports and games and art."

"I'm almost in middle school," Misha complained. "I should be a counselor."

"I could practice an hour a day," Abbie said. "If I'm not too tired from babysitting the Vandenhoffer twins."

Ellie steered into the garage, turned off the car, and let out a weary breath. Her day had been long, and she was exhausted. Abbie and Misha seemed tired, too. They took their time unbuckling their seatbelts and climbing out of the car. Once inside the house, Abbie filled a vase with water, stuffed the flowers into it, and carried it upstairs to her bedroom. Misha announced that she was starving, helped herself to a banana, and followed her sister up the stairs.

Ellie pulled her phone out of her purse to recharge it. It was still turned off, and when she pressed the button to wake it up, the message light flashed.

She tapped the icon to retrieve her message and lifted the phone to her ear.

"Ellie?" Scott demanded. "I called you on the landline and no one answered. So I called your cell, and your phone was shut off. Where the hell are you?"

I'm here, Ellie thought. *I'm here with our spectacular daughters. You're hundreds of miles away, saving the world, but I'm here, fatigued but glowing inside because Abbie played a solo and Misha was so proud of her and wanted to make sure she got flowers.*

We're here. And you're not.

DAY TWENTY

If I said my speech at the University of Illinois went well, I'd be too modest. Like the big, bad wolf, I blew the house down. (See photo below: me and a huge screen with my PowerPoint slides. The RE:CYCLE shirt I'm wearing is a clean one, not one of the shirts I'd been riding in. Hooray for laundromats, even if they consume too much water and electricity.) After the speech, the organizers hosted a reception for me. Vegan noshes and artisan beer. Several faculty members were there, as well as a lot of students who rely on bicycles to get around. The campus is as big as a city, so they put those bikes to good use. Several wanted to discuss the pluses and minuses of recumbent bikes with me.

I've been invited to give my presentation at the University of Colorado and the University of Texas. Wow! Did you know that Texas generates more wind power than any other state in the country? You may think of Texas in terms of oil production, but they've stepped up wind power generation in a big way. All that open space. All that wind.

Speaking of wind power, the funnel cloud that touched down in Iowa was nowhere near me. From what I've read, it caused no major damage. If only we could harness the power of tornadoes to produce electricity.

How about it, engineers and meteorologists? There's a project worth pursuing!

Tomorrow, back in the saddle — or on the recumbent, which doesn't exactly have a saddle seat. I'll be veering south into Missouri, where I hope to meet with members of the Missouri Organic Association. Looking forward to that.

Since a few people asked in the comments, no, I don't have any blisters. Properly fitting bike shoes really work. But yes, my butt is sore.

CHAPTER TEN

The digital clock on the microwave read 10:27, but Ellie was pretty sure Illinois was in the central time zone, which would make it an hour earlier where Scott was spending the night. He would probably still be awake.

She poured a glass of wine for herself — partly to drink a toast to her talented-musician daughter, partly to reward herself for having dealt with Carl Corrigan all afternoon — and carried it and the phone to the den. She settled into the couch's pliant cushions and tapped in Scott's number.

He answered on the first ring. "Ellie. Where were you?"

Not the sweetest, most loving greeting she'd ever heard. "We just got home from the high school. The end-of-the-year concert was this evening." She paused long enough to let that sink in and, she hoped, cause Scott a twinge of remorse, then added, "Abbie played a solo. I had no idea. She wanted to surprise me."

"Oh." Scott sounded marginally less irritated. "Wow. A solo?"

"In a George Gershwin medley. She played it perfectly. You would have been so proud of her."

"I *am* proud of her," Scott said, sounding more than a little defensive. "I wish I'd been there."

"Anyway. I turned off my phone during the concert," Ellie said.

"Right. Of course."

"Misha and I brought her flowers."

"Good." She heard him draw in a breath, and when he spoke again, he sounded hesitant. "Is Abbie angry at me for missing her concert?"

"No," Ellie reassured him. "She's proud of you, too."

His tone was much more upbeat when he said, "I may not have played a solo on the clarinet, but I did good today. Did you read my post in the Wheeling and Dealing blog? I was a big hit at the university."

"Yes, I read the post." She'd thought it best to do that before she called him, in case it contained anything important that they needed to discuss.

Apparently, his presentation at the University of Illinois was important, and they needed to discuss it. "Full house, Ellie. They gave me a standing ovation. Then they hosted a reception in my honor."

Which was probably why he hadn't phoned home early enough to catch Ellie and the girls while they were eating dinner. He could have spoken with them then, but he'd been busy being fêted at his university reception. By the time he'd called, Ellie and the girls were already at the concert and Ellie's phone was turned off.

Now her phone was turned on, allowing Scott to go on at length about his moment in the spotlight, mentioning a glitch in the PowerPoint at the very beginning of his speech and the jokes he made while a couple of students raced off to find another projector. According to him, the audience laughed heartily. He was swarmed by students after the talk. It was thanks to the video feed — he would text her a link so she could watch his speech online — that other universities invited him to speak. Several people thought he should be giving TED talks, but he believed he ought to finish his bike trip across the country first.

"This is turning out to be bigger than I expected," he concluded.

"Good for you," Ellie said. She didn't intend to sound snippy, but the wine wasn't mellowing her as rapidly as she would have liked.

Not that it mattered. Scott was awash in so much adrenaline, so high on how his day turned out, that he didn't hear the edge in her voice. "I've got to do some prep for tomorrow's ride, so I'd better not talk too much longer. Are the girls around to say hello?"

"I think they're in bed," Ellie said. Misha probably was; she had a soccer game tomorrow morning and needed a full night's sleep. Abbie was likely texting with her friends, enjoying her flowers and her own moment of glory at the concert.

"Okay. Well, give them my love. Tell Abbie I'm sorry I missed her concert, but I'm very proud of her."

Ellie promised to pass his messages along and said goodbye. She was happy for Scott, happy about his grand triumph at the university, happy that he was happy. Happy that the exasperation she'd heard in the phone message he'd left her earlier that evening had evaporated.

But she was also annoyed. She'd wanted to tell him more about the concert, about Abbie's poise, about her teacher's praise. She'd wanted to tell him about the applause their daughter had received — and Misha's rambunctious contribution to that — and about Abbie's claim that she wanted to take her clarinet more seriously.

And she'd wanted to tell him about her own day at work. But he hadn't asked about that. Not that she expected him to, but damn it, she had a life, too. She had exerted herself as much as he had, with no standing ovation, no praise, no invitations to give a TED talk. Not that she would particularly want to give one, but he might at least have shown a teeny bit of interest in what was going on in her life.

She was not a hero. She was not saving the planet. But she deserved a "good for you," too.

She would have to settle for a cold, crisp glass of chardonnay.

A week later, the roof caved in.

Not quite literally, but close.

The day dawned dark and windy, with clouds in various shades of gray skittering across the sky. Every now and then, one of those clouds would spit out a mouthful of rain, but the wind gusts dried what little rain reached the ground, which meant Ellie would have to mow the lawn that weekend. If only it rained a bit more, the grass would be too wet to cut, but Mother Nature wasn't cooperating.

Until a couple of years ago, she and Scott had hired a local landscaping firm to cut their grass. With two incomes, they could afford that minor luxury. They did all the rest of the yard work themselves: pruning, fertilizing, seeding patches of grass that hadn't survived the winter or the annual invasion of grubs. Scott refused to apply a chemical grub killer to the lawn, insisting those products were toxic for the environment. He used some sort of organic mold that was supposed to kill grubs gently — as if the grubs had nervous systems sophisticated enough to perceive that their slaughter was gentle.

But as Scott became more and more alarmed by environmental threats, he decided to stop using the landscaping service, which relied on gasoline-powered mowers, and instead mow the yard himself, pushing an old-fashioned reel mower. It was the sort of lawn mower Ellie's father had used when she was growing up — two wheels connected by angled blades that sliced the grass as the wheels rotated. Scott sharpened the blades every year and insisted that he loved the exercise of pushing the archaic machine back and forth across the yard. He laughed along when neighbors teased him about his mower's antiquated technology, and when he was done laughing, he flexed his muscles and boasted that using his own power to mow the lawn was a manly pursuit. He also lectured them on the environmental benefits of jettisoning gas-powered mowers for his clean, simple machine. He loved lecturing people about environmental issues.

He'd promised Ellie he would sharpen the blades of the reel mower before he embarked on his cross-country journey, and she hoped he'd remembered to do that. She did not want to feel manly forcing the damned mower over the grass. She had considered asking Abbie to mow the lawn — Ellie would pay her — but Abbie said she was earning enough money babysitting for the Vandenhoffer twins and didn't want to take on another job. Misha had expressed some interest in the chore, but she was only ten years old and not exactly calm and cautious. Ellie worried about her injuring herself. Strips of metal sharp enough to hack down grass could also do some damage to precious little fingers.

She had phoned a couple of older teenage boys in the neighborhood and offered to pay them to mow the lawn, hoping they would like to feel manly. Evidently, they would rather feel manly by shooting hoops and driving Jeeps with noisy mufflers up and down the street. They all turned her down.

So Ellie would mow the lawn that weekend, unless she got lucky and Shelton experienced a saturating downpour.

It was barely drizzling when she, Nakul, and Bob Kaufman from the town's zoning board met Carl Corrigan at the Mumson Farm parcel on Route 29 to see how Carl planned to grade the land for proper drainage. This on-site meeting was the sort of task Wayne should have attended, but of course he had something much more important to do — probably make a bunch of promises to the public works department that, a few months from now, Ellie would have to break. At least, given the threatening clouds and the intermittent showers, she knew he wasn't playing golf at his country club.

Carl gave a cheerful, assertive presentation. "The entry road will go uphill, with embedded drains along the way. The first building would be on that rise, and the rest of the buildings behind it, so everything will drain down toward Route 29, am I right?" he explained as Nakul and Bob took notes and Ellie picked her way carefully around a few muddy spots. She wasn't wearing boots, and she preferred not to sacrifice her most comfortable leather slip-ons to the muck. Even without a downpour, this tract was pretty spongy. Although she wasn't an engineer, she suffered visions of beautiful, expensive condominiums sinking slowly into the ground, as if it were quicksand, and burying their residents alive.

Nakul and Bob peppered Corrigan with questions implying that, unlike Ellie, they knew what they were talking about: stuff about pebble filters, berms, flood plains, and elevations. Ellie's presence merely made the meeting official. Nakul would write a report about it, she would proofread the report to confirm that it portrayed the on-site meeting accurately, and then she would hand the report to

Wayne, who would present it before the select board and receive their thanks. They would offer him their version of "Good for you" in a gloriously unsnippy tone.

Why was she so cranky? Other than the mud, the gloomy sky, the fact that she was doing Wayne's job, the fact that Scott was apparently having the time of his life on his funny little bike with his funny little Beast of Burden and its funny little orange flag trailing along behind him, and getting honored and congratulated, while she was working her tail off without so much as a thank you, and tomorrow, when she finally got a day off, she'd have to spend the afternoon mowing the lawn after spending the morning cheering Misha's team on in their soccer game? Really, what did she have to be crabby about?

Enjoying a rueful private chuckle, she let the men blather on, counted the number of times Carl said, "Am I right?" and drove with Nakul and Bob back to the town hall. On her way down the corridor to the new wing, she detoured into the ladies' restroom, dampened a few paper towels, and tried to wipe the smears of mud off her shoes. They probably needed to be polished. One more chore to add to her list.

Entering her own office, she heard voices emerging through the open door to Wayne's inner office. Whatever important thing he'd been doing instead of traipsing around the Mumson Farm tract, he was clearly done doing it now, since he rarely did anything important in his office. Ellie crossed to the doorway to let Wayne know she was back and to fill him in on how the expedition had gone — if Wayne had any interest in hearing about it.

She was surprised to see the person he was chatting with: Richard Vernon, Connie's husband. Like Wayne, Richard had on crisp khakis and a casual sports coat over a pale gray polo shirt. They must shop at the same clothing store, Ellie surmised — the Asshole Haberdashery.

"Back so soon?" Wayne greeted her without bothering to stand. Not that she cared about proprieties, but she'd been trudging around the swampy Route 29 acreage and getting sporadically drizzled on for the past three hours. She didn't think there was anything "so soon" about it. He could have risen from his chair out of sympathy.

Richard had been seated in one of the visitor's chairs, but he stood at Ellie's entrance. He knew his manners. "Hello, Ellie."

She acknowledged his greeting with a smile and a nod, then turned back to Wayne to tell him how the trip to the Route 29 property went. Before she could speak, Wayne said, "You two know each other?" He appeared shocked, as if it was inconceivable that in a town as small and cozy as Shelton, two residents might actually be acquainted.

"Our daughters are good friends," Richard said. Ellie wasn't sure whether he actually believed that. According to Connie, he was utterly clueless when it came to Merritt's life.

"They were classmates in preschool, at the Koala Cub Club," Ellie elaborated.

"Oh, that's such a cute little place." Wayne sounded condescending. "My boys didn't go there. Nancy's a full-time mom. Dying species, full-time moms," he added, winking at Richard — who was enough of a creep to wink back.

"If you're busy," Ellie said, sending another bland smile in Richard's direction, "I can fill you in later on what Nakul and Bob from the zoning board had to say about Carl's plans. Nakul will be writing up a formal report, but he won't have that done until sometime next week."

"Actually, I'm here about that very subject," Richard said. "My firm is a principal investor in Carl's complex. *The* principal investor, actually. We financed the purchase of the property. I assume everything is on track?" he asked Ellie.

If that was what he'd come to the town manager's office about, he should have chosen Ellie to speak to. Wayne was as clueless about the condo development as Richard was about his daughter. "More or less," she told him.

"Because we're investing pretty heavily in this. We want to see it succeed."

"I think that if Carl complies with what Nakul and Bob are recommending, it should work out," she said.

"You mean, the solar panels? I know your husband is all worked up about that kind of crap, Ellie, but you shouldn't be imposing his political views on a simple condominium project."

"They aren't his political views," she said crisply. "They're the state's recommendations. MEPA has issued regulations regarding the environmental burden of new construction projects."

"I'm just saying, solar panels don't come cheap."

"Neither does environmental degradation."

"Okay, okay," Wayne intervened, as if he were a referee breaking up a tussle between opposing teams. "I'd love to cut Carl a break on the solar stuff, but MEPA writes the laws. I don't."

Regulations, not laws, Ellie silently corrected him. It didn't matter. At least this time, he was backing her up, not making promises she would later have to unmake.

"I'll leave you two to finish your meeting," she said with a final, chilly smile before returning to her own office and settling at her desk. She reached for her office phone and called her house to make sure Misha had gotten home from school safely. Misha reported that she'd let Lucy out and Lucy chased a rabbit, but the rabbit was almost as big as Lucy and twice as fast, and also she had a stupid math homework assignment and she really hated base 2, and she'd gotten an email from her soccer coach saying that if it was raining too hard, they would reschedule tomorrow's game. Also, Abbie was home but she was practicing her clarinet upstairs in her room and told Misha not to disturb her. "She's so bossy sometimes," Misha complained. "She thinks just because her cyborg music teacher thinks she's talented, she can boss me around."

"Best not to disturb her," Ellie said, pleased that Abbie was becoming more diligent about practicing her instrument. "I'll be home the usual time."

"Can you bring take-out Chinese?"

"Not tonight. I've got some cod filets defrosting in the fridge."

"I hate cod," Misha said cheerfully. "We should eat steaks while Daddy is away."

Ellie laughed — and silently conceded that Misha had a point. She said goodbye to her daughter, hung up the phone, and swiveled in her chair to find Richard looming on the opposite side of her desk. Just like Wayne's office, hers had visitor's chairs, but Richard seemed happy to stand, compelling her to acknowledge his bulk.

He wasn't taller than Scott, but he had to weigh a good thirty pounds more. He had the build of a high school football player who'd reached middle age — not quite fat, but thick.

"So, your husband is still pedaling around the universe, telling people to use solar panels?" he asked.

"He's pedaling around the country and educating people about climate change."

"A strange way to make a living, no?" Richard grinned. His thickness notwithstanding, he was good looking in an indistinct, prep-school way, his hair a mix of tawny brown and silver, his complexion slightly pink, his eyes a cool, piercing blue.

"A way to make a life," Ellie said. "He's doing this for our children, not for himself." She knew that wasn't entirely true; Scott was definitely enjoying the attention he was getting, the invitations, the ovations, the receptions.

"And leaving his poor wife home, all by herself?"

"I'm not all by myself. I've got two daughters and a dog."

"Yeah, that must make you feel deeply loved." He leaned across the desk, planting his hands on either side of her blotter. "Bet you're lonely, aren't you?"

"I'm fine, Richard."

"Going to school concerts without the hubby? Relying on your little girl — how old is she, eight? — for conversation? Because we know teenage girls don't talk to their parents."

"She's almost eleven, and a terrific conversationalist," Ellie defended Misha. "So is Abbie."

"I'm just saying, it must be very lonely for you." His face was so close, she could feel his warm, damp breath on her cheeks. "If you get lonely enough, honey, I know someone who could make you feel a little less lonely."

It took her a moment to realize that the someone he was referring to was himself. She shuddered, feeling a spasm of queasiness. "I'm not lonely," she said firmly. "And at the moment, I'm very busy. Please let me get back to work." If he weren't the husband of her good friend, she would have slapped him. Or told him to fuck off. Or called him an asshole.

But out of loyalty to Connie — who would probably have endorsed all those actions — she spun away from him, tapped her computer keyboard, and pretended to be engrossed in the Shelton town website home page that replaced the screensaver swirls on her monitor.

She maintained a steady respiration, refusing to watch him leave her office. The carpet wasn't particularly plush, but it was thick enough to muffle a person's footsteps. Was he still standing in front of her desk? Had he taken a hint and departed? Would she have to slap him and tell him to go fuck himself?

Was part of her disgust and outrage due to the fact that he was right? She *was* lonely. She *did* want to feel less lonely.

Not with him, though. She'd prefer anyone, anything, even a vibrator with a dead battery, over him.

She was still fuming when she arrived home an hour later. The sky had finally committed to precipitation; hard, silver raindrops flew in the heavy wind, zigging and zagging and forcing her to switch her windshield wipers to high speed for the drive. Trees rocked and swayed and a branch thunked against the roof of her car, causing her to flinch. The drive frayed her already fragile nerves, and she took a moment to collect herself once she'd pulled into the garage and shut off the engine.

By the time she'd entered the kitchen, Abbie had finished her clarinet practice and was watching TV, simultaneously tapping texts into her phone. Misha had set up shop at the kitchen table, several math worksheets spread before her. "Do we really have to eat cod?" she asked.

"I'll cook it in marinara sauce," Ellie suggested as she set down her tote. "We can eat it over spaghetti."

"Whole wheat spaghetti?"

"With enough sauce, it tastes just like regular spaghetti," Abbie called from the den.

That was when they heard a creak and then a crack, as sharp as a gunshot — or at least what Ellie imagined a gunshot would sound like, since the closest she'd ever gotten to hearing one was in movies and television shows. The house shuddered slightly, and the wind shrieked.

"Jesus." Abbie raced into the kitchen, clutching her phone. "What was that?"

"Sounded like a bullet," Misha declared. Evidently, she'd been watching the same movies and TV shows as Ellie.

"I think something hit the roof," Ellie said. She didn't want to go outside and inspect the house for damage, but she had no choice. She was the grown-up. Scott was somewhere else.

She hurried to the entry and grabbed her rain slicker from the coat closet. After zipping it, she pulled the hood over her hair and contemplated arming herself with an umbrella. She realized it would blow inside out in the gale-force wind. She also contemplated donning boots. Her shoes were still stained with mud from the afternoon's outing, but they didn't need any additional mud. She sat on the chair beside the front door, pulled off her shoes, and wriggled her feet into her L.L. Bean boots.

Bracing herself, she eased open the front door and ventured onto the porch. The overhang offered slight protection, although the rain was blowing almost horizontally. Clasping the hood of her slicker so it wouldn't blow off her head, she ventured down the steps onto the front walk, which was flooded with puddles. Craning her neck, she gazed up and saw a tree limb resting on the roof. A huge limb, as big as a small tree, its branches covered with green leaves she would call oblong and Abbie would insist were elliptical. It must have broken off the black walnut tree near the garage. Beneath the limb, she could see a mess of broken roof tiles, as well as a patch of naked wood where the tiles had come off. Lowering her eyes, she spotted some roof tiles on the porch overhang, and some in the yews and spirea shrubs that bordered the porch.

Ellie swore under her breath and climbed back up the porch steps. Yes, she was alone. Yes, she was the only adult. Yes, she wanted a glass of wine, desperately.

"A tree limb hit the roof," she announced as she entered the kitchen and unzipped her raincoat. "It looks like the roof might be damaged. I need to go up to the attic to see if the limb actually broke through the roof and caused a leak."

"Great!" Misha leaped out of her chair. "I'll get the plunger."

DAY TWENTY-THREE

Holy crap. I almost died today.

The roads I'm biking on aren't heavily trafficked. Taking back roads means adding miles to my trip, but I've been training for this. I can handle the extra miles. What I can't handle is a monstrous SUV — probably getting about twelve miles to the gallon — being driven by someone busy texting on his phone as he's careening down the street. He missed clipping my Beast of Burden by inches — and only because I veered off the road and down a grassy slope, into a gulley that contained about six inches of rain water.

The SUV cruised on, not even acknowledging me.

It took me a couple of minutes to calm down. My shoes were soaked from the water in the gulley, but my Beast of Burden remained upright. Thank God for that. And all my possessions inside it are protected by the water-proof cover. So . . . all is well. I think by now even my blood pressure has returned to normal.

But internal-combustion vehicles have a lot to answer for. That SUV was spewing exhaust into the air. It was taking up too much width on a narrow country road. If the road had been bordered by a forest rather than a gulley, I might have veered into a tree. Or the SUV might have flat-out hit me.

Wake up, folks! Pay attention to your environment! Sometimes that environment is just air and water, flora and fauna. Sometimes it's a fellow human being on a bicycle.

CHAPTER ELEVEN

"What do you mean, the roof broke?" Scott's voice rasped with tension.

Ellie took a deep breath. She did not need him yelling at her. It wasn't as if *she'd* broken the damned roof. "A limb from the black walnut tree crashed onto the roof in the storm we had last night. I went up to the attic and found it had broken through."

"Christ. How bad?"

"I was able to nail a tarp over the damaged part so it wouldn't leak. You had that old tarp in the garage — "

"You nailed it?"

"Into the rafters, yes."

"So now there are holes in the tarp? Why didn't you duct-tape it?"

"The rafters were damp. Duct tape wouldn't have stayed glued to the boards."

"But now the tarp has holes in it."

"So does the roof." Ellie sighed. She had expected Scott to offer sympathy, not criticism. "I took a bunch of photos of the damage and emailed them to the insurance company. But it's a weekend, and I'm probably not going to hear back from them until at least Monday. It was a big storm. I'm sure they're receiving lots of claims."

"Great." Scott's voice was taut with anger. "I almost got killed by that damned SUV, and now I'm dealing with a broken roof."

"*I'm* dealing with the roof," Ellie reminded him, trying with less than total success to filter her irritation out of her voice. "And yes, I read your post on Wheeling and Dealing about your close encounter with the SUV. I'm sure it must have been scary." Possibly even scarier than hearing a tree limb smash into your roof. "I really can't talk. Misha's soccer game wasn't canceled. The field is going to be a swamp, but it isn't raining right now, so the coaches want to squeeze the game in."

"Her game is that early?" Scott asked, then snorted. "Oh, right. I'm an hour behind you."

"Exactly. We have to leave the house in five minutes. Do you want to say a quick hello to the girls?"

He did. Ellie handed the phone over to Abbie and experienced an unexpected, oddly shameful, wave of relief.

She was upset about Scott's near disaster with a bad driver — exactly what she'd feared when he had first proposed this trip. She recalled the qualms she experienced when she'd waved him off that first day. He'd looked so vulnerable on his bicycle. Abbie and Misha, flanking him on their bikes, had looked vulnerable, too, but Ellie had known they would ride only a couple of miles with Scott, and he would be watching out for them. Who watched out for him?

But beyond that, she was irritated. She and the girls had experienced their own scare last night. What if not a limb but an entire tree had fallen on their house? Apparently, the storm had left behind extensive damage throughout eastern Massachusetts. Several towns were without power, as was a neighborhood encompassing several blocks on the southern edge of Shelton. She had started her day with a phone call from Wayne, asking her to keep him updated on reports from the power company. She told him she had to deal with a broken roof and a soccer game and would be unable to contact the power company until around noon, and she provided him with a phone number so he could call the company himself. He could have looked the number up; it was on the company's website. But perhaps that was a bit beyond Wayne's capabilities. He hadn't even expressed concern about her broken roof.

Abbie, who had already announced that she would not attend Misha's soccer game because it was too wet out and she had to start studying for her finals, shouted to Ellie, "Dad wants to know if the tree limb came from one of our trees or one of Ms. Kupferberg's trees." She handed the phone to Misha, who was already dressed in her soccer uniform and shin pads, then reported to Ellie, "He says her insurance might have to pay for the roof."

"It was our tree," Ellie told Abbie. "Misha, tell Daddy it was our tree. And tell him we've got to leave so you can get to your soccer game on time."

Ten minutes later, Ellie was standing on the muddy sideline of a soccer field near the community center. She had wisely worn her L.L. Bean boots, which looked ridiculous with her denim shorts and T-shirt. The morning temperature had already reached the midseventies, and the heat caused the moisture left by yesterday evening's deluge to steam, creating a gauzy layer of mist just inches above the ground. Next to her, Jenny, the mother of Misha's teammate Marnie, wore rubber flip-flops, perhaps a wiser choice, although her toes glistened with silty brown water seeping up from the spongy grass.

On the field, the girls slipped and slid, playing a sloppy game. Ellie chose to focus her free-floating anger on the coaches who had decided not to reschedule the game despite the marshy field conditions and the dark, ominous clouds drifting across the sky. Ellie kept an umbrella in the car, where it would do her no good if those clouds opened up during the game. She should have brought the umbrella to the field with her.

Luckily, only an occasional sprinkle reached the ground. The girls galloping up and down the field ignored the sporadic raindrops, although every time one of the players skidded on the wet grass, Ellie sent a silent prayer heavenward. Sliding the wrong way could result in a bad fall. A broken ankle. A broken arm. A broken nose.

A few of the players did go down, but apparently, no one was seriously injured. Twice, Misha appeared to hydroplane, her cleats doing little to provide the traction she needed. She didn't fall, though. All that ballet training had taught her a thing or two about maintaining her balance.

Her physical balance, anyway. By the end of the game, the other team had shut Misha's team out. As soon as the coach finished her postmortem and dismissed the team, Misha stomped over to Ellie, her ponytail limp with a combination of sweat and drizzle, her shorts and socks spattered with mud, and her mouth curved downward like a bridge spanning from one side of her jaw to the other. "I suck," she announced.

"No, you don't," Ellie said, not just to make Misha feel better but because it was true. No one on her team had scored, and Misha had made a few good defensive plays that held the other team to only two points. And Misha hadn't taken a spill like so many of the other girls.

"I do. I suck. I bet Coach Sintas is going to cut me from the team."

"You do not suck," Ellie repeated, rummaging in her purse for her car keys as they neared the parking lot abutting the field. "The field was a mess. Everyone was struggling. You did your best —"

"Yeah, right."

"— and helped to make it a close game. You didn't suck, Misha. I don't even like that word, *suck*."

"It's a good word," Misha argued. "Babies suck on their thumbs. People suck on lollipops."

Ellie knew Misha was ranting from disappointment, not any lexicographical interest in the various applications of the word "suck." She yanked open the passenger side door of the car, climbed in, buckled her seatbelt, and took a long drink from her water bottle. At least she didn't point out that she was sucking on the bottle.

Sighing, Ellie settled behind the wheel and started the engine. "I should have brought a towel," she said. "You're soaking wet."

"I don't care." Misha was clearly determined to sulk.

"Maybe when we get home, you should make some noise," Ellie said. "You should be *aloud*. It might make you feel better." In fact, maybe Ellie would join her, drumming on a pot with a spatula and howling until her lungs ached. If Misha was frustrated, Ellie was frustrated to the tenth power. She had a hole in her roof; a husband who had nearly gotten killed by a careless SUV driver and who was pissed at her for having patched the leaky roof with a tarp he had probably forgotten he even owned until she'd mentioned it;

a boss who kept unloading his responsibilities onto her; a friend whose husband had made a sleazy, if half-hearted, pass at her; a daughter who all of a sudden decided to take her clarinet seriously and strain the household budget by expressing her desire for a private teacher... and another daughter who sat pouting beside her, smearing mud all over the car's upholstery.

This definitely called for some screaming and banging on things.

They arrived home and entered the kitchen. Lucy greeted them with a cheerful bark. At least she was healthy, her appetite fully restored, no more instances of vomiting. Maybe she had recovered quickly because she never hesitated to be *aloud*, whatever the circumstances.

Misha headed straight for the cabinet where the pots were stored. She pulled out two frying pans and clapped them together, accompanying that with a raucous screech as she pranced around the kitchen, her cleats depositing clods of dirt across the floor. Ellie watched her daughter, awed. She ought to be annoyed about the mud. She ought to scold Misha for failing to remove her cleats in the garage. But all she could think of was, *My daughter isn't afraid to be loud.* Misha's utter lack of inhibition delighted Ellie.

Would Misha remain so uninhibited once puberty hit? Or would she start worrying about what other people thought of her behavior? Would she opt to playact a role, like Merritt did? Or become prissy and judgmental like Abbie? Less than ten seconds after Misha had started shrieking, Abbie appeared at the foot of the stairs, scowling. "I'm trying to study," she bellowed, barely audible above Misha's cacophony. "I have finals. Shut up!"

"You'll get straight A's," Misha shot back. "You always do."

"I do not. Mom, make her shut up."

"She had a rough game," Ellie explained. "Give her a minute, and then you can go back to your studying."

Abbie eyed her mother suspiciously, no doubt disappointed that Ellie didn't rank her studying higher than Misha's noisemaking. "You actually wore that to her game?" Abbie asked, her tone heavy with contempt. "Boots and shorts? Yuck."

"The ground was wet," Ellie explained.

Abbie shuddered. "Those boots should not be worn with shorts," she declared, her arms folded across her chest and her gaze focused on the digital clock on the microwave. Clearly, she was determined to stop Misha as soon as one minute was up. Misha pranced and banged and hooted a bit more, leaping and pirouetting with pointed toes as if she were in a ballet class, and then Abbie pointed to the clock and Ellie signaled Misha to wind down. Reluctantly, Misha slowed from a dance to a walk, carrying the pans back to the cabinet and returning them to their shelf.

"Thank you," Abbie said frostily, enunciating each word. She pivoted on her heel and stormed back up the stairs.

"Everyone's in a bad mood today, I guess," Ellie said, reaching for the broom and dust pan. "Take off your cleats. We've got to clean the floor."

"You're not in a bad mood," Misha told her. "You never are."

Ellie flinched, surprised by her daughter's assessment. Of course she experienced bad moods, today as well as plenty of other times. But she was the mommy, the person who kept the household functioning, kept the family running smoothly — kept the town running smoothly, too, given Wayne's lackadaisical approach to his job. She couldn't afford to succumb to her moods, or to impose them on anyone else. At the moment, her husband was more than a thousand miles away, risking death-by-SUV while he endeavored to save the world. If Ellie gave in to a bad mood, who would keep Lucy from trying to eat the minidoughnut-shaped lump of dried mud that had fallen off Misha's soccer shoe and landed next to the dog's water dish?

Ellie experienced moods, but she contained them. She had to. She was the only adult in this house. Scott was somewhere else.

As soon as she finished sweeping the floor — Misha helpfully held the dustpan for her, catching the lumps and clumps of mud and emptying the dustpan into the trash — Ellie pulled Lucy's leash off its peg by the kitchen door. "I'm going to take Lucy for a walk," she said. "You should take a shower. Toss your uniform straight into the hamper. We'll get it washed before your next game."

"After lunch, can I get together with Viveca and Hayley? Hayley said she would teach us how to make collages."

"How will you get there?"

"Bike."

Of course. In the Gillman family, bikes reigned supreme. "Phone me when you get there," Ellie instructed her. "Call my cell, in case I'm not home from walking Lucy."

"It's raining out," Misha said. "Lucy will smell like wet dog."

"It's not raining right now," Ellie told her. "And I'll bring an umbrella. I think she and I would both enjoy a walk right now. You can make a sandwich for lunch. There's a jar of peanut butter in the pantry."

Ordinarily, Ellie wouldn't be so nonchalant about taking Lucy for a walk when the ground was wet. The pooch would likely track more mud into the kitchen than Misha's cleats had — and, as Misha warned, she'd imbue the entire house with that distinct wet-dog aroma, radiating the stench like incense. But Ellie didn't care. She needed this walk. And Lucy, who'd been indoors since her sunrise pee in the backyard, probably needed it, too.

Ellie grabbed an umbrella, her wallet, and her house keys. Lucy was already waiting by the back door, her tail shimmying with excitement. She stood impatiently while Ellie clipped the leash to her collar, and as soon as Ellie pushed open the door, Lucy lunged for what in her circumscribed life passed for freedom and adventure.

In Ellie's circumscribed life, too. When was the last time she'd taken a walk that didn't have a specific destination? When was the last time she'd gone somewhere that wasn't related to work or her daughters? Well, she'd gone up to the attic to destroy Scott's long-neglected but apparently beloved tarp by creating a temporary patch for the roof. But that was about her daughters, too. If she hadn't covered the roof's break with a tarp, the house might have gotten flooded, and Abbie would have to wear boots with her shorts, which would be a fashion catastrophe.

A walk, however... A walk with nowhere to go. A walk during which Ellie could behave just like Lucy, pausing to observe, savoring the scents of rain-scrubbed grass and trees and flowers, feeling her heart beat faster when a squirrel crossed her path. A walk that might last ten minutes or an hour, that might cover one mile or ten. She hadn't had that freedom or adventure in eons.

She would have it today.

The sky appeared ambivalent, patches of blue interspersed with intense gray clouds. Occasionally a drop of water would splash against her hair, but those drops were falling from tree leaves, not the clouds. Lucy, bless her little canine heart, avoided the puddles as she padded along the damp sidewalk and the saturated grass. Her surroundings probably smelled different to her, thanks to the rain. The markings of dogs who had gone before would have been washed away by last night's storm.

Lucy left her own markings, piddling every twenty or thirty feet until her bladder was empty. After that, she trotted alongside Ellie, sniffing and snuffling, barking at the occasional robin or crow.

They reached Shelton Middle School. It was empty, the rows of windows dark, the staff parking lot vacant. As a faculty member, Scott had a parking sticker permitting him to use that lot, but he preferred biking to work whenever possible, his teaching materials crammed into a backpack slung over his shoulders. Ellie wondered whether, once his save-the-world tour ended, he would commute to work on his spiffy new recumbent bike, dragging the Beast of Burden behind him.

Off to one side, on one of the school's playing fields, Ellie spotted a Little League game in progress, the players looking as filthy as Misha and her soccer teammates had been, the boys' white baseball pants smeared with mud and grass stains. Ellie experienced a pang of sympathy for the parents watching the game along the sidelines, some standing and some seated on folding canvas chairs or lawn chairs, most of them undoubtedly anticipating the laundry job that would await them once the game ended.

Lucy pulled at the leash. She wanted to go to the Little League diamond. So many people to sniff there. No doubt the players would be smelling pretty ripe right now.

Ellie tugged Lucy in the opposite direction, across the empty staff lot to the nature preserve that abutted the school property.

A trail cut through the wooded acreage; Scott had convinced the town's parks and rec department to create that trail years ago, and he always took his classes on hikes into the forest so they could observe mushrooms, ferns, lichens, and the critters that lived in the forest: insects, chipmunks, worms, hares, wild turkeys, finches and chickadees, the random skunk, or the occasional garden snake.

The trail was well marked, a distinct path of dead leaves and soggy pine needles meandering among the trees. She had to walk carefully, since those leaves and pine needles concealed ridges where tree roots protruded through the soil. Ferns fluttered like flags of green lace on either side of the path, and lumps of granite broke through the surface, gray bulges patched with moss. An array of fungus — oyster mushrooms, turkey tails, and chicken-of-the-woods — flourished in the dampness. Ellie heard the rat-a-tat of a woodpecker somewhere nearby, and the rustle of leaves overhead as a breeze jostled them.

Lucy was in heaven, scampering ahead the length of her leash and then racing back to Ellie, poking her nose into rotting logs and beneath soggy leaves. She would definitely smell like a wet dog by the time they got home, but Ellie wouldn't begrudge her this. As long as she didn't nibble on one of the toxic mushrooms, they'd be fine.

Deep into the woods, Ellie paused. The fragrance of pine and green life seemed more acute, thanks to the region's recent washing. Lucy stood beside her, seemingly transfixed by the dense, damp life shimmering all around them. The sky was visible in dots, a pale, whitish blue filtering through the canopy of leaves and branches overhead.

Ellie had never been good at screaming. Not like Misha. Not even like Abbie. But sometimes . . .

Sometimes a woman had to be aloud.

Standing on a narrow path, surrounded by Mother Nature, Ellie tossed back her head, opened her mouth wide, and tried to scream. No sound emerged. She felt as if her throat was plugged by some anatomical version of a trumpet mute, pressing against her vocal cords and suppressing her ability to shout.

She tried again. A strange, choking sound emerged, so muffled Lucy didn't even seem to notice it. The pop-pop-pop of the woodpecker hammering at the bark of a tree somewhere was louder than the faint gargle Ellie had produced.

She was a failure. She couldn't scream. She was too inhibited.

She felt humiliated. Embarrassed. *Just scream,* she ordered herself. *No one can hear you here.*

She opened her mouth again, and tried to force out some noise. A thin, wavering hum emerged from her, not much louder than a sigh.

I suck, she thought, echoing Misha's self-appraisal, which made her smile. *What if I encountered someone on this trail and he tried to kill me? Or rape me? What would I do if I couldn't scream for help?*

She tried once more. *Imagine a criminal approaching, a thug eager to attack you.* With that thought as her inspiration, she managed another sigh-like hum.

All right. She couldn't scream. She couldn't be *aloud.* She was too mature, too restrained. Too proper.

"Come on, Lucy," she said, giving the leash a gentle tug. At least she could vocalize those three words, in a calm, quiet voice. At least she hadn't lost the ability to speak.

Up ahead, she spotted something bright red by the side of the trail. When they reached it, she saw that it was the cap on a nip bottle, one of those miniature liquor bottles containing a single shot of booze. The checkout counter at Shelton Wines & Spirits had an assortment of nips arrayed on wire shelves above the conveyer belt, similar to the racks of candy bars at the supermarket checkout lines. Evidently, racks beside checkout counters were designed to display unhealthy products.

The nip bottle on the ground, she noted from the label, had contained a brand-name gin. The bottle was empty now, its plastic shape slightly dented.

Angry that someone had left trash on a path in the nature preserve, she picked up the miniature bottle. It was wet, and a few orange pine needles stuck to it. She wiped them off, then tucked the bottle into her pocket — not a happy choice, but she wasn't going to leave it on the trail.

Nor was she going to leave the next nip bottle she spotted just a few feet further along the path. Nor the three nip bottles on the other side of a granite rock bulging out of the soil. Nor the flask-shaped bottle, now drained of vodka.

Kids, probably, she thought as she gathered the trash. Teenagers sneaking booze into the woods, getting drunk and not wanting to bring their junk out of the preserve to dispose of properly, on the chance that they'd get caught.

She wasn't happy about underage drinking. But damn it, if people were going to do something that stupid, that reckless, that irresponsible, why did they have to leave their litter all over the nature preserve? Underage drinking troubled her. Littering infuriated her.

"Shit!" she shouted as she hooked the loop at the human end of Lucy's leash around her wrist, freeing both hands to gather the empty bottles. Scooping them off the ground, she straightened and smiled.

She could scream, after all. She could scream "Shit!" at the trash on the nature trail.

"*Shit!*" she screeched at double the volume. Lucy gave her a perplexed look, but no one else was around to hear her, except maybe some insects and birds and whatever other beasts lurked among the trees and undergrowth.

Litter made her scream. Litter — fury, rage, disgust — made her *aloud*.

"Shit!" she bellowed, and even though rage burned through her, she was smiling.

DAY TWENTY-SIX

Good news, bad news today.

First, the bad news — which wasn't that bad, really. It took three and a half weeks for me to get my first flat tire of the trip. I anticipated getting a few flat tires along the way. It happens. If you're prepared, it's not a tragedy. And I'm prepared. I've got a tire repair kit with me, and now that I've used my spare inner tube, I'll pick up another one en route. If they don't have any bike repair shops in Mississippi, they're sure to have them in New Orleans.

The tire repair messed up my schedule, and it was a filthy job. Three and a half weeks of road dirt had accumulated on the wheel. So in addition to the time it took to repair the tire, I had to spend some time riding around in search of a gas station with a public restroom where I could wash up. Not that anyone expects a long-distance cyclist to be as clean as a surgeon entering the OR, but I didn't even want to eat one of my energy bars with my hands all covered with crud.

But as I said, this sort of setback is expected on a trip like mine, and it was minor.

The good news is that I got to meet with Professor John Hsu in the Department of Earth Science at the

University of Memphis, and we discussed the condition of the Mississippi River, one of the most polluted rivers on the North American continent. We videotaped an excellent discussion, which I've transmitted back to my students in Shelton and which appears below — just click on the link. It's pretty technical, but fascinating. You'll learn as much from Dr. Hsu as I did. He also took me out for a delicious dinner with several other faculty members (yes, I'd washed my hands by then!) and contacted a friend at Action News 5, who interviewed me for a brief feature which will appear tonight on the eleven o'clock news. Once again, I'm going to be a TV star!

CHAPTER TWELVE

"Ineed you to talk to the select board," Wayne told Ellie. "They're meeting this evening at seven p.m. I'll be there, but I want you there, too, to fill them in on the status of Carl Corrigan's Route 29 project."

Ellie sighed — she couldn't help herself — but she tried to sift the exasperation out of her breath. She succeeded only partially. Wayne's eyebrows rose at the hint of a groan. "I'm a single parent these days, Wayne," she reminded him. "I've got two kids at home. Attending a weekday meeting at seven p.m. isn't going to work for me."

"Of course it will work. Your girls aren't toddlers. They're First Ladies. Obama and who else? They can take care of themselves for a couple of hours in the evening."

"Maybe, but I want to spend a little time with them. I don't get to see them in the morning, I don't get to see them in the afternoon — I want to see them in the evening." She struggled to keep her tone gentle and nonconfrontational. Defying one's boss was always a tricky matter. She didn't want to be penalized. She just wanted to stay home with her girls after work and school and practices and rehearsals.

Also, in all honesty, she didn't want to discuss the Route 29 condominium development with the select board. That was Wayne's job.

He offered an ingratiating smile, his attempt to appear sympathetic. The expression clearly didn't come naturally to him; the corners of his mouth seemed resistant and his gaze was stern. "All right, so if you stay home with your daughters this evening, you'll have to prepare a presentation for me to give the select board. I'll need all your notes. Your records. A summary of your discussions with Carl and Nick. All the information about the drainage issues there. I'll need some charts — either PowerPoint or printouts that I can distribute. Both would be best. Sometimes they don't have a projector in the meeting room. Can you put all that together for me before you leave for the day?"

Of course she couldn't, and he knew it. She had other tasks demanding her attention, and what Wayne was requesting would take hours — assuming that even if she prepared everything he asked for, he would be competent to present her findings to the select board. Stuffing Wayne's brain with information would be a feasible option only if his brain had enough capacity to be stuffed. Ellie was doubtful.

"Maybe Nakul could present our report," she suggested.

It took Wayne a minute to remember that the man he referred to as Nick was actually named Nakul. "He's an engineer," Wayne argued. "Engineers don't know how to explain anything to anyone except other engineers."

Ellie did a quick mental calculation. If she prepared Wayne's presentation, it would take her more time than she could spare. Which meant she would have to give the presentation herself.

"Fine," she snapped, deciding she didn't care if he knew how resentful she was. "I'll go to the select board meeting tonight."

Her phone rang, distracting her from Wayne's attempt to look grateful. She pivoted away from him, hurled herself into her desk chair, and tapped her cell phone.

"Hi, Mom?" Misha sounded not quite shaky, not quite alarmed, but just worried enough to remind Ellie of why she didn't want to attend the select board meeting that night.

"What's up?"

"There's this guy here. He's outside, and he wants to come in but we won't let him."

Ellie sat straighter, her annoyance with Wayne obliterated by the indignation and fear that gripped her. "What guy? Who is he? What does he look like?"

"He doesn't look like anything," Misha said, a patently untrue statement. If he didn't look like anything, Misha wouldn't have seen him. "He phoned the house from the front walk and told me he was the insurance . . . something."

"Insurance adjuster?" Ellie prompted her.

"Yeah, that was it. He said he had to come inside to look at the attic."

Ellie stifled a curse. "He was supposed to come to the house to inspect the damage to the roof at five thirty," she told Misha. She had deliberately scheduled him for a time when she would be home.

"Yeah, he said that. He said he got finished doing other appraisals early, so he came over to our house."

"Where's Abbie?"

"She's in her room with the door closed. She said she had to practice her clarinet."

This was Abbie's new excuse for avoiding tasks and chores: "I have to practice my clarinet." Ellie considered asking Misha to go upstairs and hold the phone next to Abbie's closed bedroom door, to see if any music emanated from the other side.

But she didn't have time to check on Abbie's alibi. She had to get home while the insurance adjuster was still there. If he left before she could let him inside to see the attic where the roof had broken through, she would have to reschedule him for another day, and that would push the roof repair back even farther. As it was, she'd phoned several roofing companies, and they all claimed that because of the storm, they were booked solid.

If only Scott were here, he could deal with this. She suspected the roofing companies would take him more seriously than they took her. She recalled reading a study a few years ago, which claimed that business people took phone calls from men more seriously than phone calls from women.

But Scott wasn't here. He was somewhere else.

A fresh surge of anger enveloped her, distinct from her anger at Wayne for demanding that she deliver a presentation about the Route 29 condo project to the select board this evening. Too much anger wasn't good for her. She might develop an ulcer, or high blood pressure, or her head would explode.

"I'll be home as soon as I can," she told Misha. "Don't let the man into the house. You were very smart to make him wait outside."

"He's been taking pictures of the roof."

"Good. That's what he's supposed to do. I'll be there soon." She said goodbye, disconnected the call, and swiveled in her chair, expecting to find Wayne lurking in the doorway between their offices, where he'd been standing when her phone had rung. He wasn't there now. Apparently, he had decided not to eavesdrop.

She found him sitting at his desk in his inner office, looking oddly out of place there. "I have to leave," she told him. "Since I'll be back here this evening for the select board meeting, you can't mind my leaving early now. There's a minor emergency at my house."

Before Wayne could question her, she turned away from him, stalked to her desk to gather her bag, and raced out of her office.

On the drive home, she visualized all sorts of catastrophes: the insurance adjuster breaking into the house and assaulting her daughters. The insurance adjuster giving one of the support pillars holding up the porch overhang a slight shake, and the roof caving in completely. The insurance adjuster informing her that the damage wasn't covered by her policy and she'd have to pay for a new roof herself.

If only Scott had been home... He had been the one to select their homeowners' insurance policy. He'd probably read all the tiny print on the documents, the clause buried on the last page that said the insurance company wouldn't cover damage when the home-owner created a temporary fix by hammering an old tarp across a hole between the rafters in the attic.

She spotted the man seated on her porch steps as she steered onto her driveway. Was he bored? Was his butt sore from sitting on the unyielding planks? If so, it was his own fault. He should have arrived at five thirty, when she had told him she would be home.

She didn't bother pulling into the garage; she would only have to drive back to the town hall in a few hours. And now that she'd seen the man — maybe in his thirties, clad in the same sort of business-casual attire Wayne favored, with a clipboard tucked under his arm and a digital camera hanging from a strap around his neck — she didn't want to let him out of her sight.

"You're much too early," she called to him as she climbed out of her car. Then she cringed. Criticizing him might inspire him to reject her claim for the damaged roof.

He rose and met her on the lawn, halfway between the front walk and the driveway. "Sorry. I had to do a few appraisals in town, and they took less time than I was expecting. Your daughter shouted through the door that you'd be home soon." He peered up at the roof. The limb from the black walnut tree was still balanced against the roof, one of its branches snagged by the rain gutter that trimmed the roof's edge.

Returning his gaze to Ellie, the man handed her a business card that identified him as Tim Verlander, a representative of her insurance company. "I need to see your attic," he said. "The report said the roof damage impacted the attic."

"It did." And she'd sacrificed Scott's precious tarp to patch that damage. She wondered if her policy would cover the cost of a new tarp.

She had to let Tim Verlander into the house. He didn't seem dangerous, and if he was, she supposed she could scream. If she had to pretend he was roadside trash in order to liberate her vocal cords, she would.

Tim Verlander proved not to be roadside trash, however. He nodded at Misha, who glared suspiciously at him as he followed Ellie through the front door, down the hall to the stairs and up to the second floor. When Ellie pulled down the folding steps that led to the attic, Abbie opened her bedroom door and peered out, curious about what was going on.

Ellie waved Tim Verlander up the steps ahead of her. She followed him, climbing only high enough to poke her head through the trap-door and watch him make his way across the attic to the tarp. He scrutinized it thoughtfully, then nodded and snapped a few photos. "Nice job patching it," he called over to her. "I don't see any moisture on your insulation there."

"Thank you." Yes, she'd done a nice job. She'd saved the insulation. If she'd spared Scott's old tarp those nail holes, her attic might be a soggy mess. Not only was Tim Verlander apparently not a crazed rapist or murderer invading her house with the intent of attacking her precious daughters, he'd actually acknowledged that she had done the right thing by patching the damaged roof with the tarp.

They descended the steps to the hallway, and then the stairs down to the first floor. In the kitchen, he jotted some notes on his clipboard and then riffled through the papers clipped to it until he found what he was looking for. He slid out that sheet and handed it to her. "Here are a few roof specialists we've worked with. They're all good. I know the storm left a lot of damage, but you can probably get them to at least write up estimates for you. Send them to our office and we'll take it from there."

That sounded promising. All in all, dealing with him had been much more pleasant than telling Scott about the damage. Maybe she should scream at Scott, instead. Maybe she should pretend he was roadside trash so she would be able to.

Smiling at the thought, she escorted Tim Verlander to the front door and waved him off. Turning, she found both Misha and Abbie behind her, watching her. "Is he going to fix our roof?" Misha asked.

"No, but he's going to make sure the insurance company pays for the repair," Ellie replied, then added, "He said I did a good job patching the hole in the attic."

"Of course you did," Abbie said. Why was Abbie praising her? Because she wanted private clarinet lessons or because she wanted to wear mascara?

Maybe she was praising her because of course Ellie had done a good job. Maybe it was as simple as that.

CHAPTER THIRTEEN

She didn't have time to talk to Scott that evening. "I have to go back to the town hall to give a presentation to the select board," she explained to Abbie and Misha as she threw together a supper of grilled cheese sandwiches and canned soup. It was too warm for such a meal, but the girls loved it — although Misha said she preferred American cheese to the thick-sliced cheddar Ellie had used.

"American cheese isn't real cheese," Abbie lectured Misha. "It's processed cheese."

"So it's cheese," Misha argued. "It's just cheese that's been processed."

"Any cheese that comes individually wrapped in plastic isn't worth eating," Abbie said haughtily.

"Yeah, well, I bet if you were starving to death and American cheese was the only food in the world, you'd eat it."

Ellie decided to intervene before the quarrel became toxic. "If Dad calls, you girls can talk to him. And make sure you let Lucy out for her final pee. I hope I'll be home by nine, but sometimes these meetings drag on and on. I'll have my cell phone with me if there's an emergency."

"Like a strange man trying to get into our house?" Misha suggested.

"Exactly." Ellie wished her soup wasn't so hot. She needed to get back to her office before the meeting to organize her notes, but if she guzzled the soup too quickly, she'd wind up with a scalded tongue. She scooped a spoonful of the creamy orange soup, blew on it, touched it with her tongue, and blew on it some more.

"Or a tree falling on the roof," Misha said. "Except we know what to do if that happens, since it already happened."

"You'd try to fix it with the plunger," Abbie muttered, then grinned. She was teasing, not being bitchy, and Misha seemed to accept her joke without taking offense.

Ellie devoured her sandwich as she waited for her soup to cool down. Once it did, she and her daughters finished their dinners quickly, and cleanup took just minutes. If Scott were home, Ellie would have felt obligated to prepare a full, well-balanced meal with a salad and an entrée that included protein, a starch, and a vegetable of some sort. After dinner, the sink would be filled with pots and pans demanding scouring. When men weren't around, women could eat a lot lighter, a lot faster. When women weren't around, men probably ate lighter and faster, too, and without as much attention to taste: a cheese sandwich without the grilling, soup straight from the can. Scott knew the rudiments of cooking, but meal preparation had somehow wound up being Ellie's responsibility. She wasn't sure why. He arrived home from work earlier than she did, most days. But she made dinner every night, probably because she knew that if Scott made dinner, it would be ungrilled cheese sandwiches and unheated soup.

"Okay," she said as Abbie and Misha finished stacking the dishwasher. "I'm heading back to the town hall. Wish me luck."

"Try not to get bored," Abbie said. She was at an age when boredom was more treacherous than poison ivy and had to be assiduously avoided. Thank heavens for smart phones and their infinite array of distractions. Abbie might succeed in avoiding boredom for the remainder of her adolescence, thanks to her phone.

The sky was still pale with early evening light as Ellie steered into the parking lot behind the town hall. While she wasn't thrilled by the late-spring heat — at least not when she was home and Scott was monitoring the thermostat — she appreciated the long daylight hours at this time of year. When Abbie turned sixteen in a few months, she would be getting her driving permit, a prospect that caused Ellie agita, but at least she would start her practices behind the wheel when there was still a reasonable amount of sunlight. The only thing scarier than the idea of Abbie driving a car, as far as Ellie was concerned, was the idea of Abbie driving a car after dark.

She chased that thought away as she crossed the lot to the building's side entry. Less than a foot from the door, the asphalt was decorated with a scattering of litter: a waxed paper cup with a straw poking through its domed plastic lid, a wad of silver foil crumpled into what resembled a miniature disco ball, and a broken pencil, its eraser end gone. Cursing under her breath, Ellie gathered the trash and carried it into the building. Just inside the door stood a trash can, visible through the door's glass pane. Why couldn't whoever had dropped this garbage on the ground take the five extra steps required to carry their crap into the vestibule so it could be tossed into the can?!

What was wrong with people? What was wrong with Shelton? She didn't recall so much litter a few years ago. Maybe it was a result of the years of the pandemic, when the town's residents withdrew, detaching themselves from Shelton's streets and neighborhoods and their fellow citizens. Maybe it was just the general sourness of the world — acrimonious politics, unrest in foreign countries, the proliferation of guns. Maybe it was that the planet was under threat — exactly what Scott was trying to enlighten people around the country about — and if the Earth was going to die from climate change and pollution and the extinction of species, why bother to throw away an empty soft-drink cup?

Ellie had lived in Shelton ever since she and Scott had gotten married and landed their jobs here. She loved this town. She'd made serving it her career. She soothed egos, reassured town employees, explained budget constraints to departments and tax hikes to tax-payers. When a new condo development was proposed, she made sure the ground water would be protected and the units wouldn't get flooded and solar panels would be added to generate some of the electricity the condo owners would require to light and heat their residences.

Shelton was her home. She didn't want to see it literally trashed.

On her way to her office in the new wing, she detoured into the ladies' room to wash her hands. Every time she picked up garbage, she worried about the residue of dirt and germs the trash might have left on her skin. If she was going to keep collecting the litter she found lying around on the ground, she might consider carrying a pair of rubber gloves with her.

At her desk, she woke her dozing computer and saw that Nakul had emailed her his notes about Carl Corrigan's proposed condo complex. She skimmed them for anything she might add to her own notes — which were basically a less technical version of his — and smiled when she saw that he'd copied Wayne with his email. As if Wayne would bother to read it, knowing that Ellie was going to make the presentation.

At a minute to seven, she packed up her notes, shut off her computer, and strolled down the hall to the public meeting room in the old part of the building. The room was actually a small auditorium, with a tiny platform stage on which a long table was set up. About fifty folding chairs stood in rows, facing the platform. Due to the state's open meeting laws, every meeting of the Shelton Select Board had to be open to the public, and when Ellie entered the room, she saw that a grand total of three diligent citizens were exercising their state-guaranteed right.

The five members of the select board occupied chairs at the table on the stage, along with Wayne. An American flag and a Massachusetts state flag hung from stately brass-trimmed flagpoles behind the select board. Two oscillating fans on much less stately chrome poles flanked the stage, whirring mightily but doing little to cool the room's atmosphere.

Wayne beamed a smile at Ellie as she settled onto one of the folding chairs in the otherwise empty front row. There was no room for her at the table on the stage. Just as well. If she were seated at the table, she might feel obligated to remain for the entire meeting. As a speaker from the audience, she could deliver her report, answer any questions the select board might pose, and go home.

Marshall Glavin, the portly, silver-haired chair of the select board, gaveled the meeting to order. He announced that it was being recorded and broadcast on the town's local-access channel, then led all ten attendees in the Pledge of Allegiance. Ellie had attended enough select board meetings to know the routine. To be sure, she'd been attending these meetings since the days when the board was called the Shelton Board of Selectmen, back when female members of the board were so rare they didn't need to be acknowledged.

Two of the five members of the board were women now. Ellie was acquainted with all five members. She knew that Marshall Glavin and Gretchen Webber were the most conservative members, often pontificating about how things used to be done, and how things ought to be done the way they'd always been done. Ben Bradenberg was the youngest board member and a bit of a firebrand, which Ellie appreciated. Kent Hynes was a hot-shot businessman — he reminded Ellie vaguely of Connie's husband Richard, although she couldn't imagine him ever making a pass at her. Then again, she couldn't have imagined Richard making a pass at her either, until he did.

The final member of the board, Sonia Lewis, was a sweet grand-mother who sympathized with every point of view and occasionally brought home-baked cookies to the meetings. Ellie spotted no cookies today, alas. After her rushed soup-and-sandwich supper, she would have enjoyed a warm, chewy chocolate chip cookie.

She had hoped the meeting would start with Carl Corrigan's proposed condo development, so she could give her spiel and leave early. But first the board decided to deal with a traffic light malfunction near the high school, a personnel issue in the police department, and the public works department's request for those sidewalk tractors that could simultaneously clear snow from and spray a deicing chemical on sidewalks. Ellie was well versed on all these issues — she'd already discussed the sidewalk snow plows ad nauseum with the public works department — but since Wayne was seated with the select board on the stage, she let him handle those agenda items. Not surprisingly, he assured the board that he would go through the budget again and see if there was money to buy at least one of those tractors for the wonderful guys in the public works department. Ellie knew damned well there was no money. But Wayne couldn't possibly say so. If he did, someone might think he was miserly and mean.

Being miserly and mean was Ellie's job, not his.

Finally, a half hour into the meeting, the condo complex rose to the top of the agenda. "Ellie Gillman is so well versed on this proposed development," Wayne explained, "I asked her to give this presentation."

The board directed their gazes to her. Marshall gestured for her to come up onto the stage, even though there was no place for her to sit there. "For the camera," he explained. "We want the folks at home to be able to see you."

Sighing, she gathered her notes and climbed the one short step onto the platform.

"How's your husband doing?" Ben asked. "Still biking all over the country?"

"I've been following him on that website," Gretchen said, grinning at Ellie. "My daughter was one of his students a few years ago. She told me about the website."

"I'm following him, too," Sonia said. "That poor man — he must be so tired! All those miles!"

"He's in shape," Ellie assured her. "He's doing fine."

"Well, he's lucky he's got his first lady at home," Wayne interjected. "Did you all know Ellie was named after a First Lady? In fact, all the females in her family are named after First Ladies. Including the dog."

This was not a subject Ellie particularly wanted to discuss with the select board. It was a family joke, something her parents had concocted when they'd grown tired of being asked whom Ellie had been named after. She hadn't been named after anyone; her mother had simply liked the name Eleanor, believing that it was one syllable better than Ellen. "We named her after Eleanor Roosevelt," she would tell people. And then Ellie — because she liked the names Abigail and Michelle — had continued the tradition. Lucy... well, Lucy just seemed like a Lucy. The name suited her.

"Is that so?" Marshall's somewhat overgrown eyebrows arched as he assessed Ellie. "Was there a First Lady named Ellie?"

"Eleanor Roosevelt," she told him. "If I can give my report —"

"Eleanor Roosevelt was an amazing woman," Gretchen declared. "She was Franklin's legs. He was able to be a great president because she had his back." Her gaze zeroed in on Ellie, her expression one of approval. "And your husband is able to bike across the country because you have his back. I hope you continue to help him succeed in his mission. We do need to protect the environment."

"He's doing us all a huge favor," Ben added. "Saving the planet. A monumental task. We're in his debt."

Something clicked inside Ellie, like a mouse trap snapping shut and pinching her. She didn't feel she was in Scott's debt. *He* was in *her* debt. She might not be his legs, but she had his back. Without her, he would be here in Shelton, teaching his students, attending Abbie's concerts and Misha's soccer games, fixing overflowing toilets and broken roofs. He wouldn't be hobnobbing with professors and giving presentations on college TV stations.

Scott was off saving the planet, while she was picking up litter in Shelton. And Ben thought the town was in Scott's debt?

She flashed on a memory of standing on the trail in the nature preserve, with empty liquor bottles scattered at her feet. And suddenly, the urge to be *aloud* overtook her.

"Before I talk about Carl Corrigan's proposed condo development," she said, "I want to raise another subject. It's not on your agenda" — she noticed Marshall and Kent glancing at their printouts of the agenda, evidently searching for whatever topic she intended to introduce — "but this town is filthy. There's too much litter. I've been picking it up wherever I see it, but the problem has gotten really bad lately. We need more public trash cans so people can dispose of their garbage easily. And we need to educate the town about this. Maybe we should have a town cleanup day. It's one thing to clean the planet. It's another thing to clean our town."

The board members stared at her. Sonia nodded, smiling even though her eyes glistened with tears. Marshall and Gretchen pursed their lips, no doubt contemplating whether placing trash cans around town would alter Shelton's cozy small-town ambience in some way — because, after all, there had never been public trash cans in town before. Ben nodded vigorously. Kent scribbled something on his note pad. Craning her neck, Ellie could read that he'd written *COST???*

Wayne appeared stricken. "Ellie, we need to talk about Carl's condo development."

"I will talk about that," she assured him dryly, wondering if he noticed that she'd used the pronoun "I" and not "we." "But this is important, too. Just entering this building, I had to pick up garbage that had been dumped in the parking lot near the side door. The other day, I found empty nip bottles and an empty flask of vodka in the nature preserve. I'm tired of it. We need to deal with this." *Aloud*, she thought. *I'm aloud.*

"Put together a proposal," Marshall said. "We'll take it up at our next meeting. Now, let's talk about the condo development."

As if Ellie didn't already have too much work demanding her attention — her responsibilities and the bulk of Wayne's responsibilities. As if she had plenty of free time to work up a proposal about tackling Shelton's litter problem. As if she wanted to lose another evening to the next select board meeting, rather than decompressing at home with her daughters after a long day of work.

That was the risk you took when you spoke up, when you made noise, when you were aloud. You offered a suggestion and then you owned that suggestion. It became your project, your burden, your new responsibility.

But damn it, she was right to have raised the issue, right to have forced people to pay attention. Maybe you could raise awareness of a problem by biking across the country, but actually solving the problem was a whole other thing.

And Ellie was going to do that whole other thing.

DAY TWENTY-NINE

Why didn't anyone tell me how hot Texas got in June?

Just kidding. I knew it would be hot. It's hot back home in Massachusetts in June, and Texas is way south of Massachusetts. Of course, Texas is even hotter due to global warming.

It's not surprising that there's a real awareness of climate issues here. Texas relies on agriculture, which, of course, relies on a healthy climate. Also, Texas's economy will be strongly impacted by the reduced demand for fossil fuels. It's a state that's dealt with some serious, destructive storms in recent years — hurricanes barreling through the Gulf of Mexico, ice storms in the winter, prolonged droughts The weather extremes are reaching critical proportions in some parts of Texas.

Right now, my weather extreme has me taking a break every hour or so to rehydrate and slather on some more sun block. I'm going to try to make it to Dallas today, then take a day to recuperate, after which I'll head north into Oklahoma. While I'm in Dallas, I'll be meeting with an environmental group and doing a TV interview. Neither of those activities have gotten old yet. I love talking to environmentalists, swapping information and comparing strategies, and the TV interviews help me to reach more people, which is what this trip is all about. Reaching people.

Oh, and while I'm in Dallas, I intend to try some of that barbecue that Texas is famous for! Ribs and brisket, here I come!

CHAPTER FoURTEEN

Connie's voice chirped through Ellie's cell phone: "Any chance you're free to meet me for lunch today?"

Ellie sighed. Not only was she not free to meet Connie, but she doubted she'd have time even to eat lunch at her desk. She flickered a glance at Nakul, who sat in one of the chairs across the desk from her, his laptop open on his knees and his brow dented into a frown.

"I wish I could," Ellie spoke into the phone.

"Maybe dinner, then? We've got stuff to celebrate. I just made a big sale. And today's the last day of school."

Was that something to celebrate? Ellie was already anxious about how Abbie and Misha would cope on their own, once they were no longer in school. Abbie's babysitting job and Misha's summer camp program didn't start for a week. The girls would probably be safe at home — the Vandenhoffers thought Abbie was mature enough to babysit for their five-year-old twins — but Ellie couldn't shake her worry about how her daughters would occupy their time alone in the house. Abbie could practice her clarinet only so long. Misha could ride her bike only so far.

Life was much less worrisome when Scott's last day of school coincided with theirs. He always spent a few half days in his classroom after bidding his students farewell for the summer. He had to tidy up the room, remove posters from the walls, dismantle the tubes and flasks with which he conducted basic chemistry experiments, and file reams of paperwork. But he could get home by noon on those tidying-up days, and he would spend his afternoons with the girls, keeping them busy and out of trouble. His summer school teaching would begin when their summer activities began, and Ellie didn't have to worry about child care.

They're not really children anymore, she reminded herself. But teens and tweens needed care too, even if you didn't call it child care.

"We'll make a plan for dinner soon," Ellie promised Connie. "But right now, I'm in a hole, and I'm digging." She noticed Nakul's fleeting smile; evidently, he was listening to her end of the conversation. How could he not, when he was seated only three feet away?

"You're not supposed to dig," Connie reminded her. "When you're in a hole, you're supposed to stop digging."

"Yeah. Well, I jumped into the hole and someone handed me a shovel. I'll call you when things calm down. In the meantime, congratulations on your sale." She said goodbye and disconnected the call, then sighed again. She wasn't exactly avoiding Connie — she really *was* in that proverbial hole — but she hadn't yet decided whether to tell Connie that Richard had made a vague but definitely sleazy pass at her a week ago. Telling Connie might encourage her to go ahead and divorce the son of a bitch. But it might also cause Connie to distrust Ellie, to suspect that she'd done something to invite his interest. Just thinking about that caused her to shudder.

"I really don't know why you've enlisted me in this," Nakul said, tapping the keyboard of the laptop balanced on his knees and reverting to his frown. "I thought we were going to discuss the condo project. I'm an engineer. This is not my area of expertise."

"You're brilliant," Ellie reminded him. "And I'm clearly not. I sounded off at the select board meeting, and now they want me to put together some sort of Earth Day for Shelton."

"Earth Day is in April," Nakul reminded her unnecessarily. "And it's performative. When you want to minimize the importance of something, you give it its own special day."

"Like Mother's Day," Ellie muttered.

"Right. Or Black History month. Black people are so unimportant, they get twenty-eight days."

"But see, you use big words like 'performative.' That proves you're smart. Tell me, am I crazy to schedule an all-town cleanup day?"

"People around here go away in the summer. They go to Cape Cod or Lake Winnipesaukee. Who's going to be around to clean up?"

"People go away for a week. Not everyone goes away the same week."

"Okay, then. Schedule an Earth Day for Shelton. Only don't call it Earth Day."

"Because people will think it's performative?"

"Because people will think, 'What is she talking about? Earth Day is in April.'"

"So we won't call it Earth Day. We'll call it Clean Up Shelton Day."

"Good God." Nakul shook his head. "You sound like someone's mommy, yelling at them to clean their room."

Ellie chuckled. "Maybe because I'm a mommy who yells at my girls to clean their rooms." She stared at the notes she'd typed into a new file, praying for some brilliant insights to leap out from the screen. All she saw was a bunch of text and a blinking cursor. "How about just Shelton Day?"

"Better than Clean Up Shelton Day." He studied his own computer. "Do you have a budget?"

"I have to put together a proposal and then ask for one. We have to do this on the cheap."

"How expensive is handing out trash bags and asking people to pick up any garbage they see?"

"We need an incentive. We need to make it fun." Ellie's head hurt. She probably should have gone off with Connie and indulged in a two-hour lunch, complete with wine. Under the same circumstances, that was what Wayne would do. "We could hand out cookies and lemonade when we hand out the trash bags," she said.

"Lemonade in paper cups — which people will throw on the ground when they're empty."

"We can't afford reusable cups," she argued. "That would be too expensive."

"You could give out cookies and suggest that people bring their own water bottles. Reusable water bottles," he clarified.

"Or we could distribute the cookies and lemonade once they return to the town hall with their trash bags full of garbage. They can drink the lemonade here, and we'll have a big trash can right there can so they can dispose of their cups properly. Part of the deal is to get some public trash cans placed around town."

"Have you figured out where?"

"Here at the town hall, for one place." She had already contacted the company that handled trash collection for the town. It cleared the garbage at all the public buildings — the town hall, the schools, the police and fire stations, the community center, the public works department building. The cost of adding public trash receptacles, as the company manager she'd spoken to delicately referred to garbage cans, wouldn't demolish the town budget. The company would cut Shelton a deal because it was already billing Shelton pretty heavily.

"We could get volunteers to donate cookies," Ellie said. Thinking about the reward part of the cleanup day was more fun than thinking about the cleanup itself. "What's the name of that woman who teaches consumer studies at the middle school? Scott would know her; they're fellow faculty members. She could organize people to donate baked goods. Or" — she perked up as a better idea occurred to her — "we could get Trumbull's to donate cookies as a good-will gesture."

"They should support the cleanup effort. All the town merchants should. They don't want garbage lying around in front of their doors."

"Exactly." Ellie recalled the litter she'd seen when she'd picked up take-out Chinese food the evening she'd taken Lucy to the vet.

"Okay. So enough about this little project of yours," Nakul said, making Ellie wish the project really was little. The more she thought about it, the bigger it seemed to grow. "What did the select board say about Corrigan's condo development?"

"They seemed pretty open to our suggestions: one fewer building than his original proposal, extra attention to the drainage issues, solar panels, and the other MEPA upgrades. They'll make a call within a week, and Wayne will convey their decision to Carl. At least I hope he will."

"If the board agrees with all our recommendations, Wayne will make you tell Corrigan," Nakul predicted. "Then he'll take Corrigan out for drinks at his country club to console him."

Ellie grinned. That Nakul shared her opinion of Wayne reassured her. She wasn't just a grouchy, dissatisfied subordinate. Well, maybe she was, but Nakul clearly believed she had reason to be.

They finished discussing the condo development, and Nakul folded his laptop and departed for his own office. Ellie had a pile of tasks awaiting her attention, but the Shelton Day cleanup elbowed them out of the way in her mind.

She could make this work. She could publicize it on the town website, post a sign in the Whole Foods window — and Trumbull's window, and the Chinese restaurant's window, too. And the veterinary clinic. She could map out routes for volunteers to cover, each volunteer armed with two bags, one for recyclable trash and one for the rest. The town would distribute plastic gloves if anyone wanted them. As she well knew, picking up trash with your bare hands was icky.

Her cell phone beeped, alerting her to personal email. She swiveled away from her computer and checked the screen.

Misha's and Abbie's final report cards had been sent.

Several years ago, the Shelton School District had switched from handing out printed report cards on the last day of school to emailing the report cards directly to parents, because a fair number of those printed report cards had vanished before they were delivered into the parents' hands. Abbie and Misha had never balked about giving Ellie and Scott their report cards; they'd never had reason to. They might not qualify as valedictorians of their classes, but they were solid students. Nothing on their report cards would cause them shame.

Now, however, the report cards were emailed directly to parents. Ellie tapped her phone to open Abbie's report card first. An A-plus in music — no surprise there, and Ellie really had to do some research about clarinet teachers if she was going to hire one for Abbie. An A in history, an A in English, B-pluses in math and earth science — Scott would have to put his ego aside and accept that Abbie was not the straight-A science student he had been — and a B-minus in Spanish. Too bad. *Demasiado,* Ellie recalled from her own Spanish classes.

Opening Misha's report card, she suffered a twinge of nostalgia. This would be the last report card Misha ever received in primary school. She would be attending the middle school next fall, with a different teacher for each subject. Like Abbie she would be assigned to a science teacher who wasn't her father. But her report card, like Abbie's, would present an array of letter grades with no commentary. This was the last time she would earn a complete evaluation from just one teacher.

She'd liked her fifth-grade teacher well enough. Ms. Gorshin was what the school called an experienced hand, someone who had been teaching fifth grade for a quarter of a century. She was a little bit set in her ways, but Ellie saw nothing wrong with that, as long as those ways were effective.

She skimmed the grades — all A's and B's, like Abbie's — and scrolled to the written evaluation at the end. *Misha is a bundle of energy,* Ms. Gorshin wrote. *Her enthusiasm knows no limits. She's smart and funny, and I think she'll excel if she does learn some limits. A little less talking, a little more listening, a little less energy and a little more calm will really benefit her in middle school.*

Ellie reread the evaluation, her brow aching from her frown. Did Ms. Gorshin think enthusiasm was a bad thing, something that should be limited? Did she have any idea how difficult it was for children to be enthusiastic about school, of all things? Did this quarter-of-a-century, experienced-hand teacher actually believe that Misha would be a better student in middle school if she was less enthusiastic about it?

Or maybe just if she was quieter. Calmer. A better listener.

If she wasn't *aloud.*

Hot anger rose inside Ellie, expanding like heated gas. Scott and his science students would understand the physics of it, this steamy vapor scorching Ellie's mind and soul. How dare Ms. Gorshin say Misha ought to sit down and shut up? Because that was exactly what she was saying.

Ellie reminded herself that Misha could be a bit rowdy and raucous. She wore her thoughts and emotions close to the surface. She was fearless, even when she ought to be wary. If her best friend banned her from his club, she made noise about it. If she didn't play as well as she wanted to in a soccer game, she vented her frustration. "Stiff upper lip" was not a part of her repertoire.

Because she was tired, because she was irritated, and because it was the last day of school and the girls deserved a treat, Ellie detoured to the Chinese restaurant in town on her way home and ordered their favorite dishes. She requested extra fortune cookies, even though they would probably contain vague platitudes rather than genuine fortunes. On her way out the door with the aromatic food, she noticed an array of garbage on the concrete walk extending past the restaurant and the other storefronts in the strip mall. A large public garbage can stood in front of the pet supply store at the end of the strip mall, but for whatever reason, whoever had tossed their trash onto the ground couldn't be bothered carrying it fifty-odd steps to the garbage can.

How many people had walked past this mess? she wondered. How many had sighed and clicked their tongues and rued the slovenly behavior of litterers — and then kept walking? Had they done nothing because some idiot fifth-grade teacher had once told them they should be a little less energetic?

Fuming, she left the bag of food in her car and collected the litter from the sidewalk, as she'd done the last time she'd picked up dinner from the Chinese restaurant. After disposing of it, she climbed into the car, hoping the delectable aroma of hot Asian cuisine would soothe her. It didn't. She was still seething when she got home.

After pulling into the garage, she remained in her car for a moment, trying to calm down. But really, was calmness desirable behavior in this situation? She was being energetic by planning Shelton Day, wasn't she? She wasn't sitting quietly and listening. She was doing something.

And damn it, if her daughters wanted to do something, they could do something, too. Who needed calmness when the planet — or at the very least this town — needed to be cleaned up?

CHAPTER FIFTEEN

"What do you mean, Abbie's not there?" Scott asked over the phone. "I miss my girls! She knows I call home right around now."

Actually, he'd called home about an hour later than usual, because he was in the central time zone and home was an hour ahead, in the eastern time zone. The girls had feasted on moo shu chicken, shrimp fried rice, and something the restaurant called Happy House, which seemed to have a little of everything in it. They'd dutifully read all their fortunes, which had offered such nuggets of wisdom as "Aim high and work hard," and "Brighten the world with your smile." Then Abbie had announced that she was going to her friend Mackenna's house to celebrate the end of the school year with a few friends. Ellie had told her to be home by eleven, and to call if she needed a ride. "I don't want you walking home alone that late."

"Mackenna just lives two blocks away," Abbie had argued.

"I don't care. If no one else's mother is able to give you a ride home, call me."

"Maybe someone else's *father* will give me a ride home," Abbie said. "It isn't always the mothers who do the driving."

True enough. When Scott was home, he did his share of the driving. However, he wasn't home right now. He was somewhere in Texas, throwing a minor fit because Abbie wasn't around to discuss her final science grade with him.

Ellie had summarized the girls' report cards for him. She'd edited Ms. Gorshin's written evaluation of Misha's behavior when she'd read it to Scott. He didn't have to know his daughter's teacher thought she was too enthusiastic.

"I forgot today was the last day of school," Scott admitted when Ellie explained that Abbie had gone off to celebrate that reality with a few friends. "I turned in my grades before I left Shelton, and now I feel so divorced from the school schedule. Out here, it's all pedaling and talking, pedaling and talking — and sleeping. And eating. I wish I could get my hands on some more Girl Scout cookies. They were really good."

"You should probably stick with nutritious snacks," Ellie said, then grimaced as she acknowledged how maternal she sounded. Like a mommy ordering her children to clean their rooms. "I'm putting together a special event here in town," she reported. "Shelton is looking shabby lately because of all the litter. I'm organizing a cleanup day."

"Cleaning up litter?" Was their connection bad, or did Scott really have difficulty absorbing her words?"

"You know, garbage people toss on the ground instead of disposing of it properly. There aren't enough public trash bins around — excuse me, trash *receptacles*," she corrected herself. She might as well use the official terminology. "And there's a lot of crap on the ground. So I'm in charge of turning the cleanup into an event. We're going to tidy Shelton up. No more garbage strewn all over the place."

"That's nice, but..." Scott hesitated. "I mean, no one likes garbage on the sidewalks. But the atmosphere is deteriorating. The air is filled with particulate matter. The oceans are rising. The drought areas are spreading. Dozens of species are going extinct. Isn't litter kind of trivial?"

Fury churned inside her. She pictured it as a colored fluid, heated to boiling, rising up through one of Scott's chemistry tubes until it erupted in a cloud of steam and bubbles. This colorful liquid fury was rising through her body, not through a tube, and the impending eruption threatened to blow her skull to smithereens.

She took a deep breath and ordered herself not to hang up on him. Another deep breath, and she reminded herself that he was biking through Texas, which was very hot and possibly not as welcoming to a self-righteous New Englander as some of the other places he'd ridden through. He was tired, and upset that Abbie wasn't home.

One more deep breath, and she trusted herself to speak calmly. "I'm afraid I can't make the oceans stop rising," she said. "Neither can you. But if I can get people to stop throwing their garbage on the ground here in Shelton, I'll do it. You save the planet your way and I'll save the planet my way."

He didn't respond immediately. Maybe he was taking deep breaths, too. "I didn't mean to belittle what you're doing," he said.

Well, that's a good thing, she thought churlishly. *Because in addition to saving the planet my way, I'm keeping your daughters fed and managing their lives, and waiting for the final approval from the insurance company so I can get the roof repaired, and taking care of Wayne's business along with my own, and making sure Lucy takes care of her business outside. And fending off unwelcome advances from Connie's husband.* Well, one advance, but it had been extremely unwelcome and Ellie had fended it off.

She hadn't even wanted to oversee Shelton Day, or whatever her town cleanup event wound up being called. She'd tossed it out as an idea at the select board meeting because she had found trash on the ground outside the town hall. But somehow, that project had wound up in her portfolio along with everything else, and maybe it would make a difference. It would transform Shelton into a prettier, healthier, prouder town.

It sure as hell would be easier for her to organize Shelton Day if Scott were home, seeing to it that the girls were fed and driven to their concerts and games and friends' houses, haggling with the insurance company and letting Lucy out into the yard whenever she had to empty her bladder. But he wasn't home. He was somewhere else.

Ellie could take a hundred deep breaths, but she didn't think they would calm her down enough. "Scott, I've had a long day. I need to put up my feet and close my eyes. Do you want to talk some more to Misha?"

He'd already talked to Misha once, and she was now playing catch with Lucy outside. But Ellie would be happy to bring her back into the house and hand the phone over to her if that was the only way she could end this conversation before her resentment vented out of her like toxic steam from that chemical explosion in her head.

Evidently, summoning Misha wouldn't be necessary. "I've had a long day, too," Scott said, his tone subdued. "Biking in this Texas heat is something else. I probably lost about ten pounds in sweat today."

"Then you'd better rehydrate. We'll talk tomorrow." Ellie added a goodbye and disconnected the call.

She crossed to the back door and watched Misha and Lucy through the screen. Viewing the same scene, Ms. Gorshin would probably diagnose Misha as having too much energy. In her shorts and a soccer T-shirt from last year's team, which was now a bit too tight across her chest and shoulders, Misha sprinted across the grass — which really desperately needed to be mowed — throwing a tattered green tennis ball to Lucy, who also seemed to have too much energy. The dog leapt into the air to catch the ball on the fly, raced under the shrubs that bordered the yard, and chomped on the ball until Misha wrested it from her and threw it again. They would both sleep well tonight.

There's no such thing as too much energy, Ellie thought enviously, wishing she had even half as much energy as Misha had. She was working too hard. She was stressing too much. Maybe she should have gone out with Connie tonight and skipped talking to Scott.

Except that tonight was coming after the last day of school, and her daughters deserved to have dinner, including multiple fortune cookies, with her.

"How about a movie tonight?" she called through the screen to Misha.

Misha literally jumped for joy. "I can stay up late tonight. I don't have to get up for school tomorrow." Breathless, she sprinted toward the back door, Lucy chasing her and gnawing on the soggy tennis ball as if it were an enormous wad of chewing gum. "Can we watch *Field of Dreams*?"

"We've already watched that movie twice this month," Ellie reminded Misha. She definitely wasn't in the mood to watch Scott's favorite movie tonight. "How about one of the *Star Wars* films?"

Misha selected the original *Star Wars*, which, in Ellie's estimation, was the best of the series, and inserted the DVD while Ellie zapped a bag of popcorn in the microwave. She was quite full of Happy House and moo shu chicken, but Misha insisted she was hungry. Maybe the reason she ate so much and remained so thin was that she had too much energy.

After refilling Lucy's water dish, Ellie carried the bowl of popcorn to the den and settled onto the sofa next to Misha. Misha smelled of summer — sweaty hair, grass, and fresh, hot wind. The salty fragrance of the popcorn eventually overwhelmed Misha's running-around-in-the-summer-evening perfume, but Ellie treasured the last traces of it. It was a scent she associated with youth — and carefree, youthful energy. Just as Misha's tiny, budding breasts strained against the nylon of her old soccer jersey, her entire body was straining against the constraints of childhood. Next fall she would be a middle school student. She would be well on her way to adolescence. She would start smelling like deodorant and body-wash and floral-scented shampoo.

She devoured several fistfuls of popcorn, then said, "You didn't tell Daddy about what Ms. Gorshin said about me on my report card."

Ellie glanced at Misha. Misha's gaze was locked onto the TV screen, where Luke Skywalker was learning how to wield his light saber. But Misha had viewed this movie several times; she knew what would happen next, and she could clearly navigate a conversation while viewing the movie's rudimentary special effects.

"You didn't tell Daddy about what Ms. Gorshin said, either," Ellie pointed out.

"I don't have to tell him bad stuff about me," Misha said. "I'm a kid. You're a mom. You're supposed to tell him those things."

"I'm not sure they're bad stuff," Ellie argued. Succumbing to the buttery aroma, she scooped a few puffs of popcorn from the bowl on Misha's lap and nibbled them. "Actually, I wasn't really sure what

Ms. Gorshin was complaining about. How can anyone have too much enthusiasm? Enthusiasm is a wonderful thing."

"She wants us to sit quietly at our desks," Misha said. "Well, not all of us. Just the girls." She glanced at her mother, missing a full two seconds of the movie, and then directed her attention back to the TV screen. "It's like, she would ask a question and everyone would just sit there. So if I knew the answer, I'd say it. And then she'd tell me I should wait to be called on, I should raise my hand and let other kids have a chance to answer it."

"Well, that makes sense," Ellie conceded.

"Except that boys shout out the answers all the time, and she never tells them to wait their turn and raise their hands. And it's so unfair," Misha continued, passion amplifying her voice. "Because the girls always behave better than the boys, and then, you do one thing, you shout out one answer, and she yells at you. She never yells at them."

"I'm sure she yells at the boys sometimes."

"Okay, maybe sometimes, if they're doing something really obnoxious. Or dangerous. She yelled at Aidan Rathbun when he folded a history quiz into a paper airplane and threw it out the window. He makes the best paper airplanes. He's like an engineer or something."

"Throwing it out a window would litter the ground outside your classroom," Ellie pointed out, thinking of her cleanup-Shelton project.

"But, like, she never yelled at Luke, and he would shout out answers all the time. It's just the girls who were supposed to behave."

Ellie wanted to dispute Misha's claim, but she couldn't. Not only wasn't she a witness to whatever had occurred in Misha's classroom, but she was aware of the admonishments girls received to be quiet, to listen, to behave. She'd received those admonishments herself as a student, and as a woman. "Grandma always used to tell me that if I wanted boys to like me, I should be a good listener. I should let them talk, and let them believe I was really interested in everything they were saying."

"Even if you weren't?"

"Even if I wasn't."

"Well, I don't want boys to like me, anyway. They're all creeps. Except Dad. He's not a creep."

The jury's still out on that one, Ellie thought, although she didn't criticize Scott to Misha. By tomorrow, Ellie knew, she would be over her anger with him. He had spent all day today biking through Texas and melting in the heat, after all. He hadn't meant to disparage her antilitter campaign. He'd just been wiped out from a long, hard day of biking, and disappointed that he didn't get to speak to Abbie.

And there Ellie was, being a good listener, being demure, being a well-behaved lady. Excusing Scott. Letting him say whatever he'd wanted to say, while she had pressed her lips together to keep from giving voice to what she'd been thinking. "If you ask me," she said to Misha, "you should be enthusiastic and energetic and not always a good listener. Ms. Gorshin was wrong about that."

"Really?" Misha turned to face Ellie again, her eyes wide. "I shouldn't be a good listener?"

"Well, you should be a good listener in terms of paying attention to what people are saying, and hearing what they're really trying to communicate. But no, you shouldn't stifle yourself if you have something to say. You should speak up whenever it's necessary."

"Even if I get in trouble?" Misha asked.

Ellie weighed her response, then shrugged. "Sometimes a person just has to get in trouble. And don't tell anyone I said that."

Misha grinned. Ellie grinned back. On the TV, the little, squat robot beeped and chirped and wasn't the least bit quiet.

DAY THIRTY-TWO

The Oklahoma panhandle is only thirty-four miles wide. I could sleep late and still cover thirty-four miles before lunch. Unfortunately, I'm east of the panhandle, broiling in the Oklahoma pan. It's as hot and dry here as it was in Texas. It's also pretty flat. Thank goodness for small favors.

I'm biking a straight line north from Dallas to Oklahoma City. Of course, I'm bypassing the interstate, so my route is not exactly a straight line. But meeting with environmentalists in Oklahoma City has been a challenge. The state's economy is dependent on mining and fossil fuels, not the most environmentally friendly industries. I've contacted several organizations, but no one seems all that keen to discuss climate change with me.

Just because I'm riding a bicycle doesn't mean everyone is obligated to talk to me. But even without any scheduled meetings, I can still talk to folks. When people see me on my recumbent bike with its decorated Beast of Burden, their curiosity is piqued. And we can talk one-on-one. Sometimes that's the best way.

CHAPTER SIXTEEN

Sonia Lewis strolled into Ellie's office, carrying a paper plate covered in foil. "Are you busy?" she asked, her pale eyes radiant behind her wire-rimmed eyeglasses.

Ellie was always busy, but she knew better than to blow off a member of the select board, especially one carrying a paper plate covered in foil. She tapped the keys on her keyboard to save the spreadsheet Miriam had emailed her, which summarized the town's July budget, and smiled up at Sonia. "What can I help you with?"

"I wanted to tell you how excited I am about your proposal to clean up Shelton," Sonia said. "I've been noticing the litter problem, too. It didn't use to be this bad, but I think during the pandemic, people got careless. They lost their civic spirit. We need it back."

"Yes, we do."

"I want you to know you've got the board behind you. Well, at least me and Ben. But I think the others like the idea of a town cleanup, too. Is it going to be very expensive? Because you know Kent pinches pennies."

"I was just reviewing the numbers for July," Ellie said, gesturing toward her computer screen. "I think we can find the funding for some trash bags and gloves."

Sonia set the plate on the corner of Ellie's desk. "I was in a baking mood — no idea why, it's so blasted hot out. Who wants the oven on in June? But I just felt like baking, and I was going to give these cookies to Wayne, because he works so hard. But then I thought, *you* work hard, too. And with your husband gone all summer, I think you deserve the cookies more than he does."

Ellie wholeheartedly agreed, but she exercised discretion and didn't say so. "Thank you so much, Sonia," she said instead.

"They're peanut butter chocolate chip," Sonia said.

"Oh, my God." Ellie lifted a corner of the foil and peeked at the cookies on the paper plate. "I think I just died and went to heaven."

"No, you mustn't die," Sonia said. "We need you alive long enough to get Shelton cleaned up."

"These cookies give me a reason to live," Ellie joked. "Maybe they'll give me extra energy." Unlike Misha, she didn't have excessive stores of energy to tap into. But the cookies — good lord, home-made peanut butter chocolate chip cookies! — would energize her more effectively than a Starbucks venti with an extra shot.

"Well, let me know if there's anything I can do to help with this Shelton cleanup project," Sonia said.

"Actually," Ellie said, "I was thinking about rewarding the volunteers with cookies and cold drinks after they pick up the trash. I'm planning to ask for donations from Trumbull's and the supermarkets, but maybe if you could convince some of your friends to donate baked goods, too..."

"Of course. I have lots of friends who love to bake. Birds of a feather and all that." She beamed a grandmotherly smile at Ellie. "Leave it to me. You put this project together, and I'll get the cookies for you."

Ellie was still smiling as Sonia ambled out of the office, looking younger than her years in a pair of skinny jeans and a gauzy tunic. At least *someone* appreciated what Ellie was trying to do. At least *someone* thought clearing the town's streets of litter was as worthwhile as bicycling from Texas to Oklahoma and trying to convince people who depended on fossil fuels for their income that they should shut down their oil fields and build massive farms of solar panels to replace them.

Thinking of solar panels reminded her that she had a lunch meeting with Carl Corrigan and Wayne in — she checked her watch — twenty minutes. Wayne had told her Carl wanted to deal directly with him, not with her, no doubt because he knew Wayne would tell him whatever he wanted to hear. But Wayne requested Ellie's presence at the meeting to supply the data and details about which he was ignorant. Ellie didn't have time to linger over a lunch with Wayne and Carl at the Sycamore Acres Country Club, but Wayne was her boss and he'd asked her to be there. And hell, she deserved one of those fancy lunches at the club.

She would have worn something nicer if Wayne had mentioned this lunch engagement yesterday. But he'd surprised her with the invitation when she'd arrived at work that morning, telling her to set aside a couple of midday hours on her calendar for lunch because Carl's feathers were ruffled, and she was so talented when it came to unruffling feathers.

If Carl's feathers were ruffled, they'd been ruffled by the select board, not Ellie. All she had done was give the select board her and Nakul's evaluation of about Carl's project. The select board could have rejected their report. They could have told Carl he could build as many damned units as he wanted, skip the solar panels, and flip the condo purchasers the bird when their basements grew damp and sprouted mold due to the drainage issues. The board members were the ones who had determined that he needed to respect the MEPA guidelines and construct a safe, sustainable condominium community. All Ellie had done was present her and Nakul's findings.

But...there was a country-club lunch waiting for her, and feathers in need of unruffling. Just as she wanted to reward her antilitter volunteers with cookies, she deserved her own reward for putting up with Wayne's ineptitude and Carl's resistance. She would enjoy a meal at Wayne's fancy club.

Sycamore Acres was situated on the western end of town. Steering onto the country club's entry drive, she cruised past acreage so verdant and smooth that it looked as if someone had unrolled over the ground bolts of green felt adorned with amoeba-shaped blobs of white sand, poles with their little pennant flags drooping in the windless summer air, clusters of trees and shrubbery, and carts zooming along the pathways, all of them occupied by men. The country club's main building stood at the end of the drive, which was elegantly landscaped with a border of yews and junipers. Ellie wondered what a membership in the club cost, and she wondered if Wayne wrote off his membership as a business expense — or worse, somehow got the Town of Shelton to pay the membership fee for him. She would have to ask Miriam about that when she got back to her office.

Plenty of parking spaces were empty; the golf course apparently didn't attract many players in the middle of a workday. Ellie parked and entered the building, shivering slightly in the blast of air conditioning that greeted her as she stepped across the threshold.

Inside, she walked through the entry to a spotless white counter, her footsteps silenced by plush carpeting the same intense green as the grass blanketing the golf course's acreage. Behind the counter stood a strapping young man who bore an uncanny resemblance to a Ken doll Ellie had owned as a child — tall, thin, and with hair so short it looked as if it had been painted onto his scalp. He wore a golf shirt with "Shelton Acres" embroidered discreetly over his right pectoral muscle. "I'm supposed to meet Wayne McNulty and Carl Corrigan for lunch," she said, speaking in a hushed tone because the atmosphere seemed to demand it.

"Yes, of course. They're expecting you. The dining room is down that hall," he said, pointing to a corridor beyond the counter.

Despite the clubhouse's ambiance of affluence and bland tastefulness, the young man didn't comment on Ellie's apparel. She supposed people in a venue where collared polo shirts, cotton twill trousers, and cleated saddle shoes were the standard uniform wouldn't pass judgment on a small-town bureaucrat in her usual drab but comfortable attire.

She found the dining room with no difficulty. It was elegantly lit, with broad windows overlooking a fairway. All that neatly mowed grass reminded her that she really needed to push the lawn mower around her yard that weekend. Or bribe Abbie to do it. She was old enough. Misha was old enough, too, but as Ms. Gorshin said, she was too enthusiastic. Ellie wasn't sure she wanted Misha enthusiastically messing with a lawn mower. All those sharp blades worried her.

A smattering of the tables were occupied, and Ellie had no trouble spotting Wayne, nor did he have any trouble spotting her as she strolled into the dining room. He rose from his chair and waved her over before the hostess, also clad in a Shelton Acres golf shirt and trim khaki slacks, could usher her to Wayne's table.

Two other men sat at the table with Wayne: Carl Corrigan and Richard Vernon. What the hell was *he* doing there? And would he be crass enough to flirt with her in front of Wayne and Carl?

What little appetite Ellie had had evaporated. She wished she had remained back at the office, devouring Sonia's cookies and convincing herself they were nutritious because they contained peanut butter.

"There she is," Wayne greeted her, as if she was "It" in a game of hide-and-seek. As she neared the table, she noticed that all three men already had cocktails in front of them. She had barely taken her seat when a waiter glided over and asked if she would care to order a beverage.

She requested a glass of ice water, which caused the men to chuckle. "I've got a full afternoon of work ahead of me," she said, wondering if she sounded as if she was criticizing them and deciding she didn't care. Somehow, seeing Connie's obnoxious husband seated just ninety degrees away from her at the circular table had turned this luncheon from a time-wasting but potentially indulgent outing into whatever the polar opposite of homemade peanut butter chocolate chip cookies was.

"Why don't we order, and then we can talk shop," Wayne said, filling the role of host as he distributed menus. Ellie eyed the three men before opening her menu. She wondered if they'd arranged to meet at eleven thirty and then told her to come at noon, so they could have a half hour to coordinate their strategy and guzzle their booze before she arrived. But then, if they'd wanted to plot something behind her back, they wouldn't have had to invite her at all.

She skimmed the menu. It was filled with hefty, hearty fare — beef prepared in various ways, lamb chops, ham, pasta Bolognese. A more careful perusal of the menu led her to a small list of salads. No prices were listed; she supposed the meal would simply be billed to Wayne's account.

She shouldn't have been surprised when, after she ordered a Caesar salad with grilled chicken, the men all ordered red meat. She couldn't recall the last time she'd eaten a steak. Scott liked to remind her and the girls of how resource-inefficient raising cattle was.

Then again, he was enjoying McDonald's hamburgers and Texas barbecue on the road.

"So," Wayne said grandly once the server had taken their orders and departed. "Carl was a little disappointed with the stipulations the select board attached to his condominium proposal."

Ellie sent Carl a cool smile. "Perhaps you ought to take it up with the select board," she suggested.

"The select board does whatever Wayne tells them to do, am I right?" Carl responded.

"Well, then, you should take it up with Wayne." Ellie's smile widened and its temperature dropped. She could practically feel ice crystals forming on her teeth.

"You made the presentation, Ellie," Wayne said, then beamed at Carl and Richard. "Did you know Ellie was named after Eleanor Roosevelt?"

"That lady was a troublemaker, too. Storming around the country, writing newspaper columns, riling up laborers..." Richard chuckled as he said this, but Ellie sensed he wasn't joking.

"I'm not a troublemaker," she assured him, keeping her tone as light and mild as she could. "I really do want this condo development to happen." She turned to face Carl, who was seated across the table from her. "All the select board is asking for are a few tweaks to make the project safer and more environmentally friendly."

"See what happens when your husband disappears on a cross-country bike trip to save the environment?" Richard shook his head. "Suddenly, everything looks like an ecological challenge. You know about her husband, don't you?" he asked Carl.

Carl shrugged. "He's on a cross-country bike trip?"

"To save the environment," Richard emphasized. "He pedaled off on his two-wheeler to save the world and abandoned the little lady to take care of things on the home front."

"Including the environment of Shelton," Ellie said, doing her best to sound agreeable. She shot Wayne a quick look, wishing he would join the conversation and support what she was saying. He simply grinned and sipped his cocktail. "We all know about the MEPA regulations."

"Recommendations," Carl corrected her.

She plowed ahead, ignoring his interruption. "They exist not only to preserve the environment but to protect the people who are going to be making use of the new development. Nakul and I have discussed the drainage issues with you, Carl. You don't want people moving into your condo complex and experiencing damp basements and flooded roads and erosion of all the beautiful landscaping you're planning to do. And of course, the solar panels —"

"The solar panels!" Richard bellowed, his tone heavy with contempt. "We're in New England. It's not like we have that many hours of daylight."

"Shelton installed solar panels on the roof of the high school," Ellie said. "It measurably reduced the school's electricity costs. Right, Wayne?" *Say something, you doofus. Don't just sit there nursing your drink and forcing me to do all the talking.*

"Miriam would have the figures," Wayne said. "I don't know them offhand."

"But the solar panels did reduce costs."

"If I'm not mistaken, yeah, they did," Wayne said.

Thank you for actually supporting something I said, Ellie thought bitterly.

"Look." Richard leaned toward Ellie, his boringly handsome face just inches from hers. "My company wants to finance this subdivision. We expect a return on our investment. The project has to be profitable, or it won't happen. Solar panels are expensive. They cut into the profitability of the project. You know what happens if a project isn't profitable?"

"I've taken a few economics courses," Ellie assured him, her tone just inches from sarcastic.

"Good for you." Richard trumped her, letting sarcasm drench his voice. "Then you understand that my company needs to see a profit. Carl needs to see a profit. If this project doesn't reach a certain level of profitability, that parcel of land on Route 29 doesn't get developed and Shelton doesn't get the tax revenue from it. You say you want this development to happen. If it's going to happen, it has to be profitable. That's the way capitalism works."

Richard was lucky the server chose that moment to deliver their meals: three massive plates overwhelmed with monstrous portions of sizzling meat, potatoes, and vegetables, and one ladylike bowl of greens topped with pale slices of chicken. If the food hadn't arrived at that moment, Ellie might have tossed her ice water into Richard's face. She did not need him explaining capitalism to her. She did not need him speaking to her as if she were a moron.

After staring at her salad for a moment, inhaling and exhaling with Zen slowness to calm herself down, she felt capable of speaking civilly. "I know the solar panels add to the cost of each unit. But Carl can raise the price of each unit to cover that. People *want* to live in homes that are energy efficient, that make use of the newest technology. I'm not asking anyone to sacrifice their profits." She glared at Richard, then steered her gaze back to Carl and smiled. "We've been working on this project for quite a while now, Carl, am I right?" She hadn't meant to use his favorite phrase, but it slipped out. She hoped he viewed that as homage and not ridicule. "You know I want it to go forward. So does Wayne." She favored him with a stern look, warning him not to interfere. "So does the select board. But if you build something that ignores MEPA regulations and the latest technology, it's not going to be as desirable a community. By adopting these concepts, you'll be making your units much more marketable."

"Well." Carl narrowed his gaze on her for several long seconds, then shrugged and exchanged a look with Richard and then with Wayne. "I've gotta make my nut, am I right?"

"You will make your nut," Ellie said, hearing the grit in her voice and wondering if he and his fellow stooges heard it as well. "Everyone wants this project to happen. I'm sure even the state would want this project to happen — but they'd want it to abide by the MEPA guidelines. You've developed condominium communities in other towns, Carl, and they've met the requirements of those towns, both in size and in sustainability."

"Oh, you've done your research!" Richard boomed, as if she were a school child presenting an oral report.

"I didn't have to put solar panels on the senior community in Cloverdale," Carl whined.

"If you had put them on, you could have charged at least fifty thousand dollars more per unit. Maybe more. That would have more than covered the cost of the solar panels," Ellie argued.

"You think so?" He sounded vaguely persuaded.

"Easily. Probably more."

"Her husband has brainwashed her," Richard muttered. "Did he put solar panels on his bicycle?"

Ellie thought it best to ignore him.

"Okay, look," Wayne finally spoke. "Bottom line: this project has been green-lighted and it's going to get done. Shop around, Carl. You're a construction executive. You can negotiate with solar panel suppliers. You can probably chisel down the price a bit. I mean, you don't have to put the fanciest, most expensive solar panels on your buildings. Just put *some* solar panels on your buildings."

"You're selling high-quality units," Ellie overrode Wayne. "You want to give your buyers good quality. Don't be cheap. You'll still make your profit. Because" — she gave Richard another withering look — "profitability is important, am I right?"

The rest of the lunch was more or less awful. Ellie picked at her salad while the men devoured their slabs of cattle flesh and opined on subjects she didn't care about: the Red Sox, the Patriots, the Bruins, the Celtics, golfing weather, golfing equipment, and golfing triumphs. After a half hour of listening to Wayne and Richard debate who had done better with his 5-iron on the thirteenth hole last week, Ellie excused herself and said she needed to get back to work. The salad had tasted like every other chicken Caesar salad she had ever eaten, and she didn't mind leaving half of it untouched. If she got hungry later in the afternoon, she would eat some of Sonia's cookies.

And she wouldn't share any with Wayne.

CHAPTER SEVENTEEN

By eight thirty that night, Ellie's life had improved considerably, and not only because she'd gotten to indulge in a few of Sonia's home-baked cookies when she'd returned to her office. During the afternoon, she'd received word that the insurance company had accepted her claim, and she'd been able to schedule the roof repair for the following week, using a firm Nakul had recommended. Nakul tended to be stingy with his recommendations, so if he thought this company would do a competent job, Ellie was confident that it would. If Scott had been home, he probably would have spent weeks researching every roofing company in eastern Massachusetts, checked with the state's Consumer Affairs Bureau to see if anyone had ever lodged a complaint against any of them, and scrolled through all their online ratings — and then contracted with the same company Ellie had hired. But Scott wasn't home, and Ellie was doing things her way.

Connie had insisted on visiting Ellie after dinner with a bottle of champagne. "We have to celebrate," she'd announced in a phone call. "As soon as I've got the dishes stacked in the dishwasher, I'm coming over. Tell your daughters to get lost. We're going to drink a toast to my big commission and the end of the school year."

Now they sat together on the back patio, their bare feet propped up on the bamboo table in front of their chairs, each of them holding a fluted goblet filled with chilled bubbly. In the waning evening light, Ellie could see Connie's feet, her insteps smooth and her toenails glossy with polish the color of rubies. Ellie ought to get a pedicure — her feet looked callused and dowdy next to Connie's — but when would she have the time? Saturday? Misha had a soccer game, and the lawn had to be mowed.

The night was growing darker. In another twenty minutes or so, it would be too dark to see her feet, even in the glow of the citronella candles burning in amber glass jars on the table. Their pungent scent helped keep the mosquitoes from biting.

Scott had phoned ten minutes ago. Misha had shouted to Ellie through the kitchen door, and Ellie had responded, "Tell him I'll talk to him tomorrow." She wasn't in the mood to hear him moan about the heat or his sore calves or his inability to schedule an appearance on a university campus or a television show. Nor was she in the mood to hear him crow about his triumph over the heat and leg cramps and gloat about his appearances.

She was in the mood to sip her glass of icy, fizzy champagne and talk to Connie, and to watch Lucy's silhouette as she lazily roamed the back yard, sniffing at the shrubs and rustling the too-tall grass. Ellie was in the mood to not have to deal with a man for a while.

"So Richard was at this lunch?" Connie asked her. "How come?"

"He's financing an adult condo development at the old Mumson Farm property on Route 29. That was what the lunch was about."

Connie tipped her glass to her lips and took a long sip. Her floral-print capris and her sleeveless cotton shirt were a step more fashionable than Ellie's denim shorts and T-shirt, but she looked as comfortable as Ellie felt. "I wonder who'll get the listing for those condos. I should position myself."

"You should. They won't be priced cheap. You'll make a nice commission on them."

"Especially if there are a lot of units. If I could be the listing agent for the whole complex..."

"If the select board gets its way, there will be fewer units than the developer wants. We're trying to scale back the size a little for environmental reasons."

Connie seemed momentarily lost in thought. "I might have to be nice to Richard. If I am, he could connect me with the developer."

"Ground hasn't even been broken yet, Connie. We're talking months. Maybe years before this thing is ready for a real estate broker."

"I bet that pisses Richard off. He hates having to wait for anything. Was he an asshole at your lunch?"

Ellie laughed. "He thought he had to explain basic economic theory to me. Stuff about the importance of profitability in the world of business. As if I didn't know that."

"Oh, God." Connie sighed. "Mansplaining. One of his greatest talents. If I ever leave him — *when* I leave him — I will definitely not miss his lectures. He can go on for ten minutes on the importance of checking the sell-by dates on bottles of milk. As if I haven't been doing the grocery shopping for the past twenty-five years."

"Mom!" Misha shouted through the kitchen door. She cracked it open so she could be heard, but with it open she shouted just as loudly, "Nana's on the phone!"

Nana was Scott's mother. When Abbie was born, Ellie's mother insisted on claiming the title of "Grandma," leaving Scott's mother to agree to be called "Nana." Ellie's father became "Grandpa" and Scott's late father became "Papa." The grandfathers never seemed to care one way or another what they were called, but Ellie's mother had been forceful and Scott's had been passive-aggressive, insisting she didn't mind being called Nana even though Ellie suspected that she would have preferred to be called Grandma. Iris Gillman loved presenting herself as flexible and undemanding. She never wanted to be any trouble. Everything was fine with her.

"Tell her I'll call her back tomorrow," she instructed Misha. "Tell her I have company." *And a delicious glass of champagne that I intend to enjoy.*

"She said it's important," Misha hollered.

Ellie rolled her eyes. "Go talk to her," Connie urged her. "I promise not to drink all the champagne while you're gone."

Reluctantly, Ellie stood and slipped her feet into her flip-flops. She carried her glass with her — not because she was worried that Connie would guzzle it in her absence but because she might need a few sips of wine to get through the phone call. "I'll be right back," she promised before stepping into the kitchen.

Misha handed her the cordless phone, her eyes round with a mixture of concern and excitement. Did Iris have bad news? Had she already told Misha the bad news?

"Hi, Iris," Ellie said into the phone.

"I'm sorry to bother you," Scott's mother said. "You must be so busy taking care of everything while Scott is out of town."

"Out of town" sounded much more manageable than the reality, which was that Scott was somewhere near the Continental Divide, dragging his Beast of Burden with its little orange flag behind him. "We're doing fine," Ellie assured her, not bothering to mention the hole in the roof or all the work projects she was juggling. "The kids just finished their school year. Did Misha tell you?"

"She said they both got good grades. Of course they would, with a father who's a school teacher."

And a mother who checked their homework, signed their permission slips, got them to school, practices, and rehearsals on time, and contributed some reasonably intelligent genes to their makeup. "So, what's up with you?" Ellie asked, hoping she didn't sound too impatient. "Misha said you had something important to tell me?"

"Well, I really hate to bother you," Iris repeated. "It's just that, well, I had a little fall."

"Are you okay?"

"I am, really," Iris assured her. "I'm in the hospital, though."

That did *not* sound like a little fall.

"The ER, actually. I seem to have broken my wrist. The doctor here said it's a very common thing — you fall forward and stick out your hand to brace yourself, and your wrist snaps. Apparently, I'm common."

"Oh, Iris." Ellie appreciated Iris's attempt to downplay her injury, but she needed to know just how bad her mother-in-law's condition was. "Are you in a lot of pain?"

"It's just a little achy right now," Iris said. "They can't put a cast on it because it's too swollen. The doctor said I'm supposed to see a hand orthopedist in a few days and he'll put a cast on it. In the meantime, they've given me some painkillers. But really it isn't bad."

"I'm glad you nailed your wrist and not your head. Where did you fall?"

"In the bedroom. It was all my fault. I tripped over a sneaker. I should have put my shoes in the closet when I got home from my afternoon walk with Grace Merkel. She's my walking partner. We made a commitment to walk together every day, weather permitting. We just started a month ago, and we're already up to five miles. It keeps us fit."

"I'm sure it does," Ellie agreed, her mind racing ahead. "So you tripped and fell and broke your wrist. Which hospital are you at?"

Iris named the hospital. "I phoned Grace and asked her to drive me here. But after she sat with me a while, she had to go home and fix supper for her husband. He's the kind of man who can't figure out how to make a sandwich on his own."

"So you need a ride home?" Ellie could send an Uber or a Lyft to the hospital for Iris. But that would be coldhearted. The woman was her daughters' grandmother, she was in the ER, and she had a broken wrist. "If they're ready to discharge you, I can pick you up." So much for enjoying her champagne with Connie.

"Well, that's the thing. They won't discharge me to go home because I live alone. I can't do much of anything with only one hand. Not to be crude, but going to the bathroom is going to be tricky. Have you ever tried to take off your pants using only one hand?"

"So where do they want to discharge you?"

"They suggested a rehabilitation nursing home, but I'd really rather not go there. It's just like a hospital, only with more physical therapists. They said I could avoid the rehab nursing home if I can stay with someone. I hate to impose on you, Ellie, but is there a chance I could spend the night at your house?"

"Of course," Ellie said. "I'll come pick you up and bring you back here. You can stay as long as you need to." Iris wouldn't be a bother, and she would spend her entire time at Ellie's house apologizing for being a bother.

"We'd have to swing by my house so I can pick up a few items," Iris said. "Some spare clothes, my toothbrush...I hate to be any trouble, but —"

"You're not any trouble," Ellie insisted. "I can get to the hospital in about twenty minutes. Just stay in the ER and I'll find you."

"You're an angel," Iris said, then added, "Don't tell Scott, okay? He's got so much on his mind, with that bicycle and saving the planet and everything. I don't want him worrying about me."

"You're his mother, Iris. I think he should know."

"I'll tell him eventually. But right now — I've been following him online and he's phoned me a few times, and he's so busy, and the weather's so hot, and he has all these important media people he has to meet with. I don't want to bother him with my silly little accident."

Perhaps the accident, tripping over a sneaker, was silly. But Iris's injury wasn't. She was a sixty-nine-year-old woman who lived alone and had a fractured wrist. She knew what her son was going through. He ought to know what she was going through.

But Ellie wasn't going to get into an argument with her about it, not tonight. The poor woman was in an ER, doped up on pain-killers, her arm too swollen for a cast. They could discuss when and how to inform Scott tomorrow, when the shock wore off and Iris was thinking more clearly.

"All right. We won't tell Scott yet. I'll get there as soon as I can," Ellie promised her. "Sit tight."

She disconnected the call, looked around, and noticed that Misha had vanished from the kitchen. She'd been replaced by Connie, who stood just inside the back door, champagne glass in one hand and two-thirds-consumed bottle in the other, her eyes questioning. Ellie groaned, then drained her glass. "I'm afraid tonight's celebration is over," she said.

DAY THIRTY-FIVE

The recumbent bike is supposed to cause less duress on the human body, but man, I'm sore! I took a long soak in my motel room's tub tonight. So far, that's the most distinctive thing I can say about Kansas: wonderful bathtub.

Oh, and another very important thing: it's flat. Flat means the land is easier to farm, easier to build on, easier to exploit. It means nothing stops the weather, nothing breaks up the wind. It also means that pedaling a bike is a bit easier here.

So why am I so achy? Well, Oklahoma was hillier than I expected. Texas has its share of hills, too.

But what are my twinges of pain compared to the pain our beautiful planet is suffering? I can survive cramped calves, chafed thighs, a sore butt. I can pop ibuprofen and take a bath. There is no bathtub big enough for Mother Nature to soak in, no anti-inflammatory she can swallow. The only way we can heal the earth is through human action. We need to talk the talk, but more importantly, we need to walk the walk. Walking, after all, is a lot more eco-friendly than driving an internal-combustion-engine car.

So is biking.

.

CHAPTER EIGHTEEN

"**I**t's so cool that Nana is living with us," Misha said the next morning. Ellie wasn't sure if what Misha thought was so cool was her grandmother's presence or the fact that, because Iris took over Misha's bedroom, Misha had spent the night sleeping on an inflatable mattress on the floor of Abbie's room.

Abbie didn't think that was so cool. "How can I practice my clarinet while she's in my room all the time?"

"First of all," Ellie pointed out, "she won't be in your room all the time. Only to sleep, and only until Nana is able to move back to her own house. And second of all, you don't practice your clarinet all the time."

Abbie pouted. "Why should I? School's out, and I don't have a private teacher."

It was too early in the morning for Ellie to have to deal with Abbie's adolescent petulance. After picking Iris up at the hospital last night, driving to Iris's house to pack some toiletries, clean clothing, and a hefty stack of library books and puzzle magazines — "Thank God I'm right-handed so I can do my Sudoku," Iris had said, her left forearm swaddled in gauze and ace bandages and cradled in a spiffy navy-blue sling with adjustable white straps — Ellie had gotten her mother-in-law settled in Misha's bedroom, arranged the inflatable mattress on the floor of Abbie's bedroom, mulled over whether to disobey Iris and phone Scott to update him on his mother's injury, and listened patiently while Iris repeated that she didn't want him disturbed. "He's doing such essential work," Iris had insisted. "He doesn't need to be worrying about my little mishap."

Moving Iris into Misha's bedroom didn't qualify as little. Her heavily bandaged arm, her fingertips swollen and discolored with bruising, her elaborate sling, the painkiller prescriptions they'd stopped to pick up at the all-night pharmacy on their way home — none of that qualified as a mishap. The doctor in the ER had informed Ellie that Iris might need surgery, and that she should follow up with an orthopedist within three days. That seemed just as essential to Ellie as biking through Kansas and taking a bath.

Fortunately, Iris had had little difficulty falling asleep in Misha's bed, and she was still slumbering at seven thirty the next morning, when Ellie and the girls gathered in the kitchen for breakfast. "If you want private clarinet lessons," Ellie told Abbie, "you're going to have to do some of the legwork."

"It's fingerwork," Misha joked as she poured milk into her bowl of granola. "You don't play a clarinet with your legs." She considered her words and added, "You play *soccer* with your legs."

Ellie flashed a quick smile at Misha, who was being much more pleasant than Abbie about the temporary upheaval in their household. Then she turned back to her sullen older daughter, who took a sip of her coffee and grimaced as if her mug was filled with runoff from a sewage treatment plant. She still had on the oversized T-shirt she'd slept in, the words "Shelton High School JV Volleyball" silkscreened on it. Her eyes were blessedly devoid of mascara.

"I'm really overbooked right now," Ellie told her. "If you want private lessons, go online and see who in the area is available to give them. I'm not crazy about the idea of hiring people from the Boston Symphony Orchestra. They'll probably be expensive, and I don't have time to chauffeur you into Boston for your lessons. Maybe Mr. — what's his name? Mr. Cyborg? — can continue your lessons over the summer."

"Mr. Streiberg," Abbie muttered. "I mean, he's nice and all, but I take classes with him all school year. I don't want to take classes with him over the summer, too. It'll feel like summer school or something."

"Then find another teacher. Do some research. Find some private teachers who have openings for new students, find out what they charge, look for online reviews and recommendations. I just can't do that right now."

"I'm going to be starting work next week," Abbie reminded her.

"Which gives you this week to do it." Ellie tried to filter her irritation from her voice. She *was* overbooked. And yesterday evening, when she thought she might be able to relax for a blessed hour or two with Connie and a bottle of champagne, she had instead wound up taking care of her mother-in-law.

She really regretted not being able to help Connie polish off that champagne.

Abbie continued to glower at her mug of coffee. Ellie slugged her own coffee down, burning her tongue, and then went upstairs to check on Iris. While she could count on the girls to run and fetch for their grandmother if necessary, she didn't think they could handle dressing Iris or helping her bathe. If Iris felt up to it, Ellie could wrap her arm in plastic and assist her as she took a shower, but Ellie hoped Iris would opt to skip showering today. The poor woman must be feeling more than a little rattled and fragile. A sponge bath at the sink ought to suffice for now.

Ellie inched the bedroom door open to discover Iris sitting up in Misha's bed, her eyes wide, her hair standing in silver tufts around her head, her left arm free of its sling but her fingertips still swollen and discolored with bruising. She sighed. "I feel so bad about kicking Misha out of her own bed," she said, shaking her head.

"Misha loves sleeping on the inflatable mattress," Ellie assured her. "She feels like she's camping out. I have to leave for work soon, but I wanted to help you get washed and dressed first."

"I'm such a drain on you," Iris muttered. "Just a stupid sneaker..."

"Stop apologizing." Ellie liked her mother-in-law well enough, but hearing the woman go on and on about how sorry she was grated after a while. "Let's get you ready to face the day. Putting on a bra is a two-handed operation. I'll have to help you with that."

"Oh, I'll skip the bra for now," Iris said. "I never had much in the bosom department, anyway." True enough. She was a petite woman, nearly as wiry in build as her marathon-biking son. "I brought pants and shorts with elastic waistbands," Iris continued. "So I won't have to deal with buttons and zippers."

"That was smart. How does your wrist feel? Do you need a pain pill?"

Insisting the pain wasn't too bad, Iris swung her legs over the edge of the mattress and stood. She moved slowly, a bit woodenly, but she was on her feet.

In twenty minutes, Ellie had her washed and dressed. Iris seemed proud that she was able to brush her hair one-handed. She also practiced pulling her shorts down and then up again with one hand. "I don't want to have to ask the girls for help when I go to the bathroom," she whispered, as if the mere mention of that bodily function had to be kept a secret.

"If you need help, ask for it," Ellie said. "They'll both be home today. Misha's camp and Abbie's job don't start until next week." She escorted Iris to the stairs and held her right arm gently as they descended together. Iris seemed pretty stable, but still, Ellie didn't want any more mishaps, little or otherwise. "You can call me at work if you need to," she told Iris.

"Oh, I don't want to bother you," Iris said. "I feel so bad, disrupting your life this way."

Ellie bit her lip to keep from repeating her demand that Iris stop apologizing. "The girls can help you get breakfast," she said. "There's coffee in the pot, cereal in the cabinet below the microwave, and eggs and bread in the refrigerator. Please don't trip on Lucy," Ellie added as the dog bounded into the kitchen through the back door, which Misha held open for her. Lucy raced straight to her water dish and guzzled its contents, chug-a-lugging as if she'd been wandering in Death Valley for days.

"We'll make sure Lucy stays out of Nana's way," Misha promised. Abbie only pouted. Ellie considered apologizing for Abbie's churlishness, then decided that if she didn't want Iris to keep apologizing, she shouldn't apologize either. Iris had raised a son. She knew that teenagers could be moody.

"I've got to run," Ellie said, grabbing her keys and tote bag from the counter. She would arrive at her desk late, and since she'd consumed only a cup of coffee for breakfast, she would experience hunger pangs all morning. "Don't forget to make an appointment with the hand doctor," she reminded Iris.

"And don't you breathe a word about this to Scott," Iris shot back. "I don't want him worrying about me."

"Fine." Not fine, but Ellie would honor Iris's request. She was the one with Iris living in her house right now. If she defied Iris, she would be the one to suffer for it. In all honesty, she didn't have the time or the energy for an argument with anyone — her mother-in-law, her daughters, her colleagues at work, or, for that matter, Scott.

As expected, she arrived at work ten minutes late. Hoping no one was waiting for her, hovering beside her desk, glowering at his wristwatch and tapping his feet, she jogged down the corridor of the new wing.

Someone *was* waiting for her: Sonia Lewis. Ellie slowed her pace slightly as she spotted the older woman lurking in the open doorway of Ellie's office. Sonia was not given to glowering at her watch and tapping her feet. She was too sweet, too undemanding.

"There you are," Sonia said as Ellie closed the distance between them.

Remembering the paper plate of peanut butter chocolate chip cookies Sonia had brought her yesterday, Ellie smiled. She had eaten a few of them yesterday afternoon, but she had left the rest in the bottom drawer of her desk. She wouldn't have to worry about starving all morning, after all — and she wouldn't have to worry about setting a healthy example for her daughters by consuming a nutritious breakfast of fruit and whole-grain toast instead of cookies. No one would have to know she was starting her day with a feast of chocolate and sugar.

"Here I am," she said slightly breathlessly as she led Sonia into the office. Wayne's door was closed; evidently he wasn't in yet. When he arrived, he would no doubt amble in at a leisurely pace. No corridor jog for him. He didn't mind being late.

"I have good news for you," Sonia said, adjusting her eyeglasses on the bridge of her nose and beaming a smile Ellie's way.

"More cookies?" Ellie grinned.

"Something like that. I've lined up an army to handle refreshments on Shelton Cleanup Day."

"Is that what the select board wants to call it?"

"Yes. We've scheduled it for the first Saturday in August. Sunday is the rain date. Marshall suggested that the town hall should be the launch location. We'll set up some tables, hand out trash bags and assign routes, and tell people to come back with their trash bags full if they want refreshments. Ben reached out to the hauling company that handles our trash to expand their service, although I think Wayne will have to negotiate any contract adjustments with them. We're still discussing where we want to locate the public trash cans."

"Really?" Stunned that so much had been accomplished, Ellie sank into her chair. "When did all this happen?"

"At our meeting last night. Wayne didn't tell you? He was at the meeting."

"I'm surprised he didn't ask me to be there," Ellie said, not adding that she was also greatly relieved. She was disappointed that her champagne hour had been interrupted by Iris's accident. If it had been interrupted by Wayne demanding that she attend another select board meeting, she would have been furious.

"You were there in spirit," Sonia told her. "Honestly, Ellie, everyone is just so glad you spoke up at last week's meeting. We'd all been noticing the increase in littering around town, but no one said anything about it — until you did. You said something has to be done about it, and now you're doing something about it. Your ears should have been burning last night. Even Marshall was singing your praises."

Ellie might have liked to hear that — but not so much that she would have wanted to drive down to the town hall to attend last night's meeting. What if she'd been there when Iris had called? Would the girls have phoned Ellie at the meeting and told her she had to drive to the hospital to pick up her mother-in-law? Would leaving in the middle of the meeting have damaged Ellie's career?

It didn't matter. She'd missed hearing Marshall say nice things about her, but apparently her job was safe.

"So Wayne is on board with the plan?"

Sonia chuckled. "Oh, you know Wayne. He's not thrilled by the extra work it will entail, but when all is said and done, he'll take credit for it." She patted Ellie on the arm and started for the door. "I'll keep you updated on the refreshment plans."

Ellie grinned and waved Sonia off. Then she let out a long breath and fired up her computer. Sonia was right. Wayne would complain about the extra work involved in setting Shelton Cleanup Day — and then he'd dump that work on Ellie. And he'd take all the credit.

But it would get the town cleaned up. That was the important thing.

She arrived home that evening to find a surprisingly tranquil scene: Iris seated in the kitchen, her left arm in its sling, Abbie at the sink removing the tails from frozen shrimp, and Misha at the counter, peeling carrots onto a sheet of wax paper. "We're making seafood stew," she announced exuberantly. "I'm in charge of the carrots and potatoes. Nana says we can compost the peels."

"We don't have a compost heap," she reminded Misha.

"We can start one. Right, Nana?"

"We don't have a garden. What will we do with it?" Ellie was as much in favor of recycling as anyone else, but she couldn't take on yet another project. Composting organic waste sounded like a pretty big project. Planting a garden? Forget it.

"You have to have worms for a compost heap," Abbie muttered. "I vote no."

"Mrs. Kupferman has a garden," Misha persisted. "We can give her our compost."

In spite of herself, Ellie laughed. She doubted her crotchety next-door neighbor would be thrilled beyond words to have Ellie's girls dumping their carrot peelings, apple cores, and rotting lettuce in her back yard — to say nothing of the worms. "Mrs. Kupferman grows flowers, not vegetables," Ellie noted. "She seems satisfied with mulch."

"Nana, do you have a compost heap?" Misha asked.

Iris had the good sense to look abashed. "Well, I don't have a vegetable garden. We had one when your daddy was growing up, but we didn't know about compost then."

"Daddy wasn't saving the world yet," Abbie said, sounding just sardonic enough to tickle a smile from Ellie.

"Okay." Iris squinted at the screen on her phone, then held it up for Ellie to see. "I found the recipe online, and it worked with what you've got in your refrigerator. But these tiny screens... they strain an old lady's eyes."

"You're not that old," Misha said. "You're just nana-old."

"Which is definitely old," Iris refuted her, returning her attention to the phone's screen. "It's time to get the stock started. Abbie, have you finished peeling the shrimp? We're going to cook the shells in some oil and then boil them in water to make the stock."

"We're cooking the shells?" Misha let out a shriek.

"Just for their flavor. We'll strain the broth to remove all the shells. We aren't going to eat them."

"It looks like Nana has things under control," Ellie said, nodding at Iris. "I'm going upstairs to change out of my work clothes."

It took another hour for dinner to be served. Ellie used that hour to relax. It was such an indulgence not to have to prepare dinner herself. If Iris was willing to oversee the dinner preparations every evening, she could stay at Ellie's house for as long as she wished.

The stew was delicious. Even Abbie seemed to enjoy it. While they ate, she reported that she'd texted the other clarinet player in the high school orchestra and asked him who his teacher was, even though he wasn't as good a player as she was, which was why she'd gotten the solo in the spring concert and he hadn't, so maybe his teacher wasn't so good. Iris mentioned that she'd made an appointment with an orthopedist for the following Monday, and she would take a cab to the appointment so Ellie wouldn't have to drive her. Ellie said she would take time off from work and drive her to the appointment because she wanted to hear what the orthopedist had to say. This prompted a couple of apologies from Iris, expressing contrition over interrupting Ellie's workday, but Ellie cut her off before she got carried away with expressions of how sorry she was. Misha announced that her Girls Aloud Club planned to continue meeting during the summer, even though it wouldn't be as much fun to make a lot of noise during their vacation from school, if no boys were around to hear them. "We might have to go to Little League games and make noise on the sidelines," Misha said. "Not to distract them while they're at bat or anything, but between innings. Only if we have something to make noise about," she added.

The phone rang while they were clearing the table. Misha sprang toward the phone, accompanied by a barking Lucy, who clearly judged Misha's movements as a signal that something significant was occurring. "I bet it's Daddy!" Misha announced.

"Don't tell him I'm here," Iris whispered, even though Misha hadn't yet answered the phone and Scott couldn't possibly hear her.

Misha looked bewildered. "How come?"

"I don't want him worrying about me. If you have to, you can say I came for dinner. That's all."

Misha shrugged, lifted the phone, checked the screen, and lifted it to her ear. "Hi, Daddy! Guess what? Nana came for dinner, and we made seafood stew."

Ellie sent Iris a reassuring look, then busied herself with the dishes while first Misha and then Abbie chatted with Scott. She eavesdropped on her daughters' side of the conversation, telling herself she was only trying to make sure the girls didn't leak any information about Iris's broken wrist. Scott *should* know about it, but Ellie had resigned herself to the idea that Iris ought to be the one to tell him.

Misha babbled about camp starting next week — "I'm gonna be in the oldest group. Maybe next year I can be a counselor-in-training" — and about her club, which was all-girl and beyond that she couldn't tell him anything because he wasn't a girl, and about the summer soccer season. She handed the phone to Abbie, who discussed clarinet lessons with her father. She wore a bright smile when she handed the phone to Ellie. Abbie rarely smiled that brightly for her. Only for Scott.

After drying her hands on the seat of her shorts, Ellie took the phone from Abbie. "Hi, Scott."

"So, you're available to talk today?" He sounded cheerful, but she detected a thread of annoyance woven into his tone.

"Connie was here yesterday. We were celebrating a big sale she just made." *And then I had to rush to the hospital to pick up your mother, but I can't tell you that.* She figured she could erase whatever resentment he had about last night's call by devoting tonight's conversation to him. "How are you doing?"

"I'm exhausted," he said. "I'm sore. I'm bored. Do you know how boring these midwestern states are?"

"People who live there probably think Massachusetts is boring," she said in the Midwest's defense.

"It's so flat here. And so windy. You can bike a hundred miles through farmland and never see a living soul." He sighed again. "Honestly, Ellie, sometimes I wonder if I should say I've done enough and come home. California doesn't need me to tell them how to protect their natural resources."

"Come home, then," Ellie urged him. *Come home and see what happened to your mother.*

"The thing is, California is facing an environmental crisis. They're using up their water. They've lost thousands of acres to wildfires."

"But they don't need you to tell them that," she reminded him.

"They don't need me to, but I'll tell them anyway." He sighed deeply. "I can't quit. I promised my followers I'd stop in every state in the lower forty-eight, and I can't let those people down. They're counting on me." His tone perked up as he continued. "You wouldn't believe the emails and tweets I'm getting. More than a hundred thousand people are following my journey online, Ellie. They're cheering me on. They want me to do this."

Just like idiots gathered at the foot of a tall building shouting, "Jump! Jump!" when a suicidal person stood on the roof. Ellie knew Scott wasn't suicidal, and by now she believed that the little orange flag on his Beast of Burden would keep him alive. Hell, a person could get injured just walking across her bedroom and tripping on a shoe.

But honestly, who were these hundred thousand people, telling Scott what to do? If he wanted to end his journey, he should end it. If he wanted to jump, he should jump.

On the other hand, maybe by biking past farm acreage in flat midwestern states, he was doing something important. He was training a spotlight on an essential issue. He was giving a hundred thousand people something to think about, and talk about, and tweet about.

"I've got to keep going," Scott declared. "Mike Rostoff — the guy who hosts the *Keep It Clean* podcast — wants me on again in a couple of days. It would be pretty lame if I did the podcast from Shelton."

Yes, because Shelton is such a lame town. Not at all worthy of being featured in a podcast hosted by the great Mike Rostoff.

"Ahh. I shouldn't sound so discouraged." He sighed again. "It's just been a long day. Thank God for the recumbent seat. If I was doing this on a regular seat, I'd probably be talking like a soprano now."

So he'd had a long day. All her days were long, some extending deep into the evening. Like last night. Or the night before. "You know what?" she said. "Come home. Screw the podcast. Screw the whole thing. You're tired, you're worn out, and there's plenty you could be doing here, even if it's too late for you to teach summer school. You could — " she stopped herself before blurting out that he could take his mother to her appointment with the orthopedist " — keep an eye on the girls and mow the lawn. And oversee the roof repair. That's happening next week."

"What roof repair?"

A flame of anger flared inside her. What was wrong with him? Was he so detached from home right now, so engrossed in his own grand adventure — or boring adventure, in the flat, windy farm fields of the Midwest — that he didn't pay attention to anything she said? "I told you about the tree limb that landed on the roof a couple of weeks ago. Remember? I patched the hole in the attic with your beloved tarp."

"Oh, right, right, right." He remembered the tarp. "So that still hasn't been fixed?"

"There were other houses with worse damage, and the insurance company dragged its feet processing the claim. But yes, it's being fixed next week. If you were home, you could deal with the repairmen."

For the next few minutes, Scott grilled her on whom she'd hired, why she'd hired that company, and whether Nakul really understood roof repairs. She reminded Scott that Nakul was a civil engineer and probably understood more about the construction of buildings than she and Scott combined. By the time Scott's interrogation was done, he sounded invigorated, not drained. Somehow, pretending he was managing the roof repair from fifteen hundred miles away gave Scott the energy he needed to continue his bike trip.

Well, she thought, good for him. He would not disappoint his hundred thousand fans.

She and Scott finished their phone conversation. He told her he missed her. But he didn't ask her about Shelton Cleanup Day or how Lucy was feeling or whether Ellie wanted to strangle Wayne. He probably missed her for sex, which was reasonable. He certainly didn't miss her as an audience, because she already was a part of his audience, listening to him on these calls. Besides, he had an audience in the six figures: his precious followers.

Shaking off her exasperation, she set the phone back in its recharging stand. Iris and the girls had migrated to the den to watch TV. She heard Abbie complaining to her grandmother about how her parents refused to subscribe to all the available streaming services, how the family of her friend Mackenna subscribed to KocawaTV and got to see lots of K-Pop videos. Misha bellowed, "K-Pop is stupid. I call it K-Poop." Iris mumbled something that indicated she had no idea what K-Pop was, but when Ellie peeked into the den, she saw her mother-in-law happily ensconced between her two granddaughters on the sagging couch.

She plucked Lucy's leash from the hook by the back door, and Lucy immediately sprinted from her favorite spot under the kitchen table to the door, her tongue hanging out as she panted blissfully. "I'm taking Lucy for a walk," Ellie hollered as she clipped the leash to Lucy's collar.

Not a long walk that evening. Not a walk to the nature preserve to see how many empty liquor bottles had been discarded along the path. Just a stroll around the block, a chance for Lucy to sniff every blade of grass in her path, a chance for Ellie to sort through her emotions.

Why did she resent Scott? He was her husband, the man she loved. He was smart and handsome and wonderful in bed. He took care of things like clogged toilets and broken roofs when he was around. He was a devoted father. He was doing something courageous, something important, something admirable. She should be proud of him.

She was...but somehow, his courageous, important, admirable adventure left her feeling diminished. Wasn't taking care of his mother and daughters important? Wasn't organizing a town cleanup admirable? Wasn't engaging in a battle with a developer who wanted to overbuild on a plot of land on Route 29 — and dealing, as well, with his obnoxious financial backer — courageous?

No podcaster wanted to interview her. No university wanted to broadcast her precious words on its campus TV station. No hundred thousand people wanted to read an online diary of her daily tasks and challenges.

What she was doing was just plain living her life, like all those hundred thousand people following Scott, like all those seven billion people living their lives on the planet Scott was trying to save.

Lucy spotted a squirrel, let out a raucous bark, and yanked on the leash. The squirrel dashed up the trunk of a maple tree and vanished into the foliage. Lucy didn't seem troubled by the squirrel's escape. She wagged her tail and peered up at Ellie, her mouth wide in the canine equivalent of a smile. Thank goodness she hadn't had any relapses of her stomach bug. She was healthy.

Scott could save the world. Ellie had saved Lucy — and the living room rug. Not a particularly courageous adventure, but a worthwhile accomplishment.

"Come on, girl," she said, giving the leash a gentle tug. "Let's keep walking."

CHAPTER NINETEEN

Saturday morning drifted in on a layer of oppressively muggy heat. Ellie outlined the day to Iris: Misha's soccer game in the morning, mowing the lawn in the afternoon. "If I were you," she said as she carried a tub of Greek yogurt, a box of Cheerios, and a bowl of blueberries to the kitchen table, "I'd stay indoors in the air conditioning all day."

"Oh, I'd love to see Misha's game," Iris said. "If it wouldn't be too much trouble."

As long as Iris didn't keel over from heat stroke midway through the second half, it wouldn't be too much trouble. Ellie would throw a folding lawn chair into the car's trunk for Iris to sit on.

Forcing herself to sip her black coffee, Abbie announced that she would stay indoors in the air conditioning. "It's too hot to think," she declared. "If we're not telling Dad about Nana's broken wrist, then we also shouldn't tell him we're cranking up the AC."

"Deal," Ellie said before Iris could intervene with any sort of defense of her son.

She was spooning some blueberries into her bowl of yogurt when the front doorbell rang. Iris and the girls all lifted their heads and peered around the kitchen, as if a doorbell ringing was the most unusual event in their lives. At seven thirty on a Saturday morning, it was kind of unusual, but not exactly shocking.

Misha raced ahead of Ellie down the hall to the front door and, as she'd been trained, peeked through the sidelight to see who their visitor was before she swung open the door. "Oh," she said, leaving the door shut and falling back a step.

Frowning, Ellie peered through the sidelight. Luke Bartelli and two boys she didn't recognize stood on the porch.

She opened the door. "Hello, Luke," she said, ignoring the quick rhythm of Misha's feet as she darted back through the hall to the kitchen. Like Misha, Luke seemed to have added at least an inch to his height since she'd last seen him in the crowd of well-wishers waving Scott off in May. His hair was scruffy, his T-shirt baggy, and his knees, exposed beneath the hems of his athletic shorts, had a grayish tint to them, a veneer of dirt that would require an intense scrubbing with a sudsy washcloth to eradicate. "Misha is... well, she's got a soccer game this morning."

"We didn't come to see Misha," Luke said, lowering his eyes as if the porch's floorboards fascinated him. Then he lifted his gaze to her again. "We were biking this morning and we saw your house and we thought —" he glanced behind him at the other two boys, who nodded bashfully "— maybe we could mow your grass. I mean, because Mr. Gillman isn't here to mow it, and we're trying to support him."

It was Ellie's turn to say, "Oh." Then she smiled. Luke might have wounded her daughter's feelings by barring her from his club, but here he was, offering to mow her lawn for her. "How much?"

"The whole yard," Luke said. "Front and back."

Ellie suppressed a smile. "I meant, how much do you charge?"

"We'll do it for free," Luke said. "To support Mr. Gillman."

That they would be relieving Ellie of a dreary chore would be more support for her than for Scott. But if they wanted to believe they were helping him and not her, she wouldn't argue the point. After all, she, like Misha, was a girl and therefore not aloud. Theirs was a men-only society. "Do you have a lawnmower or do you want to borrow ours?" She asked.

"I'll come back with ours," Luke said. "I sort of remember Mr. Gillman saying he had, like, one of those old-fashioned mowers that you just push. My dad's got a power mower."

So much for supporting Scott. Still, Ellie didn't care if Luke and his friends used a mower with a deafening motor that spewed pollution into the air. They were going to spare her from mowing the lawn. They could use whatever tools they wished. "If your parents say it's okay, it's okay with me," she told Luke. "We'll be out at Misha's soccer game this morning, but you won't need me at home to do this."

"Great. So we'll come back with the mower." Luke darted down the porch steps with his friends before Ellie could say anything more.

She closed the door and returned to the kitchen. "I hate him," Misha announced. "What did he want?"

"He offered to mow our lawn." Ellie lifted the phone and carried it into the living room as she punched in Sue Bartelli's number.

"Ellie," Sue greeted her cheerfully. "How are you? How is little Misha?"

"Not so little anymore," Ellie said, picturing Misha in the kitchen in her outgrown pajamas, her feet and ankles protruding from the hems of the thin cotton bottoms.

"Our kids are in growth-spurt territory, for sure," Sue agreed. "I'm sorry we haven't seen Misha in such a long time. Did she and Luke have a falling out?"

Ellie was surprised that Sue didn't know about Luke's having excluded Misha from his club. Then she decided she wasn't surprised at all. For one thing, Sue might not even know Luke had an exclusively male club of bike riders who worshipped Scott. For another, boys rarely told their mothers anything.

"One of those things, I guess," Ellie said, not wanting to criticize Luke to his mother. "Luke just offered to use your lawn mower to cut my grass. Is that okay with you?"

"Did he?" Sue laughed. "I don't know what he's up to, half the time. I'm glad this time he's up to something good."

"You think he's old enough to handle a power mower?"

"He mows our lawn, and he still has all his fingers and toes." Sue paused, then said, "I hope whatever is going on between him and Misha gets fixed soon. She's such a sweetheart."

Ellie wasn't sure that was quite the word for Misha, but she wasn't about to disagree. "I'd say Luke earned a few sweetheart points by offering to mow my lawn."

"You'll see," Sue predicted. "One of these days those two will get married and we'll be in-laws."

Maybe. Or maybe Misha and Luke would never reconnect. Maybe Luke would turn into an arrogant adolescent dude with dozens of girls getting crushes on him, and he would never look Misha's way again. For that matter, maybe Misha would mature into a striking beauty, and Luke wouldn't be able to find his way to her side through the throngs of boys gathering around her like bees around a blossom. Or maybe Misha would mature into an ardent feminist who would never waste a moment of her time on a boy who had discriminated against her in the past. Or she might discover, as she'd once wondered, that she was a lesbian because she used to be best friends with a boy.

Who cared what happened a year or two or five from today? Right now, Ellie would not have to mow the lawn. For that alone, Luke was a sweetheart.

Misha wasn't pleased. On the drive to the soccer field — she sat in the back seat so her grandmother could sit beside Ellie — she said, "How come Luke can use a lawn mower? You always tell me I'm too young to mow the lawn."

Before Ellie could respond, Iris answered for her. "You're a girl, Misha."

Ellie opened her mouth to object, but Misha beat her to it. "So what? Girls can mow lawns. Mommy was going to mow the lawn before Luke said he'd do it."

"Yes, but a lawn mower is heavy equipment. Luke's a boy. He's stronger."

"It's not that," Ellie interjected. She glanced at the rear-view mirror and saw Misha seated in her uniform, her arms folded across her chest, her legs encased in shin guards and knee-high socks, her lips curved in a decisive frown. "You can be a little . . . high energy." Ellie recalled Misha's final report card of the school term. "You can get carried away with your enthusiasm, and then you're not as careful as you need to be."

"I can be careful," Misha retorted.

"Well, maybe you can mow the lawn next time. Not with a power mower, though. With our reel mower."

"I'm not going to do it if Luke's doing it," Misha warned.

"Obviously."

"She's a girl," Iris murmured, as if she didn't want Misha to hear. "Can she even push that big mower around?"

"Of course she can," Ellie said in her normal voice. "So can Abbie, but Abbie refuses to do it."

"I'm stronger than Abbie," Misha declared.

Ellie wouldn't argue that. "You're tougher, too."

"And we're gonna win at soccer today," Misha predicted. "It isn't raining. I'm going to pretend the ball is Luke Bartelli's head, and I'm going to kick it hard."

"Sounds like a plan," Ellie said with a grin.

DAY THIRTY-EIGHT

Sightseeing!

Of course, sightseeing is a joy only if there are sights worth seeing. That's one reason we have to take better care of our planet: to preserve these places of beauty.

I'm in Colorado Springs now. Biking westward into the state, I encountered land that seemed as flat as Kansas — but up ahead are mountains. Not like those rolling hills we call mountains back home in Massachusetts, but towering, spiking, knife-edged mountains. Continental Divide mountains. When I first saw them rising up from the horizon, they were many, many miles away, but they seemed to be directly ahead of me, so close that one or two pumps on my pedals would bring me straight to them. And they seem to rise at a right angle to the ground, almost like the backdrop of a film. As it was, though, the climb was gradual. By the time I reached Colorado Springs, I was feeling the exertion in every cell of my body.

But man, those mountains are a sight to behold!

The elevation is something I have to take into account, not just because of my muscles but because the higher I climb, the thinner the air is. I'm taking it as easy as I

can, giving my lungs and my blood a chance to adjust.
I'm about a mile above sea level here.

Colorado Springs is a big military center, the home
of the Air Force Academy, among other installations.
We tend to think of environmentalists as hippies and
tree-huggers, but the military has a strong interest in
preserving and protecting our environment, as well. If
the planet degrades, it will lead to drought and famine,
which will in turn lead to huge migrations as people in
decimated regions search for more sustainable places
to live. And huge migrations will in turn lead to unrest.
Saving Planet Earth is essential for everyone, no matter
what side of the political divide you live on.

CHAPTER TWENTY

Ellie was in a chipper mood when she arrived at her office Monday morning, a few minutes past eleven. Misha had won her soccer game on Saturday morning, and they'd arrived home to find the lawn neatly mowed and raked, and no sign of Luke and his buddies — or their blood or body parts — anywhere on the property. Sunday had been rainy, but Ellie had thrown together a festive brunch — buckwheat pancakes topped with berries, and a pot of fresh Kona coffee that didn't prompt too much wincing from Abbie as she stoically drank a cup. In the afternoon, they'd all watched *Field of Dreams* together, although Ellie spent less time watching the movie than reading the Sunday *Boston Globe* and completing the crossword puzzle in the newspaper's magazine. The rain had ended by Monday morning, enabling Abbie to bike to her babysitting job for her first day of work, and Misha to her day camp, which occupied the town park adjacent to the community center, just a mile from the house.

Once the girls were on their way, Ellie drove Iris to the orthopedist's office. He took a few x-rays, declared that Iris would not require surgery, urged her to flex her fingers throughout the day, and fitted her wrist with a pastel blue cast. Ellie would have chosen a brighter color — lime green, or maybe hot pink — but it was Iris's broken wrist, and after dithering for several minutes over the array of colors and then apologizing to the orthopedist's nurse for taking so long to make a decision, she opted for a blue the color of a sunny sky.

Driving Iris back to the house, Ellie asked her to stay with her and the girls for a little while longer, at least until her next appointment with the orthopedist, a week away. "It's nice having another adult around," Ellie told her. "And Abbie and Misha love having you with us. And let's face it, Iris, as long as you've got that cast on your wrist, you can't drive."

"I'll think about it," Iris said. "I don't want to be a bother."

"You'd actually be doing me a favor if you stayed. The roof repair guys are supposed to start work on our house tomorrow. They're going to need access to the attic. If you don't stay at the house, I'll have to work from home so I can let them in and out."

"I wouldn't want to be a bother to the roof repair people, either."

"Honestly, Iris, you'd be more of a bother if you went home," Ellie said. "Then I'd worry about you being all by yourself."

"Oh, I'd feel terrible thinking you were worrying about me." She mulled over the invitation and said, "All right. I'll stay this week."

"You can stay longer than a week," Ellie told her. "Believe me, you won't be a bother."

Ellie was lucky. Some of the women she knew had dreadful relationships with their mothers-in-law. Connie...well, any woman who could produce a son like Richard Vernon had to be awful, and according to Connie, Richard's mother was awful. "She criticizes me constantly," Connie once complained to Ellie. "She says I'm after Richard's money and I'm wasteful with it, but then she says I'm a bad mother because I'm out of the house and earning money instead of in my kitchen baking cookies and waiting for Merritt to come home from school. And Merritt! Aren't grandmothers supposed to spoil their grandchildren? All she ever does is criticize Merritt's hair, her clothes, her makeup, her nose piercing..."

Ellie considered Merritt's grooming choices worthy of criticism, too, but she would never say so to Connie, or Merritt. She knew too well that if you told a rebellious teenager to stop rebelling, the teenager would only rebel more fiercely. And if you complained about a child to her mother, the mother would become defensive and resentful. If fate was kind, Merritt would outgrow her affectations in time. The hole in her nose would close up once she stopped wearing that pimple-looking stud, she'd let her hair return to its natural color, and she'd stop plastering her face with cosmetics from the Charles Addams Collection.

Thanks to Iris's doctor's appointment, that morning was a rare occasion when Wayne arrived at work before Ellie did. Ellie spied him through the open door between their offices as she crossed to her desk and roused her computer from sleep mode. Wayne was seated behind his own desk, his feet propped up on the blotter as he perused what could either be a vital document or a printout of the items his wife wanted him to pick up at the supermarket on his way home.

"Sorry I'm late," Ellie called through the open door as she stashed her tote under her desk and settled into her chair. "My mother-in-law needed to get a cast put on her wrist."

Wayne glanced up and gave her a smile that was at least fifteen degrees cooler than usual. "I'm glad you're here," he said. "Come on in. We need to talk."

If his smile didn't look so forced, she wouldn't find anything ominous in his request. He often asked her to join him in his office so he could inform her that he wanted her to discuss the month's budget with Miriam instead of discussing it with Miriam himself, or that she would have to explain to Chief Mulroney that the fire department would not be getting a new engine this year. But he usually had a jolly, host-of-the-party expression when he ordered her into his office. Not a rigid smile that was just shy of a grimace.

He gestured toward one of the visitor's chairs, indicating that she should sit. Then he swung his feet off his desk and leaned forward. The skin around his Adam's apple was pink and irritated. Razor burn, she would guess.

"Here's the thing," he said, his smile fading. "I need you to convince the select board to approve Carl Corrigan's original plans for the complex on the Mumson Farm property. The original number of units. The original driveway work. And screw the solar panels."

Ellie took a moment to collect herself. There were so many things wrong with his request, she wasn't sure where to begin. "The board has already approved the revised design. It has so much going for it."

"Carl and his financial backers are not happy with it. They need to realize a certain profit margin, and with the alterations approved by the board, they're going to fall short. They want to go with the original design."

"But the MEPA guidelines —"

"— Are *guidelines*," he completed her thought. "They aren't laws."

"They're good guidelines. They make the condo complex a sustainable project that won't damage the environment."

"Okay, look, I know your husband is doing that whack-job bike ride, and good for him. He can be the idealist, Ellie. You and I have to be realists. We're working in the real world. If the profit margin isn't there, the project won't get done. And then we've got that stupid parcel sitting there, empty, on Route 29 for another ten years. Do you know what I went through to convince Carl to build on that parcel?"

Many lunches at the Sycamore Acres Country Club, no doubt. "And now he's committed to that parcel," she said. "He's not going to abandon it. It's a beautiful piece of land."

"It doesn't earn us any tax revenue as long as it's sitting empty. We want it developed. We want to provide housing, especially for people who don't have kids to increase the burden on our school system. We want the project to happen."

"Of course we do." Agreeing with Wayne might bring this ridiculous discussion to an end. "That's what we all want."

"And the solar panels!" Wayne spread his hands skyward, as if imploring God to weigh in on the foolishness of passive solar energy. "Carl showed me an article that said they aren't cost-effective in New England because we don't get that much sunlight, or our sunlight isn't as intense, or it's at the wrong angle. Something like that — I don't know, I'm not an astronomer. But according to the article, it takes years for solar panels to pay for themselves in fuel savings in New England."

"So it takes years. Eventually they do pay for themselves. And the MEPA guidelines —"

"We already talked about the MEPA guidelines. Now we're talking about the solar panels. They're expensive."

"They've come way down in price."

"Not enough. Besides, they're ugly. Carl says if we don't use his original plans, he's not going to build the development."

"Potential buyers of his condos will be more inclined to purchase units if they honor the guidelines, and if the roads are properly graded. If we use his original plans, all the units are going to have flooded basements."

"What does he care about that? For one thing, the residents can buy insurance. For another, we have a drought every year. Didn't you get that email from the Shelton Water District? It said we should water our lawns only once a week because they're expecting another drought this summer."

"And in the winter, there will be snow, and in the spring there'll be runoff, and the basements will flood." She took a deep, calming breath. "Nakul and I worked hard on this. We evaluated every aspect of the proposal. He's trained to do this. He's a brilliant engineer, and these were his findings. I can't go to the select board and say, 'Oops, we were wrong.' That would be dishonest."

"We need this development, Ellie. It's for the town. You love Shelton, right? You want to pick up the trash? Great. Show your love for Shelton by convincing the board to go with the original proposal."

She loved Shelton enough to do the exact opposite. "The original proposal had issues. You know it. I know it. Carl Corrigan knows it."

"He's getting pressure from his investors."

"Richard Vernon knows it. They all know it. The board knows it. I can't go in there and tell everyone black is white and hello means goodbye."

"You have to," Wayne said. "Your job depends on it."

"My job?" Her breath caught. "You're saying if I don't do this, you're going to fire me?"

"I could replace you for less money than you're earning right now. We both know that."

Or the town could fire Wayne and not replace him, and save even more money. Ellie was already doing his job. He wouldn't be missed by anyone other than the colleagues he regularly treated to three-hour lunches at his country club.

"Look, hon, I'm sorry. Carl and Richard are breathing down my neck. We've got to get this project green-lighted, and this is the way they want it done." His smile was almost sheepish as he added, "I don't *want* to fire you."

Hon. He'd called her *hon*. She wanted to scream. If ever there was a time for a woman to be aloud, it was now.

But she couldn't. Her job was at stake. As long as Scott was gallivanting through Colorado on his recumbent bike, breathing the thin air and enjoying the scenery, she had to be the one earning money, paying for groceries, buying Misha clothing that she would undoubtedly outgrow in a matter of months.

She shoved herself to her feet, stalked out of Wayne's office, and closed the door behind her. Alone at her desk, she dialed Nakul's number. "Are you free for coffee?" she whispered when he answered.

"Ellie?"

"I can't talk any louder. Can you meet me for coffee?"

"It's almost lunch time."

"Then meet me for lunch."

Fifteen minutes later, they were seated in a café across the parking lot from Whole Foods. Ellie had no appetite, but she ordered a grilled cheese sandwich — the least expensive sandwich on the menu except for peanut butter and jelly — and a glass of water. Nakul chose a chicken Caesar wrap, which would have sounded delicious if Ellie's stomach weren't performing anxiety aerobics.

Nakul looked suitably concerned. "What's going on?"

"My mother-in-law broke her wrist," Ellie said. As if that was the biggest arrow in her quiver of worries.

"I'm sorry to hear that." Nakul shook his head. "They get older, our parents. I guess we get older, too. And without your husband here to take care of his mother —"

Ellie cut him off. "So I had to take her to the doctor today to get a cast put on her arm, and I arrived at work a couple of hours late. And Wayne threatened to fire me."

"Because you were taking care of your mother-in-law?"

"Because 1 convinced the select board to approve the version of Corrigan's condo development that we recommended. Not the original version. If 1 don't convince the select board to green-light Corrigan's original design, Wayne's going to fire me." The words tumbled out of her as if the dam holding them back had suddenly collapsed.

Nakul gaped at her, his dark eyes wide with shock. "Fire you?"

"Shh." She glanced around the café and was relieved to see no one she recognized seated within earshot. The waitress arrived at their table with their sandwiches, Nakul's iced tea, and Ellie's water. Ellie waited until she and Nakul were alone again before speaking. "He said he could save money by replacing me with someone at a lower salary."

"He's crazy." Nakul muted his tone. "He couldn't replace you for all the money in the world."

"You're sweet to say that."

"I'm serious. You do his job better than he does. He's an idiot. He calls me Nick."

Ellie sighed. Nakul had only spoken the truth. "1 can't lose my job. Scott isn't earning any money this summer. I'm the only income in our family." She took a timid bite of her sandwich. It wasn't bad. If only her stomach would stop gyrating from nerves. "But to go back to the select board and tell them to approve the original design..."

"That would be insane," Nakul said. He was clearly enjoying his sandwich much more than she was enjoying hers. "1 reviewed the project comprehensively. I'm an engineer. 1 can't lie about the topography of that parcel." He shook his head, then leaned forward. "1 can't lose my job, either. I'm not supposed to tell anyone this, but Mena is pregnant. She said 1 shouldn't breathe a word about it until she's three months along. Right now it's two and a half months. But she wants to take a year off once the baby is born. At least a year. Then *I'll* be the only income in my family."

"Would you alter your report if your job hung in the balance?"

He thought long and hard, frowning as he bit off a chunk of his sandwich, chewed, and swallowed. "1 could go back to private industry and make more money than I'm making now. But 1 would hate it. I love what I'm doing. I love helping to sustain a community and make it healthier. But then..." He shook his head. "If I altered my report, I wouldn't be making the community healthier. So I would be accepting a lower salary to do exactly what I don't want to do." He considered his words, then shook his head. "I don't know why that makes sense, but it does."

"You're smart, Nakul." Ellie hoped she didn't look as desperate as she felt. "Tell me what to do."

"You're smart, too, Ellie." He devoured another bite of his sandwich, then smiled. "One of these days, I'm going to learn to like hamburgers. We never ate beef growing up. My parents wouldn't allow it. I think you have to grow up with hamburgers to love them as an adult."

"Are you saying there's some Hindu teaching that can tell me what to do? We don't eat much red meat, either, but that's because producing red meat is detrimental to the environment."

"No Hindu teaching I can think of can tell you what to do in this situation," Nakul said sadly, then perked up. "Technically, you don't work for Wayne, do you? You work for the select board."

She shook her head. "He answers to them. I answer to him. They hired him. He hired me."

"Even so, they're the ones who approve the budget that pays our salaries, right?"

"Miriam writes the budget. Wayne hired her, too."

"He has too much power. Giving too much power to an imbecile is a bad thing."

"Is that a Hindu teaching?"

Nakul laughed, and Ellie forced out a chuckle, too, so he'd know she was joking. "You have to work around Wayne," he said. "Who's your strongest ally on the board?"

"Sonia. She gave me cookies the other day."

"She did?" He appeared indignant. "She's never given me cookies."

"Homemade peanut butter chocolate chip. But she's given cookies to Wayne, too. I think she likes me, but she also likes him."

"It's hard not to like him, unless you have to deal with him in a serious fashion. He's such a cheerful, amiable guy."

"When he's not threatening to fire you," Ellie said. She mulled over what Nakul had said about working around Wayne. "Sonia is really excited about the town cleanup. She's already lined up an army of friends and neighbors to bake cookies for the big event."

"So the only way I can get her cookies is to help clean up the town?"

"You've got to earn them, Nakul."

He grinned. "I was planning to participate. Now I have even more of an incentive. But sure — go to Sonia. Tell her you're getting pressured into undermining our legitimate evaluation of Corrigan's project. Tell her going with the original plan would be a disaster."

"Can I quote you on that?"

"Not by name." He gave her a doleful look. "I don't want to lose my job."

"Right." She couldn't blame Nakul for wanting to hang onto his job; he had a baby on the way. She already had her two babies, one of whom ate nonstop and wanted to learn how to mow the lawn. At least Abbie would be earning money this summer. Maybe she could support the family, if she didn't spend all her income on mascara.

"I'll talk to Sonia," Ellie said. "She's probably got the least amount of power on the board, but at least she's *on* the board. Maybe she can persuade the rest of the board to see things her way."

"She could bake them cookies," Nakul said.

Having even just an inkling of a strategy restored Ellie's appetite. As she and Nakul finished their sandwiches, they talked about how his wife felt — excited but mildly nauseous, according to Nakul, and already obsessing about nursery furniture — and what, besides cookies, Ellie planned to use to bribe volunteers to rid Shelton's streets and nature paths of litter. Ellie was glad to talk about Shelton Cleanup Day rather than Carl Corrigan's project. But as she and Nakul discussed dividing the town up into manageable segments for the volunteers to cover, and about the most appropriate locations for the public trash receptacles the town planned to add, one significant portion of her brain fixated on the understanding that she might not survive in her job long enough to see the cleanup through.

CHAPTER TWENTY-ONE

"**H**alleluiah!" Scott crowed over the phone. "It's so much cooler in the mountains! I'll take the strain of pedaling uphill any day to get out of that scorching heat."

"You sound revived," Ellie told him. She had to speak loudly; the roofing crew was still at work outside. They had completed the attic repair earlier in the day, and thank goodness Iris had been there to oversee things, because Ellie didn't want to risk being away from her desk a minute longer than it took to take a bathroom break. Wayne hadn't mentioned the previous day's conversation today, but he'd given her a few piercing looks as he strolled past her desk en route from his office to wherever he was going to waste time — probably the country club, but who knew? She didn't dare to ask.

Abbie and Misha had already taken their turns on the phone with Scott. Misha had ebulliently described her first two days at camp — she was in the *best* group, and her friends Eliza and Hayley were in her group, too, and they were going to write their own play for the performing arts unit. She didn't share with him what she'd shared with Ellie last night: that Hayley had gotten her first period and Misha had instructed her never to flush a tampon down the toilet, and then the two of them and Eliza wandered over to where a group of boys were playing basketball and they shrieked until the boys gave them puzzled looks and told them to shut up.

Abbie seemed to think that having a job aged her several years. She told Scott that the children she was taking care of were "dreadfully immature" but she hoped to "bring them along," whatever that meant. Ellie didn't hear what Scott said, but she heard Abbie's response, "I am not going to deprive them of their childhood, Dad. I'm just going to teach them the importance of using a tissue instead of wiping their noses on their clothing." That sounded reasonable to Ellie.

Iris, of course, refused to let anyone reveal that she was at the house, with her wrist encased in its pastel blue cast. Ellie assured her with a nod that she wouldn't reveal Iris's secret.

"I am revived," Scott confirmed. She strained to hear him over the constant percussion of the roofers' nail guns as they attached new shingles to the roof. She would have thought they'd stop working by now, but they said they were almost done, and the sun wouldn't be setting for another hour, so they wanted to keep going as long as they had enough light. "I've got an interview lined up with a local TV reporter in Grand Junction," Scott said, "and we're doing a big thing in Salt Lake City, with the evaporation of the Great Salt Lake and the toxicity of all that. Mike Rostoff wants me to do the podcast with him live from the Great Salt Lake."

"He's going to be there?"

"No, he'll be in Seattle, where he always is. But I'll be at the lake, discussing the deterioration of the basin and how it's affecting animal life in the region. And human life. What's that noise?" Scott asked. Evidently, he could hear the metallic chatter of the nail guns through the phone.

"They're finishing up the repair on the roof," she said.

"What repair?"

"I told you," she said, not bothering to disguise her exasperation. Sure, he was going to be on the local news, and on podcasts. He was going to save Utah from environmental Armageddon. But was the condition of his house really so easy for him to forget? "A tree limb fell on the roof during a storm a couple of weeks ago."

"Oh. Right," he said. "I'm sorry. The tarp in the attic. I remember."

She supposed he deserved a point for remembering, even though he really hadn't remembered until she'd reminded him. Again. What he remembered most vividly was his precious tarp, which the repair crew had removed and folded neatly for Iris because she couldn't fold it with one hand and because she'd made a pitcher of lemonade from frozen concentrate for them — apparently she could manage that with one hand. Even though the tarp was folded, Ellie could see the holes puncturing its four corners. If she were a better person, she would buy Scott a new tarp and surprise him with it when he got home.

She was not a better person. She was a person whose employment had suddenly become precarious because her boss wanted her to lie. If Wayne wanted the select board to approve Carl Corrigan's original design, he could make his own damned presentation to the board. He could attend their next meeting and sing the praises of poor drainage and the esthetic charm of cramming too many townhouses onto too few acres. Why did he think *she* had to do this?

Because he knew the select board listened to her. He knew they took her seriously. Either that, or he knew that withdrawing a report and presenting a different report would be embarrassing, and if someone was going to be embarrassed, he would prefer that it be Ellie and not himself.

"This whole group," Scott was saying, jolting Ellie's attention back to their phone conversation. "It was so cute."

"I'm sorry — what?

"The RE:CYCLE shirts! They saw them on my Wheeling and Dealing page and had some made up. Right there in the middle of Grand Junction. I felt like a rock star, you know? Like someone in town for a concert, and the audience shows up wearing shirts with my face silkscreened on the front and my concert tour schedule on the back."

"That's very flattering," Ellie said, forcing enthusiasm into her voice.

"So, how are things on the home front?" he asked.

She took a moment to consider her answer. They'd already discussed the roof repair, more or less. She couldn't tell him about Iris. She didn't want to tell Scott about Wayne's not-so-veiled threat undermining her employment security. "I'm coordinating a cleanup day for the town," she said, hoping she managed to keep her job long enough to run the event.

"That sounds like fun."

"Cleaning up isn't necessarily that much fun, but I hope we can make it entertaining."

"Cool."

Did he sound patronizing? Condescending? Or was she just hearing her own sour mood in his tone?

She considered sharing the other news in her life these days, news that wasn't cool or fun. Like her job situation. But what was the point of telling him? Maybe she wouldn't wind up unemployed. Maybe Wayne would come to his senses tomorrow and ask her to forget he'd ever mentioned the idea of advocating Corrigan's flawed design before the select board.

And maybe the sun would rise in the west.

But Scott was happy right now. He had groupies. He had another podcast scheduled. He was going to save the Great Salt Lake.

"That's about it," she told him. "I should probably go. I'm beat. I'm working too hard."

"Tell me about it," he said. "Biking two hundred miles in one day, at this altitude — well, like I said, at least it isn't too hot."

Not too hot at all, Ellie thought as she heard the air conditioner click on in the den.

CHAPTER TWENTY-TWo

"**H**i, Sonia — I need to talk to you."
Fortunately, Ellie had been able to arrive at work early the next morning. Wayne, as usual, was late, which allowed her to speak freely into the phone. She had been able to leave the house ahead of her usual time because Iris was there to oversee Abbie's and Misha's breakfast and send them on their way to their summer activities. Maybe it was Ellie's turn to apologize to Iris for depending on her to help with the girls.

But of course, Iris had apologized to her again that morning when Ellie reminded her to make sure Abbie and Misha wore their bike helmets and left for their respective obligations on time. "I wish I could do more," Iris had lamented. "I feel like such an imposition. Maybe I should think about going home."

"No!" Ellie assured her. "We want you here. And you can't drive. How will you be able to take care of things at home if you can't drive?"

"I could talk to the orthopedist about whether he thinks it's safe for me to go home on my own. I don't drive much, anyway, and I can ask my friend Grace to drive me if I need to be somewhere. I don't want to be burden to you."

"You are *not* a burden. Don't even think it."

Iris had subsided, and Ellie had sprinted out to the garage, climbed into her car, driven to her office, and phoned Sonia.

"If you want my peanut butter chocolate chip cookie recipe, I'm sorry," Sonia said. "It's a family secret."

Ellie allowed herself a polite chuckle, then said, "Actually, it's about something important."

"More important than cookies? I'm listening."

"I was hoping we could meet in person. Not in my office, though."

"Oh." Sonia took a moment to process this. "Do you want to come to my house? Howie is here, but I think I can convince him to stay out of our way. Trust me, Ellie, you do *not* want your husband to retire. Whoever said retirement led to the golden years wasn't a wife."

"Fine. I'll come to your house. I'll be there in fifteen minutes."

She wasn't happy about the prospect of Wayne's arriving and discovering her desk unoccupied. She didn't want to provide him with any additional excuses to fire her. She pulled a sticky-note pad from a desk drawer and wrote: *Had to meet with some people about Shelton Cleanup Day*, then entered his office and pressed the note to the center of his desk. He paid more attention to written notes than to emails or texts. Written notes, he once told her, seemed much more personal to him.

She decided this note wasn't really a lie. She and Sonia might discuss Shelton Cleanup Day when they were done discussing what Ellie intended to discuss.

She had to look up Sonia's address and enter it into her GPS, but she found the house without too much difficulty. Shelton had its share of winding roads and baffling street signage — an issue Nakul had been harping on for a year, questioning why some roads had identifying street signs at intersections and some didn't. Sonia's street was one that didn't, but Ellie found the tidy saltbox colonial. An older man in a faded Red Sox baseball cap, a baggy T-shirt, and Bermuda shorts that displayed his spindly calves and bright white crew socks was puttering around in the shrubs, armed with a pair of pruning shears. "You must be the lady from the town hall," he greeted her as she strolled up the driveway. "Sonia told me I had to stay outdoors and trim the bushes while you're here."

"They look terrific," Ellie said, gesturing toward the neatly groomed yews and spirea bordering the front of the house.

"They'll either look better or a lot worse by the time you're done meeting with Sonia," he said good-naturedly, escorting her up the steps of the brick front porch and opening the door for her. "Sonia?" he hollered into the house. "Your visitor is here."

Sonia's house reminded Ellie of Sonia herself: on the older side but well maintained. The living room walls were covered with satin-striped wallpaper, the sofa, chairs, and tables were classic colonial style, and the rug's pile had been flattened beneath years of foot traffic, but it was clean.

Sonia appeared in an arched doorway. "Hi, Ellie. I'm here in the kitchen. Come join me."

Of course. Where else but in the kitchen would Sonia be? Maybe after Ellie confided in her about her situation with Wayne, Sonia would reward her for her honesty and integrity with some homemade cookies.

To be sure, the kitchen smelled wonderful. Something was baking.

Sonia gestured toward the small table nestled into one corner of the room. "Have a seat. You want some coffee? I've got a coffee cake about to come out of the oven."

Homemade, Sonia-made coffee cake. Ellie nearly swooned.

She waited as patiently as she could while Sonia removed the cake, did her best to slice a couple of wedges even though it was still steaming, and poured two cups of coffee. Then she took a seat across from Ellie. "Now, tell me. Why all the secrecy?"

The cake needed to cool off. And Ellie needed to tell Sonia what was going on. "Wayne wants me to withdraw my report about the condo development on Route 29, and instead get the select board to approve the original design."

"Why?"

"He didn't tell me. But I suspect it's because he's buddies with Carl Corrigan and Carl wants to make a bigger profit." She took a sip of coffee. Not surprisingly, Sonia's coffee tasted better than the stuff she had brewed at home that morning. If Abbie drank this coffee, she might not grimace so much. "Nakul and I evaluated the original design and recommended the changes. The select board approved the changes. Now Wayne is pressuring me to go back and present the original design — and say Nakul and I okayed it."

"If Wayne disagrees with your report, why doesn't *he* defend the original design at our next meeting? Why does he want you to do that?"

"Because..." Ellie took a deep breath. She was confiding in Sonia. She might as well take this journey to its end. "Wayne wants to be liked. If he goes to the board and tries to sell you on a design you probably wouldn't approve, you wouldn't like Wayne so much." Another sip of that delicious, aromatic coffee gave her the courage to add, "Wayne is always asking me to do the unpleasant tasks he doesn't want to do."

"I see," Sonia said. She took a bite of her piece of cake and groaned happily. "This is so good! I got this recipe from my friend Mona. I'm going to tear up my old coffee cake recipe and just use this one instead. So moist!"

Unable to wait any longer for it to cool off — and Sonia hadn't seemed to burn her tongue on her piece — Ellie took a bite. So good. So moist.

As delicious as it was, however, she couldn't let it distract her from her mission. "I can't go to the board and present a report I consider incorrect," she said. "But Wayne is..." She sighed. "Really pressuring me."

"What kind of pressure?"

"He said I could be replaced by someone at a lower salary."

That got Sonia's attention. She leaned back in her chair and stared intensely at Ellie. "He's threatening your job?"

Ellie nodded. Actually speaking the words might make her curse, or burst into tears.

"That seems a little extreme." Sonia took another bite of her cake and issued a faint, happy moan at its goodness and moistness. "We'll have to discuss this at next week's select board meeting."

Ellie did her best to maintain a neutral facial expression. "Wayne will be at the select board meeting."

"Well, yes. We do have to hear his side of the story. The condo complex at the Mumson Farm is an important project. The town is counting on the property tax dollars it will generate. We don't want to see it fall apart."

Shit. The select board might just accept the original proposal for the development because they wanted the tax dollars. And given the opportunity, Wayne would twist everything around so Ellie would be blamed for trying to undermine the project. He would claim that she and Nakul had exaggerated the drainage problems and that she was pushing for solar panels only because her husband was on a cross-country crusade in support of environmental bureaucracy. She could already hear the growl of the bus's engine as Wayne pushed her under it.

"If you present this all in front of Wayne, he'll know I talked to you behind his back," she said, trying not to sound too pathetic. "He'll fire me for sure."

"Now, don't you worry about that." Sonia adopted her grandmotherly attitude. "We can always go into executive session if we need to exclude Wayne from the discussion. We'll get through this, Ellie. I'm sure it's all just a huge misunderstanding. Wayne would never want to fire you."

Hah! If Carl Corrigan and Richard Vernon told him to parachute from the roof of the Unitarian church, across the town green from the town hall, he would do it. If they told him to cheat on their golf cards and cancel Shelton Cleanup Day — a no-brainer. If they told him to remove Ellie because she was too problematic, he would fire her without a moment's hesitation.

"Don't you worry," Sonia said, her voice sweet and consoling. "We'll get this all straightened out. Would you like another slice of coffee cake?"

It was good. It was moist. But Ellie's appetite had vanished.

DAY FORTY-THREE

Things go well until they stop going well. Bike trips go well until a pothole the size of Montana takes out your front wheel and tire.

Well, okay. The pothole wasn't the size of Montana, but it was in Montana. And it didn't take out my entire front wheel. Just a few spokes. Enough to warp the rim, blow out the tire, and toss me onto the asphalt. I'm okay — just a few scrapes and bruises. I wish I could say the same about my bike.

Because of the Beast of Burden, I couldn't simply arrange for a car to come and carry my vehicle and me to town for repairs. I had to enlist a flatbed tow truck for the task. I did try to locate a bike club in the region; fellow cyclists always help one another out. But there was no internet access where I wiped out. I was lucky enough to have cell phone service. AAA came through for me.

So now I'm in the town of Baker. There's a bike shop here that does repairs, but they had to send out for parts. I'm stranded until the parts arrive. Fortunately, there are also a few hotels in town. Unfortunately, the one with an available room wasn't exactly cheap.

You've all been so generous with your contributions to my GoFundMe page. I can't ask you for more. But these repair and lodging expenses were not in my budget, so if you feel so inclined... I am beyond grateful. The link to my GoFundMe page appears below the photo of my sadly damaged bike. Thank you!

CHAPTER TWENTY-THREE

"**I**t could have been worse," Scott said.

"Of course it could have been worse," Ellie retorted. "You could have been killed."

"But I wasn't. And the hotel is really nice. Not as inexpensive as my usual motels, but they've got a pool. I was able to buy a pair of swim trunks at a local store. I couldn't swim in my biking shorts, with all that padding in them. They'd soak up the water like a sponge. So I splurged on trunks. Not that forty bucks is exactly a splurge."

In Ellie's view, the purchase of anything not essential qualified as a splurge. She wasn't a cheapskate, but right now, with her job teetering on the edge of a pothole the size of North America, even the purchase of a pair of swim trunks in some speck of a town in Montana — a speck big enough to contain a hotel with a swimming pool — seemed extravagant.

"The hotel also has a decent restaurant and a cocktail lounge," Scott told her. "I'm making the best of a bad situation, right?"

She tried to focus on the word *best*, not the words *bad situation*. "How much is all this costing?" she asked, praying that the bad situation wasn't too terribly bad. "Did people donate more money to your GoFundMe page?"

"About twenty-five dollars so far. Not enough to cover the damage. I've got a cushion, though. I did plan for things to go wrong. This was just a little more wrong than I'd hoped."

Come home, she wanted to plead. *My job is in jeopardy and I've got an extra mouth to feed with your mother here.* Iris didn't eat that much — nowhere near as much as Misha — and Iris was more than earning her keep, keeping an eye on the roof repairmen, welcoming the girls home from camp and babysitting every afternoon, letting Lucy out into the yard when she needed to pee or chase a squirrel, directing dinner preparations so Ellie could have a few minutes to decompress when she arrived home after work.

Earlier that evening, Ellie had driven Iris to her own house to pack up any perishables she had in her refrigerator and bring them back to Ellie's house. They harvested a half gallon of skim milk, a package of fresh mozzarella, some romaine lettuce and a few very ripe tomatoes that had made their way into that evening's salad, and from the freezer, a package of chicken thighs and a partially consumed tub of pistachio ice cream. Ellie hadn't bothered to take the loaf of white bread or the container of soggy-looking cole slaw. Her girls wouldn't eat those things, and they would probably keep until Iris was able to move back to her own home.

But she was still constrained by her promise to Iris not to let Scott know about the broken wrist. "Look what he's going through," Iris had said after she and Ellie had both read his most recent post about his accident in Montana. "He could have died."

Indeed he could have. Which should have alarmed and depressed Ellie, but mostly exasperated her.

She hadn't promised not to tell Scott about the pressures she was facing at work. But what would be the point of dumping her problems on him? If bad weather and mountains and nearly destroying his bike — and himself — thanks to a pothole in Montana weren't enough to bring him home, her own problems wouldn't bring him home, either.

Besides, he was on a mission. He was halfway to his goal. He was saving the frickin' world. What did her petty little problems about being blackmailed by her boss matter in the grand scheme of things?

Connie might not be the best person to confide in about her worries, but she couldn't share them with Iris, and certainly not with her daughters. Although it was nearly nine o'clock when she got off the phone with Scott, she dialed Connie's number. "Come on over," Connie invited her. "I'll open a bottle of wine."

"I'm going out for a little while," Ellie shouted up the stairs, where Abbie was practicing her clarinet rather lackadaisically, playing scales as if they were a dirge. Over dinner, she'd battered Ellie with demands about hiring a private teacher, and Ellie had said there would be no teacher until Abbie demonstrated she was truly serious about practicing her instrument. If this was her idea of practicing, Ellie would gladly save the fifty dollars a week her lessons would have cost.

Whether or not Abbie heard her mother, Ellie didn't care. Iris, the extra mouth she was feeding, would keep an eye on the girls. She was ensconced on the couch in the den, looking somewhat hypnotized by the television screen as Misha played a video game involving a white blob of a ghost that bounced over pyramids and collided with various birds and hammers, accompanied by tinkly synthesized music and muted explosions.

"I'm going out for a little while," Ellie repeated. Iris nodded, her gaze never shifting from the TV. "I'll have my cell phone with me if you need me. Don't let the girls stay up too late."

Iris nodded again, clearly too mesmerized by the video game to respond verbally.

Ellie arrived at Connie's house ten minutes later. The driveway to the Georgian colonial was paved with granite bricks, and the lamp on the portico above the front door was larger than Ellie's head. She pressed the doorbell and heard bells gong inside, as resonant as those in a cathedral tower summoning the faithful to prayer.

Richard answered. When he saw her standing on his broad brick porch, his face erupted in an oddly hungry smile. "Ellie," he greeted her, "feeling lonely this evening?"

She was, but she'd rather spend the next twenty years in solitary confinement at Walpole State Prison than allow Richard to ease her loneliness. "Connie is expecting me," she said coldly.

"Is that Ellie?" Connie called from the depths of the house. "Come on in, Ellie. Ignore Richard."

"My adoring wife," Richard said sarcastically, although he stepped aside to allow Ellie into the marble-floored foyer. "We could solve each other's problems, Ellie," he murmured, tilting his face so his lips were perilously close to her ear.

"I don't have a problem," she lied, then let out a breath of relief as Connie swept in from the hallway.

"I hope, for your sake, that that's true," Richard said ominously, his smile growing as hard as the paving stones in the driveway.

She didn't want to take his unspoken threat personally, but of course it was personal. He was in Camp Corrigan. He wanted his profit margins, and if he had to pressure Wayne into firing Ellie to get them, he would.

Doing her best to obey Connie's suggestion about ignoring him, Ellie followed her friend down the hall, through a kitchen so bright with white cabinetry and stainless steel appliances that it resembled a hospital's surgical theater, and out onto the elegant slate patio, where a glass-topped table held two wine goblets, a bottle of Chablis in a sterling silver ice bucket, and a plate of sliced cheese and figs with glinting silver toothpicks protruding from them. Citronella candles in cut-glass bowls illuminated the minifeast.

"I feel underdressed," Ellie joked as she settled at the table. Connie took a chair facing her. "I only came here so I could whine. I didn't know you were going to turn it into a party."

"What's a whine without some wine?" Connie poured the Chablis into the glasses. "Tell me what's going on. Mother-in-law problems?"

"No. Iris is a gem." Ellie took a sip of the dry, light wine. She realized she couldn't tell Connie about what was going on at work. Government issues, even on as small a scale as Shelton presented, needed to be kept confidential until they were resolved. And this particular issue involved Connie's husband to some degree. And Ellie's finances weren't critical yet. Even if they were, how could a woman who lived in a house like this understand why Ellie was panicking about a disaster that hadn't occurred, and might not occur?

She chose to focus on a subject Connie could relate to: "Scott had an accident with his bike. He's bruised but okay. The bike is a mess, but reparable. I'm just sick to death about this stupid trip of his."

"It isn't stupid," Connie defended him. "He's doing something so noble! How can you even use the word 'stupid' in the same sentence as Scott?"

Technically, Ellie had used it in a different sentence. "I don't know how noble it is," she said. "He's showboating."

"He's show-biking," Connie corrected her, then popped a fig into her mouth and sighed with pleasure. "How fattening are these things?" she asked, gesturing toward the plate. "They're so good, I can't resist them."

As always, Connie looked much too slim to be worrying about the calorie content of figs. "He's out there, basking in glory, getting cheered on by his followers," Ellie said. "He's asking them to contribute more money to his GoFundMe page. How does he find the nerve to do that? They coughed up all the money for this trip in the first place, and now that he's stranded in some fancy hotel in Montana while his bike gets repaired, he's asking them for even more money." If only Ellie had his nerve, she could set up a GoFundMe page for herself and the girls if she lost her job. *Suburban Boston mother of two got fired for doing the right thing. Please help her pay her mortgage. Her husband is currently enjoying the pool at a ritzy hotel in Montana, clad in his brand-new swim trunks, and can't help her.* How much money would that bring in? Twenty-five dollars from the same suckers who'd donated that amount to Scott's fund today?

"Okay, so you're pissed at Scott now," Connie said. "We're allowed to be pissed at our husbands. Me more than you," she added with a wry smile. "But still, he's a hero. You're married to a guy whose goal is saving the world. I'm married to a guy whose goal is doubling his income in the next two years, and he doesn't care how he does it. He'd happily destroy the world if that would accomplish what he wants."

Ellie wondered if Connie knew just how close to the truth her accusation was. Not that eliminating the solar panels from Corrigan's condo development would destroy the world... but in a sense, it would.

"Here's an idea," Connie said, taking a hefty chug of her wine. "I'm pissed at my husband. You're pissed at your husband. Why don't we swap husbands for a while?"

"And be pissed at some guy we're not married to?" Ellie chuckled, once again wondering if Connie had an inkling of Richard's insinuations about his willingness to alleviate her supposed loneliness. At one time his comments had seemed like silly, harmless flirting. Now they were more. She would bet good money that Richard was the impetus behind Wayne's threat. Wayne didn't have enough mental acuity or gumption to tell Ellie to change her report. He handed her orders, she obeyed them, and he expressed his gratitude and moved on. That had always been his modus operandi, until now. Until she'd learned that Richard was the chief financial backer of Carl Corrigan's condo development.

She acknowledged with a pang of sadness that Connie couldn't solve her problems. Not that she had expected her to, but it would have been nice to pass them along to someone else for a while. Someone who understood. Someone who empathized. Someone who didn't deify Scott.

Someone like the sweet, supportive Scott he could be when he wasn't trying to save the world.

CHAPTER TWENTY-FOUR

"Ⓘt's a sleepover," Abbie said, enunciating each syllable as if Ellie were hard of hearing. "Saturday night. It won't affect my work at all. I'll be home Sunday."

She had announced this plan over breakfast Saturday morning, as Ellie and Misha were racing around the kitchen, getting Misha's soccer gear together for her game in a town a half hour's drive away. Iris was doing a feeble job of rinsing the dishes and stacking them in the dishwasher with one hand, her other shifting around inside her sling as if it wanted to escape and help out.

"Who else will be there?" Ellie asked.

"Just Jocelyn and Mackenna and me."

"And Jocelyn's parents?"

Abbie rolled her eyes. "*Yes.*" As if asking a teenage girl whether there would be some sort of adult supervision at a sleepover was off-the-charts ridiculous.

"Mommy, we're late!" Misha yowled from the garage door.

Ellie waved a hand in Misha's direction to subdue her, then addressed Abbie. "Fine. You can sleep over at Jocelyn's house tonight. You'll miss Dad's call, though."

"He's on vacation." Sarcasm suffused Abbie's tone. "How come *we* never get to stay at fancy hotels?"

"How fancy can a hotel in a small Montana town be?" Ellie asked. The town had to be pretty limited, given the length of time it was taking the bicycle shop to obtain the parts required to repair Scott's bicycle.

"Fancier than any place *we've* ever stayed," Abbie retorted before sidling up to Iris at the sink and saying, "Thanks for the pancakes."

Ellie might have reminded Abbie that she, not Iris, had made the pancakes. All Iris had done was to suggest them for breakfast. But before Ellie could insist that she deserved most of the credit for having created their breakfast feast, Misha let out another screech. "Mom! Come on! If we're late, I'll miss the warm-up and I won't be allowed to play!"

She would be allowed to play regardless of what time she showed up for the warm-up, but Ellie didn't argue. She patted Iris on the back, grabbed her keys, and jogged across the kitchen to the garage.

Misha joined her team at the Framingham soccer field in time to make practice. She played most of the game, scored a goal, and made several solid passes. Her team won by two points. And when they arrived home, the lawn was mowed. "Some boys came around and mowed it," Iris reported. "They didn't ring the bell or anything. They just cut it."

"I'm old enough to mow the lawn," Misha insisted. "If Luke can mow the lawn, I can. I'm smarter than him."

She might be smarter than Luke, but she wasn't stronger. She could also be too . . . enthusiastic, as Ms. Gorshin would have put it. "Our lawn mower is a lot harder to push than Luke's," Ellie pointed out. "It isn't motorized."

"Then we should get a motorized one."

"Motorized mowers aren't good for the environment."

"I don't care. I want to mow the lawn."

Well, Ellie thought. Maybe she wasn't the only Gillman family member a little skeptical about Scott's obsession with saving the planet.

"We love the Earth," she said, and realized that was the truth. She did love the Earth, and Scott's mission to save it. She just didn't love that it was *his* mission. She wished someone else could be biking around the country, spreading the word, while Scott came home and earned some summer school income, and helped out with the kids and his mother. And mowed the lawn.

Since she didn't have to mow it herself, she took care of her grocery shopping for the week, stopping at Iris's house on the way home to empty the mailbox and make sure the property hadn't suffered in Iris's absence. Misha biked off to her friend Viveca's house, Abbie shut herself up in her room with her tablet, and Iris dozed in the den. Once the groceries were put away, Ellie took Lucy for a long walk.

On sunny July days like this, with a scattering of cottony clouds overhead, humidity low, and Lucy trotting along beside her, healthy and chipper and eager to establish dominance over every squirrel in the neighborhood, Ellie could let go of her resentment for a while. As she strolled around the block with her dog, she replayed last night's visit to Connie's house in her head. Connie idolized Scott; Richard hit on Ellie in his sleazily subtle fashion. It almost seemed like a suburban cliché, except that she and Scott didn't reciprocate their admirers' feelings. And Richard didn't really admire Ellie, anyway. He would probably hit on any woman whose partner was more than an arm's length away.

Was he the power behind Wayne's demands concerning the condo development? Was there a way to unplug Wayne from that power source? She wished she was better at strategic thinking. Nakul might be shrewder than she was, but not much. And anyway, his wife was pregnant. He wasn't going to attempt any risky, gallant moves to save Ellie.

She needed to defend herself. She needed to be loud.

Abbie sped through dinner that evening, eager to get to her friend Jocelyn's house for the sleepover. While still chewing her final forkful of three cheese tortellinis, she bolted for the stairs, leaving Iris and Misha to clear the dishes while Ellie located her purse and keys. "How come she doesn't have to help with the dishes?" Misha complained.

"Oh, I'll take care of it," Iris said, nudging her toward the den. "You go play your video games. I've got to earn my keep."

"You don't have to earn your keep," Ellie said, easing Iris away from the sink. "Go watch a movie with Misha. I don't want you to get your cast wet."

"*Field of Dreams*," Misha said as she sprinted into the den.

Good God, how many times was she going to watch that damned movie this summer? Probably as many times as she could until her father came home. Because, as Ellie heard her repeatedly explain to Iris, "It's Daddy's favorite movie."

Abbie pranced down the stairs, dressed in a gauzy blouse that floated around her torso and shorts that were just long enough not to be mistaken for panties. Her freshly polished toenails gleamed bright turquoise beneath the kitchen's overhead light, and the backpack she carried was crammed so full it bulged in spots. "You're just going to be there one night," Ellie said as she rinsed a plate and slid it onto the dishwasher rack. "What did you pack in there?"

"My pajamas," Abbie said. "Can you do the dishes later?"

"No. You can wait."

Apparently, Abbie couldn't wait, but she was forced to. She folded her arms and eyed the ceiling as if in search of a heavenly ally who would convince her mother that chauffeuring Abbie to her sleepover took precedence over rinsing marinara sauce from the dinner plates. But eventually, the sink was empty, the dishwasher was stacked, and Ellie drove Abbie to her friend's house. She watched Abbie hurry up the front walk, saw Jocelyn swing open the front door, watched Abbie disappear inside. The house looked well lit. A car was parked in the driveway. She hoped Abbie would actually get some sleep during the sleepover, and come home without too much mascara on her eyes and too much attitude in her behavior.

By the time Ellie got home, Amy Madigan was hectoring Kevin Costner about how their farm was teetering on the edge of bankruptcy while he was building his stupid baseball field. Ellie chuckled sadly to herself. To her mind, Madigan's character was the true hero of the film. She had her feet planted in reality. Costner's character had his feet planted in his field of dreams. Only in Hollywood could those dreams become more real than the reality.

Misha paused the movie when Scott phoned. She described her soccer game to him in elaborate detail, then told him about dinner and about how Abbie was at a sleepover and didn't help with the dishes. She seemed on the verge of letting slip that Iris was watching *Field of Dreams* with her, but Iris hurried into the kitchen and signaled her by tapping her index finger to her lips, and Misha nodded and instead informed Scott that summer camp was stupid but lots of fun.

Keeping Iris's secret seemed ridiculous. Misha could have divulged that Iris had come for dinner and was watching the movie without mentioning that Iris was also recovering from a broken wrist. But Iris looked hugely relieved by Misha's last-minute discretion. Once Ellie took the phone from Misha, she nodded to assure Iris that she would continue to perpetuate the secret.

She forced herself to listen patiently while Scott complained that the bike shop in Baker, Montana still hadn't gotten the parts the mechanic needed to fix his vehicle. "I'm falling behind schedule," he complained. "If I can't get to the West Coast soon, I'm going to wind up doing Nevada and Arizona during the hottest part of the summer. It's going to kill me."

"Then come home," Ellie said. "This is not worth killing yourself for."

"We're all going to die if the planet burns up," he said.

"So what is your plan? Are you going to martyr yourself for the sake of the planet?"

"I'm not going to die," he said. "I was exaggerating. Trying to get some sympathy."

She didn't have much sympathy for him while he was lounging beside a hotel pool. But she said, "Aw, poor baby. If you think you're going to die, come home."

"I'll come home," he promised, "as soon as I've finished this trip."

Great. And then he could build a baseball diamond in a corn field.

She went to bed at ten, tired from her long, busy day, tired from the anxiety that wouldn't stop gnawing at her, tired from her daughters and her husband and her mother-in-law and even Lucy, who had turned their afternoon walk into a two-and-a-half-mile trek. Sleep came easily, and Ellie was deep into a complicated dream about someone erecting a skyscraper on Route 29 while she wandered around the land it stood on, collecting the litter scattered around the base of the towering building, when her telephone rang.

"Mom?" Abbie's voice sounded small and distant. "You have to pick me up."

Ellie glanced at her bedside clock. One-twelve. The glowing digits on the clock face provided the only light in the room.

She cleared her throat, sat up, and blinked the litter-strewn skyscraper out of her brain. "Pick you up? From Jocelyn's house?"

"From the police station."

Ellie flinched. The last wisps of her dream evaporated with a jolt. "What?"

"I can't talk," Abbie said. "Just come and get me, please?"

"Are you all right? Are you hurt? Did something —"

"I can't talk," Abbie said again. "I'm using the police's phone because the police took my cell phone away." Ellie could hear irritation in her daughter's tone. "Not just mine. They took all our phones away."

"Jocelyn's and Mackenna's phones, too? Are they with you?"

"Yeah. Mom, I really can't talk right now."

"Just tell me you're okay," Ellie demanded.

"I'm okay." Abbie sounded weary, annoyed, upset, but... yes. Okay. Quite possibly in better shape than Ellie was at the moment.

Ellie cursed under her breath, then said, "I'll be there soon."

She hung up the phone, rubbed the sleep from her eyes, and shook her head to clear it. Her daughter was at the police station. Her not-quite-sixteen-year-old daughter, who was responsible enough to take care of two young children for several hours a day and get paid good money for it, and who got tapped for clarinet solos in the school orchestra... and who wanted to slather gallons of mascara onto her eyelashes. At the police station.

Pushing herself off the mattress, Ellie stumbled across the bedroom and groped through her dresser until she found a clean pair of jeans and a T-shirt. She walked out of the room barefoot, then noticed her naked feet and returned for a pair of sandals. She was brushing her hair in the bathroom when Iris appeared at the open door. "Is everything all right?"

Somehow, Ellie's mind registered that everything couldn't be all right because Iris's arm wasn't in its usual sling. It dangled at Iris's side, the cheerful blue cast striking Ellie as woefully inappropriate. "Did the ringing of the phone wake you?" she asked

"Well, that, and I heard you walking around. I'm sorry — I'm such a light sleeper."

"Don't apologize for being a light sleeper," Ellie said, then suppressed the urge to apologize for her own short-tempered response. Whatever foolishness Abbie had gotten herself into wasn't Iris's fault. It was Ellie's fault, because she was a derelict mother who had failed to raise her daughter properly, and now that daughter was in police custody. She sighed. "Abbie asked me to pick her up from the sleepover," she fibbed. "I doubt Misha will wake up, but I'm glad you're here so I don't have to leave her alone." There. That ought to make up for having snapped at Iris. "I hope this doesn't take too long."

How long would it take? she wondered as she descended to the kitchen, grabbed her bag and keys, and continued through the mudroom to the garage. Had Abbie been arrested? Would Ellie have to post bail? Would her daughter be hauled into court? Locked in a cell? Handcuffed? What the hell had she, Mackenna, and Jocelyn done? And where were Jocelyn's parents?

The streets were eerily empty at one-twenty a.m. Shelton was not known for its swinging night life. A light drizzle had begun, glazing the roadways, making them resemble stretches of black patent leather as the car's headlights reflected off the shiny asphalt. Ellie's eyes hurt.

The brightly lit police station made her eyes hurt even more. After driving past the dark houses, the dark stores and churches and the town hall, the glaring lights flanking the police station's main entrance assaulted her retinas. Wearing sunglasses into the building would probably make her look suspicious. The cops might arrest her, too. So, she simply blinked a few times and waited for her eyes to adjust.

For better or worse, she personally knew some of Shelton's finest. She often wrangled budget issues with the police chief. Maybe, if she promised him a new cruiser in next year's budget, he would cut her daughter some slack.

Then again, maybe her daughter didn't deserve any slack. Maybe she'd done something heinous and needed to be locked up.

Inside the building, the entry lobby was bustling, teeming with teenagers and adults and a few officers. She spotted Connie among the adults clustered around the counter behind a pane of bullet-proof glass where the night sergeant was posted.

"Connie!" Ellie maneuvered her way through the crowd to her friend.

Connie spun around, saw Ellie, and grinned. "You, too?"

"Me, too, what? I have no idea what's going on."

"From what I gather, there was a party at someone's house, some idiot whose parents were out of town. Half the high school was there."

A disheveled man who had buttoned his shirt crookedly — he must have gotten a middle-of-the-night bolt-of-lightning phone call, too — said, "Not half. Maybe fifty kids."

"And booze."

"Merritt was at this thing?" Ellie asked Connie.

"Why not? She's an idiot, too." Connie's gaze narrowed on Ellie. "I would have expected better of Abbie."

"So would I," Ellie muttered.

The night sergeant spoke, projecting his voice above the din of frantic parental chatter in the lobby. "We're giving most of the kids warnings," he said. "We wanted to scare the pants off them, and I think we've accomplished that. We've arrested a couple of juveniles who were apprehended trying to run away from the scene. We're going to process the rest of these teenagers and release them to their parents' custody in an orderly fashion. This may take a while, so be patient."

Ellie pretended to be patient. She listened as Connie described Richard's eruption when Merritt had phoned home. "He says I'm a terrible mother," Connie said.

"Right now, I feel like a terrible mother," Ellie admitted.

"Oh, please. Kids are kids. They do this shit. They go to unchaperoned parties and get wasted. Don't tell me you never did anything like that when you were a kid."

Ellie had broken a few rules in her youth, but none that had ever landed her in a police station.

"Then," Connie continued, "Richard starts in on her hair, and her clothes, and how he wants to ship her off to some military academy. Do they have military academies for girls? Not West Point, but high school level."

"I have no idea," Ellie said. "I can't imagine Merritt thriving in that environment."

"Or a private boarding school, so she'll be someone else's problem. Those were his words. I swear, if he sends her away, I'm filing for divorce."

Eventually, Ellie heard Abbie's name called. She gave Connie a quick hug and worked her way over to the night sergeant's desk. She signed some papers, stood silently while a petite police officer with a ponytail — obviously a recent hire, stuck on the night shift — lectured Abbie for a few minutes and handed her her cell phone, and then Ellie and Abbie were allowed to leave.

Ellie didn't inspect Abbie until they were outside, under the overhang above the main entrance. The drizzle had increased to a full-fledged rain, and in the blazing light Abbie looked small and pale, still in her skimpy shorts and gauzy blouse. Her lashes were caked with mascara, some of which streaked down her cheeks like inky tears.

Ellie dug a tissue from her purse and handed it to Abbie. "Wipe your cheeks," she said.

They didn't speak again until they were inside the car. Their hair dripped from the rain, and their shirts stuck to their torsos, but the July night air was warm enough that Ellie didn't feel a chill. Besides, she was boiling inside. Burning. An inferno of rage and fear, relief and grief.

She turned on the engine, clicked the windshield wiper switch, and twisted to face Abbie, seated beside her. "It was Jocelyn's idea to go to the party," Abbie said, her voice a blend of remorse and defiance.

"You're going to blame Jocelyn for your bad choice?"

"Well, Mackenna and I were her guests, at her house. What were we supposed to say?"

"You were supposed to say, 'No, Jocelyn, it's an unchaperoned party. Let's not go.'"

"I didn't know it was unchaperoned."

"Don't bullshit me," Ellie said.

Abbie sighed. "I wanted to fit in," she murmured, her voice breaking.

All right. Abbie was no longer bullshitting Ellie. "How much did you drink?"

"One can of beer. I didn't like it."

"But you drank the whole can?"

"I wanted to fit in," she repeated.

"Maybe," Ellie said, "you should try to fit in with people who don't wind up at the police station at one thirty in the morning." She backed out of her parking space, then asked, "So you didn't like the beer?"

"It tasted worse than black coffee."

Ellie disguised her grin.

"Mommy?" She sounded young and plaintive, no longer the tough teenager guzzling booze at an unchaperoned party. "Don't tell Dad about this, okay?"

Ellie's grin evaporated. "He's your father."

"I know, but..." She sighed brokenly, her breath catching on the edge of a sob. "I mean, it's really embarrassing, and I know what I did was wrong, and maybe if I'd run away from the party when the police showed up, I wouldn't have gotten caught. But I didn't run away because I thought running away was the wrong thing to do. And I'm really sorry. And if you want to ground me or whatever, I mean, okay. But I just..." Another deep, splintering sigh. "Dad's all the way out there in Montana, and there's nothing he can do about this anyway, and we're like — you know, we're the girls here. You and Nana and Misha and me. And Lucy. It's like our own club. The Girls Aloud or whatever. Dad isn't in our club. He doesn't have to know."

Ellie's impulse was to point out that, while Scott wasn't one of the girls, he *was* Abbie's father, with a strong interest in her actions and activities, both good and bad. But she checked that impulse. As Abbie had pointed out, he was in Montana. He'd left the family for the summer to pursue a mission he felt was more important than staying home and being an integral part of the family.

He wasn't in the club.

"I won't tell him while he's out there biking," *and saving the freaking planet*, Ellie almost added. "When he gets home...we'll see."

Abbie nodded. "Thank you," she whispered.

Those two words, uttered so softly, were as loud as a girl — as *this* girl, Ellie's fragile, frightened, beautiful-despite-her-overabun-dance-of-mascara daughter — needed to be.

CHAPTER TWENTY-FIVE

Falling back to sleep at two in the morning was impossible. Ellie lay in the big, empty bed, her legs tangled in the sheets and her brain fueled by adrenaline. Abbie was safe, tucked into her own bed after, at Ellie's insistence, scrubbing off her makeup. All was well. There was no reason for Ellie to be plagued by insomnia.

Except.

It wasn't as if she were unprepared for her daughter's adolescence. Abbie had been easing into the usual array of teenage behavior for months: the demands, the sarcasm, the hormonal mood swings, the histrionics — and the occasional bursts of heart-melting kindness, like urging Misha to make noise when Misha had been so upset about Luke's no-girls-allowed club.

Tonight's escapade didn't fall into the heart-melting kindness category. But it could have been much worse than it was. Abbie hadn't been arrested. She wouldn't have a police record. She hadn't consumed enough alcohol to engage in unprotected sex or wind up in the hospital having her stomach pumped. If she'd been honest in her appraisal of the beer she'd consumed — no doubt a cheap, no-name brand that tasted like carbonated battery acid — she wouldn't be indulging in many beer blasts in the foreseeable future.

Yes. It could have been much worse.

Except.

It was at moments like this, just as it was at moments when her daughters did something magnificent, something splendid, something that convinced Ellie she wasn't the world's worst mother, that she wanted to share her thoughts and feelings with Scott. He was her husband. He was Abbie's and Misha's dad. He was supposed to be present for the peaks and valleys, the highs and lows of the ongoing drama that animated their family. If Ellie had wanted an absentee father for her children, she could have married a hot-shot executive who had to fly to some other continent every few weeks to do a deal or network with other hot-shot executives.

But besides the fact that she loved Scott because he was Scott, she loved him because he was a teacher. He was around. He worked reasonable hours and ate dinner with the family every evening. He attended the girls' soccer and volleyball games and school concerts. He curled up on the saggy sofa in the den, with one arm around each daughter and a bowl of popcorn balanced in his lap, and watched *Field of Dreams* with them.

Except that now he didn't do any of those things. Now, on a night when Ellie really needed him, he wasn't here. He was somewhere else.

A vibrator wouldn't have helped. She wasn't in that kind of mood. What she wanted was a pair of strong arms around her, a reassuring kiss on her cheek, Scott's familiar voice murmuring, "It's okay. Abbie is safe. It could have been worse."

Instead, she had to tell herself those things, without the benefit of strong arms around her. She had to tell herself over and over, *it's okay.*

And she couldn't sleep.

By tacit agreement, Ellie and Abbie both seemed to understand that Abbie's near arrest was not an incident about which Misha and Iris needed to be informed. Over a Sunday brunch of French toast that Iris attempted to make one-handed and a very sleepy, sluggish Ellie wound up preparing, Misha asked why Abbie's bedroom door was closed. "She left it open when she went to Jocelyn's house yesterday."

Ellie responded that Abbie hadn't felt well and Ellie had brought her home. "She's resting now," Ellie said, and indeed Abbie was. She didn't emerge from her bedroom until a few minutes past noon.

Ellie could have used a long nap, herself, but she had three loads of laundry to run, and she discovered that the sack of kibble in the pantry was nearly empty, so she had to race to the store between loads two and three to restock Lucy's food supply. After a dinner of take-out pizza — not particularly healthy, and if she'd made the pizza herself she could have saved a few dollars, but she was too tired to care — she wound up falling asleep on the sofa in the den while doing the crossword puzzle in the Sunday *Globe Magazine*. "Wake up, Mommy!" Misha bellowed into her ear at around nine o'clock. "It's bedtime!"

It was Misha's bedtime, but Ellie went to bed not long after saying good night to Misha. She slept for nine hours and felt almost human by Monday morning. Abbie looked almost human, too. Her eyelashes weren't cosmetically enhanced when she bounded down the stairs, dressed in a sedate polo shirt and shorts that covered a reasonable portion of her thighs. She was smiling and chatty and didn't wince as she drank her coffee. One would think she had never seen the inside of a police station in her life.

Good for her, Ellie thought as she pulled into the parking lot beside the town hall. Ellie could not shake her own recent memory of seeing the inside of a police station, but she needed to put that memory into deep storage. She needed to remain focused on her job — assuming she didn't walk into her office and find Wayne hovering at her desk, demanding that she write and sign a letter of resignation.

She also had to pick up a crumpled page from a supermarket advertising circular, an empty paper cup with the Dunkin' logo printed across it in bright pink, and a flattened ginger ale can from the asphalt outside the building's side door. How long would the town have to wait to get the new public trash receptacles installed? Did the trash collection company intend to delay until Shelton Cleanup Day to install them? Why not install them now?

At least there weren't any empty liquor bottles littering the parking lot. Recalling the evidence of a booze party she'd found on the nature trail a couple of weeks ago, she wondered if the creeps who had left those bottles on the trail had been at the unchaperoned party Abbie, Mackenna, Jocelyn, and Merritt had gone to on Saturday night. God help Abbie if she wanted to fit in with *them*. They were litterbugs. As far as Ellie was concerned, despoiling a nature trail with litter was a greater sin than underage drinking.

She tossed the trash she'd picked up outside the town hall into the waste bin in the foyer, then strode down the corridor to the new wing, silently exhorting herself to hold her head up and her shoulders square. She would not enter her office expecting the worst. Fate would not be so cruel as to have her fired less than forty-eight hours after she'd had to pick up her daughter at the police station in the wee hours of the morning.

She was relieved that, unlike her imagined worst-case scenario, Wayne was not looming over her desk, his foot poised to kick her to the proverbial curb — or the literal one, where she would join whatever litter she hadn't picked up on her way into the building. Of course he wasn't in yet. It was a few minutes before nine a.m. He never arrived at work that early.

Still, she felt uneasy and a little wary as she settled at her desk and tapped her computer to life. As always on a Monday morning, more than twenty emails awaited her attention, but none were from Wayne or any members of the select board. Not even from Sonia, who could have sent Ellie a reassuring note listing all the many reasons the select board loved Ellie and the steps they would take to protect her job status. Sonia could have even sent Ellie a note saying she was baking a fresh batch of peanut butter chocolate chip cookies and would drop some off for Ellie later that day.

No baking. No reassurance. But no message informing Ellie that she had been given the axe, either.

At nine thirty, she went upstairs to meet with Miriam in the treasurer's office. Miriam didn't look at her strangely, edge away from her as if she were contagious, or mention that she'd been asked to screen applicants for Ellie's job, so Ellie left Miriam's office feeling marginally more optimistic. When she returned to her office, however, the door connecting it to Wayne's inner sanctum was still closed. He should have arrived at work by now. Forty-five minutes late was about average for him. He should be here.

His door remained closed while she phoned the trash service Shelton used to inquire when they would start positioning public trash receptacles around town. It remained closed while she contacted several local stores that had agreed to sponsor Shelton Cleanup Day by posting printed signs in their windows, funding water stations, and in the case of Steuben's Sporting Goods, providing water bottles with bright yellow "S's" printed on them, standing for either Shelton or Steuben's — Ellie wasn't sure and it didn't really matter. Free water bottles were free water bottles.

Wayne's door remained closed while she took a call from the town's water district office to discuss updated algae tests and chlorine levels — something Wayne was supposed to oversee, only he had somehow neglected to oversee it. It remained closed when she fielded another call, this one from Nakul.

"You're still there," he half asked, half declared when she answered her phone.

"Not fired yet."

"This is a good thing."

They agreed to meet for lunch at a local café. She contemplated how much her lunch would cost and chastised herself for having failed to bring a cup of yogurt and an apple from home to save money. But she needed Nakul's friendship and support, even if only to munch on half a sandwich — she asked her server for a bag to save the other half, which she would bring to the office for lunch tomorrow, assuming she was still employed — and listen to him talk about his wife Mena's nausea, the water table beneath Route 29, and Wayne's general asshole-ness.

When she returned to her office after lunch, the door to Wayne's office was open and the room was empty. Was he avoiding her because he was ashamed of himself? Or because he didn't want to confront her until he had all the paperwork lined up for her termination?

Did he even have the time, energy, or professional skill to fire her? He was always asking her to do tasks that ought to be his responsibility. Maybe he was going request that she fire herself.

He finally appeared, in person, at around quarter to five, as she was reviewing the revised algae-testing schedule the water district director had sent her. Wayne entered her office and gave her the sort of smile a person might manage after a bout of stomach flu — a thank-God-I'm-not-puking-anymore smile. "Busy day," he said to her.

She didn't bother to smile back. "Me, too," she said, her gaze fixed on the calendar on her computer screen.

"Don't come to the select board meeting this week," he said abruptly.

She peered up at him then. As always, he had on a collared golf shirt and twill trousers that were belted one hole too tight, emphasizing the slight swell of his paunch. His eyes appeared weary, and that phony smile sent her anxiety level into the stratosphere.

She hadn't intended to go to the select board meeting, but he had no right to forbid her attendance. She couldn't let him cow her. She had to be loud. "The state's open meeting law means anyone can attend any select board meeting. If I decide I want to go, I'll go."

Her response seemed to surprise him. "Carl's condo development is on the agenda," he said. "You've already presented your report. You don't need to be there."

"You don't want me to hear your version?" she goaded him, surprising herself.

He faltered for a moment, then smiled again, that plastic, sickly smile. "Come on, Ellie. You know we disagree about this. I don't want a showdown at the meeting." He started toward his office, then paused and pivoted to face her. "You told me you were named after a First Lady. I don't remember which one."

"Eleanor Roosevelt," she reminded him.

"Right." He nodded, as if he'd known that all along. "First Ladies stand aside when the president takes over. You need to remember that."

She might have retorted that Eleanor Roosevelt had helped Franklin run the country, that she'd been called his eyes, ears, and legs. That she'd been a journalist, a delegate to the United Nations, a champion of racial equality and women's rights. That she had hardly stood aside.

But if she said all that, her employment might not last until the select board meeting on Wednesday. So she simply shrugged and swiveled her chair to return her attention to her computer monitor. The algae testing times and dates were not all that interesting, and the rest of her calendar was filled with meetings, deadlines, and timelines for Shelton Cleanup Day. But she studied it fervently, those many neat rectangles filled with text, as if she had to memorize her schedule all the way through the end of the year.

Once Wayne was safely inside his office, she locked her desk — not that she had anything incriminating or valuable in it, but she wouldn't be surprised if Wayne poked around in her drawers in search of evidence that she'd filched something from the supply cabinet or fudged the totals on one of the budget reports, so he'd have grounds to fire her — and departed for home. On the drive, she realized that, first lady or not, she really didn't want to attend the board meeting. What would she do there, besides observe? If Wayne misrepresented the specs on Carl Corrigan's subdivision and she challenged him from her chair in the audience, the breach of protocol might do her more harm than letting Wayne present an inaccurate report. This was Shelton, after all, not Washington, D.C. Small-town governance relied on congenial relations, mutual respect, and peaceful resolutions to every major issue.

She could not imagine a peaceful resolution to getting fired.

But maybe it wouldn't come to that. Maybe the board would tell Wayne they preferred Ellie's report to his. Or maybe they would prefer his, but he would realize that if he fired her, he might have to do his own job, evaluating the tax receipts, dispensing bad news about sidewalk snow plows, and working on engineering reports with Nakul, because she wouldn't be there to do these things for him. Maybe she and Wayne would simply agree to disagree about Carl Corrigan's condos and Richard Vernon's financing, and move on. And have a festive Shelton Cleanup Day, complete with home-baked cookies.

And maybe she'd drifted into *Field of Dreams* territory, believing that if she wanted a peaceful resolution, it would come.

DAY FORTY-EIGHT

Walla Walla!

Honestly, who wouldn't want to visit a city named Walla Walla? It's arguably one of the best names of any town in the country. And after my long sojourn in Baker, Montana, I was glad to be able to cruise through that state and a sliver of Idaho and tick a couple more states off my list.

Walla Walla is an agricultural center, which means that — like all of us — the residents of Walla Walla must pay close attention to anything that might threaten the environment. This used to be a major wheat producing area, but now the region is filled with orchards and vineyards. And onions! This is the home of Walla Walla Sweet Onions, the official state vegetable of Washington. I can't believe I just missed the annual Walla Walla Sweet Onion Festival by days. But there are plenty of farmers' markets here, and I plan to sample one of those sweet onions. Send breath mints my way!

The new front wheel on my bike is performing smoothly. It's too bad the repair took as long as it did, but it — and I — are both as good as new. Thanks again to those of you who were able to contribute a little extra to my GoFundMe page. I appreciate your generosity more than you know.

Below you'll see a photo of me, with my bike and the Beast of Burden, in front of one of the wineries here in town. If I'm sampling the local sweet onions, I may as well sample the local wine, too, right?

CHAPTER TWENTY-SIX

The morning after the select board meeting, Ellie entered her office to find not Wayne hovering beside her desk, dismissal paperwork clenched in his pudgy fingers, but Connie. She was clad in her real-estate-agent attire — a tailored blouse, tailored trousers, an elegant silk scarf looped around her throat to hide the noncrepe-y skin of her neck. Ellie's smile at seeing her friend faded as she absorbed Connie's stern expression.

"Hey," she said, sauntering across the room to her desk. "You're out and about early."

"I have a relo client meeting me at nine thirty," Connie said, no warmth in her tone. "But first we have to talk."

"Sure," Ellie said cautiously. Brusque and demanding was not Connie's default attitude. Ellie waved Connie toward one of the visitor chairs. "Have a seat."

"Not here," Connie said, her gaze darting toward Wayne's empty office. Evidently, she expected that he might show up within the next half hour. All things being equal, he might.

Ellie gazed around. She supposed they could use the conference room, but someone else might have a meeting scheduled there. They could shut themselves inside the ladies' room, but that seemed terribly high-school-ish, and what if one of the building's other denizens had to pee?

"Do you want to go outside?" she asked Connie.

"It's so hot." Connie sighed. "We can sit in my car. I'll run the AC."

Allowing a car to idle just to keep the air conditioning on struck Ellie as an environmental sin. But the upscale leather upholstery of Connie's Mercedes was more comfortable than the chairs in her office. And the air conditioning was pumping away in the town hall, anyway. What was a little more air conditioning? If Scott ate enough Walla Walla sweet onions — or drank enough Walla Walla wine — that might balance the ecological scale.

She followed Connie down the hall and out of the building, automatically surveying the parking lot for trash as they walked in silence to the car. The asphalt was already gummy in the July heat, and the sun glaring off the glass and chrome of the parked cars singed Ellie's retinas. Connie aimed her fob at her car and pressed a button to unlock the doors.

"Okay," Ellie said once they were both settled in their bucket seats and the air conditioner was blasting. "What's going on?"

"What are you doing with Richard?" Connie asked, her voice steely.

Ellie blinked, then shook her head. "What am I *doing* with him?"

Connie nodded grimly.

"He wants me to retract a report I prepared on that condo development he's financing on the Rumson Farm property on Route 29. He said the changes I requested were going to cut into his profit margin. He gave me a little Econ 101 lecture about it."

Connie eyed her dubiously.

"Connie." Panic nibbled at Ellie's nerves. She shook her head again. "What does *he* think I'm doing with him?"

"Your boss asked him to attend the select board meeting last night. He said Wayne was struggling to explain the original proposal to the board, so Wayne asked Richard and the developer — what's his name? Culligan?"

"Corrigan," Ellie corrected her.

"Whatever. Wayne asked them to explain why the original design was better than what you concocted."

"I didn't concoct —"

Connie cut her off. "Richard told those people — and there were about twenty people in the audience, plus the members of the select board — that you were demanding all these costly changes because you were romantically interested in him and he rebuffed your advances, so you were taking revenge on him."

"What?" Ellie's shriek filled the car's elegant interior. "He said that?"

Connie narrowed her gaze on Ellie. "I heard about it from three people who were there, sitting in the audience."

"That's ridiculous!" Ellie might have informed Connie that Richard was the one who'd made advances on her, but Connie was already so angry — so unfairly, unreasonably angry — at Ellie, she didn't want to inflame her further. "Why would I come on to him? I'm married to Scott. You tell me yourself, all the time, what a saint Scott is."

"And right now, he's thousands of miles away, right? He's been gone for months. Maybe you're a little lonely."

"Oh, for God's sake! How can I be lonely? I've got a house full of people. My kids, my mother-in-law, my dog . . ." She didn't mention her occasional sleepless nights, or her wish that Scott was in bed beside her, making love with her — or shouldering the daily burdens of family life with her.

"Richard may not be a saint, but he's wealthy," Connie noted. "Maybe you're tired of making ends meet on a teacher's salary and whatever the town is paying you. I don't know."

"This is insane," Ellie said, relieved that she wasn't shrieking anymore. It *was* insane. She needed to address it the way a sane person addressed something that was insane. Calmly. Reasonably. Sanely.

"Richard said you were envious of our house. Yours has a hole in the roof. A tree went through it."

"It's been repaired," Ellie told her. "And it was caused by a tree limb, not a whole tree. A storm blew the limb onto the roof. That could happen to your big, fancy house as easily as it could to mine."

"And your plumbing," Connie went on. "You can't even flush a tampon down the toilet without causing a flood."

Ellie gaped at Connie. "How on earth did you hear about that?"

"Abbie mentioned it in school. She blamed Merritt for having explained tampons to Misha."

"Misha knew what tampons were. And yes, Merritt told her she should experiment with them, which was stupid because she doesn't need them yet. And yes, the toilet got clogged, and we fixed it. Do you honestly think I'd make a pass at your husband because I had to learn how to use a plunger?" She suspected Richard would not have been able to unclog the toilet as well as she had. He would probably have paid a plumber a few hundred dollars to fix it. He had money to burn, and he wouldn't want to sully his pampered, golf-club-swinging hands performing such labor. She wondered if he even knew what a plunger was.

She took a deep breath. The car's air conditioning was blasting now, chilling her. Or perhaps it was this conversation that was sending chills the length of her spine. "Connie. I don't know what's upsetting me more — that Richard would lie about me at a select board meeting in front of a bunch of people, or that you would believe him. Does he want to make money on that damned condo project? Yes. Will he make money if they build the development the right way, so the units don't flood and so there'll be some spacing between them, and with solar panels to make them more energy efficient? Yes. Maybe not as much money as he'd make if they built the condos according to Carl Corrigan's original specs, but his firm will make a profit." Another deep breath. "I didn't invent my report off the top of my head. I worked with Nakul Pawar, the town engineer. We inspected the property. We discussed our findings with Carl. We came up with a workable plan. I even gave you a heads-up so you could see if you might be the listing agent for the units. How on earth can you believe this bullshit?"

Connie sat motionless for a minute, her gaze fixed on the windshield and through it the rear façade of the town hall. The bricks on the older part of the building were darker than those on the new addition; they'd weathered to a rusty brown over the years. The old town hall building had been constructed more than a century ago, and it was a Shelton landmark. Its roof and windows had been replaced, its trim painted and repainted, but its updates had been designed so its appearance would remain unchanged, the staid, classic structure it had been since its original cornerstone had been planted in the ground. It might not be as energy efficient as the new wing, but it had a hundred times more charm.

Solar panels had their own charm, however. Triple-pane windows had more charm than double-pane windows. Corrigan could build a condominium complex that respected the land it sat on, conserved heat and electricity, and was charming. But if he did that, he and his financial backer might make a smaller profit.

Ellie had nothing against making a profit, although she didn't consider profits particularly charming. Especially not if those profits were made by trashing the reputation of a town employee who had worked so hard to assure a construction project's environmental viability.

She realized she was no longer shocked. She was furious — not just at Richard but at Connie for believing him. "This is nuts," she said, shoving her car door open. "Believe whatever you want." She swung out of the car, slammed the door and marched back into the building, wondering whether she was going to lose not just her job but her friend.

Less than a minute after she reached her office, her phone rang. "Ellie Gillman speaking," she said crisply, pleased that her voice wasn't tremulous. She was shaking inside — with anger, with disgust, with fear. But she sounded calm and professional.

"Hi, Ellie. It's Nakul," he identified himself.

She hoped she could still count on his friendship, at least. She sank into her desk chair and swiveled around, noting that Wayne's door was still open and his office unoccupied. "Hi," she said.

"I heard about last night's select board meeting," Nakul said.

She shuddered. Evidently, word had gotten out. Twenty observers at a select board meeting could easily spread gossip through a cozy town like Shelton. "So," she said, forcing herself to sound amused, "what's going to happen? Are they going to make me wear a scarlet letter on my shirt?"

"It's craziness," he said. "I was thinking, it might help if I speak to the select board. Or sign an affidavit saying none of the things those idiots said at the meeting are true."

All right. He was still her friend. "That's very sweet of you," she said. "But I don't want you to jeopardize your job."

"Speaking the truth wouldn't jeopardize my job," he said.

She knew better. He probably knew better, too. They both had been hired by Wayne. They both could be fired by him.

But beyond that, she didn't want Nakul fighting her battle for her. "I'll contact the board," she said. "I can defend myself." She thought a moment, then added, "Can you send me your notes about the property, though? I can use them to illustrate the reasoning that led to our recommendations. I don't want to provide estimates or guesses. I want your hard numbers."

"Of course." He paused. "Be careful, Ellie. They fight dirty."

Richard Vernon fought dirty. Wayne allied himself with anyone who would do his fighting for him, just as he might ally himself with anyone — for instance, Ellie — who would do his job for him. But at least one person on the select board baked delicious cookies and coffee cake. Sonia might not wind up taking Ellie's side in this war, but Ellie had no doubt Sonia would ease Ellie's pain with some home-baked goodies. Sonia, at least, had a heart.

Wayne still hadn't arrived at the office by the time she got off the phone with Nakul. After a minute, an email from him appeared in her inbox, with his file of notes about Corrigan's subdivision attached. Ellie saved them to her computer, then composed an email, copied to each member of the select board.

She could whip out memos to department heads, shoot questions upstairs to Miriam in the treasurer's office, thumb tap abbreviated texts to her daughters, reminding them to let Lucy out when they got home, and to chop up some vegetables for stir-fried tofu for dinner. But this email had to be perfect. It couldn't sound defensive, even if it *was* defensive. It couldn't sound accusatory, even if she was accusing Wayne and Richard of dishonesty. It couldn't acknowledge that they were nasty sons of bitches, even if they were.

To the members of the select board, I am contacting you with regard to the condominium development on the former Mumson Farm property on Route 29, proposed by Carl Corrigan. At Wayne McNulty's request, I have worked extensively with Town Engineer Nakul Pawar and zoning board member Robert Kaufman to make sure this project will be successful. I have reviewed the state's MEPA regulations to ascertain that the project will be in compliance. I have endorsed recommendations that will allow the project to be safe, clean, esthetically pleasing, and environmentally sustainable.

I support this project. The report I presented to the select board two weeks ago made that clear. The alterations to the original plan that I have recommended will make the project a greater success.

I have been informed that at last night's select board meeting, Wayne McNulty and the project's chief financial backer, Richard Vernon, raised questions about my motives and my integrity. Mr. McNulty had specifically asked me not to attend the meeting. As a town resident, I know I am legally allowed to attend all select board meetings, but because Mr. McNulty is my boss, I accommodated his request.

Mr. McNulty has not been in any way involved in the review of this project. Mr. Vernon's only involvement is financial. Mr. Corrigan has shared with me his dissatisfaction with my recommendations, but that does not mean there's anything wrong with them. It just means that he and Mr. Vernon do not want the project to incur the additional costs those recommendations will entail.

I am attaching Mr. Pawar's notes regarding this project. If you have any questions about the recommendations I made, please feel free to contact me. You can also consult with Mr. McNulty, but if you do, you will discover how little he knows or understands about this project. If you reach out to Mr. Vernon, he may repeat his balderdash about my motivations. I suspect his attempt to sully my reputation last night was due to his hope that self-righteous indignation would compel me to quit my job here in the town hall. That will not happen. I have no intention of quitting.

Sincerely, Eleanor Gillman.

She reread her missive and smiled. *Balderdash*, she mused. That was a very loud word.

If she was going to be fired, she would leave the building screaming. She would be so loud, Scott would hear her all the way on the opposite end of the continent. She was done being quiet.

CHAPTER TWENTY-SEVEN

"**A**re you sitting down?" Scott asked. "You won't believe what's going on here."

Ellie lowered herself onto one of the chairs at the kitchen table. She had just gotten home from having driven Iris back to her house. Iris's friend Grace had taken her to her appointment with the orthopedist earlier in the day. He was satisfied enough with her wrist's healing that he'd replaced her pastel-blue cast with a brace that could be removed so she could shower without wrapping her arm in a plastic bag. No more plaster. Plenty of finger mobility. She could drive — and she could go home.

Misha had made a big fuss over her grandmother's departure, pleading with her to stay, promising to teach her how to play various video games even though Iris pointed out that she would play those games much more skillfully once her injured wrist was completely healed and she had full mobility. Abbie was a bit more restrained — she was too mature to beg — but she did give Iris a farewell hug more affectionate than any hug Ellie had received from her in the past several years.

Ellie would miss Iris at least as much as the girls would. She'd loved coming home to discover Iris and her daughters preparing dinner. She'd appreciated Iris's letting Lucy out into the yard a couple of times during the day, so that Lucy's bladder wasn't on the verge of explosion when Misha arrived home from camp or Abbie from her childcare job. Ellie had been immeasurably glad Iris had been at the house the night of Abbie's unfortunate trip to the police station. If Iris hadn't been there, Ellie would have felt compelled to rouse Misha and bring her along to the police station, to avoid the possibility that she would wake up, find herself alone in the house, and panic. And bringing Misha to the police station would not have been a good idea. She might have been alarmed, or appalled, by Abbie's recklessness. She might have been inspired by it. Misha and Abbie were quite different, but every now and then, Misha lapsed into hero worship when it came to her big sister. Ellie would have been horrified if Misha viewed Abbie's underage drinking and near arrest as behavior worth emulating.

Eventually, Ellie supposed, Abbie could tell her sister about her misadventure. Eventually, she might even tell her father. For now, Ellie was willing to respect Abbie's request for privacy about the whole incident. Compared to everything else going on in Ellie's life, her daughter's brush with the law didn't seem quite so major.

But now, apparently, something major was happening with Scott. "I'm sitting down," she told him, closing her eyes so the pile of mail on the table wouldn't distract her.

"I'm going to Hollywood," Scott said.

"What?" Hollywood was in southern California. The last she'd heard, Scott had been planning to cycle as far south as the Bay Area, then angle southeast into Nevada and then Arizona and New Mexico. A route further south would add a day or two to his journey.

"*Hollywood*," he repeated, emphasizing each syllable. "Some movie people want to talk to me. They've been following my escapades on the Wheeling and Dealing website, and the podcasts with Mike Rostoff. They want to make a movie about my trip."

"You're kidding." Ellie knew he wasn't kidding, but really — a movie about a guy riding a recumbent bicycle around the country, sounding the alarm about climate change? She could imagine a documentary, maybe, based on his entries on the Wheeling and Dealing website — or, more likely, ten minutes on some cable news show. But who would want to sit through a two-hour movie of a guy pedaling a bike, talking to college kids and farmers, losing a tire to a pot hole, and eating sweet onions?

"They've put me in touch with an agent down in L.A. They said I'd need someone to represent my interests, and I did some research online. This agent they recommended has an outstanding reputation and he wants to meet with me, and then we'll have a meeting with the producers. Can you believe it?"

Then again, maybe people *would* want to sit through something like that. They sat through hours of so-called reality TV, with people cooped up in mansions screaming at one another or wandering naked on some island, trying to catch fish with their bare hands. They watched hour after hour of pundits pontificating on depressing news. They watched video clips of people getting hit in their groins by errant baseballs, people tumbling from roofs, people falling off bicycles. Why not a movie about Scott falling off his bicycle?

"They're going to pay my Los Angeles hotel bill, since I'll be spending some time there, going to meetings. Unbelievable. I'm going to be *going to meetings*." He laughed. "A nice hotel, too. Nicer than the one in Baker, Montana."

"Well, lucky for you, you've got swim trunks," she said.

"Yeah. I'll put them to use — if I've got any time between my *meetings*." He seemed particularly excited about the prospect of meetings.

When Ellie contemplated meetings, she felt only dread. She had sent her email off to the members of the select board hours ago, and she'd heard nothing back from any of them. Just silence. True, Sonia was the only board member who was retired, so the others were occupied with their jobs during the day and might not have even read her email yet. And sending it might have tested the limits of the state's open-meeting law. By contacting the board via email, she was raising a business issue privately. But she'd been sabotaged by Wayne and Richard, told to stay away from the meeting so they could destroy her behind her back. Would they have had the nerve to say what they did if she'd been in attendance?

If she'd been in attendance, would she still have her job today? Would Wayne be in his rights to fire her for directly defying his orders, even if his orders were wrong?

Her head hurt. And Scott was babbling about his new show-biz career.

"So my schedule is going to shift a little," Scott said. "But I mean — wow! I'm doing this trip to get the word out about climate change. What can get the word out more than a movie?"

"I guess that would depend on whether the movie gets made, and how many people see it."

Ignoring her pragmatic observation, he raced ahead, chasing his new dream of stardom. "I'm already making a list of actors who could portray me. And I'm thinking I should ask for a screenwriting credit. I've been writing the daily entries on Wheeling and Dealing. I could at least help shape the plot line. I'm *living* the plot line." He babbled on, wondering whether he'd have to get a special release from Mike Rostoff to use material from the *Keeping It Clean* podcast, or whether they could fictionalize things enough that Rostoff wouldn't demand a credit or payment. "We'll probably have to enhance certain episodes to make them more dramatic," he went on. "But the movie can be one of those 'based on a real incident' films. I'm thinking there may be some scenes on the home front, too. Who do you want them to hire to play you? Think about it and email me a list of names. Probably not A-list actresses. It's just a supporting role."

Yes. It was just a supporting role. Scott was the star.

They talked for nearly half an hour. Actually, Scott did most of the talking. Ellie listened. She kept wondering if he was going to slow down enough for her to tell him what was going on in her life. She supposed that if this movie got made — and he got a writing credit, and a producer's credit, and a book deal, and an Oscar nomination — her income would no longer be necessary.

But she loved her job. She loved Shelton. She wanted to keep working.

She was afraid.

Thanks to this detour into Show-Biz Land, Scott would be away from home even longer than he'd originally thought. Maybe only a few days, maybe a few weeks. Who the hell knew how long meetings took in Hollywood?

"So, listen, let's not discuss this with the girls yet," Scott said, finally winding down. "Until it's a done deal, I don't want to get them all excited, bragging to their friends and whatever. But I'm just so fucking excited, I had to share it with you. I wish you were here so we could celebrate together."

She wanted to point out that as of now, there was nothing to celebrate. There was no movie deal. He hadn't even met the agent, let alone signed with him. If he had bought a few bottles of Walla Walla wine, she would have been happy to open one with him and drink a toast to his potential as a bold-face name, but right now, he wasn't a bold-face name and she wasn't with him.

Still, it was sweet of him to say he wished she was. Of course, he wished she was with him so she could celebrate his success. So she could tell him how wonderful he was. So she could bask in the glow of his stardom. So, like a solid B-list actor, she could serve in a supporting role.

As soon as this phone call was over, she would pour herself a glass of wine — not from Walla Walla — and drink a toast to herself. Supporting actors deserved toasts, too.

CHAPTER TWENTY-EIGHT

The next morning, Ellie found Marshall Glavin waiting for her at her desk. The most powerful member of the select board, Marshall had always intimidated Ellie a bit. He had the build of an over-the-hill football player, one who could no longer perform on the field but who could still inflict serious damage on anyone who ventured into his path while he was charging toward a goal. His silver hair was as glossy as a mirror, and his jaw, although padded with a layer of fat, looked sturdy enough to bruise the knuckles of anyone foolish enough to punch him there.

Marshall was an executive with a huge insurance company in downtown Boston. He was nearing retirement age — perhaps he'd already passed that threshold — but he was the sort of person who would refuse to retire until he was ready to do so, and he was the sort of person no one possessing an ounce of wisdom would argue with if he said he wasn't ready.

Ellie was surprised to see him in the Shelton Town Hall at eight fifty-five, when he ordinarily would be sitting in the usual rush-hour tangle of traffic en route to his job in the city.

He had probably come to her office to fire her. Of the five select board members, he was the most staunchly prodevelopment, the most concerned with tax revenues, and he was also the chair. Unlike Wayne, he didn't send his underlings out to deliver bad news, probably because he derived some sadistic satisfaction from delivering bad news himself — that football instinct, she supposed. Wayne wanted to be liked; Marshall wanted to be feared.

"Good morning," she said, forcing a smile as she entered her office.

"We need to talk," he responded, just as Connie had yesterday. Ellie wondered if he would suggest that they sit in his car for this discussion. That wouldn't be necessary if all he was going to do was explain her severance package to her.

"All right." As she had yesterday, she gestured toward the visitor chairs across the desk from her own chair. Marshall remained standing until she'd taken her seat, and then dropped onto one of the visitor chairs. Her chair was bigger than his, she noted. For the next few seconds, until he released the guillotine blade down onto her neck, she had the more powerful position.

"The board met in executive session last night," Marshall told her, his tone as dry as unbuttered toast. "I can't divulge the details of that discussion, but I will tell you the conclusion. We unanimously agreed to terminate Wayne McNulty's contract."

Ellie hadn't realized she'd been clenching her fingers until his words clarified themselves in her mind and she realized her head was still attached to her body. Only then did she notice that her knuckles had turned bloodless white and her fingertips were numb. She exerted herself to relax her hands in her lap.

Wayne. They were firing Wayne, not her.

"We will make the announcement on Monday. He will be leaving for personal reasons, or to explore new opportunities, or some such thing. We haven't worked that out with him yet. With our announcement, we will name you the acting town manager."

"Okay." Her voice emerged as a croak.

"I emphasize *acting.* We will be working with a headhunter and executing a wide-ranging search for a new town manager. I encourage you to apply for the position. But we can't just give it to you. If there are better candidates for the position out there, we will be looking for them."

"I understand."

"This is standard protocol," he continued, as if she hadn't spoken. Maybe he hadn't heard her. Her throat was as clenched as her hands had been just moments ago. "You can't just hand out a job like that without doing a proper search."

"Of course not."

"But in the interim, you will serve as acting town manager. And again, the board hopes you'll apply for the position."

"I will," she heard herself say, more forcefully.

"Because you do have the inside track. Not that I'm supposed to tell you that." Marshall seemed not the least bit abashed that he'd said something he wasn't authorized to say. "I need to get to work. So do you." With that, he stood, nodded, and strode out of her office.

She sat immobile for a minute, trying to absorb what had just happened. Wayne was being fired. Not her. Wayne. And on Monday, she would officially become the acting town manager of Shelton.

Should she move into Wayne's office? It was more spacious than hers, with a bigger window and a polished oak desk. But his termination hadn't yet been announced. And she was used to her anteroom office and her functional, if not particularly pretty, metal desk. She knew which drawer the rubber bands were stashed in, which drawer held her spare flash drives. She knew which drawer had extra space in it for Sonia's homemade cookies, if Sonia ever brought her another batch.

She peered almost timidly at the open door between her office and Wayne's — not Wayne's anymore, or not Wayne's starting Monday. Would he be in today? She doubted it. If she received word that she was going to have to announce in just a few days that she was leaving her current position to explore new opportunities, she wouldn't waste those days trying to do the job she'd never done particularly well in the first place. She would be home, polishing her resume, or talking to headhunters, or chugging vast quantities of booze.

Would Wayne's office ultimately be hers? Would she compete successfully against whoever else applied for the position?

Marshall Glavin, who was not given to reassurances, told her she had the inside track.

A small, giddy laugh escaped her. She wanted to phone Scott, but it was barely six a.m. on the West Coast, and he would probably still be asleep. Or else packing up to begin his extended bike trek south through Oregon and California to the bright lights of Hollywood.

Would he even care? Not once last night had he asked how her job was going — or her life. He'd been so thrilled about his impending stardom, he couldn't think beyond it. He had phoned her to share his excitement with her. And honestly, she'd been a little annoyed.

Would he be annoyed if she phoned him to share her excitement?

Well, she couldn't, at least not until Monday. And even then, it would be only *acting* excitement. Not the real thing. Not unless she emerged triumphant from the board's wide-ranging search to fill the job.

She allowed herself one more minute to savor Marshall's news, and then she cleared her head, roused her computer from its overnight slumber, and reviewed her to-do list for Shelton Cleanup Day. She hadn't gotten past "Call trash company re: public trash receptacles" when Richard Vernon swept into her office.

He moved with the force of a gale wind, which surprised her, because he'd lost the battle over Carl Corrigan's condominium development. If the board was firing Wayne, it must be at least in part because they were unmoved by Richard's defense of the original design last night — or because it became patently clear to them that Wayne had done none of the work on that proposal. Surely he shouldn't be approaching her this morning with such confidence, such certainty.

"Got a minute?" he asked, not even bothering with the usual courtesies.

She bothered. "Good morning," she said, and then, "Actually, I'm pretty busy right now."

Without awaiting an invitation, he settled into the chair Marshall had vacated just minutes ago. "I heard about the select board's decision."

Which decision? To fire Wayne? To embrace Ellie's recommendations concerning Corrigan's condo project? *Had* they decided to continue to embrace it, or were they going to reverse themselves and reject her report, even though they were firing Wayne and naming her his acting replacement?

Unsure, she said nothing.

"I just want to clarify some of the things that came out at the select board meeting the other night."

"Some of the things you said, you mean?"

"It was a tactic. I play hardball, Ellie. That's how I've gotten where I am."

Where he was was in a metaphorical trash receptacle, as far as Ellie was concerned.

"What you don't seem to understand is that your recommendations for the project add up to making it almost economically unfeasible. We anticipated earning somewhat north of a hundred thousand in profit on each unit. Your report demands twelve fewer units. That's over a million in profit we're not realizing. Then you add in your solar panels, and we're talking about a significant hit."

"You already explained the profit motive to me," Ellie reminded him dryly. "Some things are more important than profits."

"Not in my business, or in Carl's. You and your engineer — what's his name? Nick?"

Ellie glared at Richard. "Nakul."

"Whatever. You should have included us in the discussions. We could have enlightened you."

"Carl Corrigan was included in most of the discussions."

"He obviously didn't get through to you." Richard sighed and gave Ellie what he no doubt believed was a charming smile. "Look. Why don't we discuss this further at lunch? We can meet at the club —"

"I don't belong to that club," Ellie retorted. She assumed girls — women — were allowed to be members of the golf club where Wayne and his cronies spent so much of their time. It wasn't Luke's club, where no girls were allowed. But she didn't *want* to be a member of the Sycamore Acres Country Club. "Richard. You stood before a select board meeting, in front of residents of this town, and claimed I was taking revenge on you and Carl Corrigan because you rebuffed my romantic overtures."

"As I said, that was a tactic —"

"Do you honestly think I'd want to eat lunch with you? Do you think I'd want to listen to anything you had to say?" It felt good to vent. Ellie kept her voice level. She kept her hands from curling into fists. She was calm. She was in control. "I have work to do. This town needs to be cleaned up, and I'm arranging to have that done. If you want to participate, you can join other Shelton folks on the first Saturday in August to help pick up the litter. We'll be distributing gloves and trash bags and dividing the town into zones for cleanup. There will be soft drinks and cookies. If you don't want to participate, don't. But right now, I've got to continue making the arrangements for that. I also have some budget issues to iron out with Miriam, and I have to talk to the school superintendent about whether Shelton can afford to hire another reading specialist, and I have to listen to some people in the public works department beg me to free up money for more snow removal equipment. I don't have time to eat lunch with you at your club and have you explain to me, yet again, that you won't be satisfied if you can make only two million dollars in profit on that development, instead of three million dollars."

Oh, it felt good, talking like that. Raging without being enraged. Explaining instead of being explained to. *I am the acting town manager*, she thought, even though technically she wouldn't be the acting town manager until Monday. Wayne wasn't here. He was on his way out, probably at his club with an early-morning scotch in one hand and a 9-iron in the other, preparing to tee off while he contemplated what new opportunities he was going to pursue once his alleged resignation was announced.

Next week, she would be conferring with Miriam and the town's attorney on how to buy Wayne out of his contract. Today, however, she would be discussing special-ed teachers and snow-clearing equipment.

She would not be discussing Carl Corrigan's condominium complex. That was done. If the amount of money he and Richard would earn on that project wasn't enough to satisfy them, they could sell the Mumson property to another developer, one who cared about flood plains and global warming.

Ellie didn't need to join a club to do this job. She didn't need to be liked. She'd been doing the work for the past ten years. The only difference was that she'd been doing it quietly.

She wasn't going to be quiet anymore.

DAY SIXTY-THREE

Well, I didn't expect to be spending this much time in Southern California. But there have been meetings. Lots of meetings. Millions of meetings.

Okay, not millions. It just feels that way.

I didn't go on this trip because I wanted to sit in air-conditioned offices in high-rises, talking to people who are uniformly pretty and fashionable and powerful. I wish I'd spent a little more time admiring Big Sur, although that was a detour for me. The coastal highway is crazy, and the drivers on it are even crazier. But it was worth the detour and the risks. Check out the photos below. The scenery was so distracting, I had to work hard to pay attention to the road.

There's so much natural beauty in California — so much beauty under threat from climate change. The redwood forests Woody Guthrie sang about are imperiled by infestations and fires. The agriculture of the Central Valley is imperiled by drought and water usage issues. The Coastal Range is imperiled by fault lines.

Yet it's all so breathtakingly beautiful.

I can't say Los Angeles is beautiful. It used to be literally breathtaking when smog was a major issue, but the city has done a fine job improving its air quality. It's an interesting city — interesting to me, at least. I'm not used to cities with so many palm trees. Back home in Boston, we don't have palm trees. And we do have a lot of very old buildings. Here in California, they consider a building old if it was built more than fifty years ago.

So we're having meetings. In between meetings, I hang out at the very nice hotel where some of the producers who want to meet with me are putting me up. Not a really fancy place like the Beverly Hills Hotel or Chateau Marmont, but a Hampton Inn, which is clean and comfortable and has a swimming pool. In between meetings, I meet with my agent (which I guess means more meetings) and we discuss strategy. And at the end of the day, I cool off with a dip in the pool.

Will a movie be made about my cross-country bike ride? Maybe. But first I have to complete my bike ride. And I can't do that while we're having meetings. I can almost feel my leg muscles going soft. The swimming helps, but I'm itching to get back on the road. I've still got a lot of states to visit.

CHAPTER TWENTY-NINE

"So," Ellie said, "you're not going to be back in time to teach the fall semester at the middle school."

"I don't see how I can," Scott said. He sounded disappointed and more than a little frustrated.

Not that Ellie felt much sympathy for him. Poor man, drinking gourmet coffee in the morning and exotic cocktails at night, schmoozing in air-conditioned office suites with people who could write checks for millions of dollars without popping a bead of sweat, listening as his companions name-dropped and hustled and dictated emails into their top-of-the-line cell phones. "Have you notified the school?"

"Yeah. They've got someone lined up to take my fall term classes. And once I get home, I can get on the substitute list to fill in for absent teachers. I'll try to pick up some tutoring jobs, too. We may not be able to put any money into the girls' college funds this year, but we'll get by. I can't hit my supporters up for any more contributions to the GoFundMe page. That's only for the expenses of the trip."

"Well," Ellie said, "there's a chance I'll be getting a raise." She hadn't brought up the subject when the select board announced her promotion to acting town manager on Monday, but once the buzz around Wayne's departure and her elevation — her *acting* elevation — simmered down, she planned to request an increase in her salary. She didn't expect to receive as much as Wayne had been earning, given the word "acting" in her new title. And it was hard to claim that she would be working harder and taking on more responsibility, given that she'd pretty much been doing Wayne's job along with her own for the past few years. But when she had been doing his job all those years, she'd been underpaid. She deserved more, and she would ask for more — in a clear, confident voice.

She would also ask for the services of one of the assistants in the town clerk's office for several hours a day. She doubted the select board would be willing to hire a full-time assistant town manager to fill her old job, since she might be returning to that old job if they wound up hiring someone else to be the town manager. But she was tired of doing two jobs. She wanted to do one job, and she wanted to get paid appropriately.

Why hadn't she demanded a raise years ago? Partly because she knew the parameters of Shelton's budget better than Wayne ever did. She knew what Shelton could afford, where Miriam could shift funds from one column to another, how giving Ellie a raise would affect the fire department's request for a new truck or the school district's need of another reading specialist.

And partly because she was still learning how to be loud.

At the moment, Misha and several of her friends were racing around the back yard with Lucy in the waning evening light, throwing a Frisbee around and watching Lucy attempt to catch it. Lucy was a small dog and not given to leaping into the air, so she hadn't caught many of the tosses. This didn't seem to matter to her or the girls, who were all shrieking and giggling and making a lot of noise. This was Misha's club, her sisterhood. They knew how to be loud.

Ellie was learning.

Abbie wasn't out in the yard with the younger girls. She was upstairs in her room with Merritt Vernon, of all people. Ellie heard Abbie's clarinet, a scale here, a run there, and Merritt's voice blending in as she sang. "Look, she's weird," Abbie had told Ellie earlier that evening before inviting Merritt over. "But I saw her at Starbucks and she told me her parents were getting a divorce. She looked real sad. So I told her to come over this evening."

Ellie had not heard this news from Connie. She had no idea if Connie still believed Richard's bullshit about Ellie attempting to seduce him, or if she was too embarrassed to reach out to Ellie and admit she'd been wrong about that. Ellie could have explained to Connie, as Richard had so snidely explained to Ellie, that his insinuations had been a mere tactic, nothing more.

It didn't matter what Connie believed. What mattered was that, at least according to her daughter, she was finally breaking free of him. And what mattered even more was that Abbie had extended a kindness to a girl she wasn't all that fond of. Her daughter had done something thoughtful and generous and beautiful.

"What I've learned," Scott was saying, "is that people in Hollywood talk a good game, but their follow-through isn't always there. My agent says things still look good, so I guess I shouldn't be discouraged."

My agent. He said that so smoothly, as if the notion of Scott Gillman, middle school science teacher and environmental warrior, having an agent wasn't hilarious.

"He's thinking we should try to get a news story — national, like on one of the network news shows. That would drive interest toward a movie. He's also negotiating an option, but he says it would probably be only about a thousand dollars."

"That's real money," Ellie said.

"He keeps fifteen percent," Scott informed her. "So we're talking only $850. *If* he gets an option." He sighed. "I want to be back on the road. Sitting around here, going to meetings... It's getting old."

His being on the road, far from home, was getting old, too, but Ellie didn't say that. "About the raise I should be getting —"

"Yeah. Wow! That's great! What's going on?"

"Well..." She paused for effect. "Wayne got fired, and I'm now Shelton's acting town manager."

"No shit?" Scott took a moment to digest this. "What happened?"

Ellie told him. She told him about Carl Corrigan's proposed condo development on the Mumson Farm property on Route 29, and about Wayne's decision to put her in charge of it, and about her and Nakul's recommendations, and about Wayne's and Richard's pressure campaign to get her to drop those recommendations, and about how their pressure campaign failed. She told him about how she'd developed Shelton Cleanup Day, and how the select board seemed to like her for having done that, and how there were going to be more public trash receptacles throughout town, and cookies on Cleanup Day.

By the time she'd finished, the sky was dark. "I need to send Misha's friends home," she said. "It's getting late. Merritt, too. She probably needs a lift home."

"Wait." Scott sounded befuddled. "Why didn't you tell me all this stuff was going on?"

A lot more had been going on than what she'd told him. His mother had broken her wrist. Abbie had gone to an unchaperoned party, drunk a can of beer, and wound up at the police station. But Ellie wasn't going to go into all that. She'd made promises.

The news about her job, however... "We talk about what you're doing," she reminded him. "You're saving the planet. I'm just keeping a small town in Massachusetts functioning day to day. I don't have thousands of people following me online and sending me money. I'm not appearing on podcasts. I don't have clubs of school children monitoring every mile I bike and crowds showing up wearing RE:CYCLE T-shirts. I don't have Hollywood agents negotiating options on my story."

"Okay, but keeping a town functioning is important, too," Scott said. Ellie wondered if he realized how patronizing he sounded.

She took a moment to compose herself, then said, "I would have told you what was going on with my job if you'd asked. You never asked."

"You should have told me anyway." Apparently, he didn't want to feel guilty. That he hadn't asked would have to be her fault somehow.

"I told you now," she said coolly.

"Well." He sighed. "Congratulations! It's really great."

"Thank you." Not coolly. Coldly. She could hear the icicles crackling in her tone. "I've got to go. I need to drive Merritt home."

And see if her soon-to-be-divorced mother is still my friend.

"Okay. I'll call you tomorrow," he said. Not "I love you." Not "I miss you." Not "I bow down to you, O acting town manager." He must have heard those icicles in her voice, too.

She said goodbye, ended the call, and lowered herself into a chair by the kitchen table. The dishes were done, the mail sorted and stashed, and the table was clear, except for a slightly lopsided but adorable ceramic vase Misha had made in camp, holding a bouquet of colorful weeds.

Her mind resembled the weeds, not the otherwise clear table: a jumble of color, possibly inappropriate but still lovely.

What had just happened? She had spoken up. She'd made herself heard. She'd been loud.

And Scott seemed . . . not happy.

Ellie shouted up the stairs that it was time for Merritt to go home. Then she hollered the same message out the back door for Misha's friends. They had ridden over on their bicycles, and they all lived within a couple of blocks of Ellie's house, so she didn't need to drive them home. When she offered a lift to Merritt, however, Merritt accepted with a smile.

Merritt Vernon smiling. Who knew she was even capable of such a thing?

Not only was she smiling, but she had scrubbed off her pasty white makeup. She was still dressed all in black — black T-shirt, black shorts, clunky black boots with thick heels — but her skin glowed and her cheeks were rosy. Only her eyes were adorned with makeup, outlines of kohl. "Abbie gave me a facial," she told Ellie as they left the kitchen for the garage.

Ellie hadn't known that Abbie possessed such a skill — or the lotions and creams necessary for the task. For that matter, she hadn't known Abbie possessed the generosity of spirit to do such a thing. Ellie's conversation with Scott might have irritated her, but seeing Merritt looking so normal, and knowing Abbie was the force behind Merritt's transformation, deleted Scott and his condescending attitude from her mind.

The drive to Merritt's house took less than ten minutes. Ellie had no idea what was going on inside the Vernon mansion — was Richard still living there? Was Connie? Was Connie still her friend? — but she accompanied Merritt up the front walk. When Merritt opened the door, Connie was standing on the other side of the threshold. She was dressed like a human being rather than a real estate agent, in denim capris and a shapeless gray shirt, her neck exposed and revealing nothing incriminating about her age.

"Oh, Ellie — you didn't have to drive her home," Connie said. "I would have picked her up. But no, this is wonderful. Come in. We need to talk. I've got a bottle of chardonnay in the fridge."

If Connie thought they needed to talk, their friendship hadn't ended. Ellie followed Merritt into the foyer and pulled out her phone. "Let me just call the girls and let them know where I am," she said.

Connie nodded, then gave Merritt a hug and said, "You look fabulous. You owe Abbie big."

"No, she doesn't," Ellie argued as she tapped the icons on her phone. The goal of being kind was to be kind, not to rack up debts. "She and Abbie made sweet music together, literally."

Abbie answered the phone.

"I'm going to be at Merritt's house for a little while," Ellie said. "Merritt's mother and I have to talk. I want you girls in bed by the time I get home. And please make sure Misha takes a shower."

"Yeah, she smells bad," Abbie declared. Evidently, she'd used up all her kindness on Merritt. She had none left for her sister.

"I don't smell bad!" Ellie heard Misha yell in the distance.

"I won't be late. Call if you need me," Ellie said, before wishing Abbie a good night and tapping the "end call" icon.

Merritt wandered up the stairs and Connie beckoned Ellie to the kitchen. Within a minute, she had two crystal goblets filled with chilled white wine and led the way to the back patio. She lit an array of citronella candles and waved her hand toward one of the wrought-iron chairs for Ellie.

Once they were both seated, Ellie raised her glass to Connie. "Here's to your divorce," she toasted.

"Definitely," Connie said. She took a sip, then lowered her glass. "I'm so sorry about the other day. I was wrong, wrong, wrong."

"You were upset," Ellie forgave her.

"No, I was wrong. How could I believe anything that asshole said? I don't know what I was thinking. That I could believe you'd make a pass at him when you're married to the greatest guy on the planet —"

Ellie's memory bank hadn't deleted her phone call with Scott from storage, after all. "He's not the greatest guy on the planet."

"The planet would beg to differ. He's *saving* it."

"He's biking around the country, getting a lot of attention. I'm not sure he's saving anything." Ellie sighed. "You think Scott's wonderful because compared to Richard, he is. But in absolute terms…" She shrugged. She didn't want to badmouth her husband to Connie. But he'd irritated her. He'd dismissed her. He'd hurt her feelings. "Tell me what's going on with you and Richard. You kicked him out?"

"I didn't have to. He left. I called him on all his shit and he packed a bag and left. I think he's at one of the fancy hotels in Boston — the most expensive one. Knowing him, he's going to spend down just so he doesn't have to give me any alimony."

"He's got a lot of money to spend down," Ellie said. "Have you hired a lawyer? You're going to need a good one, going up against him."

Connie nodded. "He's such a dick. He always said that if we split up, he'd fight tooth and nail for custody of Merritt. But then he left, without even saying goodbye to her. He hasn't even phoned her. She's coping okay, though. Doesn't she look terrific without all that shit on her face? Your Abbie is such a sweetheart, taking Merritt under her wing the way she has."

"It took them fourteen years to become friends," Ellie said, recalling their early years at the Koala Cub Club. "I hope it lasts."

"I hope our friendship lasts, too," Connie said. "I'm really sorry about accusing you. I wasn't in a good place, things were falling apart here, and I wasn't ready to believe the worst about Richard yet. I should have been, but... not that it matters. You came out on top. Richard lost."

"I never saw it as a game one of us would have to lose," Ellie said. "I want the development to happen. Everyone does. He's just not going to see as big a return on his investment as he was hoping for."

Connie drank some more wine. So did Ellie. Icy and dry, it bathed her tongue and slid down her throat, soothing her. "This is why Scott is a better person," Connie said. "He doesn't care about the return on his investments. Money isn't as important to him. Please don't disillusion me, Ellie. I've got this image of him as the perfect husband and the perfect dad."

"He can be a dick, too," Ellie said.

Connie pouted, then shrugged and smiled. "Well, he's a man. Maybe he just can't help himself sometimes."

"Maybe." And maybe Ellie had enabled him, waving him off, protecting him from all the disasters, big and small, that he'd left behind. She'd fixed the toilet. She'd fixed his mother. She'd cleaned Lucy's vomit. She'd rescued Abbie. She'd kept from him that Misha's teacher had thought Misha was too enthusiastic.

Misha *was* too enthusiastic. It was one of the things Ellie loved best about her. In fact, it was a trait Ellie should emulate.

CHAPTER THIRTY

Shelton Cleanup Day was a huge success.

Ellie had arranged for a party tent to be erected on the green in front of the town hall. In its shade, she'd set up long folding tables that held plates of cookies and enormous jugs of water. Steuben's Sporting Goods had donated not just 150 reusable water bottles with the store's logo printed on them but also a gross of duckbill caps. Since the point was to clean up the town, the Steuben bottles were far superior to paper cups or single-use bottles. So what if the store got a little publicity out of their generous donation? Ellie was fine with that.

At one end of the table, a map of Shelton was displayed on an easel. Nakul had divided the town into zones, and as Ellie distributed two bags and a pair of disposable gloves to each volunteer — one bag for recyclable trash and one for trash that would end up in the large blue dumpster just beyond the tent — she assigned the participants to zones. Misha and her club of loud girls had screeched about cleaning up the grounds around the middle school — their destination starting in September. "There's always trash there from the kids playing soccer and Little League," Misha had said. "And there's the nature trail behind the school. We can clean up the whole area. Can we have some cookies?"

Abbie teamed up with another group to patrol the high school. She arrived with her friends Jocelyn, Mackenna, and Torie, and also Merritt, who hung back a little as if she wasn't sure she belonged with them. They'd all been among the teenagers rounded up by the police at that unchaperoned party, but today they were dressed in tank tops and shorts — their outfits were a bit skimpy but not obscene — and seemed interested in doing good deeds. Either that, or they expected a group of boys to show up at the high school and were planning to flirt while they collected whatever litter they encountered there. So far, no boys had come to Ellie's table requesting the high school zone, but Ellie suspected that Abbie and her friends were motivated by more than pure altruism.

Some boys did arrive at the tent, asking to help clean up the town's commercial district. "We hear the stores are giving out free samples," a boy Ellie recognized as Luke Bartelli's older brother said. "Like, free slices of pizza if we clean up the sidewalk outside Rossini's."

"Enjoy yourselves," Ellie cheered them on as she handed them bags and gloves. "Just make sure you discard your napkins properly afterward."

"What's a napkin?" one of the boys joked. They jostled one another, filled a few of the free Steuben's bottles with water, and piled into a sunshine-yellow Jeep to drive down to Main Street.

Abbie had urged Ellie to wear a little makeup that morning. "You don't know," she warned. "A reporter might show up. You don't want your eyelashes to disappear."

True, Ellie didn't want her eyelashes to disappear. But the day was hot, and Ellie was sure to perspire, which might cause any cosmetics she wore to melt.

Not that it mattered. There were no reporters. No banners. No singers. No Girl Scouts armed with boxes of Samoas and Thin Mints. Just Shelton residents stepping into the shade of the tent, asking for a couple of trash bags and a zone assignment, and helping themselves to some water and a cookie or two. Several people returned with their trash bags full and showed Ellie before and after photos they'd taken of their zones. She viewed a photo of the stretch of roadway near the police station, with crushed soda cans and plastic bottles and empty potato chip bags scattered across the asphalt, and a photo of the same stretch with all the trash cleared away, exposing the abundance of crab grass that sprouted along the edge of the road. She viewed a photo of the sidewalk near the Calico Cat gift shop with some discarded face masks and a flattened work glove with the ghost of a bicycle tire's tread striping it, and the same sidewalk cleared of face masks and the glove.

Shelton didn't need a banner or a chorus or a TV reporter wearing pasty makeup to get cleaned up. All it needed was the publicity the downtown stores had offered, displaying posters promoting the cleanup in their windows, and the announcement on the town's website, and word of mouth. And free cookies. And, Nakul had insisted, Ellie's organizational flair.

Scott was somewhere in Wisconsin at the moment. Last night he'd posted on the Wheeling and Dealing website about how hot it was, even in the northern tier states. "Climate change is going to impact dairy production, one of Wisconsin's major industries," he'd written. "Beer is another major industry, and if you can't drink milk, you can always drink beer. But you can't make cheese out of beer."

He still had quite a few states left to go. Luke Bartelli and two of his friends had stopped by the Gillman house during the week, not to mow the lawn but to show Ellie the map they'd created to track Scott's route. "We're sort of using it to learn fractions," Luke told her and Misha as they'd stood on the porch in the waning evening light, studying the map. "For every hundred miles he rides, we ride one mile. So, he's done about five thousand miles so far, and we've done about fifty."

"Fifty-one and a half," one of the other boys said.

"That's so easy," Misha had sniffed. "We learned fractions in fourth grade. This is percentages, anyway. You're doing one percent."

"Well, yeah, I guess," Luke said, eyeing Misha dubiously.

At least Luke and Misha were talking again. Not in the warmest, friendliest manner, but perhaps they would be friends again someday.

Ellie supposed boys and girls could have their own separate clubs. She would not want Scott or Richard — definitely not Richard — encroaching on her visits with Connie. When they talked girl talk, they didn't want menfolk around. She wasn't sure what guys talked about when womenfolk weren't around — Red Sox scores? The horsepower of various car models? The relative gigabyte memories of assorted laptops? The relative attractiveness of assorted women's bodies?

They probably didn't talk about tampons. Or mascara. Or vibrators. Connie had swept into Ellie's office a couple of days ago and informed Ellie that she was going to buy one, to "tide her over," as she put it, while she and Richard worked through their divorce. "I'll let you know if it's any good," she'd promised, as if Ellie might want to buy one for herself. "They come in a variety of sizes and shapes. I'm going to get one that's a lot bigger than Richard, just to piss him off. Not that I'll tell him about it, but in my heart, he'll be pissed. You want me to buy one for you while I'm at it? Maybe I can get a buy-one-get-one deal."

Ellie had moved into Wayne's office a week ago. She still felt a little like a trespasser in it. His desk was huge, and it had taken her a while to figure out how to adjust his chair for her smaller height and girth. She had also polished her resume, accumulated references from Chief Mulroney of the Shelton Fire Department, Robert Kaufman from the zoning board, Miriam Horowitz, and Nakul, all testifying to the extensive work she'd done with them over the course of her career as assistant town manager, and emailed the entire package to the select board. It had seemed a bit too formal; they all knew her, and several of them could have written references for her, as well. But they were following protocol, and she had to follow protocol, too.

She wanted the job. She wanted it more than she'd realized. She wanted it the way she'd wanted two children. She had conceived Abbie so quickly, and then it had taken years to conceive Misha, but her desire for a second child had been a throbbing ache inside her, a desperate hunger that would not be sated until Misha had pushed her way into the world, screaming her bullet-shaped, red-faced head off. Even as a newborn, she'd been loud — and enthusiastic.

Now, her girls were growing up, her husband was in Wisconsin pursuing his dream . . . and she was acknowledging that she also had a dream. If Wayne hadn't been fired — or forced to resign — she might never have realized how much she wanted his job — *her* job, the job she'd been doing for years, only without the salary, the title, the respect, or the inner office with the bigger window and the humongous desk and the leather chair with all its screws and levers so it could be precisely adjusted to the size of the user.

She wanted it, all of it. The title, the workload, the perks, the respect. It had become her dream. And unlike Scott's dream, no one had to hold down the fort and take care of the multitude of crises, big and small, that arose while she was pursuing that dream. She didn't have the support system Scott had, but she had a dream. It was hers. She wanted it. And if she had to be loud to get it, she would be loud.

Scott phoned that evening. "Here's the plan," he said. "From Wisconsin, I'm heading south, through Illinois and Indiana, then into Kentucky. I'll cross the river into Ohio and then cross it back to West Virginia. After that, Virginia, the Atlantic coastal states and up for a final loop through New England. You can join me on the New England loop if you'd like."

Right. Just what Ellie ought to be doing when she was vying for the job of town manager: taking off a week to go biking through New England. "The girls are going to be starting school around then," she said, aware that Scott would *not* be starting school, not reclaiming his position on the middle school faculty for the fall term. "It's Misha's first year at the middle school," Ellie added. "I want to be there to help make the transition smooth."

"Of course, that makes the most sense. She should have her mother close by when she takes that big step." Scott paused, then went on. "My agent" — he uttered that phrase so easily, as if he'd had an agent his entire life — "plans to line up a guest spot for me on one of the nighttime talk shows in New York as soon as I finish the New England loop. It will raise my profile and generate more interest in the film project."

"So after you do your New England loop, you'll be going to New York City?"

"I'll be home for a while first," he said, as if this was supposed to reassure her. "At least a few days. It will depend on when and where he can get me a booking."

At least a few days. Could he spare it?

Ellie shouldn't be so negative about Scott's show-business aspirations. If someone made a movie about his courageous, quixotic mission to save the planet, the money he earned from it might compensate for his lost teaching income. Then again, the option price he'd mentioned a while back — a thousand dollars less the agent's fee — would just barely cover the increase in their homeowner insurance. Not surprisingly, the insurance company had hiked their annual premium because Ellie had filed a claim for the broken roof. Why she and Scott even bothered to have insurance, she didn't know. Any repair the insurance company covered, she and Scott wound up paying for in higher premiums in the next bill.

"I don't want to talk about your trip," she said. "I want to tell you about Shelton Cleanup Day. It was today, and it was a roaring success."

Before Scott could steer the conversation back to himself, she took over, telling him about the tent and the water bottles and the cookies, and the 173 volunteers who had come to the tent by the town hall to pick up trash bags and receive their zone assignments. More volunteers than Ellie had planned for. Many more volunteers than zones to cover. Despite her concerns about staging this event in August, when so many local families were away on vacation, Shelton residents had volunteered in impressive numbers and cleaned their town.

"Lots of people took before-and-after photos with their phones," she told Scott. "I've asked them to send them to the town clerk so we can post some of them on the town's website. Shelton really looks fabulous. And the trash company came through with public trash receptacles — lidded bins with slots to drop the trash through, so it won't blow away."

"That's great," Scott said with all the exuberance of someone who'd just been told that a root canal would probably save his tooth from extraction.

Ellie ignored his bland tone. "Yes," she said cheerfully. "It's great."

"So, what's next on your agenda?" he asked.

"Getting the kids ready for school. Running the town. Getting hired as the official town manager. Working with Carl Corrigan to reconfigure his condo development on the Mumson property. Nagging Abbie to practice her clarinet so she'll be ready once the school orchestra starts rehearsing." She could have listed more items from her agenda, but it was just life stuff. Just moving from one day to the next. Just doing what she did all the time. Not as significant as saving the planet or having an agent, but that was okay. She'd been named after a First Lady, after all, not a president.

Misha materialized at the kitchen doorway. "Can I talk to Daddy?"

Ellie nodded and spoke into the phone. "Misha wants to talk to you. I'm passing the phone along." She told him she loved him, asked him to stay safe, and handed the receiver to Misha, who immediately started babbling about her chances of making the middle school's soccer team and the fact that lately Luke Bartelli had been acting as if she actually existed, but she really thought she ought to be allowed to mow the lawn because she was more mature than he was, and also they had the best cookies at the Shelton Cleanup Day table, sort of like marble cake only with chocolate chunks as well as chocolate swirls.

Ellie smiled. As agendas went, Misha's was far more exciting than Ellie's.

She crossed to the back door and lifted Lucy's leash off its hook. Lucy bounded into the kitchen from the den — she probably could have heard the rattle of the leash from three counties away — and panted eagerly as Ellie clipped it to her collar. Then they stepped out the back door and into the hot, lavender evening. It was too late for a long walk, and the mosquitos were biting. But they could walk to the corner of the street and back.

As agenda items went, taking Lucy for an evening walk was all the excitement Ellie needed tonight.

DAY SEVENTY-NINE

West Virginia wants to think of itself as coal country, but it's not. The state's economy is wisely shifting away from coal. West Virginia has the capacity to generate more energy from wind turbines than it does from coal.

Besides all the environmental damage coal causes — both in mining and in being burned to generate electricity — it's dirty. It's ugly. And West Virginia is a profoundly beautiful state. Clean up all that coal mess — the strip mines that despoil the landscape and poison its waters, the mines that produce fuel that pollutes the atmosphere — and you're left with gorgeous hills and mountains and lush forests. Blue, blue skies. Lakes and streams and fields of wildflowers. If a movie about my bike trip is ever made, I hope they film lots of footage in West Virginia because it's just so damned pretty.

I crossed from Ohio into Huntington, West Virginia, where there are several colleges and universities and the vibe is very proenvironment. I'll be meeting with students at Marshall University later today. Tomorrow, on to Virginia.

I'm tired, but also invigorated. Wish me luck! Wish me energy! (The muscular kind, not the coal-fueled kind.)

CHAPTER THIRTY-ONE

Scott's trip ended the third week in September. He rolled up the driveway, sweaty and disheveled, his recumbent bike trailed by the Beast of Burden, which looked a lot dirtier than it had looked the day he pedaled down the street and out of sight back in May. The signs he had attached to it — "I Heart Earth" and "Save the Planet" — were bedraggled, mud-spattered, and barely legible. The Beast's zippered enclosure containing his clothing and gear was faded. Scott didn't look faded, though. His skin glowed, darkened to a gentle golden hue by the sun. He appeared lean and wiry and strong.

And absurdly sexy, but Ellie thought that just might be because she'd gone so long without sex. Connie swore she preferred her vibrator to Richard, but that said more about Richard than about the quality of Connie's vibrator. And Ellie had never gotten a vibrator. She'd wanted Scott — and now he was home.

Scott had arrived back in Shelton too late to teach his science classes at the middle school in the fall term, but Ellie had already known he wouldn't be able to teach during the fall semester. The school had hired a permanent substitute to cover his classes through January. Scott had gotten his name onto the day-by-day substitute list, so if any teacher was out for the day — English, math, physical education — he could be summoned and earn a day's pay by filling in and faking his way through the course material. He also made himself available for one-on-one tutoring. He would be earning money. Not a lot, but some.

Ellie would be earning more. The day before their trip to New York City, she had arrived at the town hall to find a frosted chocolate cupcake sitting on her desk, along with a note: *It's yours. Formal notification to follow.* Cryptic, but Ellie knew what it meant, and she understood that whoever had left her the cupcake — probably Sonia Lewis, but she wasn't sure — had been sworn to secrecy until an employment package had been put together and presented to Ellie. She'd savored every bite of the cupcake, smiling as she chewed, and contemplated what she would do once the select board made her hiring official. She would ask for a higher salary than they offered, of course. She knew what Shelton could afford, and bit by bit, she was learning how to use her voice effectively. She would ask.

Scott's agent had landed him an invitation to appear on one of the late-night talk shows, hosted by a sometime comedian who liked to tackle serious subjects with his guests. Whether Scott would be on the show as a serious-subject guest or a celebrity, Ellie didn't know. But Scott wanted her to accompany him to New York City. "The show is putting me up in a nice hotel," he said. "We can drive down, tape the show, go out to dinner, maybe see a Broadway show. It'll be a little vacation. You deserve it."

Ellie couldn't argue that. She deserved it, perhaps more than Scott did. He had been on a prolonged, arduous vacation for the past five months while she'd been working two jobs — her own and Wayne's — and taking care of her daughters. And the house. And Scott's mother. And the dog.

"Are you sure you want to drive to New York?" she asked. "Even though the car is a hybrid, it's not the most environmentally sound way to travel." She wasn't being facetious — well, maybe she was, a little — but she thought Scott might come across as hypocritical on the TV show if the host asked him why he didn't bike down to New York instead, or at least use public transportation.

"If we both go, driving becomes more ecologically reasonable. Two train tickets are pricy. And forget about flying down. All that exhaust, all those toxic contrails for such a short trip. I think Mother Earth will forgive us for driving."

"What about the girls?" she asked. "We're not pulling them out of school for two days."

"I'll ask my mother to stay with them," Scott said.

Abbie and Misha would love that. Iris would probably love it, too. Scott loved it until he saw the brace his mother was still wearing on her wrist when she arrived at their house the evening before Ellie and Scott were set to leave. Iris's brace was not the bulky, hard contraption she had worn when her cast had been removed, but an elastic wrap that gave her wrist extra support until it was fully healed. "What's that on your arm?" Scott asked when she entered the house, carrying a small overnight bag in her healthy right hand.

"Not even a hello?" she shot back. "You've been gone for months, and the first words out of your mouth are to question me about my arm?"

Scott gave her a hug, then took a step back. "Hello," he said. "What's that on your arm?"

"Nothing important," Iris said, brushing past him. "Where are the girls? Oh, hi, Lucy," as the dog sprinted toward her, barking exuberantly. She set down her bag and bent over to scratch Lucy behind the ears. "I'm sorry, sweetheart — I didn't bring you any treats."

"She doesn't need treats," Ellie assured Iris, almost adding, *and you don't need to apologize.* But of course, Iris probably did need to apologize. Apologizing was her standard operating procedure.

Ellie and Scott left the next morning after seeing the girls off to school. Iris told them to have a good time. "I don't know how to record the show on your TV," she said wistfully. "I suppose Misha and Abbie can figure that out for me. I hate to bother them about it —"

"They won't mind," Ellie said. "The show may wind up on YouTube, anyway. Lots of TV shows do."

"I hope the girls can figure out how to find it on YouTube, then," Iris said, shaking her head dubiously. "I thought YouTube was just music videos."

"Lots of TV shows are on there," Scott told her, then gave her a hug. "Thanks for babysitting. We'll call you when we get to New York."

"It's not that far away," Iris reminded them. "Just, what, four hours? We'll be fine. Don't worry about a thing."

Other than to comment on the flow of traffic and the dry, sunny early-autumn weather, he didn't speak until they'd reached the Mass Pike. Then: "Why didn't you tell me my mother broke her wrist?" He shot Ellie an angry look. "I called every night while I was on my trip. You should have told me."

"She asked me not to tell you," Ellie said, refusing to let him rile her. "She was afraid that if you knew she'd fallen, you would worry about her and fly home. She knew how important your trip was, and she didn't want you to come home just because she tripped on her sneaker and fell. I respected her wishes. I had her stay with us until the cast came off and she was able to drive and take care of herself. The girls loved having her with us. We all did."

"I'm glad you all love her. You still should have told me." He scowled. "I wouldn't have come home."

"Of course you wouldn't have." Ellie hoped she didn't sound too critical when she said that. She knew his mission was more important to him than pretty much anything, including his mother's wrist.

"I mean, why would I? You could take care of it. You *did* take care of it."

Yes, Ellie thought. *I took care of it. I took care of everything. That's my standard operating procedure.*

"So what else happened while I was gone that you didn't tell me about?"

Misha's report card. Abbie's near arrest. Ellie's fear that she might lose her job. Richard Vernon's sleazy behavior. "When you called, you rarely asked about what was going on at home. You talked about your trip. Which was obviously a lot more interesting than anything that was happening in Shelton, so I don't mind that you didn't ask. Like your mother, I saw no need to bother you about all the petty crap that was going on here." She paused, then added, "I told you about the broken roof, and all you cared about was that I put holes in your favorite tarp."

"It wasn't my favorite tarp," Scott argued. "It was just . . . a tarp. I wish you hadn't put holes in it, that's all. A tarp with holes in it isn't good for much."

"Well, your tarp isn't good for much, then. But it was good enough to keep the attic dry until the roof was repaired." She folded her arms and stared straight ahead at the cars and trucks cruising alongside them, and the blur of grass and shrubs and trees sprouting along the shoulders of the pike. She had put holes in his damned tarp. She didn't tell him about some of the petty crap that had occurred while he was away, and she never would. And if the roof ever got broken again, causing a leak in the attic, she would think nothing of poking a few more holes in a tarp. Big effing deal.

She was working herself into a sour mood, and she realized she had to calm down, mellow out, be sweet and supportive. She wanted Scott's TV appearance to go well. If it did, it might lead to a movie deal, fame and fortune and glory beyond what he'd already achieved. Oh, and maybe it would lead to a cleaner planet, although that didn't seem to be the primary objective of this New York City postscript to his trip.

"Does it feel funny to be driving after so many days of biking?" she asked, deliberately changing the subject and, she hoped, helping him to focus on the televised interview he would be taping later that day.

He shot her a look, then nodded, acknowledging his approval that she had steered their discussion back to safe territory. "The car is faster and more comfortable than the bike, for sure. Although after a while, my butt didn't even feel the bike seat anymore."

They chatted about biking for the rest of the drive. They talked about Scott. Ellie assured herself that this was for the best, that keeping him in his talk-about-his-bike-trip zone was a wise idea. Their conversation reminded her of what had attracted her to him so many years ago: his intensity. His idealism. His gloriously sexy smile. Especially now, with his body honed to lean, solid muscle after so many months of biking. He looked terrific. He had on a short-sleeved shirt that exposed his taut, tanned forearms. His hair had grown long, but it was thick and wavy, the color of caramel with a few silver strands woven through it. His cheeks were hollower than they'd been back in May, and they folded into dimples whenever he smiled.

He would look better on television today than he'd looked the day he'd ridden off on his adventure. This time he would be on national television, and as she'd told Iris, the broadcast would likely be available on the internet. Maybe it would go viral. Maybe it would assure the honchos in Hollywood that there was an audience for Scott's story.

The TV show's production company had reserved a room for Scott and Ellie in a midtown Manhattan hotel. Not the fanciest hotel in the city, but the room was clean and comfortable, and Ellie was certain it cost plenty, given its location. As far as she was concerned, the best thing about it was that the hotel had an underground garage where they could park their car — and the best thing about that was that the TV show would cover the cost of that parking space, which was nearly as expensive as the room upstairs.

Their room's window overlooked Times Square, which was so clogged with pedestrians, Ellie wondered how anyone could actually move without bumping into people. She did notice a few cyclists who pedaled their way through the crowds, which parted for them like the Red Sea for Moses.

While Scott unpacked the suit he'd brought for his television appearance, Ellie phoned Iris and let her know she and Scott had arrived safely at their destination. "The girls just got home from school a few minutes ago," Iris reported. "Abbie asked me if I would pay for clarinet lessons for her. I'd love to, but I'm retired, on a fixed income, and I —"

"You don't have to pay for her lessons," Ellie said. "She'll be studying with Mr. Streiberg at school, and we'll work something out to hire a private teacher if she still wants that."

"But Scott isn't teaching this semester. I feel so bad that I can't help out more."

"Don't feel bad," Ellie silenced her. In the background, she heard Misha screaming about something. "Is everything all right?"

"Oh, Misha is just playing with the dog. We're all fine. Tell Scott to break a leg. Not really, of course."

"I will," Ellie said.

By the time she'd disconnected the call and turned from the window, Scott had changed his clothes. He struck a pose. "How do I look?"

The suit was a little big on him. He had lost weight on his cross-country journey, and swapped some fleshiness for muscle. Beneath the jacket, he had on one of his bright yellow RE:CYCLE T-shirts, which looked goofy but cute. "You look fine," she told him, glancing at the king-size bed that took up most of the room and thinking they would not need a Broadway show to entertain them that evening after the taping. She wouldn't let resentment nibble at her. Her husband was back. He was home. He was here. They were in a hotel room, far from home, and she was going to enjoy him tonight.

"Are you planning to change?" he asked, glancing at her outfit.

She glanced at it, too: a simple sweater set and twill slacks. "I'm just going to be sitting in the audience," she said. "I don't have to get dressed up for that. You have my ticket, right?"

Scott patted his pockets until he located the pass that would allow Ellie to watch the show from the audience. He handed it to her, then lifted the room's key card from the dresser. "We should probably head over to the studio," he said.

The mass of people outside the hotel was as dense as it had looked from their room twelve stories above. Tourists kept stopping to snap photos of billboards, marquees, bodegas, themselves and one another, and whenever someone stopped, the foot traffic jammed. Scott took Ellie's hand so they wouldn't lose each other in the mob. "Do you know where we're going?" she shouted to him over the din of voices yelling, cars honking, and city buses rumbling and wheezing as they barreled down the cross streets.

"Just a few blocks up," Scott shouted back, tightening his grip on her hand.

They made their way through the throng, following a cyclist whose forward motion cleared a narrow path. How different this must seem from what Scott had experienced on his cross-country journey. Just imagining him trying to bicycle through this snarl of humanity in one of the most densely populated islands on earth while dragging his Beast of Burden behind him caused her to laugh.

Eventually, they reached the theater where the show would be taped. Inside the lobby, Scott introduced himself to a uniformed guard, who immediately whisked him away. Abandoned in the empty lobby, Ellie gazed around her. Framed posters of the show's host, a genial-looking guy in a dark suit, his eyes framed by horn-rimmed glasses and his grin bordering on manic, hung on the walls.

The uniformed guard returned alone. Scott was apparently off having another adventure, leaving her to fend for herself. "I'm Scott's wife," she said. "I have this ticket to watch the show." She displayed her pass for him.

"The theater will open in twenty minutes," he told her.

Great. Twenty minutes. She could go back outside, buy a coffee, get caught up in the dense parade of pedestrians swarming along the sidewalk, get lost. Vanish.

Or she could remain in the lobby with the taciturn guard, feeling awkward.

She chose option number two.

Eventually, more people joined her in the lobby. Twenty minutes passed, then thirty minutes. After thirty-five minutes, the doors to the theater opened and she was able to enter. The theater was actually much smaller than it appeared on TV, and the seating area was steeply sloped. She took a seat halfway up, on the aisle, which compelled her to stand repeatedly as later arrivals slid past her to fill in the row. A compact man in shirtsleeves, his head crowned by a headset with a microphone attached and his hands gripping a tablet, strode back and forth on the stage, which otherwise held a sleek desk, a potted tree of some sort, and a leather sofa in front of a backdrop of silhouetted skyscrapers. The man with the tablet squinted up at the lights, muttered things into his microphone, and finally, as the last stragglers found seats and settled in, addressed the audience. He told them to feel free to laugh at the host's jokes — "Or not, if you think they're lame, but we like lots of enthusiasm here," he clarified. He requested that cell phones be turned off. "No taping. No photos. No rings. If your phone rings during the show, you'll be arrested and sent to Riker's Island." If that represented the quality of humor on the show, Ellie didn't think she would be laughing a lot.

As it turned out, the host's opening monologue proved to be pretty funny. All around her, audience members roared with laughter. She might have laughed harder if she wasn't so nervous. But she was. What if Scott developed stage fright? What if the T-shirt he'd worn with his suit looked ridiculous? What if his story seemed ridiculous? Did the world really care about a middle-aged man pursuing a cockamamie dream? Did the planet really care about one guy who wanted to save it?

A faint queasiness churned in her throat. Maybe this whole thing was a stupid idea. Who cared if Hollywood wanted to make a movie based on Scott's crusade? Who cared if his agent — his freaking *agent!* — thought appearing on this show was a brilliant idea? She wanted to go home. Now.

She surveyed the area around her, wondering if she could slip out unnoticed when the show broke for a commercial, during which the man with the headset emerged once more and made a few more bad jokes, which the audience reacted to with raucous laughter. But no, she couldn't leave. She had to be here to support Scott. Of course.

The host returned, grinning at the audience, the overhead lights somehow failing to glare off the lenses of his glasses. "Our first guest this evening is Scott Gillman," he announced. "If you haven't heard of Scott Gillman, you've been living in a cave. Or perhaps if Scott Gillman doesn't succeed in his goal, we all may be living in caves. Because Scott Gillman is trying to save the world, and this summer he let the world know about it by bicycling through all fifty of our nation's states. What an adventure! What a story! Please welcome Scott Gillman!"

All around Ellie, people applauded. She applauded, too, even though applauding her own husband struck her as kind of odd. Did these audience members know or care about Scott? Did they care about the fate of the planet? Or were they applauding only because the guy with the headset had urged them to be enthusiastic?

Scott walked out onto the stage, and Ellie let out a breath. She didn't have to worry about his suffering from a sudden bout of stage fright. He smiled, waved, gripped the lapels of his jacket and spread it open to display his garish yellow T-shirt, and then shook the host's hand. He looked as if he utterly loved being on the stage, bathed in hot white light while bulky cameras followed his movements and recorded his smile.

Of course he loved this. He had been doing it all summer — in front of elementary school children, in front of college students, in local news studios, on podcasts, on blog sites. He had spent a week in Hollywood, hobnobbing with movie executives, taking meetings. He was a celebrity.

Ellie experienced an odd mixture of pride and anxiety. Scott was a celebrity, which was truly thrilling. But was he still the clever, enthusiastic middle school science teacher he'd once been? Could he still be the dad cheering Misha from the sidelines as she dribbled a soccer ball down the field, or Abbie when she served an ace in volleyball? Would he still take out the garbage and walk the dog and tell bad jokes at the dinner table?

"I like that shirt," the host said, taking his seat behind the desk once Scott had settled on the leather couch. "Why don't you tell us about it?"

Scott did. He explained the pun in the slogan — "my trip was about cycling — re: cycling — and also about recycling. And I've got to correct something you said. I biked through the contiguous forty-eight states. I'd have needed a boat to bike to Hawaii, and Alaska was just too far away."

"Too far away?" The host glanced at a stack of index cards on his desk. "By my calculation, you biked close to eight thousand miles this summer! I've got to ask... did you get leg cramps?"

Scott laughed. He and the host joked about muscle aches and joint pains. The silhouetted-skyline backdrop turned into a screen, onto which were projected some of the photos Scott had posted on the Wheeling and Dealing website.

The host grew solemn. "So tell us, Scott, what did you hope to accomplish with this journey of yours? Do you think you've opened people's eyes to the perils our planet is facing?"

Scott grew somber, as well. He talked about climate change, about how when societies grow complacent, you sometimes have to make a grand gesture to open their eyes to the reality around them and spur them into action. The audience applauded. Ellie doubted they were all going to leave the theater and reset their thermostats, install windmills in their backyards, and replace their automobiles with bicycles. But maybe one or two would consider carpooling, or eating a little less red meat.

The host glanced at his index cards again. "I understand you're married, with two daughters."

"Yes, that's right. My wife Eleanor, and my daughters Abigail and Michelle. They're all named after First Ladies — Eleanor Roosevelt, Abigail Adams, and Michelle Obama."

"Really!" The host seemed to think this was marvelous. So did the audience, which applauded as if the actual First Ladies were about to take the stage. "So how did they cope while you were gone for so many months?"

"Well, they missed me, I think — I *hope*," Scott said with a quick grin. "I sure as hell missed them. I called home every evening. But they're smart and capable. They managed to keep things going on the home front while I was biking around the country. I couldn't have done this trip without them. As a matter of fact, my wife is here now, somewhere in the audience. Ellie?" He cupped his hand against his brow and squinted out into the theater.

"Ellie!" The host sprang to his feet and searched the audience as well, cupping his hand above his eyes like Scott. "Ellie Gillman! Come on down!"

A spotlight swooped across the tiers of seats. Ellie recoiled, sinking in her chair — but then Scott spotted her and pointed. "There she is!"

"Come on down!" the host repeated, waving at her. "Let's hear about how you kept the home fires burning while Scott was off saving the planet. Or shouldn't we talk about burning home fires? They pollute the air, don't they? Soot and ash, and they contribute to global warming. Come on down, Ellie."

The people she'd politely stood to let into her row of seats started nudging her and murmuring, "Go! Go!" She thought about how, if she went up onto the stage, Abbie would reproach her for not wearing mascara. Her eyelashes might disappear.

Screw it, she thought. Scott and the host and her neighbors in the audience wanted her up there on that leather couch. She might as well go.

When she reached the stage, Scott gave her a hug and a lusty kiss while the audience cheered. Feeling her cheeks heat with embarrassment at his public display of affection, she glanced toward the host, who stood behind the desk, beaming at her and clapping. Scott escorted her to the couch and sat her down next to him.

"So, Ellie," the host said. "Scott claims he couldn't have had his excellent adventure without you. Is that true?"

She could be modest. She could be demure. She could be the supportive wife, fighting off the farm's foreclosure while her husband turned his corn field into a baseball diamond.

Or she could be loud. "Yes," she said, "it's true. He couldn't have done this without me."

"Tell us what you contributed to his journey," the host invited her.

She turned toward the audience and blinked, nearly blinded by the overhead lights that illuminated the stage. She reminded herself that the audience was fewer in number than she'd expected, and that she had addressed larger groups at Shelton's annual town meeting on occasion. She could do this — especially since those glaring stage lights made seeing the audience nearly impossible.

She took a deep breath, then smiled to relax herself. "You know how it is with first ladies," she said. "We operate behind the scenes. The president gets to march to the podium, with soldiers saluting him and a band playing 'Hail to the Chief.' But in the background, the first lady is making sure everything that needs to be done gets done."

"Behind every successful man is a woman," the host recited. "Did you miss him, or did you and your daughters party like crazy while he was away?"

The audience chuckled.

Ellie kept smiling, but she didn't laugh. "We all had our own jobs to do. Scott's job was alerting people to the imminent dangers of climate change. My daughters' jobs were to go to school, and then to a summer job and summer camp, and to do their chores. My job is to help manage the town we live in. I pushed to redesign a construction project so it would be more ecologically sound, and I organized a town cleanup day. There was a lot of litter on the streets. I got the town to come together to pick up that litter and dispose of it properly." Pleased at how smoothly the words flowed from her, she added, "You've heard the expression, 'Think globally, act locally.' Scott thinks globally. I act locally."

"So your town is cleaner today than it was before Scott set off on his excellent adventure," the host said. "Sounds like you might have done more to clean up the planet than Scott did."

"She's amazing," Scott said. His voice sounded tight. No one else might have noticed, but Ellie knew her husband. She could interpret the nuances, the shadings. He was not pleased that Ellie had nudged him out of the spotlight.

She reminded herself that the purpose of this television appearance was to generate interest in a movie about Scott's ride. No one was going to make a movie about a woman who organized Shelton Cleanup Day while her bureaucratic job was under threat. It wasn't exciting. It wasn't dramatic. It entailed no spectacular scenery, no mountains, no deserts, no prairies or oceans. "We need the dreamers," she said, twisting on the sofa to beam her smile at Scott. "We need the grand gestures. We need people like Scott, who can think globally and shake up the world. He's the one who's amazing."

He appeared mollified. Ellie felt her tension relax its grip on her, her shoulders loosening, her jaw unclenching. Connie might think Scott was a saint, but he wasn't. He was just a man with an ego. If she was a first lady, he was a president who needed to hear "Hail to the Chief" whenever he entered a room.

The rest of the interview went well, mostly because Ellie kept her mouth shut while Scott offered commentary about the photos flashing on the screen behind the host's desk. He talked about the pothole in Montana, the careless SUV driver who ran him off the road in Oklahoma, the breathtaking scenery of Big Sur and the threat wildfires posed to the entire western part of the country. He talked about the people he'd met along the way — touching anecdotes, funny encounters, moments of Zen tranquility and moments of nerve-twisting stress. He performed beautifully. The audience adored him. The host seemed enthralled by him. If any Hollywood producers were watching, they would probably be pulling out their checkbooks and pens soon, ready to bid on the rights to Scott's story.

He and Ellie left the theater right after the show's producers had finished taping Scott's appearance. Through the last stretch of the interview, when Scott rattled off scary statistics about climate trends and population migrations, Ellie sat quietly, feeling rather idiotic, until the discussion broke for a commercial and she was permitted to return to her seat in the audience. The bearded fellow seated next to her congratulated her, gave her what he probably believed was a playful poke in the arm but would no doubt leave a bruise, and then bragged to the woman seated on his other side about how he was sitting next to a famous person. "The wife of the guest!" he'd whispered excitedly. "She's sitting right here! His wife!"

His wife. His first lady. The woman who had antagonized him by answering the host's question about what she'd done while Scott was away. Imagine how angry Scott would have been if she'd listed *everything* she'd done. He still seemed offended that no one had informed him of his mother's broken wrist while he'd been away.

They hadn't had to inform him. Ellie and Iris and the girls had handled things.

Once the show was over, she and Scott left the theater. The sky — or at least the slivers of sky visible between the towering skyscrapers that cast long shadows across the sidewalk — had faded to pale pink while she and Scott had been inside. The crowds of pedestrians had barely thinned, however. They inched along, a sluggish river of humanity pausing to study every shop window, every poster, every neon-lit sign, every billboard looming several stories above the ground.

When Ellie and Scott reached the corner, he grabbed her arm and drew her to a halt. "What was that all about?" he demanded.

She turned to face him. "What was *what* all about?"

"Your performance on the show."

"It wasn't a performance," she responded. "I didn't want to go up onto the stage. If I'd wanted to be on the show, I would have dressed better." *And worn mascara,* she thought. "I was thrilled when I could finally return to my seat in the audience. I didn't want any of this. It was *your* dream, not mine."

His gaze was accusing. She had never realized how rich a brown his eyes were before. They made her think of dark chocolate, black coffee, licorice. She realized she was hungry. "What do you mean, it was my dream?" he asked. "You think I biked all the way across the country and back because I dreamed of being on a TV show?"

She wasn't just hungry. She was tired, and wrung out, and angry. Scott and the host had had their own club. She'd been brought onto the stage for decoration and then sent on her way when she threatened to become too interesting. No girls were allowed on that stage — and she'd dared to be *aloud*.

Now she and Scott were standing on a corner in Times Square, being jostled by the pedestrians pushing past them, crowding around them. And damn it, she was going to be aloud. "Getting a movie deal was your dream. Biking around the country was your dream. Warning the world about the fate of the planet was your dream. And just like I said on the show, makng your dreams come true was possible only because I stayed home and took care of everything that needed taking care of. If you don't like that, fine. Don't like it. But that's how come you could have your dream — because I stayed home and cleaned up all the messes that cropped up while you were away. A clogged toilet. A broken roof. A sick dog. A broken wrist. You could go off and chase your dream, because you knew I'd take care of everything."

He opened his mouth and then shut it, evidently rethinking his response. She wished he didn't look so handsome. She wanted to hate him right now, or at least resent him — and she did, a little. But she was also proud of him, dazzled by what he'd accomplished while she'd been taking care of everything.

"It wasn't as if my trip was a whim," he reminded her. "I prepared for more than a year. I did research. I raised funding. I worked hard to make it happen."

"I work hard every day," Ellie reminded him. "I've spent my entire life preparing for what I do."

"All right." He let out a long, weary sigh, the sound that husbands made when they felt obligated to humor their wives. "Next time, I'll help you make your dream come true. Just tell me what the fuck your dream is."

She had to think. What was her dream?

Most of the time, her dream was just to survive the day, after hours of making her boss look good, mollifying the town's department heads, manipulating budgets until they balanced, and ascertaining that construction projects conformed to MEPA guidelines. Her dream was to come home in one piece and reward herself with a glass of wine. Her dream was to end the day with some goodnight sex and a deep, restful sleep.

Scott could make at least some of that dream come true, if he was around. He couldn't if he was off biking through Idaho.

But that wasn't much of a dream. She needed other dreams, too.

To run Shelton? That one had come true — but she'd been the one to make it come true. Scott hadn't helped her with that.

To raise her daughters to be exuberant and noisy and just a bit defiant? She'd achieved that, too.

To have a clean planet? That was her dream as well as Scott's. But you didn't clean the planet by biking around the country, posting photos on a website and blathering on a podcast. You cleaned it by picking up a broom and sweeping.

"My dream," she told Scott, "is for you to hold the dustpan while I sweep."

He stared at her, a frown creasing his brow. A faint breeze ruffled the air, causing his hair to flutter around his face. He looked so handsome, and so bewildered.

Let him be bewildered. Let him figure it out himself. He'd never had to tell her how to help him make his dream come true. She'd known. If he thought about it hard enough, if he prepared, if he *listened*, he would know.

She turned from him and headed down Broadway toward the hotel. Maybe it was the way she moved, the way she held her head. The swing of her arms, the certainty of her steps. The noise she made, even if it was a silent noise. It was real, an aura, a determination vibrating around her.

Maybe the crowds of people milling around on the sidewalk heard it, because they parted, leaving a clear path for her.

ACKNOWLEDGMENTS

Thanks, first of all, to Jacob Paul, a staggeringly talented novelist and teacher (and also — full disclosure — my beloved nephew), who has done quite a bit of long-distance bicycling. He educated me about recumbent bikes, "Beast of Burden" trailers, websites devoted to long-distance cyclists, and the wear and tear such trips cause both bicycles and riders. I could not have written Scott's part of this story without Jacob's invaluable input. Any errors in my depiction of Scott's journey are my own.

As always, I am infinitely grateful to my editor and publisher, Lou Aronica, whose support and enthusiasm for my work keep me going, even on days when the words won't come and I fantasize about quitting this writing gig and getting a job flipping burgers. Lou, thank you for being Tom Petty to my Stevie Nicks.

Gratitude, as well, to the entire Story Plant team: Allison Moretti for keeping us all on track, Elizabeth Strong for making sure the world knows about this book, and Stephanie C. Fox for her deft, sensitive review of the manuscript.

I am blessed to have a community of friends, both writers and non-writers, who cheer me on, encourage me, sympathize with me, and keep my glass filled with wine. The Savvies, the Romexers, the Discussers, the Wednesday night group, my Ninc buddies, my Smith sisters — I could not survive without you.

The greatest blessing of all is my family: my parents, who never discouraged me when I told them I was going to be a writer; my sister, who taught me how to read and write; and my husband and sons, who remind me of the things that truly matter in life.

ABOUT THE AUTHOR

USA Today bestselling author Judith Arnold knew she wanted to be a writer by the time she was four. She loved making up stories (not exactly the same thing as lying) and enjoying the adventures of her fictional characters.

With more than one hundred published novels to her name, she has been able to live her dream. Four of Judith's novels have received awards from *RT Book Reviews Magazine* (for Best Harlequin American Romance, Best Harlequin Superromance, Best Series Romance Novel and Best Contemporary Romance Novel) and she's a three-time finalist for Romance Writers of America's RITA Award. Her novel *Love In Bloom's* was named one of the best books of the year by *Publishers Weekly*.

A New York native, Judith lives in New England.

.